Lovestoned

Lovestoned

T.P. CARTER

KENSINGTON PUBLISHING CORP.
http://www.kensingtonbooks.com

DAFINA BOOKS are published by

Kensington Publishing Corp.
850 Third Avenue
New York, NY 10022

All Kensington titles, imprints and distributed lines are available at special quantity discounts for bulk purchases for sales promotion, premiums, fund-raising, educational or institutional use.

Special book excerpts or customized printings can also be created to fit specific needs. For details, write or phone the office of the Kensington Special Sales Manager: Kensington Publishing Corp., 850 Third Avenue, New York, NY 10022. Attn. Special Sales Department. Phone: 1-800-221-2647.

Dafina Books and the Dafina logo Reg. U.S. Pat. & TM Off.

ISBN-13: 978-0-7582-1429-4
ISBN-10: 0-7582-1429-4

First Kensington Trade Paperback Printing: October 2007
10 9 8 7 6 5 4 3 2 1

Printed in the United States of America

For artists, free spirits . . .

And

The Creator of The Game,
Thanks for the inspiration.

To the realists,

"You sober people who feel well armed against passion and fantasies and would like to turn your emptiness into a matter of pride and ornament: you call yourselves realists and hint that the world really is the way it appears to you. As if reality stood unveiled before you only, and you yourselves were perhaps the best part of it—O you beloved images of Sais! But in your unveiled state are not even you still very passionate and dark creatures compared to fish, and still far too similar to an artist in love? . . . and what is "reality" for an artist in love? There is no "reality" for us—not for you either, my sober friends. We are not nearly as different as you think, and perhaps, our good will to transcend intoxication is as respectable as your faith that you are altogether incapable of intoxication."

—Friedrich Nietzsche, *The Gay Science*, I-IV (1882)

1

The game. Again. There is no truth in the game we call love. Not hon-esty, not fact or frank. There are frauds and fakes and pretenders, those who liveth and loveth a lie. There are pawns, vats, traps and whirlpools. Proprietors of end, loss, labyrinth and shame. This is what I recall. That there is no happiness in love. No harmony, no calm. There is no love in a game that everyone plays, but no one seems to win.

Please be patient with my depiction. I paint a horrible portrait. This I know. But when I think love, I see and feel shadows. Eclipse. No light. Pardon me, but that's what I remember. That there is no light in love. No sunrise . . .

Sunrise is strange. It's the most bizarre time of day for me. There is something divine—almost curative in the organic hap-penings of the few hundred seconds it takes for the sun to shake hands with the moon. Each day the earth resurrects—awakens with new perspective. New energy. If we all could be so open to change, so indifferent to difference, maybe if our perspectives were as changeable as the earth's, humanity would be a portrait I'd love to paint. In colors that would make me feel less unusual. Less strange.

I'm awakening from a dream—a nightmare, that lets me know what day it is. Every year there is the same dream. The same images. I am in a black box. Not a coffin. Not a hole. But a box. I am screaming, but there is no sound. I am crying but there are no tears. Everything in me is shaking, but the box stands still. Just me. In a box. Until sunrise. I don't know what it means, but I know what day it is. It is the day of my mother's death.

I am awake. But there are other images. Me, as a youngster, walking home from school, knowing but not knowing that something was wrong. Approaching the door to our small home, hearing my mother's voice as she spoke gently to my younger brother.

Play a game with Mommy . . .

I know that today is special. I've painted a huge portrait just for her. She, myself and my little brother. It's the first one I've ever done this big. And the first I've ever given a name to. *All We Have.* There is mother. There is my little brother. And there is me. It took so long for me to paint it. I hope she likes it. I did it just for her.

It's okay, mommy is okay . . .

Go ahead Micah,

Kick it for mommy . . .

My hands are sweaty. I know something is wrong. I double-check the painting. I hope she knows it means love.

Go ahead sweetie . . .

She sounds so tired. I can't wait to make her smile. Can't wait to be her "big man." She cried last night. And today, I promised. I will do the dishes. I will put the toys away. I will make sure Micah eats his dinner. I will give her a special gift.

There is a sound. A scream. Something's wrong with my little brother. I fumble with the key. Turn it twice to the left. Push. Still locked. Another scream. And crying. Lots of crying.

Mommy . . .

I'm sorry. I'm sorry mommy . . .

When the key finally turns and the door opens, I can't move. I can't say a word. I don't know what this is. What I see, I've never ever seen before. There is a rope. A small chair. And my little brother's arms around her legs. She wiggled. Made a funny face.

And then just hung there like a doll. All I could think of was that she'd never even seen the painting.

I remember these things and wait for tears that never fall. I reach over to the nightstand and pick up the small framed photo of my mother and me. I glance towards the corner of the room and see the gift that was never given. Every year the ritual. The dream. The photograph. The gift. I remember. Look. Wait. For a feeling that never comes.

Another morning in East London. I yawn. Stretch. Negotiate with my conscience. It's time to get up, but the chill of early day and warmth of fleece and sheets keep me still. I lay in bed, my usual morning meditation running its typical race. Except today things are different. After almost two decades of living in London, I've decided to move back to the US. To concentrate on my career as an artist. I've never truly been an expressive person, but what I can't find or feel in myself, I see on canvas. It's my connection to the earth. To the universe. And the only proof that I've been here. It is all I am. And now it's time to spread my wings. It's time for the student to leave the master.

I stare at the ceiling and breathe in. The rising of the sun encouraging me to make the change. Mother earth changes every day. There is growth. Rebirth. Spirit. Freedom. So many perspectives. I want to grow and change. I want to spread out. To be connected. To be free. But something about it—change, freedom—keeps me lying on my back this morning, thumb wrestling my thoughts.

A deep breath and much adieu, I will myself out of bed. No results. I count to three. A second attempt to thrust myself onto the cold tile proves more effective. I trot to the bathroom, take a quick wash, rinse my teeth, and almost on autopilot, adhere to the mother I've come to know as routine. A few steps to the Indonesian cloth that has seen many a humble day from this mate. Palms to the heavens. Heart in my hands. I clear my throat and face the east.

"Sh'ma Yisrael Adonai Eloheinu Adonai Echad . . ."

I take a deep breath. Inhale the false. Exhale truth.
"Barukh Shem k'vod malkhuto l'olam va-ed . . ."
As I do this—as I utilize one of the oldest languages known to man, let the coarseness of each syllable rip through me, I get a rush.
"Barukh atah Adonai Elohaynu melekh ha-olam,
she-ha-kol nih'yeh bid'varo . . .
Blessed art thou O Lord our God . . . King of the universe . . .
. . . Barukh atah Adonai Elohaynu melekh ha-olam . . ."
Deep breath. *"Amein."*

I open my eyes. The *fully* risen sun streaming rays through the large English windows in my bedroom. Windows that are probably larger than the room itself. Out of habit, I reach over and grab the only articles that have ever made me feel alive. My paint brushes. In a fingerprinted gesture, I manipulate my favorite brush, toy with my life. This is the beginning of my day. I stretch. I pray. I paint. Simple as it may sound, that's me.

The blaring scream of a ringing telephone prior to six a.m. should land one in a dirty middle-eastern holding cell. I answer it anyway. I know who it is.

"Morning, princess."

No answer.

"Morning, Yasara." I'm not in the mood for this. Without warning, she toppled bricks on an otherwise peaceful morning.

"When were you going to tell me?" She's livid. About what, is the question. I think I know. But with women it could be anything.

"What was I supposed to tell you?" I hate to be patronizing. And as intelligent as she is, it only pisses her off even more.

"For bloody sake, Islam. You are a cold bastard. I can't believe I ever fell for you. How could you make plans to leave—to move for Christ's sake and never rightfully discuss them with me? Did you ever love me? Did you ever give a fuck? Did you ever truly care enough to . . ." She's on a rant. A frantic knock on the door let me know we were in for a routine morning. She waltzed in, placed the phone on the armrest of my favorite second hand recliner and stood in the middle of the living room floor. Which also happens to be the bedroom. Which also happens to be my studio. I know I'm wrong. She knows it. I know it. I relay that to her the best way I can.

"Green tea this morning?" I ask.

"You're ignoring the issue, Islam."

"I do not know what the issue is. How can I ignore it? Are you having tea?"

"You're an immature bastard and I can't believe I'm with you."

"I don't have any honey. How many sugars?"

"Would you address the issue and stop this madness? Are you leaving London and returning to the states or not?" Her eyes were needle points at the base of my spine. Damn. I had planned to tell her tonight. That I'd decided to return to the US to focus on my career. That although there is no place in this world like London for an artist, that I needed a change of scenery. Needed new interaction, new experiences. I needed a muse. I hadn't discussed anything with her because I wasn't sure about what I wanted to do until last night. I hate having life-changing conversations under those circumstances. Being so unsure. Most times, answers to questions like these come to me at night. On the terrace, on the toilet, it doesn't matter. I get my answers the old fashioned way. They fall out of the sky. This thing they call inspiration, the other they call spontaneity—two things that seemingly dominate my life, have caused me nothing but stress. I tell her that in my own way. With a kiss.

"Islam. St-stop it with the kisses."

I continued. Her forehead. Her nose. Her left earlobe. When I got to her eyelids, they were wet. Shit. I hate it when she cries.

"Get off of me, right now." She pushed me away, the glare in her eyes less vengeful, more like I'd just sold her first born into slavery. "Are you leaving me or not?" My lover, my friend of five years, took two steps back. Looked at me like I was Hitler.

I thought about the question. Am I leaving her? Not necessarily. I am leaving London. I have to. Aside from inspiration and artistic splendor, I can't concentrate here. I can paint but I can't concentrate. Painting is only half the battle. The business side of art required focus. I am not focused in the UK. I love it too much. Love the vibe. I need to be a tad more . . . how do I say it? Bored. Less to do so I can apply my already short attention span to things of importance. Called one of my best mates—who is like a brother to her, shared the news with him and asked him not to say anything of it. So much for confidentiality. I'm going to kill him. I don't want to have this conversation with her right now. I wish I had handled this differently.

I picked up another brush and started our routine. Undressed her with each kiss. Fingered the paint brush with one hand, a very special place of hers with the other.

"I love you," she said. I thought about it, but didn't reply. I never do.

2

We lay still. She, sleeping lightly and me painting in bed. With a brief look around the flat, I take informal inventory. I've sold almost everything. All my paintings. Except for the one I'm working on and the gift, which is not for sale. That is how I know the time has come for change. I have arrived at the person I am going to be here. Although I know I will return, when I do, it will be with new perspective. Hopefully.

Right now, I'm tidying up a piece that I was commissioned to do for a large arts foundation. Funny, after all of these years of playing with color, I still find the essence of my expression on canvas in my depiction of women. The works of mine that sell, happen to be just the opposite, murals and abstract mirages of color that expose less of the human soul. It makes me wonder about people, about the state of humanity. Me, included. So I paint women, in different stages of life, and although I'm not finished, the one I'm currently working on is my best work to date. I say it's funny, because my interactions with women tend to be catastrophic.

A dab of medium red here, a smudge there and I sign my name illegibly in the bottom right hand corner of my work. Memory takes me to a distant place, where virgin thoughts of my first love almost evaded me in a place where no one seemed to be able to find value in the truest means of expression for me. In grade school, I knew. Before then, I knew. I loved to paint. But when I told this to friends, family and passersby, they laughed or looked at me in pity. How would I ever support myself? A wife? Children? What was I to do? I hadn't any idea of what or who I'd like to become other than the next Van Gogh. A physician? An attorney? High-powered businessman? They all came to mind. Those were the acceptable answers. Anything but becoming an artist was acceptable, so I concentrated on a lesser love—science. Purely for the love of the human body. And the sound of it. Instead of preparing for a white coat future and appeasing those around me, I painted all the illustrations in my books and managed to fail every course I took. Except philosophy and art. So much for mollification. I left for London, the birthplace of my mother, as soon as I'd been offered the chance. I feel closer to her here, as if she is watching me somehow.

I watch Yasara sleep. Add more color. Although I can't say that I belong anywhere, I'm here. That should stand for something. No matter who I am with, friends, women, colleagues, I cannot say that I've ever truly felt connected to anyone or anything. Sometimes I'm proud of that. The isolation. The fact that I can bear it. Not need anyone. Then in the blink of an eye, the pride is muted and I'm not able to deal with the silence in my head. Sometimes it's the most natural state of being for me. To be alone. As an artist, I prefer to live in solitude but desperately need company at times.

A stir. My girlfriend moves toward me in her sleep, as if she's forgotten the current state of affairs. We are intricately fixed, legs and sorts wrapped and re-wrapped in a juxtaposed arrangement. Both together and apart, the linen provides the only true connection between us. The sheets just as confused as I, bound by a man who wanted to be free, but had no idea of where to begin. I stare at the ceiling as usual, attempting to detangle my legs and my thoughts, desperately trying to make sense of my life as that seemed to be all I could do this morning.

The past hour has been intense. Yasara and I made our usual morning love. Prior to her leaving for work, she requests it. Whether she is upset with me or not has no effect on the session. The bedroom has never been a problem in this relationship, or in any of my others. It's the other rooms that avalanche. The ones that require conversation, sentiment and feeling. She stirs. I reach for her. She jolts. Moves away. She doesn't want me to touch her. The beautiful Egyptian goddess has awakened. So has our reality. She sighs. I savor her features. Her dark hair, olive skin, the deep curve at the small of her back. I study these imprints of female splendor that Yasara carries like an everyday handbag and wonder why she ever gave me a chance. The silence is offering me a second one. If I could explain myself, we may be able to work on things. I don't know what to say. Fuck me.

"Where is my jumper?" she asked as if making love were nothing but a trip to the local market. I don't want her to leave. I care for her and want to sort this out. Frantically searching for the right words, we are both disappointed. As usual, I turn up with nothing. I hate this. I don't know how to handle it.

"Islam. Help me look for my clothes." She eases out of bed and throws the sheets left to right. Looks under the bed. Behind it. Never once looking my way. I wish one of us would say something. She obliges.

"When I leave today, I never want to see or speak to you again. Do you understand that?" There was no mistaking the seriousness in her eyes. I knew she would hold to her word. I knew not to call her no matter how much I missed her. How much I needed her. I've seen her cut off family members who've deserved it. I guess this was inevitable. I will miss her terribly, I wish I could say that. What's wrong with me? The only thing I could do was reach out to her, attempt to soothe her pain, which regardless of how indifferent I seemed, I did care and I felt her heart break. Whenever I'd reach for her, she'd pull away. She would have no parts of me. Yasara's focus was on getting dressed, getting out of my flat and out of my life. She's that strong.

I watched her elegantly place each piece of clothing on, as if she were being judged by a panel of experts. If you weren't close enough to see for yourself, you wouldn't believe the monstrous landslide of tears making their way down her beautiful cheeks. I couldn't find the words if my life depended on it. She moved toward the door and hesitated as if she'd thought of something new to say, something to ease the ache. Then the old metal door that let her into my flat, let her out with the same dungeon-like clank. Yasara never looked back.

3

"Next stop, Piccadilly Circus . . . please mind the gap . . ."

I'm being accosted by two of my best friends, and I use the term loosely, because I don't believe in friendship, I don't consider myself to have real friends. Just acquaintances that make it a habit to be involved in my life. These two henchmen, Paul and Ahmed, were more involved with my affairs than my natural brother.

Paul is a fellow artist, a sculptor no less, who works for the same gallery as I, expertly transporting art. If I believed in true friendship, Paul would be my truest friend. We attended Camberwell College of Arts in South London together. On the first day, to a sculpting course, we were each twenty minutes late. At least twenty minutes. The instructor, known for making a spectacle of latecomers, began a typical rant. I of course, had no applicable reason for being late. I just was. So I ignored the tirade, passing seconds by sending non-verbal messages to a fit young lady on the front row. I figured that when the overly dramatic instructor tired of me standing quietly in the center of the room, he would simply ask me to sit. Paul, however, took center stage and made it clear that *if* he were the best sculptor in the room—which he was certain that he was, then it wouldn't matter if he were tardy or not, it would matter only that he had arrived. That was my introduction to the production that is Paul. Realizing that he believed every single word that he said, I laughed so hard that we were both sent off. We have been mates ever since.

Ahmed led a much more interesting life as an international deejay and music producer. I had previously been made aware of him through various adverts, festivals, and the likes as he was a headliner at most European dance music venues. We met officially at If Music, a lounge-like vinyl shop in Soho known worldwide for its elite clientele. I, having all of twenty pounds to my name and willing to spend it all on great music, hardly qualified as elite, but I loved the vibe of the place. And the music selection. Plus you could never pinpoint which world-famous deejay would walk in at any moment. Ahmed Irenai being one of them. He was getting special service at the till, as his deep Iranian pockets were good for at least a thousand pounds in great dance music, and I was trapped behind him, waiting to purchase a single CD. For some strange reason, he would not allow me to pay before him, but offered several different types of chemical stimulant to me for my troubles. I had no choice but to get to know him. Now that I do, I realize that absolutely nothing Ahmed does makes sense except music. The best parties in the world, guaranteed are his. There is nothing like watching him mesmerize a crowd of fifty thousand. He travels the world for free, samples the best food and women, and Paul and I keep him company. Keeping him off the coke is a more tedious task. The two of them are the closest to family that I have here in the UK. The closest I have period. Another reason the decision to leave London was a hard one to make.

Paul, having the most common sense of the trio, is giving me stress over my a.m. break up. Or the fact that I didn't do anything about it. ". . . So you let a woman who could possibly be the most beautiful and intelligent woman in Europe walk out of your flat and you did nothing. Absolutely nothing!" he ranted. I tried to keep myself from laughing. Not at the content of his discourse, but the drama. Paul is so dramatic. He saw the playful expression on my face and misinterpreted it.

"And you have nothing but laughter to show for your hopeless example of a life! Why do I bother with you! You are a danger to yourself! Who is off limits, Islam? Whose life wouldn't you ruin?" The passengers on this morning's Piccadilly Line glanced back and forth indirectly between the two of us. I guess it's my turn to reply.

"Is that question rhetorical?" I asked.

Paul shook his head. "No, I want to know. Whose life do you cherish if you can't even do what's best for yourself?" He's serious. Damn.

"Married women. I don't screw with couples. You know that. So at least somebody has a fair shot, wouldn't you say?" I joked. He didn't find it funny. I knew it wasn't. I tried my best at an explanation. "I don't know. She came in and already knew about the move so I didn't know what to say . . ." I answered, quite sheepishly. I'm not fragile. I just hate being put on the spot. Especially during the morning rush hour on the tube. ". . . and because I had no time to gather my thoughts, and didn't want to say the wrong thing, I . . . I don't know. Shit happened."

"Well, how did it end?" Paul asked. He took a personal interest in my and Yasara's affairs. He introduced us, and convinced her family that although I was American born, I wouldn't mistreat her. How did it end? It all happened so quickly. I attempted to answer my long time friend. As well as the tube passengers.

"She told me that she never wanted to see or speak to me again," I replied.

"And what did you do?" Ahmed decided to join us after thirty minutes of silence. Drugs are no good for even the most eclectic of souls.

"I put the finishing touches on the piece that I was commissioned for through the Royal Academy of the Arts Foundation," I answered. Paul looked at me in disbelief, Ahmed laughed. We stood in silence—the three of us, for a few minutes. The back and forth motion of the compact carriage induced a sway that should nauseate everyone, but never did.

"Do you recall the personality profile tests we took last month? Initially, I doubted the results of yours but now I see what they meant when they said you had the emotional profile of a serial killer. You're a sociopath," Paul stated in disgust. If that's what he calls my behavior—sociopathic, then I'm relieved. At least it can be defined. I'm tired of being in the dark about me.

4

Paul and I arrived to the usual morning buzz at the gallery. The down-tempo drum and bass mix of Jhelissa's "Friendly Pressure" crooned softly through the small ceiling speakers. Although I worked in my field, as the assistant director of a small gallery called John Martin on the west end, some days it felt more like play than work.

"What are you doing with that?" I asked Paul.

"What do you mean what am I doing with it? I'm taking it to the truck," he answered. He was wrapping a piece by Mark Adlington, one of our newest acquisitions, the one we were giving the next show slot to. Paul couldn't be taking that one out yet. It had just arrived. The British artist has a following but damn, this is ridiculous.

"Who ordered it? I don't remem—" the clicking of expensive heels on wood startled us both.

"—Charles Tensely did. He called me yesterday and asked for it no matter the cost. Asshole or not, it's why I looooovvvve himm!" my boss interrupted, singing the final part of the sentence in a tune particular to straight women and gay men. I took a look at the cost sheet. Eighty-five hundred quid is definitely something to sing about. "But Paul, you don't have to deliver it, we're going to have it sent over this evening special delivery . . ." She continued. The look on Paul's face said it all. *What do you mean special delivery, I AM special delivery!* Made you wonder where the cameras were. I chuckled inside. When you're working with artists, there is never a boring day. She continued to inadvertently insult him. ". . . so don't bother with it, just go ahead with some of the lesser pieces." Julia Boyd was a nutter. Paul was a gay man in a straight man's mind, spirit and body. Together, they made for an interesting work week.

My boy looked at me with one of his undercover glances. My take is, this glance stands for *"Did you tell her about leaving yet?"* A tennis match of ocular call and response.

"No."

"Well when are you going to?" he shot back.

"Not now."

"Well when?" his eyes were getting larger by the moment, aggravating me more by the second. I forgot the communication between us was a silent effort.

"In a minute!" I shouted.

"In a minute what?" Julia asked. Damn you, Paul. I wasn't counting on this being the first thing I had to do today.

"I uh . . . uhm . . ." I'd already had one catastrophe this morning, I didn't need two. Honesty. The best policy. Well, sometimes it is. ". . . I . . . have something to tell you, Julia." I uncomfortably began what would be my official salute to the UK. Job resignation.

"Make it quick, I have a morning studio visit with Liam Steinbeck, who I'm trying to secure before Albermarle or Alan Cristea does. There are almost as many galleries as there are exceptional artists these days. Is everything okay?" she asked in the middle of brushing her hair and all the other things women do every half hour in the mirror.

"I'm thinking of moving back to the States." I started, and before I went any further, I figured I'd better oblige Paul by coming correct before he had an anxiety attack over there. I re-phrased the statement. "I *am* moving. Back to the US." She looked me in the eye through her mirror. Searched for uncertainty or any indication of falsehood.

"You're serious," she stated flatly.

"Serious about what?" Mark, the other co-director walked in. Picked up where his partner left off. She answered for me.

"Serious about moving to the US. Islam is moving, Mark. He's leaving us. When?" For a moment, I saw a flash of the angst—if you could call it that—in Julia that I saw in Yasara this morning. To a lesser degree, of course, but still the same. Brought back memories of her cappuccina legs wrapped around my head in the shed downstairs.

"I haven't worked it all out. But before the month is out. I'll be here long enough to hire someone qualified for the job, so no worries." I answered. Mark sat at his desk, shook his head. Julia looked at me like we were sharing identical thoughts.

"You'll be bored, Islam." Mark replied.

"That's what I told him," Paul added. "What could he possibly do to a piece of canvas outside of Europe? Use it as a drum head?" Everyone erupted in laughter. Underneath all of that drama is a comedian who'll put Chris Rock out of a job.

The day progressed as usual. Lunchtime was busy. Ours being a more progressive gallery, offering an array of contemporary art in varying mediums from paint to video installation, tends to attract a more nouveau clientele.

My thoughts were interrupted by a clever-looking young lady standing in the middle of the gallery floor. She was admiring a sculpture of a circular structure molded in the likenesses of Venus, Earth and our Moon. A red planetary formation appeared in the distance, looking downward toward the trio with its arms crossed. The epistrophe read: *Of Women, By Women, For Women*. It was Paul's. It was weird and always attracted the attention of women. It was his way of saying you can run the world as long as you let me fuck you.

The young lady stood in front of the metal structure until she got it. The message was hidden but it didn't take her long. Obviously bored with the array, she asked of no one in particular,

"Where is Islam?"

Mark, already en route to where she was standing, gave me a hearty pat on the back and whispered,

"My God. Would you look at those tits? Islam, we are truly going to miss you, blood."

The gallery staff wrongly blames me for every decent looking woman that walks through the colorful lacquered doors. As Mark continued on toward the front of the space, he didn't mind being the first to answer the young beauty. "Yes, Islam is right over there, and he is free. Don't let him tell you otherwise," Mark flirted.

I don't know why everything is always such a stage play with my friends and women. "Can I help you?" I asked.

"I've come to personally deliver the invitation for the private studio party tonight. Velasquez Vitro's Moon Opaque, in Shoreditch. Details are provided on the invite." She delivered the lines as rehearsed and paused before her next invocation. "You look unlike what I imagined," she said, her Mona Lisa smile easy for me to read. It quickened my pulse. I know that smile well. I let one thing lead to another. As usual.

"What did you imagine?"

"The Holy Grail," she answered plainly.

"And what does that look like?"

"I'm not sure now. You've thrown me off. Surely it couldn't be this ordinary," she replied. I chuckled. Gave her trendy clothes, impressionable eyes, high cheekbones and smart nose a quick once over but issued no reply. Quite a looker, this one. She blushed. "I didn't mean to offend you. It's just that you seem to be quite popular and one wonders what one does to earn his keep." She moves quickly. I remind myself, women are the last thing on my mind today. I remind myself again. And again.

Without taking my eyes off of the scattered paperwork in front of me, I buzz the shed downstairs and ask Paul to come up and watch the main gallery for me. On autopilot, I take the young lady's hand, things to come forming a cloud in both heads. Walking quickly towards our destination, I search for that feeling again—any one will do. I almost ask myself aloud if this is freedom. If it were would I recognize it?

5

After closing the gallery, Ahmed, Paul and I walked from Albemarle Street to Soho. While my comrades spoke amongst themselves, I breathed as long and as deeply as I could. I wanted to engrave these images, people and places, into a finite place in my being. The architecture. The shops. The scents. The food. Lovers in Soho Square. I wanted to take it all with me.

A parade of tambourines and loud chants removed me from my thoughts.

"Oh no . . . It's them . . ." Ahmed gestured towards a group of men and women walking—or rather dancing—through Soho Square, dressed in biblical garb, chanting and playing instruments loud enough to deafen the deaf. They're always loud. And a bit mad if you ask me. The Hare Krishna people, the crazies of W1. Ahmed put his hands over his ears.

"Ahmed, they are no worse than your techno-rave deafening bollocks," Paul defended the outspoken group of . . . I don't know what to call them, fanatics? Free thinkers? Who the hell knew. "They are merely expressing themselves. Are they bothering you?" he asked earnestly.

"YES!" Ahmed and I answered in unison.

"Why?" Paul questioned. He always took up for eccentric personality types. Said they were freer than the average man, and should be respected not ridiculed. I simplified things to a lone theory. Crazy is crazy. No matter how many tambourines it can wave. I answered for Ahmed and me.

"They're just nutters. Some people don't want to be bothered. They want to read in peace without being reminded of—"

"Of what?" Paul interrupted. "Of reality? Of people who are different? For fuckssake, Islam, give these people a break. You may learn a thing or two," he said. We found an area to sit on the grass. Soho Square was always crowded. I complained about it most days, but I will miss it much.

An F4 growls as it zooms up Dean Street. A car the size of a trash bin sat neatly on the opposite side of the cobblestone street, daring anyone to challenge its right to be there. As the wondrous melting pot of progressive hodge-podge cursed me for leaving, my mates and I took our usual roles. Ahmed supplies. Paul rolls. They share. I try not to die from the second hand smoke. There is a vibration associated with London that can't be pinpointed. Especially Soho. Navigating the endless web of hidden streets, funky shops, modernist cafes, tiny alleyways and coves works both sides of the brain, while the eternal maze of *seek and ye shall find* opens the mind and spirit. You will change and not notice it.

Paul, Ahmed and I left the Square and had arrived for the evening, at our standard greeting place. A bar called Revolution. The dimly-lit reddish atmosphere and comfortable leather makes it easy to relax. We compare thoughts and social callings. The three of us having our own public agenda, calendars are always cramped. Deciding on what to do is a task. Paul is his usual talk-ative self, Ahmed is responding in his blue-moon nature, and I, I just can't believe I'm leaving. For the sake of enjoying our last days together, we decided to ignore my exit all together. I entered the conversation mid-sentence.

"What's going on tonight?" I asked Paul.

"Ah, I was wondering when you and Moses would come down from the mountaintop and join us mere mortals . . ." he joked.

"That is of course, always the dilemma. Ahmed wishes to entrap us in one of his drug-trafficking nights of adventure." I laughed at the expression on Ahmed's face. He actually looked hurt. ". . . I of course, have a more cultured evening to dally in, that is if anyone's interested." Paul is so. . . . I don't even know how to describe it.

"And what would that be?" I asked sarcastically. Whatever it is, I'm sure silver pocket chains, cowboy boots, and the thousand slashes in my oversized denim trousers would be sub-par the code of dress.

"The opening at the British Museum for the Michelangelo show. His drawings are on display and there are going to be some wonderful people there to know," he answered as if his face were engraved on the British Pound. Paul, Paul, Paul. This time, Ahmed was the first to speak up.

"Who is spinning?" He asked. I laughed out loud. That caught me off guard. With his habit, there was no way to tell if he was serious or not. That made everything he said hysterical.

"Who is what?" Paul is incredulous. He can tolerate anything. Drug addicts, assholes, friends who finish five year relationships without cause, but let on, even for a second, that you have no class and he will verbally reduce you to a pence. Ahmed didn't let up.

"Who. Is. The. Dee. Jay." My stomach is in knots. Paul is outraged. I'm going to miss this.

"Let's see here . . ." Flippantly turning the pages of *Time Out London*'s museum issue, he began his over-dramatized reply. Stage lights up, house lights down, Paul is . . . Paul.

". . . Ah, it appears right here alongside the advert for your favorite club, Fabric. Leonardo DaVinci in room one, spinning deep house . . . Monet with the best of breakbeat and trance . . ." I'm laughing so hard I can't breathe. ". . . and . . . of course! Van Gogh will grace the stage with his new single 'There-isn't-enough-stroke-in-my-coke'. . . so we'll simply leave life and its finery to the likes of Ahmed's beautiful mind . . ." He shook his head in disapproval of Ahmed's lack of cultural refinement, while laughter punched me hard in the chest. So much in fact, that I couldn't seem to successfully alternate the wind pattern between chest, nose and diaphragm equally. There was only one other way for the wind to break.

"Ahhhh! Bloody Christ Islam! Must you be from Brixton and Brooklyn at the very same time!" Paul exclaimed. The smell was repugnant. He covered his nose while Ahmed tastefully placed a napkin over his food and waited patiently as if he knew something we didn't about the permeability of bar food and gas. I laughed harder. And Paul, even he couldn't suppress his laughter this time. We were both in tears. Ahmed sat quietly, protecting his vittles with his makeshift gas mask as Paul wiped the tears from his eyes and shook his head. He was stuck with us. Whether I was in Soho, New York or Soho, London we would always be brothers.

Compromising as usual, we ended up attending the studio party in Shoreditch. This would ensure Ahmed's timely attendance to a weekly party he spun at a club called Cargo. He was never late for his dee-jay gigs. Music was the only thing he loved more than drugs. We decided we'd sign up for Michelangelo another day, and spend tonight submerged in north east London.

The old warehouse turned residence was impressive. Ten years ago, one could purchase an entire building in Shoreditch with a pair of trainers and two tickets to the next football game. The only group who'd even give the ghost town a chance were artists who fell in love with the lofty compounds and converted them into studio residences. Artist gentrification—as they call it—has uplifted many a sodden neighborhood. Artists can barely afford a single room in some of these areas now.

We arrived and were instantly submerged in vibe. The indigo lamps, black light and deep, rhythmic house music placed me in a trance like state. Topless women, tastefully and colorfully painted were a work of art. One placed a cherry-laced chocolate in my mouth as she passed us by. Transfixed by the atmosphere, I was moving but not. I can only imagine what Ahmed felt. No matter the path we chose, this element—this vibe, was the crossroads. I can't explain the feeling. But Velasquez had gotten it right. I'd first discovered him years ago at Central Saint Martin's as a young art student. Back then, he was known for creating an erotic and eclectic setting. Tonight, he has outdone himself once again.

"Isn't that the young girl from the gallery today?" Paul asked. Thirty degrees to my right and three steps away was my afternoon twenty-minute vacation.

"Yea." It was a flat answer. I wanted to leave today in hours past. Paul had something else in mind. He wanted to chat her up.

"Pay our respects for the invitation, shall we?" He winked. Led the way. I followed. Since he always looked as if he were personally dressed by Domenico Dolce and I, like I raided Lenny Kravitz's personal garage sale, we were a pair whose mere presence warranted conversation. We arrived at the circle of women, obviously interrupting but not.

"Ladies . . ." Paul is a charmer. I'm sure he was the serpent in Eve's garden.

"To what do we owe the presence of such upstanding blokes?" lady one asked. She was the least attractive of the group, therefore not on his radar. I could not tell if she fancied him, or if she were being sarcastic. Either way, he'd rid of her shortly.

"Are we using the word *we* a bit too freely, my dear?" Owwwwch, Paul. "The answer to your question is quite simple . . ."

He can be so cut and dry. It pisses people off. I tell him all the time about openly displaying his arrogance but I don't think he cares. ". . . we are obviously under the spell of this fine young woman right here . . ." he motioned towards . . . damn. I didn't manage to get her name earlier. ". . . what is your name gorgeous?" Paul asked, with absolutely no regard for the fact that he is ignoring the other women. That isn't my style. I made conversation with the other members of the female quad. Everyone deserves to feel beautiful, even if assholes like Paul tell them in so many words that they aren't. And I can tastefully avoid what's-her-name. She was in conversation with my friend, but her eyes were on me. Please, just let me get through this. The intelligent sex kitten expertly directed Paul's question towards me.

"Islam. Your friend asked if I enjoyed my visit to your gallery today. Would you say that I did?" She flashed a knowing look. The one that women give when they refuse to be ignored. That alone, shut me down. If we were in a private room, I'm sure you could hear a pin drop. Embarrassment struck me hard. I couldn't form the slightest of words. Paul, the only man I know with women's intuition took control of the situation. Got me out of there.

"Excuse us ladies . . . sincerest apologies. We will be back." Everyone looked confused except he and the girl.

"Islam." His tone was scolding. I know the look on my face. It was the stupid one from this morning's tube ride. "Islam! I'm going to ask you this, and I'm only going to ask it once." My comrade of almost two decades already knew the answer. I tried to stifle laughter. It was hard. "Did you bother her?" he asked. ". . . look me in the eye . . . tell me yourself . . . did you do it?" I was ashamed. But grinning. Paul hit the roof.

"Gwaaaaaaannnnn Islam! Wh-wh-how . . . when? She just came in to— . . ." and then it hit him. He mimicked me. ". . . *Paul . . . will you watch the main floor for about a score? I have some business to tend to. . . .* Maaaannn! What the hell? Did she offer herself with the invitation?" He was dumbfounded. Just as I was about to tell the entire story, something else caught my attention. An energy of sorts. I shifted focus towards its source. Moving away from Paul and closer to the energy's point of origin, I was totally captivated.

A group of boho-like artists gathered at the center of the loft space. They danced effortlessly to the rhythm supplied. Almost as if they were not in control of their own bodies. Ecstasy seemed to be the natural choice of drug here, but wasn't befitting to this group at all. They seemed to be high on something else. Something natural. Wherever it was came from a deeper place.

I watched one in particular, move freely as if it were her soul's mission to express herself that way. The look on her face was surreal, like that of women I've painted. The woman-girl's movement, dictated to her in a kaleidoscope of syncopated sound, enabled what appeared to be an ethereal communication of sorts.

She was ruled by the rhythm and she ruled it just the same. This excited me, because the feeling—that feeling—was what I've believed to exist, but could never find. I was stimulated. But saddened. I wished to find out more about this mood that I could never seem to get into. I watched and watched. So much effort, very little results. I could not capture what they were feeling. Not even enough to paint it. The woman-girl approached me like it were one of many things on her to-do list.

"Fancy Osunlade?" she asked.

"Ocean la who?" I hadn't the slightest clue to whether or not she was even speaking English.

"Osunlade. He is selecting records tonight," she answered.

"He's good. Tribal."

"You dance?"

"No."

"Sing?"

"No."

"What do you do?"

"Paint."

"What do you paint?"

"Women."

"Anything I should be aware of?"

"Doubt it."

She stood directly in front of me, her mysterious eyes allowing no escape. They were dark. The darkness matched the depth. The depth matched the discernment. I couldn't focus on anything else. Somehow or another, I had determined that I'd remain a deer caught in her murky headlights. I didn't want to escape. Funny thing is, I didn't want sex either. I couldn't put my finger on it. It was almost as if I preferred to be drawn in to her.

"You obviously don't dance," she stated rather than asked.

"I don't."

"But you paint." She reiterated. Followed by a smile that happened only in her eyes. I don't know what to do with this one. She continued to look through me. The intensity of her glare exposing my entire day—from finishing with Yasara to my afternoon soirée. I averted my glance, as to separate myself from the severity of it all. I felt exposed. As if she knew why I preferred to pray in Hebrew. And why I couldn't find the words for my love this morning. And why I don't get on with my brother. The silence between us said more than any conversation ever could. I wiped the sweat from my brow. Something was happening here, with or without my regard. I fought the urge to run. I willed the words. Just as I mustered the energy to break this . . . this . . . whatever it was, she disappeared into the sea of dark freedom, leaving me stranded mid-meditation. I disliked the feeling. I was Freud without subject. Nietzsche without subtext. The first solid thought all day, and here I was, attempting to heave into existence what seemed so effortless for the woman who saw in me things I never could. In this liberated underworld of art and free expression, I was food for thought, without a plate.

6

"Have you ever tried it?"
"Once,"
"How did it make you feel?"
"Free . . ."

The air of the night was crisp. A group of us had gathered outdoors, attempting a short break from the hedonism. Conversation and natural stimulant were passed, each responsible for elevating the consciousness of the various sects. I stood alone, staring out from the terrace onto the street, where I counted black cabs, buses and raindrops as if that were more exciting than what had just occurred.

Everything was happening inside, but nothing could be pinpointed. I could try to forget the woman-girl. As if she were no more than an afternoon soiree. That was an option. But I know it isn't true. I felt differently than I had with other women. Although we only shared a brief exchange. Basic instinctive attraction was not the name of the game. However, had she stood there any longer, I don't know what would have taken place. It was all so unpredictable. The energy was.

A black car awaited its designated passenger below. Since I hadn't anything other to do than wait for answers, I waited along with the driver. One. Two. Three. Taxis. One bus. One . . . I heard her.

"Yes, goodnight to you as well . . ." She laughed. Said something about the rain. *"Yes, it is . . . no . . . I will not make any promises, but you have my word that I will try."* I heard a male voice reply to her honest answer. I wanted to see who she was speaking to. And if she looked at him the way she did me. I am far from impulsive, so I denied those urges. Perhaps a final glimpse of her would suffice. I waited.

"Oh really? That sounds excellent. Ring me up, will you?" I watched her gather the ankle length skirt she wore into her hands, in efforts to avoid the rainwater. Her driver held the umbrella and the door as if he were born to do so. As the powers that be would have it, she looked towards the terrace. Our eyes met. And it hit me.

"Wait!" I—somebody, I don't know if it was me—shouted. Her expression didn't change. No smile. Just those dark eyes. They danced. And told me it was okay. That I wouldn't embarrass myself if I tore through the studio like a tornado, taking two, three—sometimes four, stairs at a time to meet her downstairs. That this was how it was supposed to be. That I was within my rights to want to have this time with her.

"Wait." I was outdoors, out of breath, and thankfully so, because again, all I could do was stare. I hoped she understood.

"Jules . . ." she signaled the driver. ". . . leave me for a while. I want to take a walk. I will phone you when I am ready." She looked at me keenly. Now what? I am supposed to say something aren't I?

"Care to take a stroll?" she asked. I'm not a mute. But I feel like one. Frustration set in as once again, I struggled for the simplest means of expressing thought and feeling. She placed her umbrella in my left hand, her own hand in my right. We walked. The rain poured as if it were all the gods had to offer. Nothing seemed as it were. My feet weren't wet. The temperature hadn't dropped. The feeling—the one—it hadn't returned. I was in control. Believing that was important. We walked past drab lofty buildings and Italian motorbikes parked in a row. The sound and scent of the storm, determining what and when we would speak.

She on her love for music and dance. Me on my love for art. Her desire to be more than she is. Mine to simply love who I am. I have never had a conversation like this with anyone.

Dictated by the severity of the storm, the end of our summer night stroll landed us at Refuel, the swanky restaurant café of The Soho Hotel where she'd apparently taken a suite. We sipped Earl Grey and dreamed of a world run by artists, of a country run by women—I opposed it, of true humanitarianism and no war. And when it was time for silence, there was no fear of it, as we seemed to prefer the meditative state in which we could believe what we wanted without interruption.

"What is desire?" The woman-girl with no name posed the question as if the thought had just fallen into her tea cup. I think. I'm not sure I know. I clear my throat. Attempt an intelligible answer.

"Desire. Longing. Wanting. Whether you act, react, or not, it can simply be the force of yearning. Of aspiration." Her eyes looked through mine, to my own desires. My own longings. My own aspirations and yearnings.

"Let us go upstairs." The request—if I could call it that, was met with no opposition. My desires were crystal clear.

The suite was not quite as large as one would imagine, but tastefully designed. A fine leather armchair. High thread count. Shoes neatly arranged in a row. And an easel. Canvas, paint and a few brushes. She removed her necklace. Lit a candle. I couldn't predict things to come. Desire for me is becoming something else.

I placed my bag on the armchair, leaving my hands free. Standing in the middle of the floor, facing this unique creature was an astounding experience. For the first time, I was in the presence of a woman and didn't know what to do.

"Desire is," she took my hands and slowly led my arms upward. "thirst that cannot be quenched," led them outward, "hunger that cannot be fed . . ." I inhaled deeply, and exhaled as our hands touched at all points, until hers rested at my wrists. Arms stretched to their limits, we were face to face, breath to breath—the energy flowing freely through our bodies, as our arms drifted slowly towards our sides. She, in less control than I thought, took a deep breath and continued. ". . . ache that knows no mend . . ." Inhale. "Hurt that knows no end . . ." Exhale. "Desire is . . . the truest of the true . . ." I was her Virtruvian Man. And she, tonight, was in her own way, my DaVinci. ". . . it is the drive behind the drive, the storm behind the storm . . ." Her voice took me to a meditative state. I was rooted deeply to the earth and floating above what my senses would allow. "Desire is . . . the sister of pain . . . the brother of love." Everything that I'd once known appeared and disappeared as if nothing were as vital as how I was feeling in this room. I needed this to stop. Now.

"Let me paint you." I interrupted the moment with what would in any other room be considered an odd request. I wanted to remember this night. I also wanted to gain some type of control over the situation. She smiled deliberately. Her eyes were a bottomless well of knowing.

"You'd like to paint me?"

"Yes."

"Why?"

"Why ask questions you already know the answers to." I answered curtly. It was my turn. I took her hand in mine. Led her from the center of the room.

"Please, sit." I motioned towards the bed.

"Would you like me to—"

"—I will let you know." Ah, she is used to being in control. I could see those dark eyes, fluttering at what would be the highest personal recognition—the greatest gift, from painter to subject. I moved the paint, armchair and canvas towards the bed. I would paint sitting. It would calm me. I adjusted the easel, to receive maximum light from the candles. She glowed. I reached inside my bag for my chalks. Knelt before her. And began.

"Desire is . . ." A stroke of smoke grey. "an unanswered prayer . . ." I spoke gently while I lightly moved my hands as if they were touching her skin. "an untouched heart . . ." she added. We took turns delivering the cadence to what would possibly be the most memorable night ever for me.

"an enslaved soul . . ."

"a cry unheard . . ."

"a child unloved . . ."

"a portrait unpainted . . ."

"A love unknown . . ." At that moment, she was the most beautiful woman I'd ever seen. I saw the hurt. The childhood disappointments. The vulnerability. Her acceptance of those things as they were. It was hard for me to focus on the task at hand. I wanted to drop the pencils and brushes. Love her all over. Love it all away. A stroke. A smudge. I studied her face. The broken promises. The victory. The defeat. It was all there. She wanted me to take those things away from her. Somehow, she knew if given the chance, I would.

Lovely colors were surfacing. But this was not what I wanted. I needed to be closer. I wanted to paint her eyes as they appeared. Deep. Murky. Ethereal. Desirable. I lifted her up, brought her closer to me, allowing her legs to straddle mine as she joined me face to face on the chair. Eye to eye, for a brief moment, our worlds collided. Paint brush in my right hand, the small of her back in my left, we continued our allegiance to the moment.

"Desire is . . ." she started, but didn't finish. Our desire was, at that point, was for the bodily experience of this energy. We wanted to, but didn't move. The moment would not allow it. I could see my fears in the reflection of her eyes. I could feel the heat gather in that special spot. And the wetness. Although my desire, due to pure simple differences in anatomy was made more apparent than hers, we remained still. The woman-girl and the boy-man overcome with the very thing we sought to define. I continued to paint. She, in an unbearable moment, removed her top. The rising of the sun, and the glimmering of the candles, gave new light—new perspective and meaning to life for me. It didn't matter that I was leaving the city. Or that I didn't know her name. I knew for the first time, the feeling—*that* feeling. It was no longer energy on a dance floor, or a word unspoken. If it wished to be left here, in candlelight, in bliss, on an armchair with its legs wrapped around me, wanting but not having me completely, then so be it. Its wish was my command.

7

I lay in bed, not wanting to face the day, but thankful that I'd been given the chance. I think of the woman-girl. I wonder what she is doing. If she dances in the morning instead of paints. I take a look at the desire-inspired portrait and wonder if she has the same look on her face—in her eyes right now, as she did that night. If it takes a special type of music to evoke the feeling that brings the look, or if she was born with it. I wonder if that is the look of freedom or surrender or both. If whatever she feels makes her wiser. If it makes her stronger. If it's the cause of the dance, or the dance is the cause of the feeling. I close my eyes. Try to remember the song. The candlelit room. The scent of her. Desire is all I can think of. It's all I can feel. I wonder if that is the pressure in my chest. I remember the dance in her eyes. Wonder if I will see her again.

My phone rings. It's my brother. My natural brother.

"Morning."

"Hey man! You have everything together!" He was excited. Must be the coffee.

"Yea, I just have a few more things to tidy up." I answered.

"That accent man . . ." he chuckled. "What did you say?" he asked. I slowed down the verbiage.

"I said, I have some more stuff to do today."

"Okay. I just want to make sure I have all of the details. What airport?"

"JFK."

"Good. What time?"

"Six fifteen p.m."

"What carrier?" I wondered why he separated every question. And why he spoke so quickly. I thought about the email I sent last week. Wondered if he got the itinerary.

"Virgin Atlantic." I was more patient than he was. I do remember that.

"Okay, okay, okay . . ." He was jotting it all down. We hadn't spoken in so long. I couldn't remember if it was because I was too engulfed in art, or he in business matters. It's been years.

"Alright so . . . JFK, six fifteen, Virgin Atlantic. I will be there." Goodbye was all that was left. As it was years ago.

Of my natural brother, it is only blood that connects us. Years ago, after the death—or murder, whichever plucks your fancy—of my mother, he and I made a pact to look after one another. To stay with each other at all costs, as the nature of the US social system meant well, but more often than not, left much to be desired. In terms of adoptive possibility, due to simple demographic variables, age, race, gender and the like, Micah and I posed slim chances. Separate, the chances were still slim, but better. He and I agreed that we would be better off together than apart. So, together we would stay. I would look after him as I always had. As my mum would wish.

I remember my luck, as it had improved. People loved my paintings. Prospective parents would ask me questions. They would ask none of Micah. I turned down opportunity after opportunity for love, care, an overall better shot at life because they would often want one and not the other. I got older. Chances grew slimmer. And I'd settled into the notion of being in that hellish system until further notice. One day, I'd awakened to a note, from a favorite social worker, informing me of Micah's departure. He'd apparently chosen the first lot handed to him. Never even woke me up to say goodbye.

I think of Brooklyn, of a family that never existed and a brother who never cared. I tried to conjure memories of the past. There were some images and events, like the one I mentioned, but overall the mind went numb. Some things I could recall, most I could not. For the next fifteen hours or so, I'd like to keep it that way.

The last of the day's errands took me to the gallery. There were things for me to gather, and things I wanted to leave. In the middle of ticket purchases and making living arrangements, I managed to paint small portraits for each of my friends. Replicas of famous pieces with a twist. There was Gustav Klimt's "The Park" for Paul. Except his version showed him standing in the middle of the greenery, glancing at his pocket watch. There was Braque's "The Guitar" for Ahmed, and Bearden's "Patchwork Quilt" for Julia. I left paintings for Mark and for the sandwich shop owner next door. It was my way of thanking my surrogate family. I tried to place each painting in a special place in the gallery, as if they were a part of the current show. I chuckled knowing Paul would be the first to discover the hidden pieces and put on a production as he found each one.

The knock at the door startled me, as the gallery is closed to the public on Sunday. Almost everyone who can locate us knows that. Either the guest was a thief or totally clueless. Since thieves tend not to knock on storefront windows, I answered it.

"May I help you?" I asked. An older man stood in front of me.

"Is this John Martin?" he asked.

"Yes."

"The Mark Adlington show is here, yes?"

"Yes, it is." I answered.

"May I take a look?" He couldn't be serious. An idiot would notice that we were closed.

"We are not open today. We will be tomorrow."

"Please, I promise it will be worth the trouble. I need to make a purchase for my wife." His tone was patient and controlled as if he were used to the power he had over people. His eyes said different. They were frantic and pleading. As if his wife were the one with the real power. What would it hurt? It would be my last sale to what seemed like a good man.

"You can come in, but we mustn't be all day," I said. He agreed. As he stepped through the multicolored doors, there was mischievous glint in his eyes. One that I couldn't place.

He walked around slowly, studying each piece, the soles of his shoes making love to the polished wood. He's rich.

"Can you tell me about the exhibition? My wife seems very excited about it. I just like to be informed on what I'm purchasing." At least he was honest. Something about his disposition was very comforting. Like a favorite uncle. There was also a part of this disposition that alluded to him being here for more than he said he was.

"Yes, the exhibit is called Gran Paradiso, Drawings from an Alpine Wilderness. The artist was on location in Italy, at their oldest national park where a special Alpine wilderness quarters was established to protect the Ibex, Chamois and Marmot from extinction . . ." I spoke. He walked. And walked. "The drawings of the animals are chalk—"

"—These are drawings? Amazing," he exclaimed.

"Yes. They resemble large paintings but Mark Adlington has composed a series of chalk drawings of the protected species which are remarkable and unique."

"And what about this one here? I've seen this before. Although I believe it was larger." He motioned towards my Klimt piece.

"It's a replica of a famous Gustav Klimt. That isn't for sale, sir. I'm leaving it for a friend. As a gift." I answered promptly.

"You did this? Absolutely splendid work! I imagine you are well taken care of here, else I'd invite you to work with us on a new project." A tasteful offer if I'd ever received one. The well-dressed man walked from piece to piece with little resolve, a decision nowhere on the horizon. He stopped pacing the floor. Enough was enough.

"I can't decide." He threw his hands up. Flashed his classic Presidential timepiece. Paul is so much better at this.

"Well, what does she like?"

"I hate to say it—what did you say your name was?" he asked.

"I didn't. Islam."

"Islam. I hate to say it, but I really don't know what she likes. She is the art connoisseur, not I."

"Alright. What is the occasion?"

"She is expanding. Opening galleries in the US. We are celebrating. I wanted to purchase something special for her. She mentioned this artist was showing here. He's a favorite of hers." We were not getting anywhere. He decided he'd had it. "I will take those two and let her decide," he stated, as he pointed in opposite directions towards the most expensive pieces in the gallery. Under normal circumstances I'd be excited to sell both pieces and go home. But he was wasting money in the name of impatience. I don't know how to say that without upsetting him. I try.

"Sir, we appreciate clients who are definitive in their acquisitions. However, we'd also like to ensure that your selection truly fits your taste. At almost twenty thousand pounds, it's imperative," I relayed. He looked at me. I couldn't tell what he was thinking.

"You don't want to sell both pieces?" he asked.

"I'd love to. If you had asked for two. But you asked for one." He smiled knowingly.

"That's right. But if I buy two we both win."

"But this is for your wife. It would be more special if you made the selection, don't you think?" The artist and the business man. Always a draw. He smiled an impish grin.

"You're honest. I like that."

"I try."

"Maybe I can come back tomorrow and make the choice. Will you be here?"

"No. I'm off to The States myself."

"Really? May I be made privy as to why?" he inquired.

"I need to concentrate on the business side of my career. I play in the UK. Too much to do." He nodded. Man to man, he understood.

"Ah yes, the trappings of the female kind . . ." I grinned. He's no fool. ". . . and the discotheque . . ." Now I was smiling. ". . . an artist of your caliber let loose in this city is a force to be reckoned with." Eyebrow raised, he dared me to challenge him. I didn't. "Well, if you find yourself in the States in need of work, please don't hesitate to call." He handed me his card. I fingered its suede-like texture and stared at the gold embossed lettering.

COOPER SPENCE. SPENCE GALLERIES AND ACQUISITIONS.

"Islam?"

"Yes?"

"Include one of your works as well." He began toward the door and stopped in his tracks. "And as for the drawing, you seem to be good with women, you decide. I trust your judgment," he said confidently. There was no room for debate. The old-but-young rich man was already out of the door.

I kept the card just in case.

8

The aerial view of New York City isn't what it used to be. I am not sure that I am here, although that is what I am being told. I'm looking downward, and if memory serves me correctly, I am viewing what I remember to be the Verrazano Bridge, what appears to be a tiny processional of matchbox cars on my left—the Brooklyn-Queens Expressway, and to my right—the Belt Parkway. Furthest left is where the discrepancy is. And then I experience the sinking feeling spoken of on documentaries and newscasts alike. That awful thing did happen. The towers are absent. For someone who has not been home in almost two decades, try envisioning a bright red door on the front of the home you grew up in. And then imagine it's been changed to off-white.

I reach into the front seat pocket and dig for the immigration form that was handed to me at the start of the flight. Find a pen. Surname. Ian. Given name . . . If I could lie and say it were Michael, or Todd, immigration would be my friend. I scribble the truth. Islam. The name my mum gave me while pregnant and protesting the Israeli occupation of Palestine. She'd never know the irony, that I'd be raised to pray and ask for peace in Hebrew. That small fact—the convolution—I'm sure, bought me a few additional hours at the immigration desk. Items to claim? I have nothing I brought nothing. Paint, canvas and a weird but what would be considered awesome wardrobe in another world. That's it.

"Welcome to John F. Kennedy Airport, the time is six thirteen p.m., the temperature is twenty-one degrees Celsius, seventy degrees Fahrenheit . . ."

We all but collide onto the asphalt. The passengers applaud. Personally, I think he could have done a better job. The plane landed as would an elephant sliding on a banana peel. I'm sure everyone's just happy to be here without a man's twisted allegiance to his Allah being unleashed on a group of innocent bystanders. Or his desperate response to fifty years of oppression and being uprooted from his own soil. However you choose to view it.

We progress to the front of the aircraft, like earthworms finding there was more rock than soil in their path. I eavesdrop on several conversations, and laugh quietly at jokes that I will not be able to tell my brother.

Thank you for flying Virgin Atlantic. . . . thank you. . . . thank you . . . enjoy your trip . . . thank you . . .

It was my lucky day. The man at the immigration desk did in fact, have a life. He did not take pride in ripping me a shred. I find myself an hour past landing, being inducted by tense faces, rapid pace, and angry stares to nowhere into the fraternity they call New York City. A glance forward, and I see a man who resembles me, holding what I'm sure is a rather peculiar sign at this airport. *Especially* at this airport. ISLAM. A chuckle. I wonder if authorities have already been alerted by their super-satellite to my brother's formal gesture. I'm sure they're onto him, after all, they can see me take this piece of candy out of my pocket.

I greet my younger sibling. He greets me. I mess up the handshake.

"Man, you've been away too long," he said, while laughing at my inability to profess Black American manhood.

"The handshakes change with the headlines," I offered sheepishly. Micah looked me up and down. Scrutinized my wears. My bullet-holed Glastonbury Festival tee. Gola trainers. Distressed denim. Pocket chains. Silver jeweled piercings in my ears and eyebrow. There were more tattoos than he'd ever allow for himself. A larger than life dragon on my left shoulder, performing the unmentionable on Virgo the virgin at the base of my neck. Of all my tattoos, it was my favorite.

"You've changed. I see you've taken quite well to London," he said. I wasn't sure how to take that, but it didn't matter. I haven't changed. I just stopped pretending. I took a swift look at me from his perspective, then he from mine. Shirt. Pants. Shoes. In my world, he might as well have been wearing a bin liner. Or as they say here, trash bag.

"London is a wonderful city," is all I say.

"Well, it doesn't matter. We're just glad to have you back, man. We're just glad you're here. Is this all you have?"

"Yea."

"Then let's hit the road. Traffic is crazy right now."

I am given a crash course in the crisis state of American life, from the Black perspective. Poverty ratios. Education. Prison rates. Gentrification. My brother is a civil rights attorney.

"So if we can just come together as a people . . . you know what I'm saying?" He carries on. I try to give at least the illusion of interest. My mind wanders. This place requires such intense focus on everything. Even in the comfort of a monstrous luxury vehicle. While he rants, I get a craving for that feeling. The look and the feeling. I glance at the time. Think of the woman-girl. Ask myself if she has fallen asleep yet. What her life is like. If she has thought of me since then. I concentrate. Push thoughts of her from the frontal lobe, to the brain stem. Try to focus on what my brother is telling me. I notice we are going in the wrong direction.

"Micah. Aren't we going to Fort Greene? That is where the

flat is, correct?" I'm sure that's where he told me I would be staying. It's the area I knew best. He laughed.

"Islam, take a second look. The faces have changed, but the streets are the same," he smiled knowingly. I paid closer attention. Lafayette. Washington. Dekalb. Adelphi. Three fifteen Adelphi was the address to the flat.

"This is Fort Greene?" I belted out. I was speechless. Vintage shops. Candle lit restaurants and cafes. It resembled a particular neighborhood in London called Notting Hill. Not where a childhood friend was shot in the head close-range for his trainers. Didn't a famous filmmaker own a shop right there on that corner? Dekalb street. The Technical High School. Yes, this is it. Damn.

"Yes, Islam. This. Is. Fort. Greene. My brotha . . ." he over emphasized the now obvious, as we unloaded duffel bags and canvas tubes from the vehicle with more horsepower than a British rail train. "Here are the keys to the studio . . ." I was in awe. Knowing my financial situation, and the road I was attempting to venture down professionally, my brother offered marginal rent for a studio flat in a Victorian or as they say *brownstone* that he owns. One of many I assumed. I looked upward. The mahogany door. The large windows. He's been too generous. I wish I felt gratitude. I do not.

"So get acquainted, or should I say re-acquainted with the hood. We are meeting for dinner in a few. Here's the number to the cellie—"

"The what?"

"The cellie. Cellular." He pulled a razor thin object out of his pocket that resembled a phone.

"Oh. Your mobile."

"My what?"

"Mo-bile. Like bile. The bodily fluid. Bile. Mo-bile." I spelled out for him. He chuckled.

"Yea, right. Well, you have the number. Dinner's at nine," he replied. What made him think I wanted to be bothered with such plans? It's starting already. The pressure to conform. Do what the group is doing. I'm tired. I don't feel like assaulting my cheek bones by smiling for hours on end. I don't feel like answering questions. I don't want to go. But if I don't then I'm being rude. This bullshit again. I sigh. Opt out of the panicky artist drama and tell myself that it's not what I think, that it won't be so bad.

"Where?" I asked.

"A few blocks from here, over on Lafayette. A place called Gia."

"With whom, may I ask?"

"Just myself, Lydia—I told you about her, my wife. And possibly one other guest." He answered.

"Male or female?" I must have asked as if my life depended on it. He smiled as memories came rushing back.

"Female, Islam. For you my brother, female."

"Alright. See you at dinner." He extended his palm. I got the handshake right this time.

9

I step out onto the tree-lined street feeling a sense of adventure. Welcoming the new experience. Although not as diverse as Camden Town, or as unique as Portobello road, the buzz in Fort Greene is singular to the area. It is very ethnic, if I may say so. Very Black. As if Black owns ethnic. In Europe, the word isn't specific to a particular group. It can mean Indian, Slavic, German or Arabian. Thai, Ghanaian, Sudanese or Czech. On the corner of Dekalb Avenue and South Elliot Street, I survey the culturally relative and specific characteristics of America's number one 'ethnic' group and wonder if they know they are not alone.

I make way past windows that display wooden artifacts and basketball players better than the ones on television. I am greeted, either with a simple head nod, or by beautiful women who glance, who smile, but do not speak. I almost get run over—the traffic here comes from the opposite direction than it does in London— noticing woman after woman. So many hues and textures. I share a private joke with myself as I wonder if this move was a good idea after all.

I approach a restaurant at sixty eight Lafayette Street. Where I would watch crap games as a child is now a French American fusion get up. The ambiance is posh. Chic clientele over small black tables and candles. I do recognize the Nicola Conte remix of Fertile Ground's "Yellow Daisies" and it makes me feel good. Hearing the rich voice of the female vocalist offer peace and blessings to the stylish crowd assures me that all is not lost here in the Big Apple. I must admit, it will take a while to adjust to the changes. But I like them. I'm not sure what that means, since Micah seems to refer to the newness negatively. I see them immediately to my right. My brother stands.

"Ladies, the prodigal son. This is my long lost brother, Islam." He gestures towards me. I take a look around and wonder if I should have changed. "Islam, this is my wife Lydia, and a friend of ours, Lia." I nod. Kiss the one he introduced as Lia on both cheeks. Did the same to Lydia. Lia was flattered. I affixed her chair, so she could seat herself more comfortably.

"Awwwh, he's such a gentleman!" Lia exclaimed. I'm not sure where the accolades are warranted. It's standard in Europe to treat even a dog-faced woman with a shred of dignity. "Did that hurt?" Lia pointed to the outline of one of two pierced chest nipples.

"Not much," I answered sheepishly.

"I love your tattoos . . ." While Lia complimented me and my brother sat himself, I held the chair out for my brother's wife. Something was different about the energy I received from Lydia. A shift. A move. A bit of hesitation to sit on her part, then I got it. The flash. That quick shot of heat a woman sends to you when there is a bit of, how do you say . . . interest. I'm sure I am misinterpreting things. Women are different here.

"We haven't ordered entrees, but we've got a round of appetizers here so help yourself," Micah stated. I looked at the spread. And remembered the monster sized vehicle we taxied in from the airport. Excess. All excess.

"Islam. Micah tells me you are an artist. A painter." Lydia began the inevitable. Flash again. I ignored it.

"Yea. I consider myself somewhat of an impressionist, but not really," I answer.

"Impressionists, if my memory serves me correctly, paint the same figures from different perspectives, right?"

"Somewhat."

"And what do you like to paint most? What captures your attention long enough for you to paint it several times over?" She was obviously very interested in art.

"Women." I answered curtly. Lydia blushed. There was an awkward silence at the table.

"Yes, Islam studied art at a well known Arts College in London and has traveled Europe extensively," Micah added. He made it sound so big. I haven't done anything different than any of my colleagues.

"Have you been to Prague? Is it as beautiful as the pictures?" Lia asked.

"Yes to both." I answered quietly.

"Where's that again? Germany?"

"Yeah, that's Germany, right bro?" Micah attempted to answer Lia's question.

"It's the Czech Republic," Lydia and I answered in unison.

"Are you an artist?" I asked her. I decided to stop ignoring her and have what would be my only shot at an intelligent conversation.

"No, well kind of. I've loved film all my life. I've shot a few shorts, a documentary or two, but that's it," she said solemnly. As if it meant nothing.

"You speak of it as a love lost," I probed. "What do you do now?"

"She's a doctor. A psychiatrist," Micah interrupted.

I could tell she wished to speak more openly. I know the feeling. "That is respectable. You must be proud of yourself." I say. I know she isn't. She's a closeted artist. It's hell.

"Some days I am." The look in her eyes asked me if I understood. If I sympathized. Women communicate most thoroughly with their eyes. I looked towards my brother who was tapping a slim metal pointer onto a small plastic screen vigorously, as if his life depended on it. I understood. I understood that she was trapped. That she was not pleased with her choices. And that she saw no way out. I said nothing to console her. There was nothing to say.

We all pretended to be truly enjoying the two scallops in a pretentious serving dish. Just as the combination of jet lag and utter boredom threatened to force my head onto the table, a familiar voice wrapped its arms around my ears. It was British. Music to my ears.

"Should Britain's finest, meeting twice in such a short period of time, be considered fate or a trick of the gods?" He was standing behind me to my right, and I didn't have to look to place the voice. It was Mr. Spence, my last client at John Martin. Lydia and Lia's faces told it all. If *GQ* had a Windsor edition of their magazine, he'd easily grace the cover.

"I don't believe in fate, but I'll take the piss on it for the occasion," I replied candidly. Stood up. Extended my hand for a shake.

"Ah, a nonbeliever!" he playfully exclaimed, tastefully surveying the scene at the table. He wouldn't be rude even if I was. "Ladies . . ." A courteous bow toward the table, ". . . and sir," a firm handshake, "the pleasure is mine. Sincerest apologies for interrupting your supper, but this man right here is an artistic genius." Micah looked at Mr. Spence, then at me. The expression on his face read: *Who? Him?* I ignored it.

We spoke amongst ourselves.

"She loved the painting."

"Drawing."

"Oh, yes. Drawing. Painting, whichever, she loved it. I could watch Beckham's World Cup debut uninterrupted." We laughed.

"So he did come back? Did we win? I haven't had time to catch the match." I asked of my favorite sport.

"They're not showing it here?"

The question was rhetorical. No one at the table had the slightest clue as to what we were talking about. Nor did they pretend to. They were far more interested in how we were saying what we were saying instead. I continued.

"So she fancied the work. Good. I'm glad. You here on holiday?" I asked.

He chuckled. "Unfortunately my driver takes more holiday time than I do, business calls."

"Really?"

"Of course. You remember I told you. We're expanding. More galleries, larger clients, major purchases, etcetera."

The fascination with our accent, pace of conversation and overall ease of flow was apparent. Eyes shot back and forth like tennis balls. Lia smiled. Lydia shifted in her seat. I was just happy to have been offered a break.

"You said art was her gig, yea?"

"It is. I handle the financial aspects. Property acquisition, council taxes, banks, those sorts of bollocks." I nodded in understanding. He continued. "We are to do something completely different with our US galleries, and I am here to lay the foundation."

"I didn't know there was that much money in art," Micah volunteered his ignorance as if there were a top prize for the most happily unaware. Mr. Spence gave me a knowing look. I tend to separate myself from ignorance. It's contagious. I let him handle it.

"Art. If there were less finance in art, society would be in far better condition." He's a pro. "Now if we could just get Islam to join us in these matters, we'd be sorted."

"As an artist or gallery director?" I asked.

"Both."

"As an artist I would love to, as a director, I'd have to respectfully decline. I left London to focus on my career as a painter. My career as a gallery director was already on its own. But if you—" The rear of the restaurant. It caught my eye. Was that her?

"Excuse me, please." I made my way through the small candlelit restaurant as quickly as I could, to its rear. I looked from left to right. I could have sworn I saw her. No, I know I did. Embarrassed by my impulsivity and even more so by my desperation, I pushed all thoughts of her as far away from me as I could. Just then, I remembered Borges' short story of the Islamic tale, "*The Zahir*". About the object that drove one mad upon a single glance. That the greater the attempt to rid oneself of thinking of it, the more one became obsessed—to the point of madness. I had thought of her almost every day, certainly every night. Of the feeling and the look. I had raced through a studio to get to her. Now I was a continent away, racing through a small restaurant. Although I knew madness was out of the question, I would not have this . . . this obsessing over a woman that I didn't even have sex with.

Enough is enough. I returned to the table to find arbitrary chatter back to preferred levels and Mr. Spence long gone. Ignoring the concerned looks from Lydia, I grabbed Lia's hand and decided that she would help me get the woman-girl out of my system once and for all.

"Care to join me?" I asked.

I already knew the answer. She was just as desperate as I to feel something other than what she had been.

10

"*Will you be having anything else, sir?*"
"*No, thank you, tea will be just fine . . .*"

They say that if you can make it in New York, you can make it anywhere. I'm not sure how the concept relates to me, but if the statement is true, then I might as well quit while I am ahead.

Two months of personal adverts, invitations, handshaking, hustle and bustle have landed me here, at a local pub slash underground gallery slash performance space, sipping designer tea with a bunch of other artists who were also good, but just couldn't seem to pull it all together.

I sip. Stare. Sip. Wonder what the hell I'm doing here. Wonder what I'm missing. I look around at the art work on display here at Sputnik, and find myself way above the norm. Some of these pieces, I could paint with my eyes closed and a brush between my teeth. There must be another way. I think of what I've accomplished so far. I did manage to put on a small studio show at the flat to somewhat of an audience. My brother, Lydia, Lia and one unsuspecting girl who happened to ring the wrong doorbell. Micah suggested placing the works outdoors, to which I vehemently refused. I am no sidewalk artist.

So I am here, at what could invariably be considered a turning point for me. I could say fuck this. Apparently you have to be on the "inside" of the various social circles and scenes in order to be taken seriously. Even if you can't tell a paint brush from a toothbrush. Or, I could move forward. Figure this out. What I lacked in determination, I retained in ego. I am better than. I am well trained. I know the difference between The Tate Modern and Tate Brit. Constable and Kandinsky. MoMA. and The Met. There is that whimsical situation, where the artist is discovered on a street corner or a shopping center. Then there is the one who has studied to show himself approved. There is Mickey Mouse. And then there is Miles.

I gather my things. Head towards the only refuge I have here in Brooklyn.

Greene Street is a peaceful collection of homes, trees and foliage. I knock on the door and wait. The foxtrot of two very large but beautiful dogs greets me first, each one sniffing, initiating me into their space. Then, the man himself appeared. He's got more grey hair than I remember.

"Well, well, well . . . look at what the cat's drug in." He said. Danny Simmons. The epicurean connoisseur of the western world. The only man I know here with his ear to the ground and his arms to the sky. He is talented, dedicated and true. A sight for sore eyes.

"Good afternoon." I stood there like a wanker.

"Well what are you doing standing there, come in!" he exclaimed. Walked off leaving me standing in the doorway, in a way that only Danny could. You'd have to understand the gesture. It was one of invitation. Of trust. It was the best I'd felt since I'd arrived in New York. I walked through the narrow hallway, past what people know to be The Corridor Gallery of the Rush Philanthropic Arts Foundation, to his ridiculously obtuse studio flat. I took a look around. This was the real deal. There was so much art, in so many mediums from literally everywhere. I'd almost forgotten why I was here.

"Islam, my man. It's good to see you. Make yourself comfortable." He stated.

I was completely submerged in his collection of black and white photographs. "Huh?"

"I said get comfortable. What brings you to the city?" he asked.

"I've moved."

"Why?"

"It was time."

"Uh huh. How's Julia?"

"Fine."

"I bet she is," he laughed. "And Mark?"

"Good."

"And what about that other one . . . the gay one."

I chuckled. "Paul, he's not gay. Everybody's fine." I located a piece purchased from our gallery in London. The goddess Isis in clay. One of my favorites. "I forgot you had this." I told him.

"Yeah, she's still holdin' on."

He let me roam the large flat for a while. One thing I've always appreciated about him. He's perceptive. If something is twigging you, he'll let you sort it. A few minutes passed. I sat. Twiddled my thumbs.

"I can't get my work out." There.

He joined me in the main area. "What have you done so far?" he asked.

"Everything, it seems. Studio show, passed out adverts—"

"Passed out what?"

"Adverts. Flyers. I've been to all the shops. Galleries. Been to Chelsea. Lelong. Cristea. Rare. Miller. No one will see me. Even with my credentials." I was frustrated to say the least. He could see that. I watched him clean his brushes. With all the activity on his end it never seemed as if he were listening. But he always was.

"Who do you know here?" He smudged the synthetic bristles. Patiently worked the color out of each one. "Besides me." He finished.

I thought. Not too many. In London, I primarily dealt with purchasers directly, people who were on the cutting edge. Julia did the ball-cupping.

"Honestly? No one I can imagine at the moment." I thought harder. Surely there must be an option other than nepotism. "Is this entire scene about who you know? Does anyone care about the work?" I asked. I was green. I knew I was.

"Yes!" he yelled. "Now who do you know? Let's start from there."

"I met the director of the Studio Museum last week at a showing and talk for the Gordon Parks retrospective. She used to direct the Whitney."

"Thelma Golden?"

"Yea."

"You get her contact?"

"No, it was crowded and she was a bit too popular for me. I don't engage in those sorts of bollocks. Ass kissing etcetera. I left prior to making arrangements with her." I answered.

"Get to know her. She knows everyone."

"What? Shag her? She's a bit old for me, yea?" He laughed. I guess that's not what he had in mind.

"Man, I'm sure she wouldn't be interested, your reputation precedes you. Just get to know her socially." He laughed. "I'll give Derek a call at RUSH in Chelsea, you know we'll run a show for you here. I know your work. But you need to establish yourself with your clique."

"My what?"

"Clique. Cohort. Group. New York is cliquish. What you paint is forward contemporary, modernist, but European influenced. You need support from people in that area." He was right. "Anyone else you can think of?" I pulled the card from my wallet. Handed it to him. He scrutinized it dearly if I may say so.

"You know Cooper Spence?" he asked incredulously.

"Yea. He was my last client at John Martin. I chose a piece for his wife. She loved it. He offered me a gig here, but I can't. I've got to get my career off the ground."

"You know Cooper Spence." This time, it was a statement.

"Yea." I wondered why he was making such a big deal out of it.

"THEN WHAT THE HELL ARE YOU DOING HERE!" he yelled. "You know the heir, the estate manager of one of the most influential aristocratic families in the world! What, his father is a Lord or a Duke or something like that? Friends or family of the King, you should know all of that royal shit. Art? Please. The man has his hands in more oil than a Kansas City shop mechanic. Get your ass on the phone and take that job. What does he want you to do?"

"I don't know. Help him and his wife set up things here. They are expanding. Opening galleries in the US." I answered solemnly.

"You mean his wife is opening galleries. He's into other shit. Spence has made a mint using smoke screens. If he's here, he's got a plan." Danny assessed. The conversation wasn't heading in the direction that I'd hoped. The last thing I wanted was a political talk, and I cringed at the thought of another gig. This was always the toss up for artists. Can't support yourself and commit to your art. If you are full time in art, you have no money, no contacts and virtually no hope. If you work, you have no time to create, no art to show for the money you've earned. Fuck.

"But I can't work. That's what I was doing in London. If I take the job, then I surrender to the system. Besides, you know more about him than I do." I reasoned.

"Let me put it mildly. If Dick Cheney was out of politics, twenty years younger, a bit more understated, and say, a few— make that several hundred million dollars richer, he'd be Cooper Spence. With Tony Blair, Texas and parts of Iraq on tap, he's one of the youngest of that upper circle to make moves in the way that he has. Lots of respect from the higher ups because of how he got to where he is. That's a ruthless motherfucker. The only thing he loves as much as fucking people over is his wife."

"How do you know all of this?" I asked.

"I've got cable," Danny made a face that asked: *What can I say?*, as he laughed with the statement.

"Why do I feel like I've been under a rock? I should know this."
I prided myself on being informed. Not that it would change my
mind about work, but I'd at least know who the man was.

"Cooper Spence doesn't peek his head out from the molehill
unless it's absolutely necessary. And I don't know many artists
who can afford three hundred channels of bullshit so I'm sure
you're not alone. Just take my word for it. He's a snake. But a
powerful one. If you can get in and out unscathed you'd be on
your way. At least make some good contacts and get your work
out. Whichever the case, it wouldn't matter. Your shit would go
through the roof. Like that." He sent his hands off in a mock air-
plane gesture. Seemed he was sorted on the matter. He pulled
out a small piece of canvas and began working around and about
color as his signature style would indicate. I sat still, weighing op-
tions. Oblivious to an environment that would normally inspire
me.

Nothing in me seemed to be able to find the capacity to report
to work again. There must be another way. I needed to change
the subject. The current one was depressing me. Danny had gotten into a groove painting. I hated to interrupt him, but there was
something else I wanted to ask.

"Danny."

"What." He answered bluntly. As to say: *what other matters of
life and death have you actually discovered you've got the answers to?*

I chuckled. Asked the question anyway. "When you paint. You
get a feeling, yea? One that of course, we can describe as a high,
given there has been nothing extra curricular ingested."

"Yeah. Go on," he said.

"And this high . . . how would you describe it if you had to?"

He thought for a moment. "Connected. Spiritual. Free."

"And have you felt it otherwise? Outside of painting?"

"Of course," he answered.

"When?"

"That's my business." We both laughed. "But I can tell you,
when you're connected to that thing—your thing, you get there.
You feel it. It takes you to where you need to be. Most artists

have it, man. It's the thing that separates us from the masses."
He seemed so sure. I was ashamed to tell him that I'd only felt it
once. In a hotel suite. "Why do you ask? Something else on your
mind? 'Cause I'm about to start charging you by the hour." We
laughed again.

"No, not at all. I was just wondering." I answered him as honestly as I could. Wondered if I was what he called connected. If
that's what she—the woman-girl was. If that is what I saw in her
eyes. Spirit. Freedom. If it's what I felt. I closed my eyes. Allowed myself into a meditative state. I remember desire. And
that it is thirst that cannot be quenched. Hunger that cannot be
fed. I breathe in, and recall that it is ache that knows no mend. As
I contemplate it further, I remember it is a heart untouched. A
cry unheard. I tried to induce what I felt that night. The sister of
pain. The brother of love. Came up with nothing. Again.

11

The rain poured. I climbed the stairs quickly, happy to emerge from the underground or as New Yorkers say, train station, without succumbing to respiratory failure. It's filthy. However, it runs twenty-four hours, and is air-conditioned. That's more than any Brit can say about our ridiculously primitive transport system in London.

New York is alluring in the rain. Since I wanted to learn the streets of Soho here as I knew them in London, I opted for the train instead of taxi into Lower Manhattan. The R train to Prince Street. West Broadway to Broome. Four twenty-one would find me at the Spence Gallery of Contemporary Art. My first day as . . . actually I don't know what the title is. Sir Spence, happy that I'd chosen to assist him in his art buying ventures, made an offer I could not refuse. I'd be working with him and his wife to build the repertoire for the US galleries. If there was one thing I knew, was where to find cutting edge work. I'd work with Mr. Spence on the financials, and Mrs. Spence with everything else. It was great because I could work a schedule that would allow me time to paint. Select exquisite works in a variety of mediums from artists all over the world. Compensation that exceeded my expectations. We'd work out the minor details at a later date.

The large metal door was tightly sealed. There were four large windows but no displays. I located the appropriate doorbell. The gallery was apparently several stories up. As the elevator rose to its designated floor, I must admit to being a tad nervous. This was all very new to me.

The space was huge and smartly designed. There wasn't as much art around as one would suppose. I guess that's why I'm here. I stood patiently in front of what appeared to be a reception desk.

"May I help you?" A beautifully raspy voice asked as she took the empty seat at the desk in front of me.

"I am Islam," I said.

"Oh, why yes. We are expecting you. Please. Take a seat in the office to your right. She will be with you momentarily." She. I forgot Mr. Spence was already back in the UK. I was meeting with the Mrs. We would be working closely together. Building the collection for the gallery here. I waited patiently. Noticed the Mark Adlington piece—the one I had chosen, hanging neatly on the wall behind her desk. Restless, I stood up, walked towards the huge window. Stared through the rain, onto the street. One, two taxis. One bus. One, two, three taxis. Another bus. One—I felt it. The power. The connection. I wondered what triggered it. The sound of her voice froze me in place.

"Yes. Yes. We will try . . ." I didn't have to turn around. The energy. The feeling. The voice. I knew it was her. I stood facing the window. I didn't know what to do or say. When—if I should turn around. If I should run, or just walk out of here. The room was quiet. The door shut. She stood behind me. Silence. For what seemed like an eternity.

"You are Islam." Statement. No reply. There was too much adrenaline running through my veins. If this were a job interview I'd be finished. I turned to face her. Those dark eyes ripped through me. I did the only thing I could do. I stared. After a few minutes, I resolved to stop acting like I'd never seen a woman before. The words came.

"You are Mrs. Spence," was all I could muster.

"I am."

We stood there.

* * *

The rain was unrelenting. There was no music. No talk. Just the pounding of the water. Everything inside me said run. Which was baffling because it also said grab her. Touch her. Paint her. I'd discovered the feeling again, but a complicated one it was. There was north and south. Coming and going. Having and being had. But no resolve. They all seemed to coexist.

"We will be working together," she said. I questioned her struggle. If there was one. She seemed unaffected. I answered her statement-question.

"Yes."

"Portugal. Italy. Spain. Prague, possibly more," she offered. "Will you be content with that? The travels?"

I knew there was some traveling involved. I know it's my job to find, her job to acquire cutting-edge art. I say this the best I can. "Yes."

"Good. Here is your key. Also one for upstairs, the corporate flat. In case of emergency . . ."

I wondered what type of feeling this was. That it would allow my senses to betray me. I didn't want to, but I heard her. In another time. On another continent.

"*Desire is . . .*" I willed it away before it overtook me.

"*A love unknown . . .*" My nerves. Get a hold of yourself, Islam. Stop acting like a bitch. Her natural voice interrupted my reflections. Thank God.

"And we will be in our travels at length, sometimes for undisclosed periods of time."

"Yes." I should have written the one word answer on my forehead. Simplified things.

"The schedule is not fixed," she told me.

"I need time to paint," was the first sentence of mine.

"I know. That you will have without fail."

She said that without so much as a slight inflection in voice. I want to know what she feels. If she feels this. It's so hard to tell. She made her way around me, to the window seat. Sat. Removed her shoes. Let her feet swing aimlessly back and forth. She looked towards the large chalk drawing of the endangered species hanging on the wall behind her. Then at me.

"Of all the pieces in this collection, you chose my favorite," she said. I was affixed.

I wanted to know her name.

I wanted to know her heart.

I wanted to know her spirit.

I wanted to love her.

12

The day was short but long. The sun is set. I am at home covered in contemplation, the sound of the rain my only accomplice. I hadn't a congruent thought since I saw her this afternoon. There were no other women. No Paul. No Ahmed. No parties. No escape. I did the only thing I knew to do. Faced the east.

Barukh atah Adonai Eloheinu melekh ha-olam,
Blessed art Thou O Lord Our God, King of the universe . . .

I prayed for might.
Ozeir Yisrael bigvurah . . .
I prayed for strength.
Ha-aotein laiya'eif koach . . .
I prayed for discernment.
Asher natan laskhvi,
Vina l'havchil ben yom
U'vein lailah . . .
I prayed and prayed until I started seeing shapes and color behind my lids. I needed Him to hear me right now. Deep breath.
Amein.
I got up from the kneeling position covered in sweat. I am not a practicing Jew. Anymore. But there are still some things that I

do religiously. I try to at least acknowledge the Sabbath and Holy days when I can. I follow the dietary laws. And I still pray in Hebrew. It's the only time besides the time that I paint that I feel close to God.

When I'd first arrived to London, the family that arranged to take me in were Orthodox Jews. They were a wonderful family who loved and fed me as if they'd brought me into this world. But they were strict. Upon my arrival, I hadn't any money or address other than theirs. I had no choice but to love and obey. No more pork. Duck. Shellfish. Friday evening at sundown, inside. Prayer. Sabbath candles. Saturday, synagogue. It was different. The language. The laws. To them, it didn't seem to matter that I was unusual. That I was withdrawn. That I loved to paint. When I stepped off of that plane, I was family. Family ate, prayed and worshiped together. To be honest, after my mother surrendered her life, I never really had anyone who loved me enough to enforce anything like that. I was happy to oblige.

I started working on a painting of a woman who'd caught my eye in London. A troubled one. This particular goddess portrait is a favorite of mine, because of how it's coming along. I'm using color differently. Trying new things, even if I'm not sure of how or if they'd work. A woman painted in earth tones stares blankly at me from the canvas. I mixed and re-mixed several shades of color. Browns, oranges, yellows. The clock ticks while I try and get into the woman's head. Into her heart. I can't. I'm distracted. Although I'm trying desperately to pretend that today was a day just as any other, I am failing miserably. What to do under these circumstances? There were no answers. None that I wish to accept. The phone rings. I almost knock over the canister of paint thinner trying to answer it.

"Hello."

"Hey, Islam. This is Lydia."

"Hello, Lydia."

"I—we just wanted to see how you were doing in the rain," she offered.

"I am doing well. It seems to only rain in London, so I am used to it." I answered.

"Oh, yes. That's right," she laughed nervously. "Well, feel free to come by and hang out if you need company."

"Thank you for the invite. I am painting, so I am quite occupied. But during the next storm count me in." I offered as diplomatically as possible.

"Am I disturbing you?" she asked. As if there were something else she wanted to say.

"Yes and no. Yes in that I am in a groove. No in that you are always welcome to ring me up. Whenever you need to." I answered. Felt her blush.

"Why thank you, kind sir. I'll take you up on that one. Have a good evening. Happy painting." She said.

"Ciao." I replied. Returned to the subject at hand. The situation. The circumstances. What to do? How did this happen? The job, it's a dream job. I travel the world discovering great art. The gallery, whose owners happen to be ridiculously connected in the art world—in the world period, represents my work. They are on a totally different level than I could ever imagine playing. The art that I visit in museums around the world, the works by famous artists, they actually own. I cannot give this gig up. And for what? A woman? A feeling? Fuck, no. I might as well have stayed in London with Yasara. At least she was mine.

So it's sorted.

There is no situation.

There are no circumstances.

I returned to the only woman who was not giving me trouble. Tried layering a bit of crimson between the umber. It's not working. Tried blending the color with my fingers. Damn it. I'm turning what could be a masterpiece into a finger painting. I am definitely distracted. Distraction is an understatement. Phone rings again. I'm frustrated and want whomever it is to fuck off. I prepare to say that in so many words.

"Hello."

"Good evening . . ." A pause. "It's Adrianne."

"Who?"

"Adrianne . . ." I knew who it was. ". . . Spence." So her name is Adrianne. I tell myself I don't want to feel anything. I don't want to feel like this. I pretend not to.

"Yes, how are you." I was as formal as Prince Charles.

"I am well," she answered. I said nothing. The pause was uncomfortable.

"Am I disturbing you?" She—Adrianne asked me as if she didn't care if she was or not, it was simply the proper thing to ask.

"Yes."

"Would you care for tea?" I was right.

"No, thank you. I'm painting." I was being strong. I was being an asshole, but strong.

"Would you prefer that I leave you to your work?" she asked. But she already knew. I hate this. I am the master of my urges. Not the other way around.

"Yes, please." I lied.

"As you wish." We hung up. I stood near the phone. Awaited the inevitable. It rang again.

"I can come to you," she said. There was no pause. The information tumbled out before I could stop it.

"Three fifteen Adelphi, between Dekalb and Lafayette. Fort Greene." We disconnected. This is not what I planned. I am not one of those people. I wish I were in London. I'd shag the very first woman I could get my hands on. Get my mind off of this . . . this . . . foolishness. I pace. Open a window. Shut it. Open it again. I tell myself. There is no situation. There are no circumstances. This feeling. It is not freedom. It is not spirit. It is not connection. It's what you feel prior to throwing yourself from an office window.

There is a moment. A moment in one's life where a definitive choice is made. And you know, that no matter what lies ahead, that you will not be the same after making it. For it is not the choice that made you into someone you didn't recognize, but the fact that you considered it.

The glare of high beam Xenon bulbs reflecting off the walls of the studio made me aware of the moment. I looked out onto the street. A black car. Driver in front. Female passenger in back. She was here. I made my way down the stairs, to the front door. Walked to the curb and waited. Dejavu.

She was dressed differently than earlier. I am realizing that she has many looks. No bohemian ankle length skirt. No cashmere jumper or business wear. This time, black, sleek, everything. Classic. A small solid gold timepiece. Paul would be proud. I on the other hand wore a paint stained tee shirt, and yesterday's— possibly the day before's—denim.

I waited. The driver insisted on helping her out of the vehicle, as if one needed a black belt in letting a woman out of a car.

"You're wet." She took the umbrella from the driver, handed it to me. Silently, we marched up the wooden stairs into the candle-light. There was nothing to say. I wanted her.

"I love the space." Adrianne handed me her coat, kicked off her shoes and waltzed around the flat. It was a mess. Shit was all over the place. Ask me if I noticed. Ask me if I cared. I was some-where else. For what seemed like an eternity in seconds, I wrestled with my demons. *Surrender. Liberate. Touch her.* I heard the angels. *Refuse. Control. Will.* The candles, the open windows, the rain. The sights. Scents. Sounds. They all got to me. That's it.

"Islam. We need to ta—" I kissed her. Gently, at the back of her neck. Then deeper in other places. I wanted to ravish her. But I wanted to savor this. So I moved slowly. Aside from moving her hair aside, I haven't touched her. She made a slight sound. Followed by another. Then a moan. I kissed her neck, her shoulders, the back of her head. Buried myself in her hair. Breathed in. She turned to face me. Placed her hand on my cheek. My hand on her heart. And I lost it. I fucking lost it.

Before I knew it, I was all over her. What the hell was wrong with me? I kissed her as if I were on a hunt and the object of de-sire was buried deep inside of her person. I was much rougher than I had ever been with a woman. If I weren't careful, I'd shred her to pieces trying to find whatever I thought I was looking for.

She kissed my cheeks. Calmed me. We stood still for a moment, me quite embarrassed, as I am not in the habit of losing control. I'll have to make up for this. I'll love her to submission if necessary. Aware of the need, she gently placed my hands where she wanted them to be. I obliged her for a moment, then moved them to where I knew would cause her to fully succumb. I felt her body tense. Then relax. Tense. Relax again. She was struggling. Wrestling with her own demons.

There were two voices breaking the stillness of the room. Adrianne's moans and small cries saying but not, *I don't want to be broken . . . I want to control this . . . I want to leave as I came . . .* and mine saying just the opposite. *Surrender. Lose yourself. This is freedom . . .* I paused to make sure she was okay. Oddly enough, she would not look at me.

"Adrianne." I said softly. No response. "Adrianne." I called her again. She placed her forehead on my chest. Exhaled.

I could feel the heat radiating from that special place as I did when we were in the suite in London. This time, I let my fingers trace their way to the place women have no power over. I moved in slowly at first, her spot smaller than what I'm accustomed to, I wanted to be sure that I was where I needed to be. She let out a low but piercing scream. There was no more restraint. She moved against me. Slowly at first, then more and more aggressively until her back hit the wall so hard that I was concerned it would bruise. As Adrianne approached the place where only women go, I stopped. Not yet. A frustrated scream. A chuckle. She could kill me, I know. But she doesn't. She kisses me instead. Unbuckles me. I remove her top. Her beautiful bra. We were naked. The picture was stunning enough to paint.

Arms around my neck, legs around my waist, I carried her towards the back of the studio and placed her on the seat of an open window. The rain, more violent than it was when she arrived, hit her bare back in a massage-like manner. She looked confused. I knelt.

"Islam. What are you do—" She groaned mid sentence. I'd placed my hands around her waist. Held her in place. Started at her breasts and found my way south. My connection, my free-dom was in a window seat, her legs wrapped around my head, not able to move forward or backward. The restraint drove her mad. She lost all sense of what it meant to have strength. The scratches. The screams. Desire. Control at this point was the least of her concern.

"Sto—stop. Please," she begged breathlessly. I stopped. "No. Don't. Don't stop . . ." her indecision, the tone of her voice, it af-fected me in a way that I hadn't been in the past. Her cries . . . I had never heard such a beautiful thing. I wanted to make love to her. I wanted to fuck her senseless. I wanted it all. I listened to what she wanted. What she needed. Gave it to her as if I were Adrianne, giving it to herself. But better, because there was no precedence. Water streamed down her shoulders. Collected in her belly button. Trickled down to where I was and mixed with the wetness. She was loud. Unrelenting at this point. I felt the trembles. The small waves. The beginnings of what would signal an orgasm, and came to a halt.

"God! Damn! You!" she screamed between breaths. I laughed. Adrianne thought none of it was funny. "You're mad. Get away from me." She tried to push me off of her, forgetting that she was actually a few stories above ground level. I chuckled. Her hair was wet. Her back and legs were wet. I picked her up, grabbed a towel, wrapped her in it and laid her on the bed. She kissed me like she meant it. Like I was born to please her. I loved having her here. Kissing her like this. She stopped. Let out a light chuckle and said, "Darling, you are a lesbian."

I laughed at the implication. Held her tighter. Kissed her deeper. Loved her hard. Soft. In between. Allowed myself the luxury of being me. We made love until the sun came up.

13

The sun streamed through the extra large windows signaling the beginning of a day to remember. I lay still, replaying tidbits of last night. Afraid to move, as if moving would erase it all. Did it happen? I look to my left, at the wondrously elegant creature sleeping beside me. It did. I ask myself this morning, if I am any different. I check to see if the feeling, the one that started all of this is still with me. It is. I try to pin it to one or two of the chosen classifications. Desire. Connection. Spirit. Freedom. Is it one, or a combination of them all that allows me to feel this way?

Adrianne sleeps peacefully. There is an air of calm, of comfort in the room. She, with simply a gold watch on her wrist, was a sight to behold. Her sexual appetite is quite ample for a woman. And it doesn't take her long to climax. Aside from how different I feel with her, it's what I like best. However, my back is sore. For one, I'm not in the sexual Olympics of New York, as I was in the UK. I glance at a box of condoms that wouldn't ordinarily have lasted a week at home let alone a month or two. I laugh at me. At the adjustments. At the newfound soreness. One thing about Adrianne. She likes to be made love to deeply from start to finish, and although it can wreak havoc on the lower back muscles, I am not in the business of ignoring such preferences. I take another look at her lying next to me. Try to keep from staring. I am weak, but satisfied. Inspired. I reached for a pencil. Grabbed my sketchbook from off of the nightstand. I wanted to remember this.

A quarter hour into the sketch, my *belle époque* tossed a bit. Turned. Groaned. "Hmmh . . ." she made her morning noises. Stretched that marvelous body. "It's bright . . ." Her voice had a lovely raspy quality to it. She's obviously not a morning person. "What time is it?" she asked.

"Seven." I answered.

"In the morning?" She yawned. Stretched again. "Come to bed," she said, gesturing with her eyes. A sly hand ran across my lower back. Those hands. They were liable for so much pleasure last night. But I wanted to complete the sketch.

"I am in bed," I replied. I felt her move into me. Now there were two hands, with various other parts and sorts massaging places that spoke for the group. The hands and heart wanted to draw. Capture the moment. Everything else wanted to live in it. Hands and heart nil. Everything else won. "Alright. For a minute," I told her. Like I actually owned an ounce of control over the situation. I'm a man. I have to at least act like I have things under control. She grinned slyly. I grinned back. Adrianne was woman enough to let me believe for the sake of the moment that it was my decision. I turned towards her. Played with her hair. Her nose. Her dark eyes like an inkwell, invited me into them. It's amazing how she can accomplish so much with a simple look.

"You are an interesting man." Strands of our hair wrestled each other for space. She held mine behind my head. Kissed my face.

"I . . ." Kiss. "don't . . ." Kiss. "think. . . ." Deeper kiss. "So." I answered. I could melt into her. I wanted to.

"You . . ." Kiss. "Are . . ." Lick. Tongues play. A moan. An incoherent mutter. The facets of physical love are so fluid between us. We tossed and turned and played. Moved with the current. Her climax was gentle and tender this time. Not as vigorous as the ones from last night. She laid atop me, breathing deeply but softly. Moved around a bit. Climbed and squirmed and shifted.

Stretched her body all over mine. This is so different from what I am accustomed to. It's so . . . so free. She fell asleep. I got up. Put the kettle on. I need a moment to myself.

Sitting on the counter top, waiting to intercept the tea kettle before it whistles, I think. Play with my manhood. Think. Play. Glance across the studio. Play with it some more. Glance again. Feel the heat go straight to my gut. See it gain in size about two inches. Three. Then I force myself to think of something, anything other than her. Circumcision. Circumcision. Circumcision. Ru Paul. Deflation. I laugh out loud. Adjust my boxers. If it were my style, I'd kick up my damn heels. This is some shit. I feel alive. Well, I am alive, so the feeling should come with the territory. However, for so long, and in many cases it has not.

The water's boiling. Carefully, I pour it into a thick of herbs. Let it sit. Her naked body in plain view, I remind myself of my reality. No matter how I feel—how alive, how limitless and unbound, that this lovely woman-spirit-creature is not mine. This is a fictitious account of what I could have, maybe of what I should—of what I deserve, but not what actually can be claimed. If it all disappears tomorrow, at least I know that I am still here. That I didn't die while breathing.

My attention shifted. I want to work on this goddess portrait of mine. I mix the required teaspoons of honey and take the steaming ceramic cup over to my easel. I sip. Stare at the half-painted lady before me. Ask her to tell me what she wants. How she wants to be portrayed. Like lightning, it came to me. Dropped right out of the sky. Much quicker than usual. I say a silent thanks to Him above and to the woman staring at me from the canvas. I glance towards where Adrianne is lying so comfortably. Thank her as well.

I placed the cup down and picked up a brush. The colors I chose, the strokes I used, were so different. So airy and new. I didn't question anything. I just let the creative forces that be, use me. It's weird. When one gets into a zone, no matter the artistic venture, there is a notion that each one of us will agree to. You lose you. Somewhere in the process, someone or something else has come in, and whatever it is, is powerful. Besides true love, it is the most veritable form of surrender known to humanity. You wake up to portraits you could have never painted. Techniques you've never studied. Ideas you've never had. And theories that have yet to be hypothesized. All in the name of inspiration. In the name of art. It is a god in itself.

The combination of my already existing talent and newfound connection places me on such a spiritual high, that I don't feel as if I am controlling the brush strokes. I add, blend and arrange color in a way that proves I am not. I feel the energy flowing through me. I feel my own trinity: mind-body-spirit succumb. I can comprehend the dedication of an elderly Christian woman. The fervent prayer of a righteous man. I've never truly understood the energy of the Holy Spirit, but if it is anywhere near what I am feeling, I too would desire to give my life. I'd be fanatic. After all, I would give so much just to feel this again.

I painted for what seemed like hours, but truly must have been no more than one. The sound of the water from the bathroom startled me. She's up.

"Good morning," she says, her bare feet making a small pitter-patter sound against the hardwood. I don't turn around, but I smile at her relative account of morning.

"Good afternoon." I reply. Hear her in the kitchen area. "There is tea in the cupboard. I don't have much in the lines of food," I said bashfully. She didn't answer. Minutes later, she appeared beside me, cup in hand, sipping gently. I loved to see her in my paint stained shirt.

"You are painting." Statement-question.

"I am."

"You are painting well," she said with praise. Adrianne stood beside me, watching the various techniques that are singular to my style, unfold. I don't usually allow onlookers. But I don't mind her being here. I want her to be. "I don't want to disturb you," she said. As she turned to leave, I lowered the palette, took her arm and placed her in front of me, between my legs. As if she were ashamed of the level of comfort she felt in that position, she hesitated before she sat, then released her back into my chest. If I could paint like this everyday, I'd be a happy man. Minutes passed.

"You use color so freely."

"I try."

"Who are your influences?" she asked. "I think I can tell."

"PBL." I answered.

"I'm sorry? I've never heard of any PBL."

I chuckled. Underneath all of the freedom and spirit, I could hear the pomp and circumstance that comes with aristocracy. It's a tone of voice and dialect thing. "Cubism. Think."

"Cubism . . ." She paused.

"Picasso, Braque and Leger," we said in unison.

"I would have guessed correctly. At least two of three," she stated.

I put the palette and brushes down. I can paint anytime. I wanted to enjoy her.

"When do you have to return to the city?" I asked.

"Late. I haven't any plans today." Her head was thrown back onto my shoulder, and as she turned to look at me, her lips brushed the underside of my jaw. I was hard as a rock. We both laughed.

"There is such thing as too much, Islam," the cause of my embarrassment scolded playfully.

"As what? Too much noise? Too many screams? Too many scratches?"

She blushed. Got up. Gave me a strange but sexy look. "It's a beautiful day and I'm famished. Let us go." A pat on my leg was the signal all women give no matter their social disposition. It simply meant: *Now*.

If this were to only last a day or two, I wanted to enjoy it too.

"Alright. Let's go."

14

We sat in silence, at a small table outside a popular French bistro called Chez Oskar. It was Saturday, and Dekalb Avenue buzzed with shoppers and passersby. Adrianne seemed to be in her own world, watching each person who walked by quietly as if she were observing cells in a Petri dish. We've been here for almost a score of an hour and haven't had much exchange. Having gotten used to being the silent one, it was interesting to be with someone who spoke less than I did.

The waiter brought our servings.

"Salmon and Tuna Tartare for the Misses. Musclar salad for the mister." He placed various plates and dishes on the small table and filled our glasses with still water. I watched Adrianne prepare herself to eat as if it were a special process. A plate here. A fork there. Water over here. Glass over there. Unable to tell if all this was due to aristocratic upbringing or a seriously detail-oriented personality, I was amused at how methodical she was.

She removed her watch, bracelets and the ring on her right hand and placed them all on the table in a neat but unorganized pile. Just as I was about to comment, a small and ridiculously cute child whizzed past us at top speed. She, with a bushel of wild curly hair and a mother with the patience of Mother Teresa ran to the corner, then made a direct turn back towards where we were. She stopped at our table. Adrianne didn't smile, but the twinkle in her eye gave the little girl all the encouragement she needed.

"Leave those nice people alone, sweetie," her mother yelled from a distance. She was tastefully ignored.

"How are you today?" I asked in a make-a-child-smile tone. The tot never even turned her head towards me. I chuckled inside. I'm not used to being disregarded by women no matter how short they are. Totally transfixed by the pile of expensive jewelry in front of her, she made her move.

"What's that?" the little girl asked Adrianne, her sticky fingerprint smudging the face of the Swiss piece I know costs more than the average American car. Paul would have had to be taken to the emergency room. Adrianne didn't flinch.

"It's a watch."

"What kind of *wotch*?" The little girl mimicked Adrianne's accent and examined the piece as if she were doing an appraisal. I had to laugh. She was a clever little one.

"Franck Muller." Adrianne answered patiently. The adorable little girl looked at Adrianne. Then at the watch. Then at the pile. As if the pronunciation was too much for her miniature soul, she put it right back. Picked up a bracelet.

"Is this a dragon? What's this red thing? Is it a crystal? Can I wear it?" she held the ruby bracelet up to the sky and bolted questions in a row like a prize-winning journalist. Adrianne positioned herself more comfortably, as if she were preparing to answer as many questions as the little inquirer asked. Just as I was beginning to enjoy the exchange, the child's mother scooped her up.

"I'm so sorry. Did she—Omigod. She didn't ruin anything did she?" The young mother asked anxiously.

"I was looking at the wotch, Mommy . . . wotch . . . wotch . . . wotch . . ." the tot continued in her best British intonation.

"Apologies unnecessary. She is a wonderful child. With expensive taste." Adrianne and the mom exchanged short pleasantries.

"Byyyyyyyyeeee Miiiiissssss Fraaaannnkk Mooooollo!" The child yelled as her mom carted her off. I laughed aloud. This got more interesting by the moment.

"Do you always remove your jewelry before you eat?" I asked her.

She tossed the avocado on her salad around. "Sometimes. Depending on how I feel."

"And how do you feel today?"

"Like I don't want to wear jewels while eating." Adrianne winked. Smiled. Dug into her salad. Smart ass. "No, it's just more com-for-ta-ble," she said playfully, accent personified. "Here, remove yours." Reaching across the table, she began to unclasp the huge Thai-silver dragon from my wrist. "And your ring." Her fingers and mine intertwined, I wished she'd just place them in her mouth and get it all over with. Adrianne's ways, they were more convoluted than my own. She was naturally seductive. Removing jewelry at a dining table could just as well be foreplay. It felt like it. "There. Now you can relax."

Those dark eyes met mine and my body responded in a way that said I had less control than I thought I did. Adrianne did something different to me. Before she was tackled and fucked silly on Dekalb Avenue, I changed the subject. "Do you want children one day?" I asked.

"Absolutely not," she said without so much as an explanation. She chewed, sipped, wiped the corner of her mouth and added, "Do you?"

I didn't have to think about the response. I've never had a family of my own. Besides success in my art and a bit of self-understanding, it was the only other thing that I wanted in life.

"Yea. Children deserve love. I want the opportunity to give it," I replied. She nodded slowly, stretched her legs under the table and elevated them so that they landed in my lap. Eventually, they were moved to the small space between my legs. We ate quietly, enjoying the sun and the buzz of the neighborhood. The tribal music in the background made all the difference.

"Would you mind stopping by the park when we've finished?"
"Not at all." I answered.

We approached the entrance of Fort Green Park at South Elliot Street. On the way up, you could see Frisbees and kites flying high, blankets and baskets on the grass, smell the aroma of
freshly spiced and grilled food, and hear the tribals. Tribal music
thumped. Soulful house music. Afrobeat. Latin. I've heard of the
Soul Summit house parties in the park during summer week-
ends. Tabu, one of the deejays, is a good friend of Ahmed's. Of
all the big named super-clubs Ahmed plays worldwide, this small
event is one of his favorites. He won't miss it. No party drugs
here for him either. He says the high is in the vibration. I can see
what he means. It reminds me of the outdoor summer music festivals in Europe. The feeling is one of emancipation and identity.
I guess today is my lucky day. In more ways than one.

Although I wanted to, I didn't know if it would be proper to
hold Adrianne's hand. The man in me took it anyway.

"Did you know about this?" she asked rhetorically, eyes straight
ahead as we approached what seemed to be a sea of free dancers.
Beads, locks, ankle length skirts, they were all over the place.
The thumping sound of the music and the airy sound of the
conga drums made it hard not to move your body to the rhythm.
Even while walking. She was almost dragging me towards the
epicenter of the dancing crowd. The look in Adrianne's eyes was
different. Girlish and playful. As if she couldn't wait to jump into
the sea of freedom in front of her. While we stood at what would
unofficially be the entrance of the dance floor, she moved in front
of me, sort of like a sway. Almost as if she were warming up. I was
enjoying her enjoying herself, but a thought came to me. What
the hell am I supposed to do? I hope she doesn't think I'm going
out there with her. I don't dance.

While I rehearsed excuses, the music lowered. Thank God. I
needed more time. There was an intermission or introduction of
sorts, to what seemed to be a fired up crowd.

"Y'all ready to party Brooklyn?"
"Yeaaaaaaaahh!"
"Soul Summit would like to welcome . . ." Thump. Thump. Thump.
"Lady Almaaaaa!!!"

The crowd roared. A shapely woman, resembling a favorite aunt, sang the first few lines of a song that I've heard many times in the UK.

Hold it down . . . Hold it down . . . Move your body. . . .

As if that were all Adrianne needed to hear, she immediately began navigating her way to the center of the dance area dragging me along with her.

I had to let her know that I wasn't into this. "Adrianne. No. Adr—" She couldn't hear me. "Adrianne. Adrianne!" We were at the heart of the dance floor. There was nowhere to go. People were sweating to my right. Sweating to my left. She threw her head back. Moved her body without abandon or reserve. I figured I'd try one more time.

"Adrianne! I don't dance!" The fire in her eyes had returned. She smiled. Took my hands in hers. Locked her fingers into mine and slowly raised my arms above my head as she did that night in her London suite. With both hands in the air, I stood there watching her and everyone else dance like they were possessed. As I began to call her name one last time, she pulled herself into me. Used her lips to silence mine. And her hips to guide me. She twisted and turned, pulling out and then using my strength to pull herself back into me. I liked the way she felt. I figured I'd try a two-step. I had to laugh at this shit. I can't dance.

At this point, my arms were wherever she was, and she was moving so fluidly, that I had no choice. I closed my eyes and let the music into me.

Thump. Thump. Thump. Hold it down . . .

First, my head. Then my feet. Parts of me were moving faster than I could keep up with. As I let the sound run through me, it seemed as if the feeling from my toes was intent on meeting the one from my head. I wanted to ignore this shit. But I couldn't.

The music was infectious. Ahmed always said it was. I grabbed Adrianne. Brought her close to me. Released her. I still didn't know what I was doing. But whatever it was felt good. She laughed out loud, brought my face to hers and stared right through me. Adrianne Spence was intent on bringing everything I had out of me this afternoon.

"You are a natural," she whispered in my ear. We began to edge our way through the tight crowd. When we finally got to the grass, I hit the ground hard. I was exhausted. And hot. "I'll be back." I watched her walk towards a man selling bottled water, grin as he chatted her up, and return with two iced down bottles of Evian. She handed me both bottles to open, sat next to where I lay and said, "Drink." I felt her hand on my leg as I downed the twenty-ounce bottle as if it were a shot of tequila. I could get used to this. I had to remind myself not to. Somewhat of a pleasant surprise, Lydia and my brother appeared it seemed from nowhere.

"Islam! What's up bro? We didn't expect to see you out here!" Micah exclaimed. It would be he whose presence wouldn't be expected. Micah wouldn't know this music or vibe if it were giving him a blowjob. These people didn't seem pretentious enough for him.

I didn't respond. Instead I focused on the silent exchange between Adrianne and Lydia. If looks could kill, Lydia would be serial. What's wrong with her? "Lydia, Micah, this is Adrianne." I introduced her to the unbalanced couple.

"Good afternoon," Adrianne offered properly. A slight nod of the head was all she gave. Lydia replied cordially and Micah of course did everything he could to win her affections. He could see beauty and smell money.

"You have a lovely accent. Where is it from?" He was sure to sweep the world championship in ignorance.

"Thank you. It's British," was all she said.

"Is this your first time here?" he asked.

"No, not at all."

"Are you on vacation?" He smiled. Looked from Adrianne to

me. Then back at her. Was he trying to chat her up in front of me
and his wife? I didn't treat women that I was simply sexual with
like that.

Adrianne drew a few circular shapes on my upper leg with her
fingertips, then allowed her hand to linger in place for a bit before replying. "I suppose you can say, I've been on holiday." She
was good. Not one smile, but cordial as the Queen. She handled
him and Lydia briskly. Turned towards me and began to position
herself to lie down. I snickered inside. She'd had enough. There
were a few moments of uncomfortable silence before they noticed that she was through with the exchange.

Lydia did not appreciate that. It was all over her face. Or something was. She took control of the situation. "Okay Islam, we're
going to head over to the other side of the park. We're meeting
friends and we're late. You guys enjoy the rest of your evening."
She kept her eyes on me.

For some reason, I felt the need to make her feel better than
my brother had. "Yes, thank you, we will. Oh. I am doing some
art research this week. If you'd like to take a break from the sci-
ences for a moment, feel free to join me, yea?" It was a sincere
offer. Besides Danny, Lydia seemed to be the only other I could
imagine friendship with in this city.

Her face lit up. "That would be great!"

"I will phone you later about it." I answered. Micah wasn't even
paying attention. His eyes were on Adrianne. We exchanged final
goodbyes and they were off. Adrianne lay quietly on my chest. I
wanted to know what she was thinking. I thought it smarter to
wait until she offered her thoughts.

Without moving from where she lay, she asked, "Why don't
you get along with your brother?"

"I never said that I didn't." I do not want to talk about this.
Not even with her. She picked up on that instantly, because she
didn't push me.

"And between the two of them, there is no love." Statement-
question.

"Lydia is his wife. I'm sure he loves her." Another pause. A longer one. She lightly traced her fingers around the border of my lips and over other areas of my face as if she were reading me in Braille. It felt so good. Too good.

"And what is love, Islam?" She asked that question in a way that implied answering was non-negotiable.

I tried for the sake of the conversation to forget or better yet ignore that I was lying on my back, in the park with another man's wife. "Love is . . ." More finger traces. They were affecting me. I pulled her atop of me as to hide my ever-so-obvious expression of that affection. As usual, she made herself comfortable and awaited my reply. "Love is . . ." Unlike the night we mutually defined desire, I came to a halt. I can't say that I truly know what love is. "I don't know. I can't answer that," I offered. She moved upward, allowing us to be able to look at one another. Or rather her to look at me. She could see I was telling the truth.

"Would you do something for me?" she asked.

"What would you like?" I hoped the request was sexual.

"Close your eyes, forget that I am here, and imagine yourself at your purest moment."

I did as she said. At first there was nothing but blackness and the sounds and smells of the park mixed with her own wonderful scent. I allowed myself to relax and meditated on what she asked. In moments, visions of me smearing paint on my mum's face appeared. Fade out. Me presenting her with my first portrait as a young boy. Fade out. Fighting bullies for Micah. Carrying him home on my back. Fade in. Adrianne. The look she gave me at the party.

"Love is light." I said. "It's light. It's liberty. It's freedom. It's what it means to be you. To be loved is to be accepted. To be accepted is to be free. It means there is no repercussion for being who you are." I paused before continuing. There was a part of me that wanted to know if she was loved. If she was free. If she were, would she be here with me? Or does the fact that she is here with me denote her own sense of freedom. Her own acceptance of self. Of choice and perspective. I wanted to know but not. How does one ask another a question like that? Thinking about whether one is or is not loved is disturbing enough. Especially under these circumstances. I had to remind myself again that there were no circumstances. This was for the moment. I asked the question the best way I could.

"Are you free?"

"Are you asking if I am loved?" She cut right through the mask of the analogy.

"I am asking if you are accepted for who you are."

"Is anyone? Does one even accept themselves for who they are?" She answered my question with one of her own. A worthy opponent.

"Some do."

"Well then love cannot exist by your definition."

"Explain."

"To love oneself truly, to accept everything one has to offer, is to go against the grain of society."

"Uh. Huh."

"To go against the grain of society, one must give up the basics of life. Of survival. Food. Water. Shelter. Etcetera. It's sudden death. Suicide."

"Not in all cases," I responded.

"Yes. In every case. We are all made differently. Therefore it is not natural for us to agree with the simple rule set implemented by bureaucratic doctrine, which is the spine of what we know as modern society. For one to express himself freely, means he has agreed to disagree with society. At his own expense." She made a good point.

"The rich are not dependent on such rules. Money can buy love. It can buy freedom." It sounded idiotic, but I said it anyway.

"Nonsense. A rich man is even more susceptible to such influences. One cannot become rich without relinquishing freedom, acceptance and the likes. The illusion of buying those things is worse than the reality of them not being within reach. It is not possible. To love or be loved by your standards and definition."

"I disagree." I did. I couldn't base the rebuttal on anything concrete, but I knew I thought she was wrong.

She took a deep breath. "Islam . . . freedom. Liberty. Complete autonomy means telling your supervisor he is incompetent. Or your clients that you do not wish to be available. Or your lover that he is not pleasing you."

"Or your husband that you are not happy." I added.

She shifted uncomfortably. Ignored the implication. "One accepts another on condition. That condition surrenders the possibility of the love you wish to believe in," she finished. I thought about what she said. I refused to give up hope. That there is a feeling out there, a depth. I'm feeling it as we lay here. I try to express that.

"Then there is connection. Spirit. Freedom in a different sense," I added. "The feeling you get that can't be rationalized. It's what the painter or the dancer or even the number cruncher who loves their job feels when they've broken through. It's what a mother feels towards a child. It's what I—" I stopped right there. Changed course. "I've never felt the connection with anyone before. But I believe in it," I said. Paused. Looked her in the eye. "So do you, Adrianne."

She looked at me intently. Her eyes said so many things. I couldn't successfully place them all. But I recognized a few. There was flame and intensity. Darkness and indecision. A flash of hurt. A glimmer of vulnerability. A flicker of strength. She was a complicated soul. Nestling her head between my chin and shoulder, she reclaimed what has become her usual position of comfort.

"I must be going. I have an early day tomorrow," she said aloud. I didn't answer. Figured she would get up when she was ready. To my surprise, we lay still, until the park was just as quiet as we were. Until there were no more music, drums or dancers. Until everything that appeared was either a shadow, or a shadow of a shadow. We lay on the grass, in the park until my favorite time of day. Until sunrise.

Sunrise is strange. It's the most bizarre time of day for me. As I watch first hand, the organic perspective change of the earth in effect, I wonder how much my own perspective has changed. I wonder if I appear in colors that I'd love to paint. Or if by allowing this wonderful feeling—this freedom, I've become someone I detest. I play with the theories of the afternoon, and wonder if society is right. If there should be rules. If by chance we were all so open to change—so indifferent to difference, if we'd truly be free. Or simply slaves to our impulses.

I feel her atop me. I love the feeling. The high. I want to feel this again. After this day. I think of the implications of those feelings, of the reality they possess. Of what I will do—of what I have already done, to have these moments with her. I feel a slight sense of liberation, because I have released myself from human opinion and judgment. Even my own. But on the contrary, I am beginning to feel a bit affixed. I feel as if I cannot let it, her, this go. Everything is so vibrant right now. My art. My spirit. My life. I'm doing and feeling what I've always wanted to. I watch her sleep peacefully on my chest. No, not yet. I will, but I can't let it go at the moment. I feel the pressure gather in the center of me. The heat spread to my gut. As adrenaline seems to replace the blood streaming through my veins, I ask myself a question that I don't want to answer. Is this the feeling of freedom? Or slavery?

15

It is a beautiful summer day. Lydia and I are returning from a special studio visit for a Russian artist named Eteri Chkadua, whose paintings were even more stunning in person than they were in her portfolio. The level at which she expresses detail is unsurpassed. We spent a few seconds attempting to remove what had appeared to be a small insect on one of her works portraying rural life, just to be informed that the insect was a part of the painting. We both had to double back to the piece. This artist is amazing. She can capture a single strand of hair, or a lone blade of grass as if it were the centerpiece of the portrait. Lydia was astounded. As was I.

We walk through Brooklyn's Prospect Park, enjoying the sunrays and the greenery. This is the subtle side of Brooklyn that isn't regularly seen or appreciated by the masses. I breathe in, feeling the beginnings of what I've come to know as connection and smile inside because I know I'm making spiritual progress. Lydia, spellbound by Eteri's work, couldn't stop herself from raving about it. I smiled for her, because she is making progress too.

"So, I mean, how much would one of those cost? If I wanted to buy one today, how much do you think she would charge me?" she asked excitedly.

"How much would she charge you or how much is it worth?" I

asked. As an artist I tended to think in terms of public versus personal value. Sometimes the cost of a piece will be lowered in efforts to get it out—to help establish a name for the artist. Maximizing the influence and reputation of the Spence Galleries worldwide, I intend to focus on the latter value of the work. I want the artist to get what they deserve. That's what I relay to Lydia. "I would ask for ten thousand British pounds for any one of the *Shane* works, and slightly more for the self-portrait." I answered. She thought.

"Ten thousand pounds . . . ten thousand pounds . . . Islam when was the last time you made a purchase with a pound?" I laughed. I knew where she was headed with the question. "If it's not a mo-bile, it's a wanker. If it's not knickers, it's a jumper!" I laughed aloud at her rant. She grabbed my chin and turned me towards her. "Repeat after me. Cellular. Asshole. Underwear. Sweater. Can you pleeeease start using American references!" I was in knots. I had no idea she had such a sense of humor. After a really good laugh, I obliged her.

"Twenty thousand dollars for any one of the *Shane* pieces. Slightly more for the self portrait." I said.

"DAMN! I'm certainly in the wrong business." We shared another laugh. My brother doesn't deserve her. There is a lot that he doesn't deserve. "Well, if there is a friends and family discount, then let me know. I'll be the first in line." She added playfully. We'd approached a man selling grilled food from a small metal cart. I wasn't particularly hungry, but it smelled wonderful.

"I'm going to get something. What would you like?" she asked.

"What is he selling?"

"Sausages, hotdogs—I'd stay away from the hotdogs. And knishes."

"Ka-what?"

"Knishes."

"Oh Kh-nish-es. Just one syllable. Knish."

"Islam. Don't get me started again. It's mashed potatoes wrapped in dough. Okay? Ka-nish. There. How's that for anti-Brit pronunciation?" she said mockingly. "The sausages are good. That's what I'm getting."

"Are they kosher?" I asked.

"No, I don't think so, just get a knish. They're great." We walked the trail of the greenway, food in hand, conversation to a minimum. She sighed.

"Thank you for inviting me today, Islam. It was amazing. I'm learning so much, and I can say that for the first time in a long time, I am inspired," she stated sincerely. Flash. The heat. I ignored it. Again.

"I am happy for the company." I paused. "Surely you must take advantage of what New York has to offer with my brother." My newfound friend sighed again.

"Micah . . . I love him but he is interested in Micah. We tend not to do as much artistically as I'd like. He doesn't see the value in it." I am not surprised. That is what I tell her.

"He is certainly more interested in what is going on outside of him as opposed to the goings on inside. However, he wasn't always that way." I added. She didn't know that Micah can capture the very rhythm of a heartbeat with a pencil and paper. Growing up with no parental support, he and I were forced to make choices in life. We are products of those choices. I reached into my pocket. Glanced at the small digital screen. No missed calls. I wondered what she has been doing for the past few days. I haven't heard from her since she left Brooklyn.

"That is the fifth time you've checked that screen in the past hour." Lydia said. "Who has you glued to your cell phone?"

I noticed a man with a bushel of roses in hand. I decided to ignore or better yet divert the implications that I was affected by Adrianne the way I knew I had been. I signaled the gentleman, and chose a white rose for Lydia. "For you, Mademoiselle." I handed it to her.

"You are such a gentleman," she beamed.

"I am no different than any of my friends. It's standard," I answered

"Lia is completely taken by you, you know."

She informed me of something that I already knew. That was a one-night stand I'd wished to forget. I didn't think bad sex was possible. "I'm sorry to hear that." I replied. She and I laughed at my dry humor. I glanced at the time. Decided I that it would be good to head back to the house. I need to prepare my first presentation for Spence. "Lydia, I need to get back to Fort Greene. There is work that needs to be done—work that I enjoy, but work nonetheless. If you do not have a prior engagement, feel free to join me. You can help choose the pieces for the presentation." I said.

"Really? I'd love that. I've never been so involved in art like this. It's exciting for me." She said gratefully.

I didn't mind, she was helping me keep my mind off of Mrs. Spence.

"Honey or sugar?" I was pouring tea and wanted to know what Lydia's preferences were.

"You have any coffee?" She saw the look on my face. Interpreted it correctly. "Sugar's fine." She flipped through the large portfolio slowly, taking in each piece. "I like this one. This would be good to show."

I glanced at the selection she'd made. Good taste.

"That's Shane number two."

"As opposed to?"

I chuckled. Good question. "Shane, number one. It's a member of a series," I answered. "Good eye. Which others are interesting to you?"

"This one right here, the one we saw, the self-portrait. That would grab my attention." I looked at my phone again. Not one missed call. Where the hell was she? Lydia continued. ". . . and I like the one of the woman holding the dagger."

Damn. She's better than I thought. Outside of Eteri's Indonesian inspired works, those were my top three selections. "Dowry. That one's called Dowry." I glanced over her shoulder to get a better look at what she was seeing. Tried viewing things from her perspective. "You're good at this." Just as she was about to reply, my phone vibrated. I almost jumped out of my skin. Checked the screen. Double-checked it. It was the alarm. Nothing more. I don't like how this feels. I consider it karma for past indiscretions.

Lydia smiled knowingly. "Call her, Islam."

"Call who?"

"Put yourself out of your misery and make the phone call. I don't know why men are so . . ."

"Stupid?" I asked.

"Yes!" She laughed heartily.

"Just because you told me to," I offered. I retreated to the rear of the studio and dialed the number to the gallery.

"Good afternoon, Spence Gallery of Contemporary Art, New York . . . to whom may I direct your call?"

"Adrianne Spence."

"Your name and the nature of your call?"

"It's Islam."

"And the nature of your call, sir?"

I didn't know I needed one. "Prospective artists meeting. I need to schedule one." I obliged the gatekeeper.

"Please hold." Albeit briefly, I waited. Impatience getting the best of me, I tapped an ink pen against the table enough to be annoyed with my own nerve-laden behavior. This is not me. The voice that returned was the same that left. "Mrs. Spence cannot speak at the moment. She will return your call as soon as possible." She what?

"Did she say when?" She can't be serious. Maybe she mispronounced my name. "You did tell her that Islam was calling." I stated-asked.

"Yes, sir, you are new to the group, correct?"

"Yes."

"As I said, she said she will return your call as soon as she can. She is tied up at the moment." I said thanks and hung up. Walked back to the kitchen area.

"What's wrong?" Lydia asked.

"Nothing," I replied.

"Liar." She didn't believe me for a second. "You know I do this for a living Islam," she added.

"Read minds?" I asked.

"Smart ass." Lydia punched me playfully on the shoulder. "No, I know when something's wrong, you can talk to me if—" Phone rang. Startled us both.

I picked up on the first ring. "Hello."

"Good afternoon." It was Adrianne.

I didn't know if I should dive straight into business matters or not. I wanted to know where the hell she'd been. Why she hadn't called. If she thought of me while she was away. If I could love her until she fell apart tonight. All of that tumbled out in one short, "Afternoon."

"You called?"

Is she serious? I decided to take the business approach. "Yes. Uhm, I've completed my first round of artist visits and have selected two. When should I present them to you?"

"Hold, please. I need to check the schedule." Am I or she, the nutcase? "Thursday. Half past one," she stated calmly. There was an awkward moment of silence between us. Under normal circumstances, I am far from impulsive in these matters. I have seldom been the protagonist. These circumstances—now that there are circumstances, are far from normal. I didn't care if Lydia was listening. I asked anyway.

"How are you?"

"I am well." She hadn't a trace of familiarity or sentiment in her voice at all. Did I do something wrong?

"Are you sure?" I asked her.

"Yes. I am well. Busy, but well." And that was it. That was all she said. I've had enough. You would have thought I was speaking to a stranger.

"Alright. I will see you on Thursday." I finished. We hung up. I sat for a moment, then began sifting through the artists' portfolios looking but not, at the work. What was wrong with her?

"Hello, Islam. What happened? Are you okay? Your entire

mood has shifted." Lydia was concerned. She was also sensitive. Most women are. Well, some of them.

"All is well," I said. Obviously it was not, but she didn't intrude. I appreciated that. I thought about desire, connection, freedom and spirit. No one mentioned the downside. Fuck this. What we had, we had and that is all there is to it. For the first time since Adrianne and I met, I didn't like the way I felt.

16

Emotional landsca-a-apes, they puzzle me . . .
The day is grey. I listen to one of the most eclectic and essential artists of all time—Bjork, tell me that she is in a state of emotional emergency. I hear the pain in her voice and the nervousness associated with uncontrolled passion. As she lets out a piercing scream from the depths of a soul that seems to have no bottom, I wonder how she got there. She is so open and free, definitely connected, but all I ever hear in her melodious cries are pain and torment. Then I hear her say, of this permanent state of emergency that it is a beautiful place. She sings of it as if it were an oasis. Then says that it's where she wants to be. I listen. Hum one of my favorite tunes and try to make sense of wanting to be in pain.

The large metal elevator door to the gallery opened slowly, and although I am not in a state of emergency, I am nervous. This is very different than what I am used to, my behavior.

"Good afternoon, Islam. She is expecting you. You can wait for her in the office." The receptionist, one if I had been in London, perhaps in a different state of mind, would have been shagged already, gestured towards Adrianne's office. As I walked towards it, I felt a bit edgy. That was an understatement. The nervous twinge underneath my armpits told me so.

Her energy, her vibe, was all over this place. I sat. Stood. Sat again. Resisted the urge to stand back up. No one I knew would believe me if I told them that I was acting this way. It is unbelievable to me. I credit the behavior with the novelty of the thoughts and feelings inside. This is new to me. Once controlled, I will be back to normal.

I didn't hear her approaching the entryway of the office. The sound of her voice startled me. So did her wears. Tattered ball cap. Ripped denim trousers. Belts and buckles in disarray. A navel piercing that I'd somehow overlooked. And a tiny tattoo on her inner wrist. Today, she was rather boyish. Except for the off-shoulder top, she was the female version of me.

"No, Eli, that is not what I said." She paused. Listened intently. "Absolutely not," was her sole reply. I could tell she was displeased. She is so collected, even when she is angry. "That piece is of my grandfather's estate, and is priceless. It will not be auctioned." Eli. Eli . . . I run through the mental rolodex of gallery names, agents, collectors . . . Is she speaking to Eli Broad? The billionaire art collector?

"Well Larry did not give you the correct information. You must take this issue up with him. I haven't any additional say of the matter." Larry. Larry Gagosian. Gagosian Galleries. Purchaser for Eli Broad. She and Mr. Spence are on a first name basis with these people? It actually seemed like the other way around. They were calling her. A flood of excitement rushed from my head to my feet. This is heaven. Or luck. Whichever it was, I wanted in. My career would take off meteorically—instantly. This is what I've worked for, what I've dreamt of and it fell right into my lap. I could kiss Danny for pushing me to do this. Alright. Of the soiree, it was splendid, I'm more in touch etcetera etcetera, but things are now in the proper perspective. Adrianne and I are history. Affair over, back to business. Off the phone, the piercing look radiating from those dark eyes said '*what do you want?*'

"It's half past one." I stated dryly. The ocular message continued.

"*And?*"

"We have a meeting." She could at least act like she was happy I was here.

"Oh, why yes. I apologize. We are discussing Eteri and your French discovery." I attempted to look through her for a trace of something . . . anything that indicated we were recently ensconced on a wet window seat. Nothing. This is insane.

"How do you wish to present?" she asked.

"Powerpoint." I answered flatly. She handed the applicable cords to me in one sweeping gesture.

"The outlet is here." She signaled behind her. "And here is an adapter."

The room was silent except for the fumbling sound of cords and footsteps. I now know what Adrianne meant in the park, when she implied that there could be no love by my definition, if it meant freedom—if it meant acceptance. I want to talk. I want to stop acting like I am okay with the silence. I want to ask her what is wrong, if I can fix it. I don't want to be penalized for the inquiries. I have never wanted those things before, so the entire experience is above my head. I don't think I've ever truly encountered freedom, therefore I've never been without it. I must say, it is difficult to return to dormancy. I wondered how she faired so well.

Adrianne sat atop her desk, awaiting the introduction of my presentation. One more plug, and I'd be sorted. I reached around her to the underside of her workspace and connected my laptop to the projector. Flash. I felt the heat. Smiled inside. I am not alone.

We began. I confidently swept through the various aspects of the presentation with ease.

"Here, with Eteri's 'Man and the Sea', old age and youth are given immaculate contrast, with images of a young man and an older woman in a moving exchange. Next we have—"

"The realism, the detail, is almost hallucinatory." Adrianne interrupted. "Can we go backward for a moment, to the Shane series?" I was happy to oblige. No matter what our differences in opinion or perspective, the midpoint between us was art. The fire in her eyes had returned, and I was just as excited. "This . . . this looks familiar." She paused. Thought. I figured I'd wait for a moment. I wanted to see how well she knew her art. "The men in this piece, they are addicts. They are in a drug house, correct?"

"Yes." I answered patiently.

She leaned forward, "Yet . . . yet the poses. The poses of each of them at the table are likened to DaVinci's *Last Supper*." She looked disgusted. Then aroused. Then intoxicated. I was proud. She got it.

"Yes," I added quietly. Let her take it all in.

"Look at the passion in their eyes, the anguish, the desire . . . it's pious." I waited for her to fall in love with the work as I had. "Is she on drugs?" She asked earnestly. I laughed out loud. She grinned.

"Not that I know of," I answered, still chuckling.

"But she has likened the high, the feeling to a relentless spiritual passion—the passion of Christ. They will do anything to separate themselves from pain, yet they will also do what is necessary to become closer to it. The pain, and the passion associated with the high cannot be lived with or without. It is not a feeling to them, but a drive. A cyclic exchange that ends as soon as it begins. As is thirst or hunger."

"Or desire." I added. I was ignored.

"She captures the basic want . . . the neediness and confusion so well." I nodded. Adrianne had arrived at the special place where art lovers dwell. Where the soul of the artist has captured you, and for a moment, you exist inside of the painting, photograph, film or dance. It is the quintessential grounds of artistic foundation. To feel. To express and enlighten. I can't say how much I loved that she understood and adored it on her own. She paused. Adjusted her position on the desk.

"You've gotten it," was all I said. I could have taken her right then. I didn't.

"I love it. But can we sell it? Her work is a tad on the edge."

I could see the business side of her shifting into gear. I decided to bring her back to where she seemed to prefer being.

"I haven't heard you complain about being on the edge."

She began a reply, but came to an abrupt stop. Ingested the insinuation. Blushed profusely. Silence, the principal means of communication between us, said more than a simple look or comment ever could. "No, you haven't. I have not complained," was all she said.

Everything changed. Her tone of voice, her body language, mine. I continued with the presentation. Finding myself distracted by minor gestures of hers. A shift in posture. The uncrossing of her legs. I don't know if I have enough control for this. I don't know if I want to.

We were interrupted. "Good afternoon, ladies and gents of the court." Mr. Spence entered the office bright and in a positive mood as usual, and here I was, about to pounce on his wife. "How are you Islam? I hear you are adjusting well," he said.

Shame. That was the first one. Loathing. That was the second. I hated myself. I repeated the mantra from weeks ago.

There is no situation.

There are no circumstances.

"I am adjusting, Mr. Spence. Thank you." I avoided eye contact with Adrianne. I felt like a child pornographer exposed.

"Very well. I am glad you are being taken care of," was his earnest reply. He patted me on the back, then walked over to where his wife was seated and placed what I thought was a luscious kiss on her lips, but it was hard to tell as his back covered her entirely. Kiss or not, the mere thought of Cooper touching her in any way sent the first of what would be myriad confusing but authentic emotions through me. The beginnings of one in particular surfaced, one that I haven't been privy to in times past. Anger. As the so-called kiss progressed, so did the emotion. Anger. Anger. Anger. Rage. Visions of me ripping him off of her flooded the creative areas of the mind. I dismissed them. What has gotten into me?

"Excuse us." He said. Another quick kiss on the cheek. I wanted—I needed to see what she felt. I tried to look into her eyes, but Mr. Spence's body was still blocking the effort. "Whew! Okay. Apologies for the interruption. Back to the presentation. Where were you two?" Albeit a bit out of breath, he was content.

I seethed. Wrestled with the most recent imagery. Found my place in the presentation. Cleared my throat.

"We reviewed—Eh-em—we were reviewing the work of Eteri, a US based artist and were moving on to my next recommended acquisition." I was so angry that I began to sweat. I could smell the twinge that alerted me to my deodorant working overtime. I don't recall ever being this upset. I shouldn't be. It is not my place.

Adrianne picked up where I left off. "The first recommendation is atypical of what we have shown, but exactly what we are searching for. The second artist, is actually based in the UK but is in residence at Gallerie Chappe in Paris. Islam will schedule a studio visit on our behalf. Is that correct?" She looked at me.

I focused on the screen ahead. I didn't want to see her. I didn't want to touch her. I didn't want to know she existed. "Yes."

Mr. Spence.

"Sounds like you have been working hard, Islam." Involved in my own thoughts and feelings, I ignored them both. He continued. "Adrianne . . ." He said her name like his mouth was filled with peanut butter. I hated the sound of it. "Isn't the meeting with Mohammed Siddiq in Paris coming up?"

"Yes, but he's cancelled," Adrianne answered.

"Again?" Cooper asked incredulously. I assumed he was not used to cancellations.

"Why?"

"He did not say." Adrianne was in a world with Cooper that was their own. I was invisible.

"Why did you let him? Is it impossible to get him into a single meeting?" he asked in irritation.

"What am I to do? I cannot force him to meet with you." Her voice lost the softness of just moments prior. She answered him in an "all business" tone. Still heated over their kiss, and subsequently my reaction to it, I was here but not.

"He will do whatever you ask. You managed to get him to—"

"Islam." Cooper was blatantly interrupted. The conversation was over. Adrianne apparently didn't take well to being interrogated.

"Yes," I answered nonchalantly.

"When is the artist expecting you?" she asked softly. From where I was standing, Cooper was still sucking the life out of her. I loathed the image.

"Within the month." I answered dryly.

Cooper stood behind his wife. Massaged her shoulders in apology or something else. I couldn't tell. I was still seething.

"Fine. Why don't we schedule the studio visit for a month from now," he added. "If there are any acquisitions to be made, we will all be there. There is also business that I need to tend to during that time in France, so it all makes sense," he finished.

I heard but didn't hear the dialogue between them. I was a child who had taken his first steps, concentrating on managing these newfound appendages with care. My emotions. They were running rampant. I didn't want to be anywhere near either of them now or later. I just wanted to get my head together and focus. I was asked a question to which I'd given my standard default reply.

"Yes."

"Well then it's sorted. Islam will accompany us to France. This will give us the time to get to know each other better and streamline a trip the two of you would have had to take anyway. Plus, I will introduce you to the various collectors and such who I'm sure would love to acquire some of your own work, Islam." He stated assuredly.

I was here, but not. I remember shaking hands. I remember gathering my things. I remember wanting to get as far away from her as I could.

* * *

I was back home, in Brooklyn, painting feverishly. It was as if I had been lifted to another plane. I was painting and completing quality work as I never had before. One after another. Woman after woman. Every nerve ending at attention, I was angry but drenched in stimulation. This is greater than inspiration. More powerful. I don't know what to call it. I don't like it. But the canvas does.

In front of me, in vivid color, I saw her boyish clothes, slight grin, the ethereal look on her face as she described what the paintings meant to her. I saw the wanting in her eyes as I brought her close to the edge, and the kiss that she received from her husband. That's where I stopped. All roads led to my freedom, my connection being kissed by someone else.

For the first time since I'd gotten home, I glanced at the time. It's late. Almost ten hours have passed, and I am nowhere near stopping. Painting is all I can do right now. I thought, maybe I should say a prayer. Just as I was about to turn in the direction of what would in hours to come, bring morning sun, my phone vibrated.

Adrianne. I ignored it. I don't want to confront the goings on of today. I don't want to make love to a woman who isn't mine. I don't want to be free. I don't have enough energy to be connected. And desire is rubbish. The phone vibrated on the countertop unrelentingly. I don't want to take this trail. The course of a Kamikaze.

Maybe, if I tell her that I am finished, I will return to a state of normalcy. A swift glance around the flat, at the level at which I'd managed to perform under this type of stress, and another confusing feeling crept in. Craving. Yearning. The desire to hear her voice.

Another vibration. I picked up the phone this time. "Yes?" No answer. "Adrianne." Silence. "Adr—"

"Hello." Simply stated.

"Hey."

"Are you available?" she asked. She sounded tired. As if the day had worn on her as well.

"No." A pause.

"Today. I didn't mean—"

"I know," I answered.

"You—are you well?"

Her voice. The tone. The vernacular. It ate away at every ounce of will I'd managed to muster. I tried hard not to let on.

"I am."

"Is that all?" she asked.

I decided to take the opportunity to tell her that we would go no further. I have a career to launch, she has a husband—who happens to be the god of my livelihood right now. Financially and artistically speaking, the risk is too great. I love the feeling she brings. She taps a nerve, something inside of me that allows me to let go. Allows me to dig deeper than I ever have. I am forever grateful to her for that. For unleashing the truth inside of me. The spirit. The connection. The desire. I know I can feel. I just don't like what it does to me. I'm siding with society.

"Adrianne."

"Yes."

This will be difficult. "I lov—I enjoy your company."

"Yes." Our default responses were identical.

"You have reached a place inside of me that I could never."

"Yes."

A pause. Images of us holding hands, of playing in each other's hair appeared. I felt her lying atop me in the park. Bringing me close to her while she danced. I closed my eyes, and saw the twinkle in her eye while she spoke to the inquisitive child. I wrestled those images to the floor.

"You know that this . . . I have a career."

"Yes, you do."

"And you . . ." I walked toward the window. I looked out onto the street. Attempted to count cars, taxis, buses—anything to stall the moment. I did not want to let go.

"I wish you were here." I meant it more than anything. She didn't reply. I saw, but didn't, the driver's side door of the black car open. I was caught in the throat of my own emotion. It felt odd to acknowledge the word—emotion, even more so to align it with me. "And if I could, I'd let you sit between me while I paint. If you wished. If not, you could simply sleep. And I'd—"

My newfound expression was quietly interrupted. "I am here, Islam," she stated calmly.

"Where?"

"I am here."

I doubled back to the front window. And there she was. Standing there. On the pavement. Patiently. Near the passenger side of a black car. She looked upward. Our eyes met. And every belief, every theory or idea that I'd managed to construct in a lifetime disappeared. All that mattered was the way I felt. Not sure if I should run or stand still, I just stared. I couldn't believe she was here.

"What—how long have you been—"

"Not long," was all she said.

Lightning hit me for the second time today. And I all but flew through the studio and down the stairs. As these moments seemed to appear randomly and without warning, I did not want to waste a second. I turned the knob of the century old lock. And there she was. Houdini couldn't have done it better.

Before I touched her, before I let her know just how happy I was that she was with me, I wanted to take it all in. Savor the moment. I took special notice of everything from the understated necklace she wore to the buttons on the cuff of her jacket. Her attire, different from the afternoon's playful garb, was dark. Classic. As I've come to prefer. The sight of her. My God. Just the simple sight of her was—it defied description.

There was nothing to say. The vibration between us was loud enough for all of New York to hear. The look in her eyes was one of confusion and longing. *Love me. Rescue me. Release me.* I'd forgotten that I was upset. I'd forgotten my rehearsed speech. I couldn't recall the rationale for leaving her be. I took her hand. Brought her into me. Moved her hair from her face. The cycle. Pain. Love. If that is what this was, was hard.

I recalled all of the times in life where I searched, wanted and waited for a feeling. Any feeling. Something to let me know that I was indeed a viable force on earth. All of those times. Mother. The chair. Micah. The dreams. All I wanted to know was that my soul had not gone numb. Everything about the way I kissed Adrianne said thank you. Thank you for this.

She returned the gesture. Her hands on my face, at the back of my head, she roamed aspects of me without reserve. She was thanking me, in her own way, for things I may never understand. Possibly never believe. I understood the relationship between passion and pain. I felt the connection. The drive. And saw life differently. Became more tolerant of addiction. Of the search for connection and spirit. For freedom. The semi-conscious state of being placed me on high, altered my perspective in many ways.

I held her. Kissed her. Protected her from things past, and those to come. Let her know that it was okay. That she could let go. She could fall into me. I would be there. I had no choice.

We fell asleep. On the floor. In the hallway. In our clothes. Pain. Pleasure. Anger. Inspiration. Longing. Love. I wanted to do it all over again.

17

I am awakened by the sun, to Adrianne's intense gaze. She does not avert her eyes. She will not act as if she was not studying me. She would continue to search, and I'd welcome the discernment. If she were looking for truth. For acceptance. For love. She would find it.

"Would you like to go upstairs?" I asked, mid-yawn. Gently, she shook her head and placed it on my chest. I smiled. "Adrianne, we can't lie here."

Those beautiful eyes looked at me with the innocence of a child on her first day of primary school. "We can't?"

"Uh-uh."

"We are not bothering the neighbors. I am com-for-ta-ble here."

I chuckled. She's comfortable on a cold, hard, dirty floor and I am not. I wondered who was the child of the aristocrat and who was the bastard. "Adrianne." A kiss on her forehead. "People will begin going to work soon. As you should." She moved upward. Another kiss. A longer one. "Let's go upstairs." I didn't wait for a response. I hoisted her over my shoulder and began the trek. With her waist exposed, I couldn't resist a tickle.

" St-Stop it! Is-lam. I swear! Ah! You!" A shriek. A scream. A slap. She couldn't get away. She kicked her feet. Giggled like a little girl. I threw her down onto the bed and attempted to fall into her, but she moved away. "Don't touch me. You're a raving lunatic!" she exclaimed. The look in her eyes said just the opposite. If she wanted me, then me she would get. She must have sensed my next move, because she waved her hands in a "move no further" motion.

"Islam, it is too early for—" I tackled her. She laughed. Yelled. I thought back to Yasara cursing me, and waking up to nameless faces in a row after nights of average sex. Above all, this was my idea of a good morning.

We tossed each other around, rolled, laughed, held one another down like children playing in a sandbox. Adrianne was stronger than I thought, but a man is a man. I was winning. After minutes of futile effort on her part, I let her pin me to the bed.

"Who is boss?" she asked. Grinning ear to ear. She was.

"I am," I answered. She dug her nails into my wrists. "Owwh! Now you've got to pay!" I flipped her over, she giggled, and unlike previous attempts to out maneuver me, she easily obliged.

"What is the cost?" she asked slyly, cutting those gorgeous dark eyes at me like a pro. Instant hard-on.

"What are you willing to give?" I couldn't hide my arousal. Nor did I want to. She moved up toward the head of the bed, and spread her legs ever so slightly. The gesture was suggestive enough to insinuate but not enough to appear vulgar. Just what I liked.

"I will give as much as you—" She was interrupted by a loud and annoying mobile ring.

"Don't get it," I told her. "Don't pick it up." I was about to burst. I positioned myself between her legs, hoping the contact would direct her attention back to me. No avail. Fuck. Still in her trench, she wiggled the phone out of her coat pocket. A quick glance at the screen. I didn't like the look on her face.

In a final and desperate act, I tried to kiss her, in all of her special places at once.

"I have to answer," she said earnestly. I watched her open the small device and issue her signature, "Good morning." The voice on the line was male. "Yes, darling . . ." she replied. Instantly, she squeezed out from under me and walked briskly to the kitchen area. "Really?" she added every few seconds.

It could only be one person at this time of morning. Cooper. Apparently, our morning play wasn't on anymore. I ignored the sinking feeling within, got up, and went into the kitchen area. As though we were in relay, she moved from the kitchen to the opposite side of the flat. That pissed me off. I didn't know how I was supposed to feel in this situation, but I was fuming. Instinctively, I sought to repress the emotion. But the freedman in me let it seethe.

"And did you correct them?" she asked him amiably. Although I was two steps from community service and anger management course sentencing, I found a few things interesting. There was no special look in her eyes. There was reserve. Form. Cordiality. She was not disconnected, but you could tell she was used to her position in her husband's life, and took it on as a duty. Whether of love or obligation, I couldn't decipher. I have yet to understand the reality of our own interaction. She said her goodbyes. Closed the mobile case. Removed her coat, untied her hair, walked across the studio and climbed into bed. Never once did she look at me or offer an explanation. What type of woman is this?

"Are you coming to bed?" she asked. Silence. I was thinking. This woman—this whatever, is in my house, in my bed, and although I love what she does for me, I haven't an idea as to who she is. I don't like this. I don't like being on the outside of her life.

"Islam." She called me, but I was in another place.

"How long have you and he been married?" I blurted out.

She didn't hesitate to answer. "Twelve years."

"And how long have you known him?"

"Since we were children."

"Where did he attend university?"

"Eton."

"And you?" There was no rhyme or reason to these questions. It was just what I wanted to do. It was my natural reaction to how I was feeling.

"Rhodine," she answered.

"And did he play sport?"

"Yes."

"Which?"

"Rugby."

"Did you attend the games?"

"Some."

"And what about him, did he attend yours?"

"There were none," she answered calmly.

"What did you do?"

"I danced."

"Ballet?"

"Yes."

"In England?"

"And France," she added.

"And how many were at the wedding?"

"Many."

"Any royalty?"

"The prince. They are friends," she said.

I wasn't finished. "Where is he?" I asked. If looks could kill, she'd be on the back of a milk carton.

"At home. In Belgravia, in London."

"Where does he think you are?"

"I don't know."

She answered every arbitrary question that I asked. One after the other. Until I tired of asking. The mood of the room lost the vibrant color of just minutes before and had become pale. Still. You could crack it and nothing would come out. We were silent. The look in her eyes told me to ask as much as I wanted. That she would hide nothing. How can one be trustworthy and fraudulent at the very same time? The annoying ring blared for a second time. The phone was on the countertop nearest me. I picked it up. Tossed it out of the window like a baseball. You could hear it shatter on the street. The adrenaline pumped through me so hard, that I had to clench my jaw to keep my teeth from chattering. Where was this coming from? From Adrianne, there was no movement, no reaction. She just looked at me. I saw shock. I saw defiance. I saw arousal. Don't ask why I did it. I just did. It felt good. I wanted to ask questions without interruption. If I weren't top priority to her, I didn't want it thrown in my face. She was still. I was still. Our eyes fixed on one another's.

"How do you feel when you're with him?" I wanted to know.

Her steady gaze told me that she was also, a victim of freedom. That anything I asked, she would answer. She gently bit her bottom lip. As if she had to think about it. "Like his wife," she said calmly.

"How do you feel when you're with me?"

"Like a madwoman."

"Do you love him?" I asked.

"Yes."

"How do you feel about me?" She sat still. Stared, but gave no response.

I let up. Left her on the bed. Went into the front of the studio, wet a brush, and dipped it in paint. Does she love me? The million dollar or in this case I should say billion dollar question was do *I* love me? Am I here, in Brooklyn, in the arms, sense and spirit of a married woman because I love me? Because I am a newly freed man? Because I love being free, I love what it does for me, I love how passionate I've become? Or am I here on the contrary? I was in the mood to ask the hard questions. But I was not in the mood to answer them.

The light and ethereal guitar strings of Lauryn Hill's much debated live network concert drifted through the studio, holding a full-length mirror to my inner consciousness. It showed me who I was and who I was becoming all at once. I remembered clearly, Paul and I purchasing the double CD, almost running to my flat and tearing it open like hungry wolves. It had been a while since we'd heard from Ms. Hill and the world was waiting for a break from the bullshit that it seemed to perpetuate. I recall each track as Paul would describe it—one ridiculously tedious acoustic set. How could she just play the same song over and over and over? Furthermore, he had a much more serious bone to pick with one of his favorite world artists. *What the hell happened to her hair? And her wears?* He swore that this was not Lauryn, but some horrible prank played by Wyclef and Pras, as he'd heard they weren't on good terms. Drugs? It couldn't be, he said. No. Not his Lauryn. So he stuck with the Fugee conspiracy theory. All she needed was a day off of that bloody island with him at Harvey Nichols and she'd be sorted.

I laughed at his rant, and somewhat agreed. Lauryn was indeed different. There was something in her eyes. In her voice. It radiated throughout herself from a bottomless well of being. I could not put my finger on it then as I was, and possibly still am completely lost, but I recognize it today. It was the energy of the dancers at the loft party, and in Fort Greene Park. It was what allowed me to do, say and paint what I felt. She was liberated. All it took was a break. Something to bring you to your knees, where you realize society is but a minor chord in a major composition of a song that is only yours to create. I can't imagine what she went through to get there. Could she be any more connected than she was on the debut of her first solo work? Surely *The Miseducation* was figurative. I was one of the majority who needed to believe that. Because if Lauryn was searching, if *she* was being re-educated, then humanity hadn't a chance. I listen to her tell us that our spiritual leaders are pagans and idiots, and that our present condition needs serious recognition. I nodded my head in agreement and chuckled. It would be natural for us to imply that she'd gone mad. To acknowledge her would mean we'd have to keep up.

"*It's freedom . . . It's freedom time now . . .*"

Again I am wreaking havoc on canvas. I am utilizing a technique that I've never seen nor heard of.

"She is beautiful," Adrianne says, referring to the painting. I didn't hear her come into the front and did not acknowledge her presence in the slightest. Unsure if I was still irritated, I didn't want her to know either. She has an effect on me that distorts my concentration. I wanted to think in peace. After a few seconds of silence, she solemnly retreated into the bedroom. Instantly, I missed her. But I didn't get up. I continued to paint. Pondering the reality that I'd created. I'd thrown the woman's phone into the street. I was becoming someone that I loved and loathed at the same time. I feel, I express, I react. I do all of these things from the current that is soul. I do not care to consider repercussion. Or rebuttal. I say and mean from the deepest part of me. I feel so connected to everything going on. So aware. But I went off today. She could have walked out on me immediately. She'd have been within her rights to. Although I thought about that on down time, when I am in the moment, I could not care less. I have changed. For better or worse is what hasn't been deciphered. I'd like to say for the better. I just need to learn the balance between self-control and free-expression. Is there one? Wouldn't one cancel the other? Questions portend questions.

On the subject at hand, if I am real with myself, I know what I want from Adrianne. It's simple. I do not want her to be with anyone else. Although technically, *I am* 'anyone else', I want that to change. I want all of those 'darlings' and 'reallys' to myself and I never want to be put on hold. I never want to see her kiss another man again. I know what I've gotten into. I've made a deal with the devil and now I want to break it. Apparently, he is not letting me out of it that easily.

My reflection was interrupted by a familiar voice.

"Yo! Islaaaaaaam! Islaaaaaaaam!" I had to laugh. Of all the people in Brooklyn to befriend, I had offered my hand to the neighborhood mad man. I got up, and walked to the front window.

"What's up, blood?" This culture of shouting from the window was new to me. But it added a familial aura to a cold place. He scratched himself openly. Apparently he has no care either.

"You got any soda bottles?" he asked.

"Bottles? What would you need of bottles?" I asked.

He looked at me as if he should be in the studio painting and I should be on the street. "Change man! Change! They gon' give me change for 'em!" Oh.

"I'm painting!" I yelled down.

"So! Just see what you got and throw the bloody things down here!" was the reply. I laughed so hard that he laughed with me. He's heard me use the term *bloody*, and informed me that he needed new curses to add to his 'reper-twah.' I laughed all the way to the kitchen. I looked in almost every cupboard, but only came up with a few cans. Tossed them down to him. He caught all three.

"This all you got?" he asked.

"Yea."

"A'ight. To da queen!" He tipped his hat and walked off as if he were the Duke of Westminster. I busted out laughing. If nothing else, this place had character. My veteran friend was the lead.

The neighbors treat him harshly, as they believe he's mad and hadn't an ounce of intellect to add to their John Madden and *Sex and the City* lives. I've however, found just the opposite. After a long conversation on a beautiful night, I found him a more worthy source of life force than my own brother.

I returned to the easel. Picked up where I'd left off. The reality of the situation is simple. She has been married for over a decade. To a billionaire. To a friend of the Prince. Happy or not, my chances were slim. And I'm not really sure about what she wants. I ask myself how I could trust a woman who is making love to me as if I am the only one in her world, when I am not. Sometimes, she looks at me like I am the center star of her universe. And no matter what I thought, felt or decided prior to that, she becomes the center of mine. How to deal with this? The choice is ultimately my own. Leave her alone and suffer. Stay and suffer. Which proves the greatest reward? Is this a matter of reality? Of what society says reality is for me, that there is ultimately no hope for a situation like this, or is it society who has misfired?

I am an artist. A creator. Made in the image of God himself. Although Adrianne would like to ignore the side of her that is most real, she is a creator as well. Shouldn't we create our own world? Our own reality?

Earlier, I was beside myself—frankly gutted—that she could talk to Cooper as if I didn't exist. Right now, I wanted to lie with her. I wanted my reality to be the only one that counted. I laid the brush down. Stared at her reflection in the extra large window. She is in my business shirt, on her computer, working. I am so sorry about the phone. That's what I get up to tell her.

She noticed me walking toward the bed, and glanced up, but didn't stop what she was doing. I didn't know what that meant. Did she not wish to be bothered? Did she want space? I was jealous of Cooper for knowing her well enough to be able to tell these things in an instant. What to do?

"I apologize." I said it and meant it. No response from her. I tried again. "Adrianne. Babe. I'm sorry. I don't know what got into me . . ." She stopped, pulled herself up onto her knees, into a half-stance and came to the edge of the bed. I continued. "I haven't been myself lately and . . ." A kiss. Then another. Then another. Hands grabbed fistfuls of my hair. She was kissing me all over. "I will pay for the ph—" Her lips on mine almost made me forget where we were. I placed my arms around her waist and kissed her like a hungry man.

This was right. It felt right. It felt right yesterday and today. Maybe tomorrow's right would be different. As of now, today is all that counts. I kiss her as if that were all I knew how to do and tell myself that this is real. There is no Cooper, no career, no conscience, no truth other than ours. This is the reality of today. Tomorrow after all, is not promised.

18

The soul of Fulton Street on a summer afternoon. A young man on the steps of the Brooklyn Academy of Music donning a tattered *She Hate Me* tee shirt and Marvin Gaye's best, courtesy of Leon Ware, crooning from a handheld electronic device. He is handing out adverts for a free summer event. I am in a daze as an—I don't know what nationality she is—woman, issues a gentle hello and asks about my trainers. I tell her they are FLY, I bought them in Camden. She nodded, smiled that smile. Flash. The heat. Replied. After I assured her that the original Camden is indeed north of London and not southern New Jersey, she wants me to say a few extra words as she loves my accent. Although proper British intonation can give a barnyard animal an attractive edge, I am beginning to appreciate the hard vowels and soft consonants that resonate from the New York female tongue. On a normal day, this woman would be at the flat in five minutes or less, asking me to say and do more precarious things. I let go of her hand, and wondered why I did, never minding that, as I'd forget her face the moment another appeared in plain view. My god. Women to the left, women to the right. Straight hair, long hair, curly hair, short. Naturals. Skin, skirts, legs, thighs, bloody hell. How one makes it to the bodega without mistakenly falling into a vagina is a hat trick.

Returning from a very interesting studio visit, a performance artist who will absolutely not be considered for Spence—as I am not such a fan of yards of toilet paper strewn about aimlessly in protest of genocide anywhere, no one deserves that type of protest—I am back in the neighborhood today, running errands. I recall Micah complaining about everything being so accessible in Brooklyn, and that it was a "trap" set by "the man" designed specifically to keep "us" in our neighborhoods. I happen to think it's convenient. And since every train in the known universe stops at Atlantic and Fulton Avenue, it seems as if travel to Manhattan, or Queens, or California for that matter would be easily attained.

I, only needing a few things here and there, am thankful for the shops in a row today. There are items that need to be replaced. Water, orange juice, condoms. Definitely condoms. Adrianne has been with me at the flat for three days now. She has not reported to the gallery, opting to work from Brooklyn instead. She makes calls, speaks in different languages, kisses me and occasionally asks a question. I paint, visit artists and underground galleries, leaving her to her own devices. At the end of a day, when she closes her computer, she will walk into the front of the studio with a cup of tea and sit between me while I paint. She will not speak, there are no interruptions, just silence.

I have painted for hours with her like that, and have in fact become used to the studious and ever-so-slight moans of acknowledgement she gives when I have done something new or uncustomary. When I am finished for the evening, and not a moment prior, she will massage and stretch my hands, before placing them where she loves them most. After knowing what it is like to feel her muscles—those muscles—suck me inward and out like a Hoover, I try to apply at least an inch of the discipline I showed on our first night together. It will always fail, and we will finish intense sessions in a row, seeing the sun each morning anew. I say a prayer. Tea. Nap. Work. Love. We have been like this for days, on occasion forgetting the trinity, breakfast, lunch and dinner exist.

I try and quarantine images of her, at least long enough to chat up a fashionable woman in large earrings, many bracelets, god forsaken heels and shorts, but the images prevail. All I see is Adrianne in my clothing, shirts, sweats etcetera, as she seems to prefer mine to her own. Bless her for having such a sex drive. If I weren't so weak, I'd somersault to the corner. I thought to send thanks in Hebrew but decided it to be somewhat blasphemous. I snickered inside instead.

Racing through the small Spanish shop, or as natives say, *bodega*, I bag my own items and insist that the dark haired clerk keep the change. I can't wait to get back to the flat.

There are people all over the place and I wonder where they all manage to sleep. I walk a long city block. Turn a corner. Turn one key. Then another.

"Adrianne . . ." I call her name. As I take the stairs two at a time, I hear her. "Adriaaanne . . ." I called her again, I wanted her right away. The aroma of freshly grilled something-or-other sent a smoke signal to my stomach. It growled. I hadn't eaten properly in days. I grabbed Adrianne by the waist and kissed her.

"I thought you would be later," she said as spices accompanied a large wooden spoon into a wok filled with green leaves. I moved her hair from her neck and kissed her there. "Islam!" she laughed and screamed. "Go into the studio. I will call for you when I am done," Adrianne signaled in the opposite direction with the spoon in her hand. She was scolding me.

I didn't want to leave. I wanted to tackle her onto the countertop. "I am not hungry. Not for food," I grinned.

"Go!" she yelled playfully.

Retreating unwillingly into the studio, I lit a few mood-altering candles, figuring I'd pass time that way. Keep my mind off of the obvious. Minutes turned into what seemed like an hour or so of painting. My phone rang. I glanced at the screen. It was Cooper. I picked up immediately.

"Evening, sir."

"Good evening. Are you available?" he asked politely. Sensing this would be a more important conversation, I drew the large wooden parlor doors to the studio shut. It was weird, how in an altered state of reality—my reality, I'd been able to actually separate my world with Adrianne from his. At least for today. It's amazing what a change in perspective will do. Normality, or my perception of, is shifting. I answered the question.

"Yes. I am available. Is all well?"

He seemed preoccupied. "Yes, I need to know if you've completed a collection as of yet."

"Almost."

"Good. Have you set a range?"

"In price?"

"Of course," he answered.

"Not yet. I have to apply the finishing touches. Why do you ask?"

"Do not set cost without consulting me, and try and complete a set prior to the France trip. There are some special people I'd like you to show your work to," he said earnestly.

"To whom, may I ask?"

"The Jumeirah-Siddiq group."

Jumeirah . . . Jumeirah . . . Essex House Hotel on Central Park South? The Burj Al Arab in Dubai? Christ's sake. The Arabic gods of the hotel industry. "The hotel group, yea?"

"And oil. I was in a meeting and was asked of your work." I am speechless. Seconds passed with my jaw dropped. The parlor doors were pulled slightly open. Adrianne squeezed through them and fumbled around behind me. I heard her but didn't. My God. Jumeirah? Siddiq? He wants to show my work to *them*? What type of luck is this?

"Islam," Mr. Spence called. Adrianne appeared beside me, freshly showered and dripping wet. I can do this. I can tell her to get the hell out. I can tell her that I am about to possibly become the Allah of the Arabic art world, if she would just get her damn hands off of me. "Islam. Are you there?" Mr. Spence asked.

Just as I had gotten my head wrapped around what he'd stated and her hands away from a major nerve center, she removed the phone from mine and gently pushed the casing together. "Are you done?" she asked softly.

"That was important."

"That is not what I asked," she responded calmly. "Have you finished your work for the day?" One hand traveled the length of my chest. Lightly.

I could tell her that her husband was on the phone. I could tell her that I'm not sure about this. That I didn't know if what I felt right now was guilt, nervousness, fear, or stimulation. If it was the excitement of watching the only thing that I've ever wanted and worked for in life begin to take off, or if it was simply the blood rushing to my pelvic area.

I reached for the phone, but was startled by a hard bass line, dreary drums, and deep ambient vocals. Slow, sinister mood music. Allowing her body to drift back and forth in a hypnotizing motion, Adrianne's eyes locked on mine. She was determined to get what she wanted. Watching her belly button move in small tidal waves was crucifying. Belly dancing was unfair at its usual speed. Slowed, and over infectious music, it was treacherous. Accompanied by the sight of dripping wet skin, and wondrous curves, it was all too much at once.

"Help me put on my clothes," she ordered. I didn't respond. I was transfixed. Adrianne held in hand, a single candle, and moved slowly with the bass line as a snake to a shaman. The voice of an underworld artist that I knew well filled the room.

I'll teach you to lead . . .

Coming from an artist who confessed his sins in a way that alluded pride over atonement, Tricky's dark and deceptive voice sounded like the devil himself, egging you on to do things that only he could appreciate. The music was twisted and deep. Eerie. Love was not what came to mind when the Brit's raspy vocals hit Marilyn Manson-like bass lines and chords. Ice picks. Pitch forks. Chains. The sounds were sadistic. It was what I played while painting anguish either into or out of a subject. Adrianne was steps from me, inviting me into a world she'd created. Wrists above her head, her waist stirred intelligently in front of me, as if seduction were an everyday thing. Wax from the dripping candle fell gently onto her shoulder. She maintained her eyes on mine. I was fascinated. Intrigued enough to watch, but not enough to wait, I reached for her. She backed away. Another drip of wax. A more delicate area of her body. A more sensuous series of movements. I liked this side of her. She wasn't the primary school girl of the morning. She was an angel with a dirty face.

"What is imagination?" she asked in the voice that sent ripples through me. A low-toned sexy one that let me know that a more adventurous Adrianne had arrived. One who had a propensity for the twisted. The weird. One whose own imagination never ceased to amaze me. I didn't answer. I decided I'd show her instead. Belt buckles and trousers hit the floor. I walked towards her.

Her tongue snaked outward and in, a tiny silver ball buried into its center. The piercing was a beautiful surprise and I felt the increase in stiffness, as if I could become any more rigid than I already was. Candle in hand, Adrianne allowed the tip of her tongue to cut slowly through the fire. Back. Forth. Back again. She backed up against the glass of the front window, smiling that Mona Lisa smile, watching her effect on me trump any restraint I'd managed to muster. I stepped towards her. The candle lit a path to a place that I could easily find in the dark. She pulled it closer. I wished she'd move that thing. The flame was in the way of where I wanted to be. It seemed as if she liked the heat. Or rather the danger of being burned down there. I reached for the candle and Adrianne intercepted my hand, linked it with hers.

"Taste it." She captured my other hand and slyly edged them both behind me. One hand cuffed my wrists in a singular, fluid movement. How'd she do that? This was sick.

"Come on, A," I begged. I was used to restraining, but not being restrained. I took a look at the flame standing patiently between my love and hers. If I did what she asked, my tongue would cut the small blaze, and its tip would barely brush her most sensitive orb. The danger of it . . . the restraint would drive us both insane.

There were Adrianne's half-moon eyes, and Tricky's deceptive voice enticing me to do things that made me nervous. I felt a gentle heat run along the tip of my manhood and almost had a heart attack. Fire? There? Hell no.

The heat passed under and over me again, and to my surprise, a quick sting. Wax. I yelled like she'd cut me there. She chuckled. Used her tongue to quiet the sting. She was playing with me. My dirty little thing—that's what I'd call her tonight—placed the candle behind me, for my restrained hands to hold. The wax burned as it overflowed onto the tips of my fingers, and Adrianne finished the job she'd started. I gritted my teeth at the combination of pain and pleasure. My voice took on a feminine quality that I'd never heard before. I was high pitched and losing it. To give in to the pleasure and move my pelvis, increased the overflow of wax onto my skin. Increased the pain. Standing still wasn't an option either. The pleasure was too much. Hypnotized by the music, the slow movement of her head and the expert way she loved me down there, it would be difficult to convince me that I hadn't been abducted. That I wasn't on another planet. Stars circled my head in a dizzying array and I'd resolved that I might die this way tonight.

Ashamedly amidst an asthma attack, I heaved, but felt too good to be embarrassed about it. This . . . I don't know what this is, as I've never *ever* felt this shit before. It's not an orgasm. I know orgasms and this is not one of them. Fuck. My legs are shaking.

"What is desire?" Adrianne came to a halt, and grinned like the devil's wife. I yelled like a man being tortured. If my hands were free I could strangle her for this. She let the tip of her tongue linger on the only true connection to mankind that I had. A gunshot to the head. A quick and painless death would do. It would stifle the agony, the relentless torment and anguish of the moment. I'd flirt with the idea, as she'd write her name all over the very core of me. I'd almost prefer to die than deal with this. She'd ask me of desire once more and chuckle at the slightest notion of a response from me. I didn't answer her. I couldn't. Besides, all of the riposte she needed was right here, shaking like a leaf, too strong to buckle, too weak to stand. I am too young to have a heart attack . . . I am too young to have a heart attack . . . I repeat the mantra until I begin to believe it and let her wet body lead me to Babylon. Desire is a fucking demon. That's what it is.

We lay in the studio, on the second-hand sofa, covered in sweat and other bodily fluids. I didn't even bother to get up and wet a cloth. After days of this, we were both exasperated. She is already on her way to sleep. That is always what a man wants to see. There is something about a woman heading immediately to sleep after sex that makes one feel like he's king of satisfaction. If she leaves you, you know it had nothing to do with your abilities. Sleep is proof.

Adrianne was purring peacefully, as I can assume that all was thoroughly enjoyed on her behalf. After she all but crippled me—I can't even remember certain aspects of the session—it was only right that I returned the favor. I found out that she was more of an exhibitionist than I thought. Definitely sadist. Hair was wrapped and re-wrapped in my fist tightly. The notion was not to hurt her, but to hurt her. She hurt me. It was only right. I held her to the window, and we pounded it so hard, not only did all of Fort Greene see us, but the notion of shattering glass, the danger of plummeting several feet to the ground, did something to her that I've never seen or heard of any woman. She was exceptionally loud this time. To no objection of mine, all of New York could hear her voice.

All was still, as smoke clearing after a gunfight. My love lay on my chest sleeping peacefully like a newborn. Still wired from moments prior, I was too disturbed to join her.

"Islaaaaaaaam!" Oh no. Not him. Not right now. I will ignore him. "Islaaaaaaaaam! Islaaaaaaaaam! Aye! IS-LAM!" Does he ever quit? I tried my best to slide from underneath Adrianne without disturbing her.

"What!" I yelled.

"You got a quarter? And a pair of sneakers I ca' borrow?" Is he fucking serious? What a nutter.

"No and no." I answered curtly.

"You ain't got a quarter? How you payin' na rent?" he asked.

I stormed toward the kitchen area, swearing. Fucking quarter and trainers. I gathered every piece of silver I could manage to find. Placed it all in a small brown paper bag. Tossed the package down to him. Back into the studio, picked her up, slid her back atop me.

Five seconds later, the bloody phone rang. From the sound of it, the call was international. I reached over and picked it up. Music to my ears, I'd know that voice anywhere.

"Oh and what does one possibly know about fine French cuisine, when he can't tell a baguette from a bin liner!" Paul. "Yes . . . What? Well, you do that. And manage to get the hair in your nose trimmed properly, would you? You are working with food for Christ's sake! Or am I the only one who has taken notice of that as well . . ." He has not and will not change. "Islam. Are you there?" Voice, tone and vernacular perfectly restructured, you would have no idea that he was swearing just seconds ago.

"Yea, man. Who are you cursing?" I whispered.

"Why are you whispering?" he asked.

"I just am."

"I'm sure. And which poor, unsuspecting dame is having the best sleep of her known life beside you today—or tonight. What's the time difference again?" I laughed quietly. With intuition like that, I am sure this is the only incarnation where he has been male. I rubbed Adrianne's back. Ignored the implication made by my comrade. He continued. "Oh you're just going to play mute anyway . . . listen. Ahmed and I will be in New York shortly. He is playing tonight with Thievery Corporation. It was last minute. A major gig for him, as he has managed to make at least one twenty-four-hour period without doing a line." The sarcasm that is Paul. I heard Ahmed's slow slur of a voice in the background. "He says hello, of course," Paul added.

"Where are you now? And what are the details of the concert?" I was excited about seeing my boys. I needed a break.

"Montreal, Canada. And this airport might as well be a mausoleum. Not a decent shop in sight. I can't even get a proper meal. Fucking waste of natural material, these Canadians."

"Paul. Focus. The details." Adrianne stirred. Made herself more comfortable.

"Why yes, of course. Madison Square Garden. Tonight, nine pm. Your ticket and pass will be at the side entry gate."

"One or two?"

"One. Why?"

"I need another."

"Then she'd better bring a friend," he stated.

"I'll see what I can do."

"Cheers."

"Ciao."

We disconnected. Adrianne yawned, then asked in the girlish tone and voice that she uses when she wants something, "Are we going to see Thievery?" she asked of the eclectic world music group. I didn't know she was awake.

"Can you?"

"For Richest Man in Babylon? Of course, I can." She said that as if it were an absurd question to ask. As if she'd forgotten that she was married. That would make day four. I guess I am not the only one in an altered state of reality. "Who was the man at the window?" she inquired.

Damn. She heard that as well? "A friend."

"Is he gone mad?"

"Define mad," I responded.

"Mad. Insane. In need of confinement," she replied.

"Those are synonyms. Not classifications."

"Really?" That classic Brit intonation of hers ever so pronounced. It did something to me. "Well, then. Why doesn't the expert define it for me?"

I chuckled. She earned that one. "Well," I began. "Everyone, every philosopher, every scientist, Freud, Jung, Nietzsche, even Aristotle has taken a stab at defining what it is to be or become mad."

"And?" she asked.

"Lately, I am most in tune with Nietzsche's characterization."

"Which is?" she asked wide-eyed.

"Madness to him was simply the eruption of arbitrariness in feeling, seeing, and hearing. The enjoyment of the mind's lack of discipline, the joy of human unreason."

"Go on." She climbed further upward, as if I were a rock mountain.

"He disagreed with the forced discipline of the mind that was and still is the embodiment of mankind, and believed that the contrary impulses that are human nature are more powerful than the over simplified law of agreement that served as a universal binding force for humanity."

"Yes . . ."

"Slower dredging spirits were the proprietors of this binding force. Those, who continually found pleasure in their wisdom. They who refused to seek, as fear of finding kept them in a state of spiritual paralysis. In his eyes, the greater majority lacked an intellectual conscience. They would never ask, would never challenge—even their own views. They questioned nothing and articulated no doubt. They laughed when nothing was funny and smiled when they wanted to cry. In Nietzsche's eyes, they themselves were the truly mad. For they were incapable of free expression, and would never know what it is to be liberated, thus confusing freedom and unconventionalism with madness. With insanity. They, the spiritually and socially repressed were the least free, but the most powerful because they were the majority."

Adrianne was silent for a few moments. It seemed she was taking in all that I said. "Enlighten me. Of these slower dredging and bound spirits, are there any counterparts? Any unbound spirits?" she asked honestly. I answered.

"Yes, in fact there are. Artists, the most unsobering force of mankind, the most incapable of any type of binding or containment, yet the most gifted in the art of reason, spirit and the likes, are most able of passion, of connection, of real-life articulation, as it is their natural birth right, a talent that gives them an unfair advantage over their bound counterparts." She nodded, the look she gave me was hard to place. I continued. "Of artists, they are challenging, fanatical, overly concerned with liberation to the point of obsession. They endure great pleasures and pains to get to where they are most comfortable—on high, yet they however, are also most often misunderstood, thus most easily gone mad by society's standards. As of the moment, I am not sure that the society in which we live is credible enough to define madness, or reality or any matter of the heart or spirit. What do you think?" I asked.

She paused. I could hear the wheels between the logical and artistic sides of her turning. "Friedrich Nietzsche was a madman himself. He couldn't manage to use the toilet without suffering migraines, outbursts and the likes. He was obsessed with proposals to a lone woman who was smart enough to refuse him continuously. What we've witnessed is the immaculately written tantrum of that refusal. There is nothing worse than one who has made excuses for poor behavior. He was lovesick, friendless and mad. Perhaps gifted. But mad nonetheless." Adrianne added. Threw her hand and wrist about in a tisk.

I knew she didn't believe that. "Nietzsche was possibly the greatest philosopher of all time. A scientist, perhaps one of the best alchemists known to date, above all, considered himself an artist."

"Do tell," she said.

We adjusted ourselves on the old sofa. I have found it such a joy to discuss the deepest aspects of me, my fears, beliefs and philosophies on life with a woman. With a person period. I carefully removed myself from the sofa, and reached for one of my favorite philosophical volumes. *The Gay Science.* I prepared to read one of many favorite passages. "Ready?" I asked.

She—everything smiled. Her eyes, her lips, her entire being it seemed. She was full of light over there. She was beaming. "Yes. I am ready." She sat up, allowing space beside her for me to sit.

I took my place on the sofa, and Adrianne surprised me. She

straddled me as she had the first night we met. While I painted her in the suite of The Soho Hotel, I thumbed through the worn paperback, the many underlined pages catching but not keeping my attention. I arrived at the appropriate section and read the heading. "We Artists . . ."

The look in her eyes was that of the night at the loft party in Shoreditch. It was pure. Untainted. I continued. "It is quite enough to love, to hate, to desire, simply to feel—and right away the spirit and power of the dream overcome us, and with our eyes open, coldly contemptuous of all danger, we climb up on the most hazardous of paths to scale the roofs and spires of fantasy . . ."

She gently closed the book, and looked into my eyes. Locking her fingers into mine, she picked up in the passage where I'd left off. "Without any sense of dizziness, as if we had been born to climb . . ." She half-smiled as she recited from memory one of my favorite excerpts. ". . . We are somnambulists of the day . . ."

"We artists, we ignore what is natural . . ." I chimed in. In what had become signature for us, we traded lines back and forth, a rhythm much like ours in bed.

"We are moon struck and God struck . . ." she added.

"We wander, still as death . . ." Me.

"Unwearied . . ." She.

"On heights that we do not see as heights . . ." Me.

"But as plains . . . as our safety," we finished together. As she joined me for the last line, I thought—no, I knew, we were one of a most peculiar kind.

"How did you know that?" I asked her.

"I could ask you the same."

We sat still, legs over and under one another, Adrianne's fore-head to mine. I'd determined that the darkness in her eyes wasn't darkness after all. It was knowing. Maturity. It was her accepting me, loving me, although I have so much of this journey left to travel, the look that she gave on the night we met, and tonight was one of patience and understanding. Of tolerance.

Yet another indescribable feeling crept in. This . . . I don't know what to call it, interaction, for lack of a better word, has me so high, too high in fact. So much that I do not feel comfortable. Meditation usually brings me down. So, I closed my eyes. Inhaled deeply and exhaled fully. The breath in my body flowing freely through the channels of each meridian, from the base of my spine to the top of my head, and back down again. I did this over and over, as I was used to it calming me. However, something else happened instead.

Still forehead to forehead, her hands cupping the back of my neck, Adrianne also breathed deep. And gradually, as she relaxed and quieted her own thoughts, our bodies rose and fell slowly, at the same syncopated pace. I am used to meditation. I am used to breath. Besides painting, it is how I have maintained myself all of these years. I am not used to this. I am floating. Holding her and floating. I am aware of the fact that we are separate, as parts of me can feel parts of her, but overall we are breathing as one entity. We flow it seems, into and out of each other's spiritual space. Instead of coming down off of a high that I feared not being able to control, living in and through her breath gave me additional strength, and I climbed higher. I feel things that I do not want to feel. She has been hurt. She is in pain. At a meditative zenith, I feel what she doesn't want to remember. What she will never tell me. This is not what I wanted to happen.

The bell rings. As does the mobile phone. We do not move. After a few minutes, I open my eyes. Hers are still closed. I wait for her, and watch the makings of a tear drop that never falls. When she opens her eyes, I do not pretend that I wasn't looking. I let her know in so many ways that I was. That I saw everything.

"Is that your mother?" she asked quietly.

"In the photograph?"

"In the painting."

"No." I answered flatly. I wanted to avoid this conversation at all costs. Adrianne wouldn't allow it.

"The subject resembles her."

"How do you know?"

"I saw the photo of you and her together." She paused. "What happened," she asked. I don't talk about this. Half of me doesn't know what happened. It's the other half I'd like to avoid. I think back. She used to cry a lot, I used to make her laugh. She loved my father. I don't know if he loved her. She loved me. I loved her back. She adored my paintings. Bought my first brushes. And she never saw the painting that day. It was my best one.

"She died."

"I know." Adrianne said. "How?" Why is she making me talk about this?

"Killed herself."

"With what."

"With a rope. And a chair. And a boy who should have never been born."

"Your brother."

"Yes." I didn't notice the rain on my face, as to call these monstrous tears drops would be a severe understatement.

"You are her first born, yes?" I nodded my head.

"And you were close?"

"Uh-huh."

"And the small painting, you did that for her?"

I couldn't answer. Every image, every unspoken word, was either caught in my throat, or rolling down my cheeks. I could see my mum, the half smile, the funny look on her face as she hung there. And the stillness. On the inside and outside of me. Nothing moved for a very long time. And every day afterwards that didn't hurt, days where I went numb or apathetic, caved in on me all at once. I cried so hard that I couldn't find time for embarrassment. And Adrianne rocked me. Held me in place. Sex I could handle. This I could not.

I held her to me. Attempted to wipe some of the wetness off of her neck and shoulders. She moved my hand. Kissed my forehead.

I needed to get out of here. "Have you eaten?" I asked.

"Not yet. I wanted to wait for you, of course. You were working," she responded.

"What is it again?"

"Salmon. Yours is made to Hasidic rule." I smiled. I love her. God, I love her.

"Let's eat and get dressed. The concert is on at nine. Ahmed will play first."

"Alright." She smiled back. We helped each other up, and headed into the kitchen area.

There is a moment. A moment in one's life when a definitive choice is made. And you know, that no matter what lies ahead, that you will not be the same after making it. For it is not the choice that made you into someone you didn't recognize, but the fact that you considered it. I have considered life with this woman. And life without her. I have considered the implications and varying realities of my choices, free will, passion, spirit, desire, discipline and the likes, and the decision is obvious. I will not move from her. Where I am, she is. That is final.

19

Madison Square Garden, a mystic of coliseums, although not the most beautiful, surely she is the most desired, the Aphrodite of performance venues. On the night of a performance, you could feel the heart of New York skip a beat, as the anticipation of possibly witnessing history flows transiently through the air. Something about this venue brought out the best in artists and game players alike. I hoped tonight would be no different.

The music in The Garden was live and airy. Drums, horns, strings, Thievery Corporation was one of many world groups performing tonight and it showed. Although their show had not begun, there was no other word to describe the vibration here, than flavorful. Tonight there would be music from all over, Brazil, Germany, England, India, Iceland. As we moved from escalator to escalator, we could hear the faint sound of whoever was on before Ahmed, making their mark on New York City. I was particularly excited about one performance, a Brazilian jazz singer that I'd met several times in London, one that I knew fancied me, and vice versa, but we never quite made the connection. Not that it mattered now, but a good look at a fine female specimen never hurt.

We rode escalators almost endlessly. The Garden, making a habit of testing the patience of those who were in a rush to be seated, boasted lift after lift, a metaphoric stairway to entertainment heaven. Life-sized panels of historic moments in music and sport donned the walls like masterpiece paintings. Jackson. Jordan. Springfield. John. It was all a part of the experience. Adrianne seemed excited. She placed her keys in my hand as she thumbed through the program booklet.

"Your friend, what is his name again?"

"Ahmed."

"Ahmed," she repeated, "must be extremely talented. He has quite a spread in here," she said, referring to the performance program. "Zero Seven and The Roots are here tonight as well, this is amazing . . ." She went on about the show while I almost tripped over trying to figure out how much time it took the woman passing us to get her extremely long legs into the sliver of material I'm sure she mistakenly referred to as a pair of shorts.

"Islam." Adrianne called.

One more look, and I swear I will answer every question she—AH! A sharp knife-like jolt traveled through my upper leg and groin area simultaneously.

"Ad—ri, AHHH!" The couple behind us laughed. I bit my lip and held my breath as Adrianne's claws pinched my balls. I felt like I was being ripped in two.

"She is nice, but she's a man," she stated calmly. Her impish grin was easily interpreted: *You will learn not to stare at women in front of me.*

"Yes, Ahmed is talented," I answered, still in pain. Why do women do that? I bet she'd be sorry if she'd ruined something down there.

We'd finally arrived at our assigned box, where none other but Paul, the aesthetic disciple himself, awaited us with open arms. We kissed each other on both cheeks. Something European men do without a second thought. I'd gotten used to it. Paul's lived in England all of his life, but his family is Italian.

"Islam! Blood! What the hell took you so long? I am sure there are at least chariot horses in this city, not to mention rail trains and vehicles!"

I laughed aloud and hugged him again. I missed this guy.

"And the lady . . ." He took Adrianne's hand and kissed it prior to the introduction. Paul. "A proper introduction please." Paul signaled me to introduce the two. I already knew, the bag, the heels, the jewels, she is his type to a point of fanaticism.

"Paul, Adrianne. Adrianne, Paul," I responded.

"Why hello, Paul." Adrianne said, grinning ear to ear. If Paul liked you, he made a production of it. If he hated you he made a production of it. Paul himself was a production, so it followed.

"Has anyone seen the most exquisite woman in the known world? Excuse me . . ." he tapped the arm of the security guard standing nearby. "I am looking for the most exquisite, the most beautiful woman in the—oh! Never mind! Why here she is right in front of us!" Adrianne smiled brightly.

"Paul. Enough is enough," I interrupted.

"How do you manage with him?" he asked her.

"I try," she answered. They shared a light laugh. He'd made his impression. You'd either love or hate Paul. Adrianne loved him.

"Alright, alright." I interrupted. Took her hand from his. It's funny how hypersensitive I am to small things, like whether or not someone is holding her hand, her waist, who she's talking to, no matter who it is. I have never been like this before. So protective. "Are we up here the entire night?" I asked Paul of the sky-box.

"It depends on where you and the lady want to watch the show. You can either watch it from the behind the stage, the floor or the box. Your choice," he answered.

I looked at Adrianne, pulled her to me. Asked her what her preference was. Paul gave me a weird look. He'd just taken notice of my behavior. It didn't register. Under normal circumstances, I did what I wanted to do without considering anyone else. These were not normal circumstances.

"I'd like the opportunity to meet the artists." Adrianne responded in the calm but *this is final*, tone of voice that I've become accustomed to. My hands were around her waist, her back resting lightly on my chest, I inhaled that magnificent spicy vanilla scent of hers and pulled her tighter to me. Paul's jaw almost dropped. I had to keep myself from laughing.

"We are going down," I told him.

"Yes, Islam, that has been made quite apparent," he replied. The ocular call and response between us would start at any moment. We made our way to the elevators.

"What the hell is going on?" was the first look he gave.

"Nothing!" I shot back.

"Yes there is!"

"I will tell you later!" I hoped he would let it go. The elevator doors opened.

"You'd better!" The look in his eyes was a mixture of amusement and utter disbelief. I thought to myself. I am not *that* bad off. Am I?

Paul took the lead, navigating through sterile corridors and passageways that housed recording artist after recording artist. He thought it would be good for us to go to the artists' lounge and get a drink or two, as that seemed to be the central meeting grounds for the performers. He was right. Upon entering the lounge area, we were pleasantly surprised. Everyone, I mean everyone was there. Shifting and moving about. There was Meshell N'degeocello, Questlove and Black Thought of The Roots. Mark Mac of 4 Hero, Mark de Clive Lowe, Tricky, Radiohead, Bilal—my favorite soul rock star from Philly, British singer Corinne Bailey Rae, Ceelo and Danger Mouse. Andre and Big Boi. The UK's Uprock crew—I knew them personally—and Gilles Peterson, the only international deejay who had a larger and more devout following than Ahmed. My head spun attempting to figure out who I wanted to meet first. As we approached a small table, a tall man with shoulder length locks wiped his fingers on a napkin, eyed Adrianne and gave me a pound.

"Sup man, where've you been?" Vikter Dupleix was one of the world's most eclectic creators of sound and a good friend of Ahmed's. One whose soft crooning soulful vocals have landed me many a female "most memorable moments" in the past. He stood, I extended my hand. He gave me a hug instead.

"I've been around," I answered with a smile.

He looked Adrianne up and down, smiled back and said cynically, "Yea?" We were both on the verge of laughter. My female woes were much the topic of ridicule with him and his crew.

"Yea. Just trying to get this paint gig off the ground." I answered honestly.

"Seems you already have the inspiration," he joked.

After properly introducing Adrianne, we made our way through the crowd of A-class world music producers, musicians and culture icons. New Brit producer Aaron Jerome, Kenneth Crouch, Missy Elliot, Pharell Williams, Kanye West . . . the list was endless. Ahmed came out of nowhere and jumped on my back. We play-fought like brothers. I introduced him and Adrianne.

"Wowwww," was all he said. And that was it for Ahmed. We were lucky to get that much.

Adrianne's phone. It wouldn't stop ringing. She pardoned herself and answered it.

"Who is that? I have seen her before." Ahmed's Iranian-British accent plus his signature slur, gave him a unique disposition in any conversation.

I thought about his question. Honestly, I couldn't really answer him. I didn't know what to call this. "A friend," was all I said.

"Have you . . . you know." Ahmed gestured inward and outward with his fingers. Normally I'd laugh, but I was interested in something else. I watched Adrianne's expression as she spoke on the phone. I didn't like it.

Paul dropped in on the conversation. "Yes, that is what we'd all like to know! Who is she and have you plunged into that—that remarkable creature of a woman!" I didn't answer. My attention was still on the opposite side of the room. "Islam. We are your mates, we've been on a bloody plane for an entire day, we haven't seen you in months and repeat after me . . ." Who was she talking to? "She will not fly away," Paul said sarcastically. Ahmed laughed. "Never mind the finer details, Ahmed, do you know that Islam hugged and kissed her publicly? With total disregard of any of the other women in the building he may have been with? And America or not, we know there are possibly fifty of those unsuspecting women here tonight." Ahmed laughed. Paul continued. "He actually showed *affection* to this woman. Can you believe it? We are surely in the last days."

Ahmed's infamous, "Wowwww," was all he added.

I was about to defend myself, when none other than Brazilian jazz singer Bembe Segue broke up our little party. She hadn't seen me in quite some time. Wanted to know how I was doing. If I was selling art. How long I'd been in the States. She's a beautiful piece of work this one. With a sultry voice that made you want to pluck her right off of the microphone. Although I've always wanted to, I've never slept with her. Some women are saved for special occasions. Paul and Ahmed left us to catch up, as they wanted—no needed to see me speaking to someone other than Adrianne in order to believe that I was still Islam. In a way, I needed to prove that I was.

I was careful not to be disrespectful, but male-female interaction boundaries are so unclear from woman to woman. I gave my favorite Brazilian singer a big hug.

Adrianne appeared like the ghost of Christmas past. "Hello," she stated blankly.

Caught. I hadn't done anything, but there is something about these situations that makes you feel exposed. The introduction. This one would be tricky. Tone of voice was everything. Keep it general. Adrianne first. "Adrianne, this is Bembe, who is performing tonight. And Bembe, this is Adrianne, who will be enjoying the performance." There.

"Hello, Adrianne." Bembe extended her hand, she was blatantly ignored. There was no reply, no cordial phrase or gesture. Just air that seemed to get thicker and thicker as moments passed.

A slight glance in Adrianne's direction and I saw what could easily be categorized in a single word. *Venom*. Ah, I have learned something. Adrianne had a jealous streak worse than mine. She just hid it better than I did.

"I would like to watch the concert from the floor," Adrianne said out of nowhere.

"Why?" If looks could kill there would be nothing left of me.

"It is my preference," was all she said.

Damn. I wanted to meet some of the other artists. "Alright. I will tell Paul—"

"No need. I have already spoken to him. Your name again?" She gestured to my friend.

"Bembe."

"Yes, well luck wished in whatever it is that you do," Adrianne hissed. Her back was already towards us both, as if she had much better to do than endure the company of this woman. As my own luck would have it, Paul stood off to the side of us grinning as he watched the entire exchange. As I sent a swift and silent apology to my favorite Brazilian songstress and followed Adrianne to the elevator, I heard a remote laugh.

"We'll see you downstairs, man!" I yelled to my best friend attempting to save face.

He just shook his head and laughed. "I'm sure you will," he replied. I grinned to myself. I will not hear the end of this.

The deep bass, strings and organic drums of Thievery Corporation's signature reggae-femme sound caused the crowd to erupt into a fit. We couldn't see them, but we could hear soft French perfectly spoken and sung, over a hard bass line. If you could imagine the hardest of Rasta dub beats hitting you in the chest, then a most sensual French voice and lips lightly tracing your ears, you'd have been robbed blind with the eclectic sound that is Thievery Corporation. The house lights were low. Adrianne swayed. The mood was exotic and beautiful.

"Le Monde. I love this song," she whispered.

"What is she saying?" I asked. I spoke French. I knew. But I wanted to hear her say it. She tossed her head back onto my shoulder. Moved her hips in a slow, circular motion.

"I love to move with you," she said after the first choral line, slowly and sensuously moving with her interpretation. "I love you inside of me . . . I love what it does to me . . ." I could tell her that I spoke the language and knew the song, that what she said to me was not what was being sung, but I declined. I was interested in this. It was a different side of her, a most natural one.

The vocalist purred softly, while Adrianne allowed herself free range of movement around and about me. It took all that I had, but I maintained. What was being said was much more important than what was being done. Her hands found their way to the back of my neck. Her lower body found its way elsewhere. She moved fluidly.

"I am so free . . . you make me . . . you make me that way . . ." My love's faux interpretation and movements had me enthralled. "I'd love to lay with you tonight . . ."

That was it. To keep from ripping her clothes off right there on the concert floor and humiliating us both, I turned her towards me, and told her in perfect French, that she could have whatever she liked. She could lay with me, she could have me. I would do whichever, whatever she wished, right now, tonight, whenever. Freedom would cost her nothing. My love wasn't for sale.

Cheeks reddened. It was hard to decipher whether or not she was embarrassed at being found out or stimulated by my reply. She can be so shy at times. So shy but dominant. Dominant but demure. So connected but so distant. Moments passed. The sounds emanating from the stage area were intoxicating.

"Monsieur, vous parlez français, alors vous comprenez ceci." She retained the haute demeanor that is characteristic of Adrianne Spence and spoke the type of French that could have only been taught to her as a child. It was natural and unforced. As beautiful as the woman's on stage. And to her statement, yes, I would understand whatever she said perfectly. Her eyes danced mischievously.

Adrianne reached for my hand. Led it to a place that I've come to know all so well. She reached upward, and whispered in my ear, "Prenez-le. Faites ce que vous aimez," French for, *Take it. Do what you like.*

She only had to ask once. She had absolutely no idea. I would do exactly as she asked. I searched for the nearest and darkest space I could find. Found it. Took her hand in mine, the caveman in me almost dragging her to our destination. Bless these stage passes.

There were horns and people and darkness alternating with colored light. There was Adrianne pinned against the wall of her choice. There were our noses and lips into each other, as gently and aggressive as the music playing. There were fingers in mouths and hunger, as I couldn't be with all of her at once or into her fast enough. And then there was the bloody phone. The damn thing hadn't stopped ringing all evening.

"Turn it off."

"I can't."

"Why?"

"I just can't," she said. Picked it up. One hand on my jewels, the other on the receiver. Irony. I hoped she would put it down the way she had earlier. This was a hell of a mood to interrupt.

"You are here?" the look on her face was one of utter shock. "Where?" Then fear. "Outside? Alright. Alright. I will be there shortly." She hung up. I hoped what she said didn't mean what I thought. It couldn't. "I must be going." She rearranged her clothing swiftly. The look in her eyes upset me. She walked.

"Adrianne." No response. Was she insane? She couldn't leave now. "Adrianne!" She walked briskly to the exit. I ran. Grabbed her arm. "Where are you going?" I was calm. But I felt it coming.

"I will call you later." She answered in a huff.

There it was. "Fuck do you mean you'll call me later? Tell me what's going on!"

"Release my arm."

"Not until you tell me what the issue is."

"Islam, release my arm." She was as calm and curt. As if I were an employee who needed firing. That hurt. I tried but I couldn't let her go. She closed her eyes as to further compose an already too composed woman. "Cooper is here. I need to meet him. Now let me go." That stung. I could hold this inside. Save face, or I could keep the promise to me and be free. Do what I felt. Milliseconds of deliberation in place, I heard her words in French, and saw the lustful look in her eyes as she told me what she wanted. I listened to conversations of spirit and matters of heart. Saw the tears from earlier today. Hell no. I'm not letting her go. Two seconds of calm, the rest was a blur.

"Really? Cooper is here? Take me to Cooper, Adrianne. Take me to him."

"Islam! Stop it!"

"Stop what?" I didn't see security heading our way. Had no idea I had her backed into a corner. I would never hurt her, ever. Not lay a single hand on her, but they didn't know that.

"Sir. Let the lady go." Hands were on guns and clubs. I didn't care. I couldn't stomach her being with him tonight. Any night for that matter.

"Sir, we are going to have to escort you from the premises if you do not let her go."

In one ear, out the other. "Adrianne, tell me what the problem is. No. Tell him you will not see him tonight. Tell him that he does not make you happy. Tell him . . ." I hadn't taken notice of the crowd of onlookers, or the extra guards. I hadn't noticed that I was holding her tightly. I did, however, hear Paul asking the guards not to maul me, in his own way.

"Alright already! Please! An ounce of civilization! Is it too much to ask? He is not Rodney King for Christ's sake! Leave him be, I will handle him alone," he stated. I saw but didn't, him standing next to me.

"Islam. If you cause me to miss this concert you will pay. Adrianne?" he asked.

"Yes," she answered solemnly.

"Must you be going?"

"Yes."

"Islam?" I didn't answer. "If you get into trouble here, I will not be able to leave this godforsaken country, and I'd be damned to even think of living in this uncivilized mess of a place. Let her go. Now."

I did. I watched her walk to the exit, no kiss goodbye, no anything. A thought, a wonderful one crept in. I had the car. Her car. To the garage. I grabbed Paul's arm.

I was focused. There was no way she was staying with him tonight. "Islam! Where are we going?" Paul yelled. "Islam, you are a nutter! What the hell is wrong with you, she is only a woman! There are plenty of them here, remember?"

He attempted to reason, as I all but dragged him to one of possibly fifty black Mercedes in the lot. Which one was it? I sounded the alarm from the key ring. Found it. We wouldn't wait for the valet, I was ready to leave immediately. Fuck. I forgot. I don't drive. In cities like London and New York, you don't have to.

"Paul. Drive." I handed him the keys. Got into the passenger side of the vehicle. Which to a Brit can be quite confusing, as the passenger side happens to be the driver's side in America. Everything is backward here.

"Islam! Drive? Where? I can't drive this thing! Not only am I on the opposite side of the car, the bloody traffic moves on the opposite side of the streets! Now, calm down and let's talk—" He attempted reason.

There was no logical approach to this. I was in a zone of spirit and heart. "Fine. I'll drive."

"You can't even drive a British vehicle, what has gotten into you?"

He was ignored. How do you start this thing? I fumbled around a bit, until I realized all it took was proper key alignment. The pushing of a button. There. I can't drive but I will learn. I almost ran Paul over trying to back out. He was waving his arms and yelling. He is in the way.

"Move. I will try and drive this thing. You've gone mad. You have surely gone mad," he said as he backed the car out of its space. Upon exiting Seventh Avenue, not only did we take off like a space rocket, but we turned in the wrong direction and were facing oncoming traffic.

"AHHH! DAMN YOU IS-LAM!" Paul screamed. A truck the size of a small house almost split us in two. Tires screeched. Harsh words exchanged. All I could think of was Adrianne with Cooper.

"Go that way." I pointed in the most impossible direction.

"I can't!" Paul exclaimed. "It's a one way, or haven't you noticed since we seem to be attracted to those types of streets!"

"That is the way I know."

"To where, Islam? A speedy death?" He attempted a ridiculously wide turn at thirty-third street. Turning right from the right lane was so awkward for him.

"Can we go faster?"

"Do you mean can we see Christ any sooner? Absolutely not! There are at least three nicely fit backup singers awaiting my attention at The Garden. I'd like to live long enough to give it to them. Which way!" he yelled. I pointed. I saw the intense look of concentration in his eyes, as he maneuvered the gears, and this crash course—for lack of a better phrase, manually, under award winning pressure. "This better be worth it . . . I, myself must be in shock or else I wouldn't be involved in this madness. . . ." he muttered and reasoned to himself.

There is something about this freedom. This love, this passion, this spirit, this pain, that pushes you to the limit. Pushes you past it. As it does for those around you. I didn't know if it were good or bad. Sane or insane. It was simply what I felt.

"That way." I pointed. He turned left from left. He'd gotten it. We hit the West Side Highway and I felt the engine open up on this thing. I'd pretend not to notice the grin on his face as he gunned this baby like a pro. Paul was in the trenches with his friend, yes, but spreading the wings of a super fast luxury vehicle, in a foreign country, on the wrong side of the car, and the wrong side of the road, manually. I guess he'd surpassed a limit or two as well.

A left onto Houston. Right on Sixth. Left onto Broome. Four twenty one. The Spence Gallery of Contemporary Art. I watched Paul's eyes widen like saucers as he read the gun-metal inscription.

"That's why she looked familiar. She's Adrianne Spence. Awesome, Islam. Fucking awesome. We'll be either dead or in a Guantanamo holding cell by the end of the week." He lowered his head onto the steering wheel, as to figure out how to talk me out of this. I remember reading a book about a man who did as he felt, who chased a woman when it made no sense to anyone except him.

I remember the literary analogy to mile twenty of a marathon. Where it hurt more to stop than it did to keep going. I see why the American author sold so many books. One wouldn't admit it, but mile twenty, whether in the form of love, freedom or ambition, comes more often than not. I watched the floors above the gallery light up, as the inhabitants of the enormous multi-level loft made themselves at home.

Paul lifted his head off of the steering wheel. "You do not fall in love, Islam. We've been through this," he said. I felt his intense glare. "And if you do, then you know you can fall out of it." Through the window, I saw her. Parts of her that I wanted to touch and feel, teased me. The look must have surfaced on my face, one of longing and want. Possibly need. Paul has always been intuitive. "And if you find it troublesome falling out of love, there is management. You can manage, Islam."

In the window, there was Adrianne and her husband. In society's reality. Not ours. Arguing, discussing private matters. Twelve years of exchange, of confidentiality between them. How could I compete?

We sat there in her vehicle for over an hour. The scent of her, in seats and on buttons. As I watched them, pain ripped through me. I felt so powerless. I hurt so much, that I wished for numbness. I wished for restriction and apathy. For constraint. For limitation. Tonight, I would openly denounce liberation, as it had been a Gemini of a friend, causing laughter and pain, as if they were one in the same. Paul must have felt really bad. He patted me on the back and didn't say a word. There was nothing to say. I had discovered the deepest part of me. The part that would allow desire, craze and spirit. Connection. Freedom, expression and the likes. And there she was, with another, in a world where all of what I'd discovered was irrelevant. That hurt.

"Let us go, Islam." Paul stated calmly.

"No. Not yet." I watched her drink tea, and read. I wondered what she thought. How she felt. I'd decided that if I could look into her, the answers would be there for the taking. I pulled the door handle.

"Islam. Wh-what are you doing?" Paul asked, his calm demeanor bordering fanatical.

"I am going to see her." I stated simply. As if it should make sense to him as well.

"No, you are not!" He got out of the driver's side, attempting to meet me on the sidewalk. All I thought was if I could see her, I'd know for sure. If she was happy, I'd leave. If she wasn't, I'd take her with me. Logic, rationale, existed, but in another dimension.

There were stairs, stairs and more stairs. And there was Paul, yelling at the top of his whisper voice. "This is insane! Islam, do not—do not do this!" Paul was ignored. "You're acting like a fucking suicide bomber!" I didn't care. I'd arrived at the private entrance to the main loft. Keys in hand, I remembered being given a key to the loft upstairs, in case of emergency. The thought came and went. I rang the doorbell as if it were the most natural thing for me to do.

Paul gave up reason, and moved to a viable plan b. "Your career. We've worked so hard, Islam. Don't toss it on account of this." He made perfect sense. I rang the bell again. The lock turned.

"Islam! How are you? To what do we owe this visit?" Cooper exclaimed.

"Jesus Christ." I could hear Paul behind me.

"Can I speak with Adrianne, sir?" I asked politely. Everything was so surreal. I was in me, but not of me.

"It is a bit late, but of course you can." He motioned for us to step inside. For reasons unbeknownst to me, I did not feel guilt or remorse. Only focus. Paul introduced himself. Dropped his jaw at the splendor of the ridiculously large loft. As Cooper went to retrieve my love, my heartbeat—his wife, everything in the look Paul gave me said that he disagreed with this, and that I was a madman for risking so much.

She appeared less ethereal than she had at the concert. Ponytail, house wear, in a state of luxury and comfort that seemed so natural for her. Paul talked openly to Mr. Spence about matters of men. The World Cup. Business. The impact of the World Cup on business. The two of them built a relationship while the one I valued most stood still in time.

She walked towards me. "You wished to see me," she asked-stated.

I just stood there, trying to make sense of what I saw. In her eyes, there was grey. Blankness. Void. As if there never was a connection between us. And for the first time in a very long time, I couldn't find the words. I just stood there and searched for an inkling of what was made so richly available to me just hours ago. I heard Cooper's laughter in the background. Paul was being Paul. But even more so as to allow Adrianne and me time together.

"Are you happy, Adrianne?" The words didn't flow, they were forced. But they'd arrived nonetheless. In her eyes, first was nothingness. Numb. However, I was determined to drag out kicking and screaming the passion that I knew was there. She couldn't hide from me. "Somnambulists of the day right?" I quietly recalled one of the Nietzsche verses so easily spoken by her earlier this evening. In her eyes I could see it plainly. *How dare you? How dare you hold me to my own standards?* And for a second I saw light. Love. Pure, untainted love. And I knew it was possible. If my love—if our connection was strong enough, I knew we were a possibility. That flash of hope was what I needed. Then as if she couldn't bear the energy it took to show herself, there was coldness and reserve again.

She replied coldly, "There are some finer points to your performance, Islam, that I could be happier with, but overall, you are doing splendid work for the gallery."

My heart sank. I know that the upfront nature in which I am expressing myself is considered a bit wayward. But this. *This is crazy.* I am staring it in the face. Day in and day out, how can one being of complete universal energy and spirit, live in a body and mind that is not her own?

Paul tapped me on the shoulder. "Are we ready?" he asked, cordially kissing Adrianne on both cheeks. He treated her with as much favor as he had earlier. She half smiled. He nodded. Spirit recognizes spirit. Hers was firey. It vibrated loudly. As did his. Except while she, for reasons unbeknownst, would toss a war blanket onto the sound, hoping to muffle it, Paul on the other hand turned his up, blasted it for all to hear. Literally and figuratively I was amidst the two, desperately trying to configure accuracy in theory. Paul, although well dressed, technically is a starving artist. Adrianne wouldn't know the word starve if it were a face in a mirror she looked into everyday. Who is right and who is wrong?

I placed the keys to the vehicle in her hand. And if nothing did it, the contact did. She closed her eyes. Paul saw it. I did. He understood everything. It was bold, and wrong, but I held her hand anyway. Allowed her time and space in a world where only she mattered. I held on until my friend pulled me away. We walked. "You know you're asking much of her," he stated. I was silent. "She knows her potential, but having it thrown in your face when you are in fact immobilized is tough. Her husband is literally the Gotti of modern day business. Even if she wanted to leave, she couldn't," he said empathetically. He made sense. I was still so new to all of this. My friend of years held the train doors for me and continued. "I'd never thought, not even for a moment that I'd be talking to you on matters of spirit. I know you went through much as a child and I also noticed over the years that you weren't interested in reaching inside. It's amazing to see what has surfaced since you've chosen to let go." I heard him but didn't. "People are in our lives for a season, Islam. In each lifetime, groups of spirits flock together, each one helping the other learn lessons that will enrich the soul's journey through this incarnation. I know the connection that you feel with Adrianne is deep. It is also new. She, being placed in your life for a finite period of time, to assist you in getting to where you need to be, can be a matter of forever, but often times is not. Seasons change." He paused. "And from the looks of it, she may need you more than you do her."

I sat in silence for the rest of our train ride. Paul continued to enlighten me on matters that I've read about but never experienced. This connection, these spiritual vibes, being in touch with the god—the truth within is very hard. I wanted to smile and have sex. I wanted to paint average abstract art. I wanted to ignore depth. I wanted to go back to the old me so badly. But I don't. I can't. In matters of time, seven can never become six.

We'd reached thirty-fourth street, Penn Station. The stop for Madison Square Garden. Prior to taking the thousand little stairs that led to the entryway, I took notice to the Tourneau Rolex digital clock behind us. I wanted to remember this. The day and the time. I've never felt so low in my life.

"Are we alright?" Paul asked. I shook my head back and forth. I wasn't. He smiled knowingly. "That is exactly what I wanted to hear," he said. "At least you aren't telling yourself otherwise."

When morning sun has risen, and one awakens, there is always the desire to return to the cousin of death. The sun—my sun, shedding light on an otherwise dark and lost soul, is demanding acknowledgment. Demanding that I rise with it.

As the very core of me acknowledges that I am in fact, awake, I do not recoil. I do not retreat. I do not negotiate with my conscience. I allow the renaissance that is feeling, to restore the universal properties of organic me. I feel pain. I feel pleasure. I feel stronger because of those things. If I am not a member of the society in which we live, due to acknowledgment of the sun, the awakening within, then so be it.

Paul and I watch the last of the concert. Thom Yorke of Radiohead took us home with eclectic but weird arrangements that he had become renowned for. Ahmed appeared from behind us, asking of our whereabouts. Paul handles things as my thoughts were elsewhere.

I think of her. I see her. I smell her. I do not try and decipher all of what I feel, as to simply feel is enough. I do know one thing. I will not move from her. Where I am, she is. It is the only thing in which I am certain.

20

It is morning. Whether I feel like it or not, I pray. I am not sure
of how or what I should pray as I am unsure that any direction,
the road most or least traveled is the right one. I face the east and
hope the words come.

Barukh atah adonai Eloheinu melekh ha-olam,

I begin morning prayer as usual, and open myself as I've
learned to do. Direction comes.

Modeh ani l'faneykha, malech chai vekaiyam,
Shehechezarata bi nishmati,

I pray and sweat. I don't know what else to do.

I thank you, living and eternal King,
For returning my soul within me, compassion.
Great is thy faithfulness.

I hope this morning's prayer removes the horrible feeling
within. It doesn't.

It's been weeks since I've spoken to her. Since she's laid on
my chest or sat between me while I worked. And I can say, now
that I am opening to feeling, I know the difference between feeling alive or dead.

Memories of a subdued Islam who took everything as it came,
who was neither here nor there, flashed before me this morning.
Where is he? I relished in his return. Because this Islam was out-

doors at earliest morning, waiting for the shades of the main loft at four twenty one Broome Street to be drawn.

"Good mornin', good mornin'!" A plump, sugar filled middle aged woman wearing a pair of plastic frames with missing lenses, appeared seemingly from nowhere. She smiled, exposing tonsils and possibly yesterday's lunch. Her breath was like a warm breeze from a landfill. "You shoulda called first! You know I don't get up this time'a'mornin'!" It would be easy to confuse articulation with the clearing of one's throat. Threatening to expose her entire rib cage, the jack-o-lantern smile widened. She shook her head and continued on. "You wanna see, don't cha? Here, use these." She removed the broken frames from her face and pushed them towards me. This one was a nutter.

"Oh no, thank you. I'm okay. I don't need those," I replied softly, refusing the plastic lenses she offered. She has the wrong idea. I am not crazy. I'm not a stalker. I just want to see my love. I've stood here every morning. Across the street. To the left of the gallery. In the alley. About an hour passes, and Adrianne draws the blinds. She is served tea. She eats fruit. She reads yesterday's Evening Standard from London. She checks herself in the mirror. Sometimes she is in cashmere. Sometimes pinstripes. And sometimes, she dances a bit. On those days, I smile.

The smell of cheese feet and a voice of a meat grinder tossed my thoughts into a brick wall.

"Well if she does sumthin' sexy and you need a lil' privacy, feel free to use my space. Mi casa is su casa!" The woman winked as if it had the possibility of summoning a dentist.

"Privacy?"

"Yea. Privacy. Like private. You know. Personal. Privates," she gestured. It took a second but I'd gotten it. I am not crazy. I am not neurotic. I am not perverse. I just want to see her.

"No, I'm not here for that." I replied.

"Uh huh. You come he-ah ev-er-ry single day. This is *my* house!" Her hands said, *voila*.

I surveyed the space. Two milk crates. A patchy, single pound cat with undeterminable color. A trail of radioactive green city-trash-slime oozing down its path and comfortably hardening into what in any other natural habitat would be volcanic rock. A life sized metal bin that read *New York Dept. of Sanitation*. And there was us. Or rather me, visiting.

"I've never seen you here," I said.

"'Cause I'm sleep this time a mornin'!" I'd pissed her off.

"Sorry for awakening you."

"Uh-huh. You wanna see? Well you just make sure you run that way . . ." She pointed towards a sliver of a space between two concrete slabs of building. Run where? What the hell is she talking about? ". . .'Cause they'll let the dogs loose on ya'." Apparently the same went for screws. Wait. What am I doing? I thought to leave—I should, but not after Adrianne raises the blinds.

"What's ur name sweetie," the woman asked.

I was in her house so I guessed it rude not to answer. "Islam."

She looked upward and to the right. "There she go!" She laughed loud and uncontrollably. I followed her gaze. And was appalled. She was right. Adrianne had just drawn the blinds. "Pretty gal." The middle aged trash-alley-condo owner ad libbed as if we were in cahoots.

"What's ur name, sweetie," she repeated as if Islam was not a satisfactory answer.

I heard her but didn't. There was toast, an egg, juice and fruit. She would eat the toast but not the egg. She would eat the fruit but only drink half the juice. I know. I know, by now, what she does. What does that make me? The woman was losing patience with me.

"You heard me? I said what's ur na—"

"Islam," I repeated.

"Is she one of your wives?" The woman scratched and scratched until I myself felt a twinge of itch. While I watched Adrianne, she waited for my answer as if it would be the most interesting thing she'd heard in a decade. I had to chuckle at the implication. Islam. Polygamy. She wasn't too far off. Anyone who knew me would slap her five.

"No, she is not my wife."

"So then you *are* gonna need some privacy," she said.

"No."

"Then what? They just let you out?" she asked earnestly. I waited for Adrianne to gather her things, as that would be my cue to leave the trash-alley-condo and transition to what would become a daily ride of shame back to Brooklyn. She can never find her keys.

"You he-ah me?" the plump woman reiterated.

"Yes."

"Let you out from where?"

"No. That's not what I meant. Yes, as in I heard you. I'm not . . . not . . . you know."

"I know you ain't *you know*. You already told me who you are. You're an Arab. I asked if you just got out, that's what I asked."

This thing is getting the best of me. I am in an alley, being interrogated and subsequently offered the private accommodations of one luxury trash bin. And still, I won't leave until she finds her keys. She does. Five minutes. Down from seven yesterday. I salute my plump, trash-condo friend and am on my way.

The A train is packed with morning rush. I ride and wonder how many others in suits and stripes have done things that they'd rather not admit this morning. I exit Lafayette street station and see my veteran friend, sitting on the stairs, simultaneously playing guitar and singing his heart out. Aside from the fact that there was no actual guitar in hand, all was standard. He would tell me I looked like shit and offer for me to join him, as it would help relax me. I'd decline and say that I don't play strings and he'd call me a fool—a bloody one, as there were obviously no lessons needed to play his. I'd half heartedly laugh. Locate a delightful glint in the eyes of my friend. The same for the trash-condo owner. Of all the solemn and abhorrently morbid faces on this morning's train ride, they seemed to be the happiest of all. Ignorance or freedom. I wondered which one was bliss.

I walk into my studio flat and smell her. I plopped onto the bed. Tucked my arms behind my head and lay back. Staring at the ceiling would replace sport as a pastime. If there is still something there, something between us, I wish to know. But she won't talk to me. There is seemingly, nothing that Adrianne wants with or of me. It's eating me up.

The communication between Adrianne and me has been modest, and that was being generous. There was an email, instructing me not to report to the gallery, and to postpone any studio visits until after our Paris trip. I was to utilize the time painting, applying finishing touches to the collection that I finally named: *Amour de vie, Amour de Femme.*

The phone rang. I didn't rush. I'd given up hope of it being her.

"Good day," I answered.

"I got your message. All I can say is I told you so. You went from a two guest studio show to hanging your shit at the Louvre," Danny answered. I didn't want to talk. All I wanted to do was lie here and pretend that Adrianne was lying next to me. Or on top of me fast asleep. Or on top of me doing something else . . .

"Islam. What's up? Did I interrupt something? I know how you like to celebrate," he added playfully.

"No. I am here." I sighed.

"What's the problem? You should be bouncing off the walls."

I thought about whether to explain my dilemma or not. I am not excited. I feel trapped and don't know what to do about it. "I just feel so . . . in a box. Like it is impossible to do what I wish, to live from within. I guess I am taking time to adjust," I answered somberly.

Danny muttered something arbitrary to one of his two canines before returning to me. "When has living from within ever been a concern of yours?"

"I don't know. I feel different. I don't want to but I do."

"Well do us both a favor. Feel different after the showing. Better yet, hold off for about a year or two. Get some head. Do what you have to do, but don't cross these people. You read about Chavez and the Citgo oil pullout?"

"Briefly," I replied.

"I told you, if Spence is here he has a plan. Do what the man asks, nothing more nothing less. Use them to your advantage, go along with their program, and get what you're supposed to out of this."

"Alright."

"Stop sounding like your dog died. Congratulations and good luck. Call me when you know something." We hung up. Before I could take a step, the damn mobile rang again.

"Good morning, sir!" It was Paul. He is handling the transport of my collection from New York to Paris. I have been so pain-stricken, that there hasn't been a serious digestion of things to come. I am showing my work in *Paris* this week. I want to be as excited as Paul, but I miss her so much.

"Good morning."

Paul can never have one conversation at a time. Geminis. "Yes . . . and do you have these in size thirty two? Would you be so kind as to fetch them for me? Yes . . . thank you. Islam. Are you there?"

"Yes."

"Hold on." He continues on with a sales associate. "I'm sure Etro makes them in that size . . . yes . . . I have several . . . you're so kind, thank you . . ." I wait. Read her email for the hundredth time. Possibly the thousandth. "Alright, I'm back. Quickly, are the works to be retrieved in Soho or in Brooklyn?"

"Brooklyn."

"You can't be serious."

"I am."

"You want me to send someone to Brooklyn to carry by hand, twenty works of art? Are you nuts? They'll never make it over the bridge."

The words float gently across the screen. Teasing me. Daring me not to read them again.

Do not report to the gallery. Perfect your collection for the Paris showing. . . .

"Islam."

. . . Make sure your work is complete and transport has been arranged by the fifteenth of the month.

"Islam, are you there? These dodgy mobile phones . . . Islam!"

I will see you in Paris.

. . . see you in Paris.

. . . see you in Paris.

"Islam! What the hell are you doing?" Paul asked.

"I'm here."

"Listen to me. Get your head from between your legs and focus. You are showing your work, not one, but twenty pieces to a small group of people who could possibly fill the gross national debt of the country in which you—for whatever reason—have chosen to live and still have enough to blow on hotels that stand in the middle of the water in one of the wealthiest places on earth. Get off your ass. Get her off of your mind. Answer my questions," he went on. He was right.

"Transport the paintings from Brooklyn. They will be safe."

"Will do. And the receiving address?" he inquired.

"Ninety nine, Rue de Rivoli." I answered.

"Ninety-nine . . . Rue . . . de . . . Rivoli . . ." Paul repeated the address as he jotted it down. There was a pause. Then an eruption. "The Louvre? You are showing at the Louvre! What! How? How could you keep this from me! You can't be serious—"

"Paul," I interrupted the theatrics, "I am not showing at the Louvre. That is simply where the meeting is, the museum has absolutely nothing to do with it."

"I didn't know they had dinner there."

"They don't. Dinner is at Le Tour D'Argent. Cooper had business matters to tend to in the area and in terms of tools and hanging, it was just more convenient. These pieces are larger than my usual, and they thought the environment would add to the essence of the show. It's just a small room with cocktails."

"Amazing. These people are amazing." This was his type of thing. I was just doing as instructed.

Moments pass. I don't say anything.

"How are you handling things?" Paul asked earnestly. He has always been concerned with Ahmed and I. Although we were basically identical in age, he was more the big brother in the group. I've always appreciated that.

"I am okay."

"Really." That was a statement. I could be honest. But what am I supposed to say? That I've gone to the gallery every day, just to watch her through the window? That I sat all night through a rainstorm simply to see her turn pages of a book? That I've called several times daily, just to hear her ask me to leave a message? What would he think, if he knew that I set up an entirely different e-mail account, and posed as a potential client, just to have contact with her? No. I've seen what expression, what freedom can do. It alienates. I feel ridiculously helpless and sick. I don't want Paul to patronize me or treat me differently, as the neighbors treat my veteran friend. I don't feel safe expressing myself to anyone right now.

"I said I am okay," I answered.

He mumbled something about fine linen trousers and returned to the conversation. "Make sure you block your number when you ring her up for the thousandth time. And try to limit your messages to two. No more than three. I don't want any orders of restraint violated, as I have limited myself to only one episode of debauchery per annum," he added.

I smiled lightly. The first in weeks. "I will."

"How many calls today?" he asked.

"Eleven. But down from twenty-six yesterday." It took more energy to pretend than it did not to. I chuckle inside as I remember when things were quite the opposite with me.

"She pick up any?"

"Six."

"You don't do any of that serial killer shit and breathe into the phone do you?" he joked.

"No!" I laughed. "I just rung her up a few times." I was a bit ashamed, but couldn't stop laughing.

"Do you think I'm crazy?" It was a sincere question. I wanted to know.

"No, I do not. To hold this in, force it down your throat, just to show up to one's place of work and blow everyone there to God's dust is crazy. You are channeling, streaming emotion. What goes into us must come out. It may be different, inconvenient, but closer to sane than what's respected amongst men," he added wisely.

"Have you ever been this way before?" I asked.

"No. But I've always wished to be. Consider it a blessing. Let it come out in your work," he responded. I nodded.

We disconnected and I sat there for a moment, replaying all of what he said. To hold this inside, this grief, this agony, would be torture. It would ultimately lead to true insanity, the crossing of physical, intellectual and spiritual wires.

I toy with a mobile phone that has received far too much attention from me in recent weeks. Call her. Don't call her. This would be number twelve. It is not as of yet, afternoon. Don't call. Don't act as a madman. I think of madmen of times past. Einstein. Newton. Nietzsche. Of eclecticism and differences. DaVinci. Michaelangelo. Kahlo. I recall genius works, displayed in museums and classrooms worldwide. There is a method to the madness. I hit speed dial one. She picked up on the second ring.

"Good Afternoon, Adrianne Spence," I want her close. I want her to look into me. I want to watch her sleep. "Hello," she tried. Again. I hung up. Again. I call back. Again. She does not answer.

I know that Cooper is back in the UK. I know that business is not overwhelming at the gallery. I wonder what she is doing and who she is doing it with. I try to account for hours of her day, the many possibilities in which she could possibly spend them. I know of the nature of her sex drive. I wonder who is satisfying it. If she holds the back of his neck as she climaxes. If she scratches him and breathes short light breaths that progress to longer deeper ones. I envision someone else tackling her onto the bed. I am fuming and have to remind myself that I have imagined these things.

I align my work along the walls of the flat. Rows of color, cadmiums, umbers and ochre, smiled abstractly, bringing out the beauty in each piece. I walked the length of the studio, determined to spend quality time with each piece, as if they were daughters. I am proud. I have *never* painted like this before. So much in so little time and so passionately. That made me happy, and for a second, I would completely disregard Adrianne and bask in this newfound artistic height.

Lydia calls, tells me that she will be here in an hour or so. She wants to see the paintings before they are sent off. She double-checks my departure details for Paris, she is taking me to JFK and will need to work patients around road time. My friend asks if I am okay, says that I do not sound like myself. That I haven't for weeks. I tell her that we will talk when she gets here. A deep breath and a much needed walk through the neighborhood calls. I grab my keys and head out.

21

I find myself waltzing through the neighborhood. There is Chez Oskar, where Adrianne and I had our first brunch. The small park on Cumberland, where she'd asked me question after question on American basketball. The corner open-air market on South Portland that she loved. B.A.M., where we'd sit on the steps and kiss like teenagers, and the park. Fort Greene Park is where I found myself lying face up, in the spot on the grass where we slept a night away in each other's arms.

My attention is diverted to a man—a well dressed one, walking through the park. He yells out at the top of his lungs, as would a fiery Baptist preacher. But there is no church. There is no choir. There are no devoted members to encourage him on. Yet he shouts as if every ounce—every bit of his existence depends on it. He carries an attaché. He is clean shaven. Signs of employment and life by society's standards. But he roars like crazy, and we all can't help but stare. I, with everyone else wondered if he were insane. Or, if he had such a day at work, that if what went into him didn't come out as violently as it entered, perhaps we'd be watching him on the evening news instead. He hollered obscenities totally unaware or simply apathetic to what any of us thought. I wondered, if the norm was to scream like a banshee after work, to release the stress that your life and livelihood depended on you holding within, would the one who remained quiet, reserved and unaffected be the crazy one?

I searched the sky for answers that never came. A pleasant voice left my thoughts where they were.

"Well, hello there, mister." It was Lydia, I'd asked her to meet me here instead of at the flat. She looked good. Fashionable. I stood up, gave her a hug.

"I see someone has hit the shops on Prince Street," I complimented. I haven't seen her outside of business casual attire since we'd met. She wore wooden bracelets and beads over a mix of color that any painter would appreciate. An oversized bag. Tight jeans, ripped in the right places. I didn't know she had it in her. "Have a good day at the office?" I asked. Trying very hard to ignore a bottom that I had no idea was there. She blushed.

"Yes, it was shorter than usual, but crazy," she answered.

"When a psychiatrist uses the term crazy to define a work day, one worries." I added playfully. She laughed. We walked.

"Well, I started the day with an MPD—"

"A what?"

"MPD. Multiple personality disorder," she clarified, "and ended up with rounds at Bellevue."

"Is that a mental hospital?" I asked.

"Yes, it is. One of my patients actually needed detaining."

"Detaining? What did he or she do?"

"I needed him to sit and talk. He wouldn't. Things progressed and got out of hand, he was detained," she said simply.

"Did you ask him to sit?"

"Yes. But he was preoccupied with the nurse, he was a bit too obsessed with her to listen."

I thought of me at Madison Square Garden. Of the guards who asked more than once for me to let go of Adrianne. Guns, clubs and all, I wouldn't listen either. I had my reasons. There are truly more than a few existing realities here. I wonder what Lydia would have thought of me if she'd been privy to my behavior that night. If she would have had me detained. "So what do you have to do to be forced into detainment?"

"Misbehave."

"And who or what defines misbehavior?" It was an earnest question. After all, she is a licensed professional. If she can't answer my questions, I might as well give them up entirely.

"The DSM four." She answered as if that should sort it all. I'd heard of the biblical mega manual of psychological associations large and small. To me, many of the premises for diagnosis were a bit dodgy.

"Ah, yes. I have seen remnants of the premises on adverts throughout the city. Are you tired? Feeling depressed? Suffering insomnia? . . ." There was an outburst of laughter from my good friend. I grinned and continued, "If you perhaps, have experienced five or more of these twenty eight symptoms, you should give every cent you've managed to earn in recent years to Lydia Blackwell. She accepts all methods of payment." Lydia was in stitches. I was laughing too. "No honestly Lyd, who wrote this DSM four? What is it based on?" She stopped. Looked at me. Realized I was serious.

"Well," she began slowly. "I'd say this. Evolutionary theory can tell us how to differentiate between a diseased mind and a healthy one. A diseased mind tends to interfere with an individual's natural functions, or pushes them to exhibit behavior that is not in the nature of the species," she answered. I still was not satisfied. My behavior was in times past not considered normal by my best friend. To finish a five-year relationship abruptly, to express not even the slightest of emotions other than contentment was atypical to him. Now that I am more expressive, he seems to think I am more normal. Lydia I'm sure, would have me detained. They were both credible to me. This was so confusing.

"I see," We'd come to the stairs leading to the entryway of my house and sat. "Let me ask you this. When it comes to said definition, how much of this assertion is value-driven? Surely culture, ways of the majority must have at least the slightest influence on what is considered typical or atypical of a group or person."

"Yes, Islam, some of what we do in this field is value-driven. It can be based on what we know and have experienced ourselves as professionals. But you'd have to agree that there is behavior that is normal and behavior that is abnormal. The patient of mine this morning was abnormal," she stated. I was not challenging the credibility of psychiatry. I was merely trying to make sense of my own life.

"I believe there is repression and there is release. Both are a form of coping. Whichever one chooses affects them in ways that society—depending on where theirs falls culturally, explains that."

I thought about my mum. "There is at first trauma, yea?"

"In most cases," she replied.

I thought of the years in which I felt nothing. Absolutely nothing. "And one can choose to repress, or maybe it is not a choice, but a means of survival. Disassociation, I believe you professionals call it."

"Yes, we do," she replied.

I thought of loving Adrianne from top to bottom. Of crying on her shoulder. Of not wanting to let go of her. "Or, there is a second option, release. Whether a matter of choice or subconscious coping, one can take this road as well."

"Uhm-hmph."

"Which would you say, as a professional, is the most healthy route to take?"

"I'd say release. That's what we are here for."

"Yet, when one, say a child, releases him or herself, say they lash out or throw tantrums, they are quarantined, and penalized. Something is either given or taken away involuntarily of the child. Punishment of their sole means of coping pushes them in the opposite direction, to repression, which we have established is in fact the less healthy option."

She signaled to make a point. "If the child's behavior is excessive, if it affects others negatively then yes, it is dealt with appropriately. What are you getting at?" she asked.

I decided to change course. "Have you ever been to a worship service of a Holy Spirit filled Pentecostal or Baptist church?" I asked.

"Of course," she said with confidence.

"And when the woman sitting next to you screamed out to a Lord that no one could see, when she mumbled things in a language that no one seemed to understand, when she jumped up and down uncontrollably, did you flinch? Did you order her detainment?"

"No, I did not."

"You do understand, that in many cultures, even ours, had she exhibited the same behavior in a public space, as would a temperamental child, without the support of her church group or reverend in sight, she would be considered mentally ill or at least escorted from the premises. Now I ask, why is that behavior deemed valid in her chosen place of worship? The answer is simple. It is supported by the majority. The group who if nowhere else but in that stained glass building, makes the rules. So you are telling me of this psychological definition, of this DSM four, that the premise is simply, majority defines what it is to be insane." She shook her head.

"You are simplifying it beyond its means, Islam. It is not simply that society defines normal therefore it defines sanity. The woman I saw earlier is by all standards crazy. It's bad for me to say that but it is true. There is no way around it."

"I am not saying that insanity does not exist, Lydia. I am merely suggesting that there may not be enough classifications of accepted behavior. Perhaps where there are five categories of norm, there should be ten. Perhaps where there are ten, there should be fifteen. There are many who suffer unnecessarily due to society's inability to accurately define or accept their behavior as normal. I am not sure that it is just for the man who cheats at the game, to referee it." She nodded intently. We walked up the stairs in silence. Insanity, DSM fours, theories would have to wait. I am showing in Paris a day or so from now. For the first time in weeks, I was excited about that.

"Thank you." I kissed her neatly on the cheek.

"For what?" She seemed surprised at the gesture. I didn't reply. I was sorting things out in the studio for a first time viewer. Lydia was out of plain view, the clanking of bottles suggesting she was fighting the fridge for one of many Coronas. She yelled from the kitchen,

"She's not worth it, Islam." I heard her clearly, but didn't respond. I wish I felt the same.

22

Paris is burning. In the dead of summer, the dry heat of the artistic capital of the world will scorch every thought one has that isn't of water or ice. But I am happy to be back. It's been years since I've been able to fully appreciate the aesthetic master-piece in full. There are beautiful women. And then there is Paris. As attractive and alluring as she is intelligent, she touches—brings out the passion, the infatuation of life and love in entrepreneur and epicurean alike. If you've been here you know. The spell. There is no escaping it.

While a university student, I took residency at The Gallerie Chappe in Montmartre, an area second to St. Germain, known for its bohemian artistic mores. I think of the year I spent finding myself artistically. Of the beautiful Parisian artist who brought me as close to true love as I'd ever been at the time. Of the mornings we spent in cafes and the evenings in Brasseries. Of painting and making love all day. I would do more than just see her while I was here. If all went well, the talented artist would be our next acquisition.

"Uh, Six fremiet d'avenue, Sezz d'hotel," I reminded the driver of the address.

"Oui, Monseiur." One left turn, and a half block in, we arrived to a small and chic boutique hotel called Sezz. Situated on the Seine river, right across from the Eiffel tower, the tasteful mesh of chrome, concrete and color is not what one would expect in this old guard district of Parisian wealth. Christophe Pillet's modernist design rivaled that of any metropolitan establishment worldwide.

"If you need anything else, do not hesitate to call." My personal assistant courtesy of the hotel offered.

I fell backward onto plush sheets and pillows and let out a deep breath. After weeks of painting all night and morning trash alley visits, I was shattered. Thank God there wasn't much on the schedule today, except going to the Louvre to see that the paintings were hung and displayed properly. The showing wasn't until tomorrow evening. My studio visit in Montmartre was the following day, and I hoped all went well. The phone interrupted my thoughts.

"Hello."

"Good afternoon, Islam." Cooper.

"Good afternoon, sir."

"Had an easy transport and check in?"

"Yes, no worries," I answered. He fumbled around with papers, made a few disgruntled sounds. Back to me.

"Listen, I would like to meet with you briefly today. There are finer points in need of going over for tomorrow's showing. Some things you should know going in."

"Alright."

"Can you meet me in the bar of your hotel in an hour?"

"Yes, no problem."

"Alright. See you then," he said. We disconnected.

I would begin what has become the ritual. Block out the fact that he has spoken to her. Omit the fact that he sees her daily. Erase the fact that he has slept with her. That he kisses and touches her. That he knows so many things about her. On the way down to the hotel bar, I tried to block it all out.

Cooper entered the bar area as usual, seemingly unaware of

how far from indigenous he truly was. I stood. We shook hands. I'd see a slight mark underneath his shirt collar, and wonder if it were from Adrianne. I had to remind myself to focus. Focus, Islam. Focus. Repress. Do what you must. But maintain. He sat opposite me in a leather chair that was way too comfortable for any bar. Gave me a weird look, as if he wished to express a concern but decided against it. The bartender poured his glass, and refilled mine. We exchanged pleasantries.

"So, are we ready for our presentation?" he asked candidly.

"I believe so. I haven't been to the museum yet. I've just gotten in."

"You'll be in before closing, yes?"

"Yes, to double check things. But I'm sure all is well."

"Alright." He took a deep breath. "Of this Jumeirah-Siddiq deal, I have an earlier meeting with members of the group. Upon dismissal, we will file in for the showing. They will inspect the work, for which they've already expressed interest. I'm just assuming they want to confirm a few things."

I was distracted by the mark, and the extra effort it took for me to—I don't know what I was refraining from, but whatever it was couldn't have been positive. He continued.

"And the deal, each piece at one hundred thousand US dollars each, for a total of two million dollars." He concluded.

I saw his mouth move. But I didn't hear anything coming out of it. How much? "Cooper. What was that?"

"Dinner will follow the meeting." He referred to his notes.

"No. Not that. The amount."

"Oh. Two million. I know it's not much, but it is a start, don't you think?" Think?

Think? I was having trouble breathing. Two million fucking dollars? Champagne was sprayed across the table. The bartender rushed to pat me on the back and help get it up. "Are you okay?" Cooper asked.

"Uh . . . yes, Sir. Wrong pipe." I coughed ridiculously. This has got to be a dream. " Yes, it is more than—more than enough. Thank you," I stammered.

"No need. A well-collected art director adds to the prestige of the gallery. It is a mutually beneficial gesture," he replied. "Any questions?"

"No." I couldn't believe this.

"Good. Well that sorts it all. The art director for the group's name is Mohammed Siddiq. He's the son of oil magnate, Abu-Salaam Siddiq, and a long time friend of Adrianne's. His sister, Kharet, will be in attendance as well. She is the curator of the collection. Mohammed will review your work in protocol, but Kharet makes the decision."

I was still caught up. Two million dollars? My head was swimming.

"Well, that is all for our meeting," he said. "Let me know what you and Adrianne decide of the acquisition here. She has the budget. I have to fly South this evening for a meeting, back here tomorrow for Siddiq and then back to London after the showing." He had to go, but didn't move. There was that weird look again. "Would you mind if I asked you a question?" he said.

"No, not at all," I answered.

"You . . . I've checked you out," he said smiling.

"And?"

"I underestimated you."

"In what way?" I asked.

"Your reputation with the ladies. Where there is smoke, there is fire." He rubbed both hands together in somewhat of a nervous gesture. "I knew you were somewhat of a ladies man, most artists are, but my God. Every woman in the UK, possibly in Europe knows who you are." He chuckled in the way that wealthy men do. I felt a twinge under my armpit as I wondered where he was going with this.

"I wouldn't say that, sir." I answered modestly.

"Oh really? And the modesty just adds to the allure I suppose."

"What is your question?"

"In recent months, I've been overwhelmed with business matters and Adrianne and I haven't spent much time together.

As women often do, she has become impatient with my constant travels and has become a bit, should I say . . . distant. For Adrianne to be any more vague than usual is saying much, as she has always been somewhat of a mystery, that woman. Since you spend more time with her than I, tell me, have you noticed anything peculiar of her behavior in past weeks?" He reclined in his chair and waited for a response as if it would pave the way to the fountain of youth.

I sat back a bit myself. "Perhaps she is simply distracted." I stated. Cooper half-smiled.

"Perhaps, indeed." He ran his finger alongside the collar of his shirt, further exposing the mark that infuriated me.

"Has business picked up in New York?"

"Somewhat."

"Has she been happy with it?"

"Most definitely."

"Have you?"

"There are some areas needing improvement."

"And which would those be?" he asked.

"Acquisitions. I'd like to be more aggressive in acquiring work that I am passionate about," I said frankly.

"A wise man knows when to acquire and when to fold. And passion as it relates to business can leave one in a field of personal and financial land mines," he said smartly.

"Depending on the world in which one lives."

"We are all of the same world, Islam. Passion is not the rule. It's the exception."

"I am king of my world. I make the rules," I stated simply.

"As am I." Cooper replied. We were at a draw.

Cooper tipped his glass upward and placed it lightly on the table and chuckled.

"Well, I'd like to do something special for Adrianne. I don't like it when she is unresponsive. Can you offer a suggestion? I know you're good with women and as I mentioned on the day of our meeting at John Martin, I am at times unsure of what she likes."

That was a curve ball. I thought about what Adrianne liked and a shot of heat ran straight to my gut. I could tell him that sometimes she likes it rough. That other times she wants to be made love to very deeply. That it all lies in a simple look. She will look at you a certain way, hours before. Way before the notion of sex is on the horizon. It could be at a meeting, or over breakfast. You get the look, and you know.

"What she likes . . ." What she likes is sitting across the table from him. In this altered state, this reality where passion and freedom are foremost, I could say what I feel. I could tell him these things. Take that route. But I don't. I concentrate. Focus. Repress. Give the world what it wants. It fucks with me.

"I don't know, sir. I can't profess to know of Adrianne's or women's preferences more than any other bloke." I stated blandly.

There was a weird look, and a weirder half smile. You could never tell what Cooper Spence was thinking. He slept wearing his poker face. We shook hands, he gathered his things and chuckled as he looked at me.

I glanced at the clock. It was time to get to the Louvre.

23

Deciding to take the train, I walk leisurely down Avenue du Pres. Kennedy, and admire the Upper West Side of Paris. The terrain, although not as green as London's, makes up for it in many other ways. There is art everywhere. Even the way people dress to ride the train is a work of art.

A few stairs, and a right turn out of the station, I enter the largest and grandest of museums in the world. I am overwhelmed with awe. It doesn't matter how many times I've been here, as an artist, walking the regal corridor passage of the Richelieu wing, I all but bow at the splendor of the architecture of this place. There are stone carvings on walls and on ceilings. Golden gates and fountains. It is almost too much to take. I stop and admire a beautiful sculpture garden to my right. And it hits me. I am at the Louvre. There is two million dollars on the table. For *my* work. I could have never imagined this. Not in a million years.

Through the corridor, to the main courtyard, I shuffle past DaVinci Code clutching tourists, who are more concerned with the Mona Lisa, murder trail and plot of the book than they are the six thousand years of art housed in the former palace of Charles the fifth. At the pyramid entrance, there is a queue to rival that of a Michael Jackson concert in the eighties. I wait. Give my name. I am to report to the Denon wing of the museum, floor one. I walk for what seems like a season and make my way up the circular grand staircase, past the huge marble sculptures and signs for Venus de Milo. I get caught up at the congestion that is now the Mona Lisa, pay homage to the greats, Botticelli, Rafael, Veronese, and look for the small room where the meeting is to be held tomorrow night. I find it.

"Are you Islam?" the pleasant gentleman asks.

"Yes."

"Right this way."

The door opens, and again, my breath is taken away.

"Monsieur, your friend Paul left this for you."

"He was here?"

"Yes. He couldn't stay. His train is leaving for London as we speak. We offered to hang the paintings, but he would hear nothing of it. Quite an assorted young man, he is." The older gentleman chuckled and placed a small piece of paper in my hand. It was a handwritten note, in Paul's almost impossible handwriting.

I hung them each by my standards, by myself. Do not, I repeat DO NOT, let anyone tamper with or re-hang anything. We are proud of you. Knock them off their feet. –P.

I was overwhelmed, but in a different kind of way. Friendship, true friendship, presents itself at the right time, just when it's needed most. I realized that tomorrow is special in a way that is most unique. It is not only my showing, but Paul's, Ahmed's, Julia's and Mark's. I felt the support and the love.

"Yes, Paul is quite assorted. It is his special quality," I responded.

The gentleman smiled. "I will leave you to your own devices. If we do not see each other again, good luck to you," he smiled, patted me on the shoulder, then made his exit quietly as if the works on the inside of this small room were just as precious as the ones on the outside.

I walked slowly past each piece, trying hard to digest all of this.

"Brilliant collection, wouldn't you say?" There was the slight sound of heels on marble. And the spicy vanilla scent that I've come to know so well. Another surprise. I don't answer. Moments pass. I stand in front of a piece that was most difficult to paint. The first one I painted in New York. I felt Adrianne standing slightly behind me

"I'd say the artist was a madman in need of detention," I ridiculed. She chuckled lightly. In all of this back and forth, I'd almost forgotten the sound. It was music to my ears.

"Correct, but according to the collection in this building, he'd be in excellent company," she claimed. A pregnant pause. I turned towards her, and there was a split second. One of which I wouldn't recall grand museums, special showings or hangings. I'd only see her, and have to wrestle with reasons not to scoop her into my arms and run away from all of this.

"This is one of my favorites," she said, stepping closer to the piece. Under normal circumstances, I'd stand behind her, wrap my arms around hers and she'd melt into me. We were adjoining pieces of a complicated puzzle. It was a known fact. So why are we standing here acting as strangers? I could act as a freedman would, and tackle her. Kiss her. I could tell her to drink her juice in the morning, that half a glass isn't enough, to put her keys in one place, as to make them easier to find. I could lift her, club her, drag her to a nearest cave and love her until she couldn't say anything but yes. It was all an unfamiliar struggle. The new you? Or the old you, Islam. I'd remind myself of a simple fact. Two million dollars on the table. For *my* work. Logic over love, Islam.

"I'm glad you like it," is all I say.

"Is all to your liking?" she asked simply.

"Yea, I couldn't ask for more."

"Paul, he is fascinating." She blushed.

"You've spoken to him?" I asked.

"Yes. While he was here." She waltzed over to one of many windows looking down onto the sculpture garden. Looked outside. Then at me. There was that piercing look from the loft party. The one that started all of this. And stillness.

She hurriedly interrupted the quiet.

"Have you eaten? I suppose you are famished, having just gotten in," she said, walking briskly toward a small corner door. I have seen many things of Mrs. Adrianne Spence. Nervousness has not been one of them. She disappeared, reappearing with a stately gentleman, pointing in a few directions, then came back to where I was standing and asked-stated,

"We'll dine here."

"I thought eating was prohibited." I knew it was.

"It is. It is impossible in the main wings. In this room, it is not recommended, but we will eat over there, by the window, away from the art," she pointed. I guess that was final. As a very small table, two chairs and two covered dishes were escorted out, we were made comfortable and I chuckled at the ways of the wealthy. I couldn't sneak a candy bar into this place.

"You are spoiled." I removed the top from my dish and found a colorful salad.

She blushed. "I am not spoiled. I am hungry. There is a difference."

"You are hungry and spoiled." And desirable. And intelligent. And the rose of my heart. I do not say those things. Instead, I watch her remove her jewelry before picking up her fork.

"How was your trip?" she asked.

So we are going to do this. We are going to play this game. We are going to repress everything and act like there is nothing between us. Fine.

"It was well."

"Did you sleep?"

"Yes."

"You could have flown on the jet."

"I prefer Virgin Atlantic."

"As to flying privately?"

"Yup."

"Why?"

"I just do."

She was about to stretch her legs out under the table and place them in my lap. She stopped herself.

We ate in silence. For a while, the tossing of lettuce was all that could be heard.

I can't do this. "Adrianne. Babe. We need to talk." She doesn't answer. She doesn't look up. I took her hand in mine. Slid my fingers between hers. Eyes cast downward, she pushed leafy lettuce from one side of her plate to the other. "A . . . you know I love—",

"Let me show you something." A swift interruption. She got up from the table, and signaled for me to follow her. I did. We'd take several flights down to an area that didn't appear on any of the maps I was given of the museum. She used a series of keys and cards to open door after door, and when we reached our destination, my jaw dropped. Nothing could prepare me for what I saw. Rows and rows of works by the masters.

"This is Monet." She gestured towards a large piece. "And Van Gogh. And Kahlo." We walked slowly through the tight space together. It was almost hard to breathe. You read about pieces like this. You don't get this close to them. She continued, "This is my grandfather." She gestured to a piece we were approaching.

"He was painted by Modigliani?" I was incredulous.

"Yes. This over here is—"

"Kandinsky," I answered. There was no need to narrate. I knew every single one of these artists as if we'd played football together. If there weren't enough shock, I found myself standing in front of what I am sure was a priceless combination. Picasso and Braque. Almost identical works. They worked so closely together at one point, that it was hard for either of them to tell which piece had been painted by whom unless they were immediately signed. I've never seen them side by side like this.

"What is this?"

"It's my family's collection. My grandfather was an extreme lover of art as was my father. They worked and collected. Collected and worked. Both were high government officials. My father was the Duke of Wellington. Grandfather was French. He actually designed, or should I say re-designed, the Louvre after parts of it were destroyed in the first war. Thus our relationship with the museum."

"So this actually belongs to you." I was astounded. The nearest seat was a dusty folding chair. I wiped it off and sat.

"Not exactly." A few steps down, she stopped in front of a portrait of a younger version of her grandfather, which I would assume was her father. There was a pause. "My father was killed."

"By?" Her eyes asked me if I really wanted to know. In my own way, I assured her that I did. I grabbed the dark-haired beauty by her waist, drew her into me and sat her on my lap. She sat stiffly at first, as if the feeling of being this close to me was brand new. Hesitation passed with moments and Adrianne relaxed into me as she answered my question.

"It was an accident. He was never quite as careful as he should be."

In the midst of her confessions, I found it hard not to relieve her, to touch her, to express myself intimately with the woman who would rather sleep atop me, than beside me. My hands left her waist, exploring gingerly on their own, from the sensitive place beneath her navel to the deep curve at the small of her back. There was a minor flinch, the slightest stiffening from her, as if my hands brought more heat than pleasure.

"I'm sorry." I replied to the non-verbal signal that said I'd gone too far. Or that she wanted me. I couldn't tell these days. Everything was so . . . I don't know how to describe it.

She continued. "And father left an exorbitant amount of debt. Everyone in Europe was in financial distress after the second war. From the Royal House on down. He spent years climbing out of it. Along with a small investment in what was then a new Middle eastern oil company, his collection was all he had left, half of which was offered to his business partner as collateral before his death. As well as a dowry."

"Dowry?"

"Yes. A monetary endowment typically given to a bridegroom in anticipation of marrying a daughter of the house."

"Your marriage was arranged?" I asked.

She half smiled. "Yes and no. It wasn't as banal as it sounds. I had a choice."

While she spoke, that spicy vanilla scent of hers flooded my senses, filled my body with yearning and intoxicated me with none other than purest desire for this woman. Against will and better judgment, my hands and other members of me took on personalities of their own, allowing—in fact welcoming the pleasure. Adrianne suffered an identical betrayal. The power of mind yielding to that of body and soul. The tone of her voice changed. As did her rhythm of breath. The short, light breaths between select words let me know exactly what I needed to. This wasn't over.

In an almost choreographed gesture, she turned her body towards mine, allowing herself into a favorite and more comfortable position. There was no smile, no moan, no other indication of wanting than the minor beads of sweat forming on her upper lip. Legs straddling mine, she continued.

"As for the other half of the collection, it was sold all over Europe by Mother after Father's death. She hated him *that* much." She narrowed those eyes that I've come to love so much.

"Why?" I wrapped my arms tighter around her waist. Pulled her closer to me. I wanted her to stop this nonsense and give in.

"It may have had something to do with his fixation with his favorite daughter," she added.

"You?" She nodded.

"We were incredibly close. Too close." For a moment, a dark wave passed over her eyes. The moment as usual, was short lived. She continued the recollection in her typical subdued nature. "There was so much freedom and affection between us, which was irregular for a man of his stature in government. But he said that I reminded him so much of himself."

"How? I mean besides the obvious."

She slid her arms around my neck, and went on, "Well for one, I was a bit odd as a child."

"*Really?*" I mocked. She cut her eyes at me.

"If I wasn't dancing or spinning in circles, I asked question after question."

"Uh-hmm." Listening but not, my hands ran up and down her

back slowly, drudgingly, as I was ashamed that they had more control over me than I had them. I wanted to focus on what she was telling me. I wanted to be stronger than I was. But this was torture. I was sweating. Other bodily functions were giving me away. I could not deal with the reality of having the most desirable woman in my world on my lap, and not being free to express myself with her. All of the resolve, self-help books and conversation, logic and reason would grin impishly at my demise. A simple twinge of a yearning had turned into a desire to devour her. Fuck it. I decided to comfort her the best way I knew how. She pushed back for a second, a second only, then yielded completely, every single muscle of Adrianne's melting into mine.

There were fingers and lips, hums and moans, light and beautiful sounds, mine and hers mixing, making lovely music. A natural orchestra of desire and freedom, our lips and tongues licked and teased, roamed and explored, moving into and out of one another in their own repertoire of intercourse. We explored each other as if it were a first time. She tasted so sweet. We'd part momentarily, only to rejoin, as breathing had become secondary to the freeing feeling. A stroke, a light chuckle, they all reverberated through me, as extensions of our being played like children in a sandbox. I was free again. It felt so good. A kiss of her forehead, her eyelids, a slight nudge under her chin. I'd pull away, and see her eyes linger shut, as if she was more lost in the moment than the memories. The stillness between us prompted her to continue.

"Th-the ritual was for us, after school, I'd run, jump into his arms, he'd hold me to the mirror and point out ways in which we were similar. A dimple, a lighter strand of hair, small things that no one would ever notice but us." She chuckled as the memories flooded in. "He would point and show, I'd ask him question after question. One of which would change things between us forever," she said sadly.

"I'm listening." This time I truly was. The melancholy in her voice had my full attention. I didn't like it.

"There was one question in particular, of habits and things of his that I would ask him to explain. I remember the look on his face when I asked. Shock. Pure shock. Then fear. Then disapproval. He'd grab me, shake me and accuse me of things that I could never even fathom as a child let alone implement. He'd demand of me not to ever speak of them again. Freedom, love and trust, were replaced with silence and shame. I was crushed. I never meant for that to happen. He was the only one that I loved the way I did," she paused.

"What did you ask?" She didn't answer.

"I was there when he died. And I had to live with that. With knowing how it happened. That I could have done something. But what? What child could handle all of that?" She was in a far off place. I asked a question, but was ignored. "I withdrew. My family attributed my behavior to one of many 'eccentricities' and eventually, I'd be placed in the care of a child therapist. For behavior my father understood perfectly."

"Who killed him?" I asked again. There was a half smile that never managed to reach her eyes.

"There was a manhunt throughout England for the head of his assassin. But he was never found," she said calmly.

"But you were there," I reiterated.

"I was." The look in her eyes was disturbing. I held her tightly. I couldn't do anything about the past. Or the future. But there was now. There was now between us. And in this small shaded room, in this reality of ours, where nothing exists but us, I wanted her to feel protected. I wanted her to know that I was here. And whatever came, however it did, no matter how large or small, would meet me first.

"Is this the entire collection?" I asked.

"No. This is half. The half that my then, husband-to-be's father was given as collateral for debt."

"So you married Cooper to recapture what was lost?" I asked. If so, there was hope. Her heart belonged to me.

She smiled knowingly. My leading question had been filtered. A sigh. And an even moreso leading answer. "Not exactly," she said in a vacant tone. "There is more to our story than that.

Cooper has always loved me," she added. "I was always his special girl."

I didn't want to hear anything that would take me out of this space with her. Not at all. I changed the subject. Quickly.

"Where is the other half?" I asked.

"Spread out over the world. I've managed to recoup some of it. I am working on the rest. The collection was the pride of my father, and his. It is a life's work, piecing it back together," she chuckled lightly, as to downplay the magnitude of her goal.

I recalled a similar outpouring, after a meditation that would prove too much. Connection. Questions. Answers. And tears. Mine were everywhere. Of Adrianne, her arms were around my neck, her forehead to mine. Her eyes dark and penetrating, she smiled her signature half crescent. Not a teardrop in sight. The emotion. Where did she put it all? I decided to lighten the mood a bit.

"Do you think grandfather would mind?" I asked playfully.

"I'm sorry?" she didn't get it.

I let my eyes wander the length of her, and linger in a few special places. I continued,

"I've lost practice. You know it is not as simple as riding a bike. One needs to train daily if he is to play with the pros of the game."

"Of course." She was grinning almost a mile wide.

"Would you say I am good enough to play professionally? If I am not, then I will happily work on it for you. We can begin promptly if you like."

"You are better than professional," she smiled, then shook her head in a, *what will I do with him* motion. Suddenly, her expression changed.

"What are you wearing tomorrow evening?" she asked seriously.

"I can't wear this?" I motioned towards my signature ripped trousers, pocket chains and army shirt. She laughed and laughed. And I held and tickled her until she couldn't take it anymore.

I could ask questions. I could fight this. But I don't. I allow myself down a road that has no end. Desire. Passion. Pain. Connection. Freedom. There were these things of me, all of them, like moths to a flame.

24

It is the morning of the showing and I am not at Sezz. I am on Avenue Emilie Deschanel, in the penthouse, on what would be considered my side of the bed if we were in Brooklyn. After a night of marathon love and cups that runneth over, Adrianne shows better than tells how much she's missed me. I watch her turn and stretch, as she reaches for me in her sleep.

There is a morning newspaper on the nightstand that could double as sculpture worthy of museum showing. I reach. Thumb through the pages. Try and relate to the headlines of the day. What happened on the day of my first major showing? As I retrieve answers, excitement should be at the forefront. But it isn't. Something else looms in its place. Shock, horror, I guess that is what one would call this feeling.

Thirty-seven Lebanese children died in an Israeli missile surge on the village that they've grown, laughed and played in. The village, Qana. The epicenter of the attack was unanimously an extended family of sixty huddling together in an underground space, coupled with elderly and children who were ill, handicapped, deformed or simply too poor to make the single-road journey out of the identified war zone. So they camped in the basement together and at 01:00 hours, were detonated in their sleep. I recall similar headlines of similar targets. The ill, handicapped, deformed and poor, trapped and drowning in a swamp basin of the most powerful country in the world. A legitimate act of civil war crime it would seem, but the notion itself suffered a death as immediate as that of the Lebanese family. Is this the world that I should surrender to? Are these the realists? The integrity seekers, who sanction, start and finish war crime at will? The ones who make the rules? Who determine sanity?

Page three.

A RABBI RISKS HIS LIFE PROTESTING AGAINST ISRAELI AIR STRIKES IN LEBANON

I was raised by Orthodox Jews, therefore I should take sides. I should be okay with this. I should side with what's acceptable—with the majority. But I don't.

As I thumb through pages and imagery, I try to ignore a photograph of a young girl dangling lifelessly from the arms of a Red Cross volunteer. And when I put the paper down, prepare to sell paintings, pretend not to love, say what I don't mean, mean what I don't say, live for nothing, because nothing is what you gain when you are not true to yourself, I am reminded of a simple truth. People are dying to be free.

I face the east. Lift my palms to the heavens. Pray for possibilities and things I've never known to exist before today, then open my eyes. When I do, I am eye to eye with the Eiffel Tower, inhaling the scent of life and love. Behind me, my Aphrodite sleeps lightly. Peacefully. As if everything is happening in its place.

Of this relationship with her—because no matter what we tell ourselves, that is exactly what it is—we are not ethical. We are not honorable. We are not right. We are however, in love. By society's standards, there is no morality between us and I am crazy for loving her enough to risk so much. Of all the back and forth and over analyzing, a lone question hangs daintily in front of me. Who the hell is society?

I have an idea.

"Babe." I trot back towards the bedroom. Kiss her lightly. I know it's early. But it can't wait. "Baby," I call. She stirs. Eyelids flutter gently. There is an instinctive pucker for an invisible kiss that is missed. Then back to sleep for her. Mornings are not her specialty. I know what to do. Under the duvet, a special kiss in a special place. And another. And another. She moved delicately. The type of tremor that could be felt prior to a minor quake, progressed to full, seismic movement.

"Are we awake?" I asked.

"Yes." She answered sharply and out of breath, while pushing my head back.

"I have an idea." Another unwanted pause. The sound of exasperation meeting air. I chuckled at her frustration.

"T-tell me, late . . . yes love, yes . . . god . . ." Pause. Moans. A scream that seemed not to be able to find its way out of her.

"I just wanted your atten—t"

"ISLAM!" she yelled. I laughed. Went back to work. Brought her to where she loved being. A series of beautiful sounds, pants and profane utterances later, I pulled myself upward the bed, and lay beside her as she catches breath that is too quick for one with morning energy. There were beads of sweat on her nose, her upper lip. Yea. I feel good about that one. She wants to lay on me. I oblige her.

"Good morning," Adrianne says happily. Now she wants to talk. Women.

"Good morning," I answer. There is so much love, so much light in her eyes. Her hair plays with mine. This has all become so normal. I want to make it permanent. We kiss. She says my lips smell like sex. I lick what's left of her off of them, say something about nourishment and kiss her again. We laugh.

"Babe."

"Yes?" Eyelashes batted.

"How do you feel when you're with me?" I really wanted to know.

"Like I've lost my mind."

"But you're still here."

"Yes, I am."

"What does that mean?"

"I am unsure."

Her answers were given so honestly, I found it hard to ask for more. We were eye to eye as usual. The energy and connection between us, thriving in the silence. I wanted to feel this every morning. Prayer. Painting. Passion. Not exactly in that order. I decided to tell her just that.

"Be with me, A. Not just a few days at a time. For as long as we can be. After this contract is signed, I want to wake up to you for as many days in a row as we can live. I will massage you. I will wake you every morning as I did today, if you wanted. I will take care of you. I don't have billions, but I will take care of you. We'd grow together, spiritually. I'd love you from the core of me. You know that, Adrianne. You feel it. You know it's true." Silence and stillness. You could hear a pin drop. A dark look replaced the light in her eyes. I don't know where she went in that moment. As she stared into me, confusion, uncertainty and sadness crowded her eyes, all of them fighting for space. Moments passed. They seemed like millennia. "Say something, A."

"It is not that easy, Islam."

"Nothing worth having is," I reasoned.

She sat up. "You are thinking with the mind of an artist. You must think further than that."

"How much further, Adrianne? Do I need to think further than what you mean to me?"

She sighed. "Life is more than love."

"Is that why you're with me? For more than love? Or for more than the life that you live? Because I can and will offer both." I wasn't letting up. This conversation was long overdue. For a moment, everything in her eyes said that she wanted to believe me. The moment came and went.

"He and I have been married for over a decade, it is more complicated than you suggest," she answered. "These things are not simply a matter of living in a world one has created."

"So I am to be your side man? Your weekend lover, Adrianne? Is that what you want? Because I am not anyone's bitc—"

"That is not what I want."

"Then what is? What are you saying?"

"Stop it."

"Stop what?"

"Stop pushing me. When you do not have your way, you get upset and act as if only what you want matters."

"Well if you told me what you wanted, if you didn't leave me to guess, maybe I'd have an idea as to what mattered to you."

"What I want should be clear."

"Would you stop speaking in parables for fuckssake?" I was frustrated. She did all but hiss at me.

"We will review this only once." Eyes tight, index finger raised, she used it to remove a lone lock of hair from her eyes. "*Do not* swear in front of me. I am not one of your little singer-tramp-whores. Do you understand that?"

"I understand that you are selfish."

"Do you, now?" she reverted to a cut-throat British intonation that was just as sexy as it was unnerving. If I weren't so pissed I'd fuck her into submission. "I am selfish? I? Am selfish? Are you mad? What do you call your little tantrums and sorts? Do you call that love, Islam? Really? Do you refer to it as freedom? Well I have news for you, it is selfishness! You only know what you want! Let's be together . . . have you stopped your childish rant even for a single moment to think about what I may want? What I may be capable of giving you? Or that I may not even know what I want? The bloody *nerve* of you . . ." I've never seen nor heard her shout before. The shock of it almost took me out of the argument. She pushed the sheets aside and kicked those gorgeous legs to the side of the bed. Entirely naked, Adrianne stood, and continued to mumble to herself.

"Islam. Bloody Islam. Only knows or cares about what he himself wants. If he does not get his way, then the known world ends . . . he calls it freedom . . . passion. Bollocks. I've fallen for a primary school boy." She threw her hand in a tisk.

I was shocked. The old, less passionate me watched the episode, a spectator as opposed to a participant. Adrianne walked her ballerina walk, towards one of the many oversized studded leather bags that I've seen her carry. She reached inside for a tiny box and pulled out an even tinier slim of neatly packaged cancer.

"You don't smoke." I offered as if the observation would set her free. Something needed to. I was ignored. "You don't smoke, Adrianne."

"I do today," she snapped.

Paul used to say that it wasn't his arrogance that made people upset, it was the fact that he saw through to the very bone of what they were trying so desperately to hide. People on average wanted to be, but did not have the balls to be free, he would say. They resented him not only for his unabridged liberation, but for seeing the blemish in theirs. They'd rather call him crazy, eclectic or an asshole for speaking his mind, than acknowledging a possible admiration of his persona. I understood what he meant now. Everything in me knew and believed that Adrianne and I would be together. I also knew that she wanted that. Whether or not she knew it had not been determined.

"After this contract is signed, you can leave Cooper," I said.

"Oh?" she said incredulously.

"Yes. You can stop this nonsense and leave him."

"You are not Allah, Islam! I know that it comes as a shock to you, but you do not control everything and everyone!"

"Do you not want me at all? Because there is but so much of this back and forth one can take! A day with me, a day with him. What man would deal with this shit? Make a selection, Adrianne!"

"What if I hadn't come to a conclusion? In all of your tantrum throwing and order issuing, has that run across your passionate, liberated mind?"

"Don't give me that shit. There is no way you can leave my bed and—"

"And what?"

"And want anyone else to touch you but me. I see the dry pecks you give him on the cheek, Adrianne. You belong to *him*? Please. You don't even kiss him the same."

"You are so full of yourself. Fucking painters. I can't even believe we are having this conversation."

"Look me in the eye and tell me otherwise, Adrianne. Tell me that he—that anyone makes you feel what I do. In or outside of the bedroom. I am not speaking of ego. It is connection between us. Spirit. I'm not afraid of it, A. Why are you?"

For a moment, I wasn't the crazy one. Only a moment though. The epoch was short lived.

"Islam. You are impatient and controlling. How is one to deal with this daily?" She threw her hands up in surrender.

"I am more than patient, Adrianne. As patient as one can be in this situation. I am not Gandhi."

"Patience is relative. In my reality, you are not patient. You yield a second, and no more, for one to reconcile differences that would ordinarily take a lifetime to resolve."

"I cannot wait a lifetime to love you. It's absurd . . . this, wait, wait, wait. I love you *now*. You speak of your reality? Well in mine, I am free. *I* make the rules. I am not Allah, I am Islam, and you are my love. You are my reality. It is that simple to me."

Everything stood still for about a millisecond, for which I could have sworn I saw a break in stride, an acknowledgment in her eyes and body language that she agreed with me. Maybe she questioned herself, her fears, maybe for that split second, there was reconciliation of the concept that we did indeed belong together.

"Alright. Since we are speaking on freedom, on parallel realities, then I would be free to create my own paradox, my own irony, yes?" she asked.

"Yes." A small surge of victory ran through me. I was swaying her.

"And your reality would compromise with mine in order to create an agreeable world in which only what you and I want and need matters, correct?"

"That would be correct."

"Well, then. What to say of a woman who wants her lover *and* her husband as a part of her world?"

"What?"

"Would you love me if I were free enough to want you both?"

I was speechless. Not only had the question tipped the alarm of every single livewire my sympathetic nervous system had to offer, but it had never even crossed my mind as a possibility. Want us both? There was rationale. Resolve. Reservation. I could retreat to one of the three. Answer in a controlled and patient manner. But I don't.

"How the fuck can you say something like that? How do you think that makes me feel? Each time, you leave me and go to Cooper as if nothing we've shared matters! What the hell do you think this is, Adrianne? When I see him kiss you I want to just . . . argh!" My hands moved in a motion that signaled strangulation. That was an understatement. "I'm not a fucking escort, Adrianne!" I shouted loud enough to be heard in Hamburg. The thought of another day of her in Cooper's arms drove me nuts. "Cooper is a billionaire, so what? So bloody what! With all of his billions, he doesn't know what to do with you! He can't put that smile on your face! I do that! Not him! Both of us? Get real. You're so fucking selfish!"

We were in that stage of listening not to listen, but to reply. She jumped at the chance. "Selfish! In your so-called liberated world, I should be able to create my own reality! If freedom is truly what you are after! But it is not, Islam! You cannot even live up to your own standards! That is not passion . . . it is not love, it's selfishness! You are acting as an egotistical, self-centered child!"

"And you are acting like a whore." I said it too quickly. I started to apologize, but the sound of glass shattering diverted my attention from the apology. The crystal flute barely missed my head. As did the mobile phone.

"Adrianne! What the fuc—stop it!"

She launched any and everything she could get her hands on. We were down to emerald and ruby bracelets and rings hitting the wall, the glass doors of the terrace.

"Whore? How! Dare! You!" I didn't know there were this many tossable objects in the room. One hit me directly in the eye. Shit hurt like hell.

"A! Babe! St-stop it!" I dodged glasses and books and brass knobs. When the opportunity presented itself, I launched at her. Tackled her onto the bed.

"Get your hands off of me. Right now." If smoke could exit one's ears, it would hers like a steam from a kettle.

"No."

"Islam. I swear before my father and grandfather, if you do not remove yourself from me you'll regret it."

"I didn't mean to call you a whore, A." I saw her wince at the mere mention of the word.

"I don't care. Get off of me."

"Not until you . . ." An ill, almost nauseated look spread across her face. I felt her body and her stomach heave.

"Are you alright?" The look on her face gave all the answer I needed. I shifted my weight to give her more breathing room. "Adrianne, baby, what's wrong?"

"I . . . the toilet . . . I need to get to the toilet." In an instant, I scooped her up and ran her to the bathroom. I placed her feet on the cold tile and before I could ask another question, last night's dinner was all over the place. Luckily she was facing the Jacuzzi. I held her hair away from her face and wiped the sweat from her forehead. We stood through several heaving sessions, until there was nothing left to throw up.

I felt so bad. "Baby, I apologize. I didn't mean for this to happen. I get beside myself and—" she shook her head from side to side.

"Not you. You weren't the cause. I have been feeling odd all week. This is the third time in four days that I've awakened to a queasy stomach."

I fumbled around with towels, mouthwash and small cups of water, alternating each at her lips as needed. She accepted the care, but not the kiss given. I attempted to carry her to bed, but was interrupted.

"I can walk," she said with a calm curtness that confused me. She wasn't raging anymore. The tone of voice she used with me was so distant from her natural state. I let her down, happy for the moment I'd have to myself in the bathroom while I cleaned up. Minutes passed, each one leaving me more uneasy than the next. I returned to the bedroom to find her laying on her side, staring into nowhere. I felt so bad.

She was first to break the silence. "You've insulted me. You speak of me as if I am some pawn in the game of life, when you cannot live up to the standards which you require of others. Either I am selfish or free. Or a whore. If you think I am not to your standards, then it is best that we do not—"

"Don't say it."

"Islam, I cannot deal with you on this level. You have no patience and love to control. I am not to be controlled . . ."

I listened to her tell me that I lived in my own head and that it was at times, unbearable. I'd realize why discipline wasn't as horrible as I'd made it out to be in recent months. She would not let the whore comment go. A bit more self-control would have stifled a comment that hurt her to the core. I didn't mean it.

". . . And if that is what you feel, maybe it's best that we end this prior to things going further down hill." She can't be serious.

"It was one argument, Adrianne."

"It was one that I never wish to repeat. I want to sever this. If we can find it in us to be friends, then I will be the best that I can be to you. But this . . . what happened this morning . . . it's madness."

I sat beside her, on the edge of the bed, a shell of my former self, words and thoughts in gridlock.

"Will you leave me please?"

"Adrianne."

"Please. I do not wish to suffer a torrid rebuttal to a simple request." She turned her back to me. Silence filled the room with an eerie calm. I did the only thing there was to do. I got up.

Clothing, papers and objects strewn about, I find what belongs to me and reluctantly, set off to make my exit. Before I turn the doorknob, at my feet, is the photo of the small Lebanese girl, the one whose life had been shortened and exchanged for the notion of a freedom that may not exist. I wanted to follow my heart and live for her. Fight for sovereignty with the passion and heart of a Palestinian solider. But it seems as if I'll never win.

25

"So what happened after that?" Paul asked between muted laughs. I was on my mobile, in a taxi, en route to the Louvre, trying my best to explain to him how I ended up with a darkened eye on the night of my showing.

"She kicked me out."

"No shit."

His snickers and laughter were irritating me. "What do you mean no shit? She said she wanted to sever things and you think it's funny? Whose side are you on?"

"You called the woman a whore, Islam."

"I did not call her a whore. I said she was acting as one. There is a difference. And I didn't mean it." I answered. We took a right turn onto the Champs Elysees. Paul continued his irritating laugh. "You are truly getting a kick out of this," I said.

"Yes, I am finding this more than amusing. I don't think you've been paying attention to yourself over the past fifteen years. I'm just imagining the panty sniffing Islam that I know, dodging—what did you say she tossed at you?" He laughed at the anticipation of my reply.

"A crystal goblet." He hit the roof. Laughed loud enough for the taxi driver to hear him. "And her mobile." Louder. He laughed and laughed until I couldn't help but laugh with him. "And her jewelry." That stopped him.

"Whoa. Not my favorite watch," he said semi-seriously.

"Might as well have been. I got it all. Cartier bracelet crashed against my forehead like an F-16 jet into a wall." He roared. I let him have a few additional minutes of comedic reverie before I told him that I was approaching my destination. "Paul, I'm about to head inside. Wish me luck." I said. I knew I'd need it. I had no idea what I was walking into. Cooper. Adrianne. Arabs. It was all a hat trick. Paul calmed his laughter, the big brother in him taking the event as seriously.

He cleared his throat. "Islam. Listen to me. This is important. Remember the night our heat went out, and we sat in the cold imagining all of the wonderful things we'd do with a million pounds?"

Sure, how could I forget? "Yea." I answered.

"Well, you're about to find out. Do not lose yourself in there. There is a lot of money on the table. She is just a woman. A beautiful woman with a massive temper but a woman nonetheless. You are where you want to be, this is what you've prayed for, so please don't get in there and act like Jeffery Dahmer in a meat locker. Yasara's Islam tonight. Not Adrianne's." I chuckled at the reference. Funny, I don't even remember what that Islam did or didn't do. I remember life being unquestionably simpler. That, I do recall.

"No worries, mate. She's done with me anyway. It won't be that difficult." I reply, wanting terribly to believe what I was saying. I placed ten euro in the hand of the taxi driver, and thanked him for a safe and timely arrival.

"Did you dress for the occasion?" Paul asked. I glanced swiftly into the rear view mirror, giving myself a quick once over. I looked good. At least I thought so. After I left Adrianne's, I spent an hour or two in the steam room and spa of my hotel, trying to figure out what the hell had just happened. When I returned to the suite, there was a handwritten note, and a black American Express card on the nightstand.

Go to Rue Marbeuf. Corneliani. Get something presentable. –A.
That's what I did.

"She sent you to Corneliani?" Paul's tone altered on disbelief and admiration.

"That is the place. I look like you," I joked, as I stepped out of the vehicle and adjusted the linen sport coat I'd picked up this afternoon. A nervous rush washed over me. I tried to assure myself that this was a normal eve at the gallery in Soho. That it was a simple showing. Nothing more, nothing less.

"She must love you," he added. Damn, Paul. Italians and fashion. Love was determined by how many double-initialed letters accompanied a gift.

"I don't need to hear that right now man, I need to hate her," I said seriously. Friends always say the stupidest things at the worst moments. "I need to hate her and I need to find a woman to sh—" What I saw stopped me mid sentence. A dark luxury vehicle. Cooper's hand in hers, both of them in black, complementing each other as if this were an everyday thing for them. Her legs were long and bare, heels were high, and her hair . . . so many ringlets. I wanted to touch them all.

"Islam, you there?" Paul asked. I heard him, but I was too busy figuring out how I'd make it through the night.

"Islam!"

"Yea." My tone lacked the confidence and luster of just moments prior. "Paul, I've got to get inside," I said. I knew I sounded exactly how I felt.

"She looks like a million bucks doesn't she?" His intuition is always on.

"A billion, bloke. A fucking billion." I answered.

"Deal with it later. Focus now. Just get through the night. I don't want to read about you in tomorrow's Evening Standard," he chuckled.

Nothing in me could find laughter. I could barely find one foot in front of the other.

*　*　*

I walked behind them for what seemed like miles, too sick to be jealous. As I approach the entrance to the show room, I am greeted.

"La droite cette façon, monsieur," said a slim, immaculately groomed middle age man. He directed me toward the showroom entrance.

"Merci beaucoup," I responded, a bit distracted. What was yesterday a completely empty space, seemed smaller as people that I didn't know, and some that I had seen only briefly before, filled the room. There were more people here than I thought would be.

"Good evening, Islam. Man of the hour," Cooper said as he headed towards me with his wife in hand. A nightmare if I'd ever had one. She was speaking to another woman—a beautiful one—over her shoulder and didn't know that he was bringing her to me. When she realized it, she didn't flinch. She didn't break stride. That stoic, grey, glazed over look replaced the heated one of this morning's wake up session. She was an expert at hiding her feelings.

"Good evening, Cooper," I responded casually.

"Everything seems in place," he said, lacking the vibrant tone of voice that was his usual. He looked at me oddly, and I wondered what sparked the change in his demeanor.

"It seems that way, yes." I answered stoically, trying my best to ignore Adrianne.

"Good evening, Islam." She was collected and calm.

I responded just as casually. "Good evening, madame." The former me—the one who never turned down an opportunity to touch a beautiful woman—took her hand and kissed it. The shift in her demeanor suggested that a kiss, or any sort of contact was the last thing she expected. There was no change in look or mannerism, but her energy betrayed her.

"Did you inventory the pieces?" she asked.

"Yes."

"And the transporters are taken care of?"

"Last week," I answered.

"Alright. Well I suppose we are well prepared," she'd say looking but not at me.

"Isn't she splendid tonight?" Cooper asked, pulling her closer to him, planting a quick kiss on her cheek. This, I didn't think I could deal with for hours on end. I scanned the room for the small bar station that I knew was here.

Just as I was about to make a swift comment and exit, the gorgeous woman whom Adrianne was speaking to prior to this debauchery approached the group. Damn, she was striking. A disposition likened to Adrianne's with a bit more haute, less artist. Wide doe-like eyes. A lone stream of blacker than black hair, trailed a bare olive back, and rested lightly at her tailbone. I've had my share of women but she was stunning. Not as my love, but close enough. If nothing else, I was happy for the distraction.

"Is this Islam Ian?" she asked in a tone of voice identical to Adrianne's but different accent. I decided to answer for myself.

"Yes, I am."

"Splendid work. I am Kharet Siddiq." She extended her hand and I kissed it. She blushed, but maintained the equanimity that was signature to women of this class. There was no more to the introduction, as all it took was a name to rightfully place her in the proper position. Curator of the collection, sister of director Mohammed Siddiq, daughter of a man who could easily cause the two most powerful countries in the world to stand still for a day with a simple nod of his head. I've read about the Siddiq family, oil was inherited, art was natural. Abu-Salaam—the patriarch and oil magnate played several instruments as did many of his children. His youngest son and daughter were the executors of the art collection. Art was a weak spot in the family. Cooper is a smart man.

"You are a ladies man." She gestured towards the walls adorned with women I've painted.

"I am unsure of the verity of that statement, but yes, I paint women." She gave me a look that stated her position. I don't think anyone else noticed. There was no bashful grin, or note passing. Her eyes said simply, *I am interested.*

Adrianne interrupted the exchange with a brief apology.

"Pardon us," she said as she placed her hand into her husband's. "We must greet the arriving guests." Did she not care that this woman was interested? Did she care at all? As they walked off hand in hand, I couldn't help but rest my eyes on places my hands and other parts of me wanted to take recess in. My imagination, for a second, ran wild.

"Islam, are you okay?" the Arabian beauty asked.

"Yes, I am fine."

"You want Adrianne, don't you?"

"What?"

"I said, do you wish to show me your favorite piece?"

"Oh, yes. I apologize. Right this way." I gestured to the first piece I'd painted in New York. The first one Adrianne watched me arrange.

"Amazing. Reminds me of Modigliani's earlier nude works, but a bit edgier. Very passionate, the look in her eyes," Kharet said in awe. She's acting like she's never seen it before. "The color and texture are so rich. And you capture light as a true master impressionist. What was your inspiration for this?" Was she sober? The inspiration for this piece is well known between us. In the distance, I heard her begging me to touch her. I felt her body on mine. I saw that full moon smile—the rare one, replace the crescent after I loved her as deeply as she wanted to be loved.

"You know what inspired me," I said softly.

"No, I am sorry. I do not," she answered coyly.

"You did, Adrianne." There was a slight look of confusion, followed by a light chuckle.

"You called me Adrianne," she said.

"What?"

"Adrianne. I am not Adrianne," Kharet said in a playful tone of voice. "But do not worry, we are mistaken for one another all of

the time. It has been a constant since we were young. When I am
in London, I am called Adrianne. When she is in Paris, she is
called Kharet." The beauty tossed her mane over her shoulders
and grinned playfully. "However, I will take credit for the inspiration," she laughed lightly. I called her Adrianne?

The clinking sound of silver on crystal solicited the attention
of the entire room.

"Welcome to the first of many showings for the Spence Gallery's
international director, Islam Ian." Cooper addressed the small
crowd, and gestured to where I was standing. There was applause
and an announcement that we would not dine at Le Tour D'Argent, in the interest of time. The most elite restaurant in Paris,
where presidents and Kings dined, offered to cater and staff the
small event. The first course would begin shortly. Wine goblet in
hand, Kharet moved onto the next piece. I was still sifting through
nouns and verbs from moments ago. I called her Adrianne?

"This is the one that most interests me." She gestured toward
a particularly large piece that was actually the centerpiece of the
exhibition. It was an abstract of Adrianne, lying comfortably
naked, in her favorite position on my old sofa. "I find it fascinating, the contrast in color and impasto especially here . . ." Kharet
spoke intelligently, interpreting aspects of the painting as would
a curator beyond her years. The image that I'd see in front of me,
was not of the abstract piece, but of what happened *after* I took
color to the canvas.

"I'm painting."

"I know."

"What happened to Plato?"

"He is fine where he is."

"And you?"

"I am interested in something else right now . . ."

"The colors are so warm, but her eyes . . ." Kharet pointed to a
dark area on the canvas ". . . are so dark. The contrast alludes to
the relationship between truth and illusion, appearance and reality . . . you blend color so effortlessly, it would be hard for one to
decipher where it ends and where it begins," she said astutely.

"Kharet. Please excuse me for a moment, I will be back." It would be in my best interest to spend as much time with the young curator as possible. She was, after all, the buyer in her brother's absence. I wanted to stop them, but my feet were moving at a pace that suggested they were going to do what they wished. I stood in front of Cooper and his wife, wordless.

"Hello, Islam." Cooper offered. "Are you and Kharet finding each other well? She seems very interested in your work. That is a good sign. Mohammed will be here shortly. He will miss the showing but I'm sure Kharet will inform—"

"Excuse me, Cooper. I need to speak to your wife."

"Can it wait a moment? She and I were—"

"No. It cannot wait," I answered swiftly. I'm tired of waiting. Of Adrianne, there was not a sentiment in her eyes. Not fear, nervousness, intrigue, worry, love. Nothing.

"Well it will have to," he answered back.

"Well, it will not," I retorted.

"What do you wish to speak to me about, Islam?" Adrianne asked.

"Business matters. Excuse us, Cooper," I grabbed her by the arm and attempted to escort her outside of the small room. Cooper was still holding her hand. I pulled harder. He held her. And before I knew it, I'd dropped her hand and placed both of mine around his neck. I would squeeze her love out of him if I had to.

"Oh my god, Islam!" There was a gasp and shriek. I told him that I wanted to talk. That was all I wanted. I told him that. I heard screams and plates crashing to the floor.

Paul was going to be pissed at me. "Islam!" I heard my name but people, sounds, paintings . . . they were all a blur.

Kharet's voice seemed to be the loudest. "Islam! Oh my god are you alright? The waiter took a nasty fall, but don't worry, it is only wine, it will come out of the jacket. What's important is that you're all right," she went on.

What is she talking about? A brief look around and things were . . . different. Especially because I was looking at them from the ground up. I was on the floor, Kharet and a gentleman who I assumed was a part of the staff attempted to help me up. How'd I get down here?

"Someone should speak to the waiters about tending to so many requests at once. One can only balance so many glasses at a time before they all go crashing to the floor. He walked right into you," Kharet said, as I was helped onto my feet by the man standing next to her. "Are you alright?"

"Uh, yes, I believe so," I said more confidently than I felt. What is going on? I glanced at Adrianne and Cooper. They were in the same position as minutes ago. Face to face, discussing matters intimately. I am not sure as to what was happening. Moments ago, I was strangling Cooper. This—whatever it was—wasn't good. I will ignore it. That's all that seems to work in this life. Everyone ignores everything.

"Apologies for that. Where were we?" I asked, hoping Kharet hadn't noticed anything other than the faux pas of the waiter.

"I was commenting on the piece," she replied. Intent on allowing her beauty to distract me, I focused on her eyes. The shape of her lips. The angular nature of her cheekbones. The longer I stared, the more she blushed. "I'd merely suggested that the contrast in color yielded more than meets the eye, no pun intended of course," she smiled. "For our collection, it is the one that I am most interested in," she answered.

"Ah, yes, this one here. Well, you've enlightened the artist on his own work. Many times the depiction of what is felt comes before the knowledge of the feeling."

"Well, Islam, there is much feeling in your work. I find it interesting that a man of so little words and emotion feels deeply enough to produce work on this level. One simply wonders who or what the spark is behind it." The smile in her eyes was suggestive.

"Maybe I will answer that question at a later date," I answered.

"Maybe you will," she took a light sip of wine, "but for now, shall we move on to the next one?" It was a question and a statement. I'm finding it to be common of women who are used to getting what they want. As would a gentleman, I placed a light hand at the small of her back and attempted to escort her on. We were interrupted.

"It would be fair to assume that the two of you are getting on?" Adrianne asked innocently.

Kharet answered her. "That would be a fair assumption, yes. Mr. Ian here is quite the talent." I don't know what it is between women, but whether they are companions or enemies, the undertones in communication are more complicated than Scotland Yard code. There was something going on, but it was apparently over my head. It was all in Adrianne's eyes. Less to do with me and more to do with Kharet.

"Yes, he is. Isn't he?" Adrianne answered contemplatively. Those cerebral wheels were turning. She stared past me into Kharet as if I didn't exist.

"Very passionate in his approach. But distant. Unobtrusive. Exactly what we are looking to acquire," Kharet responded. Adrianne didn't. "By the way, Mohammed will be late, but he will be in attendance, albeit briefly." She said as moreso a personal cue to Adrianne of her brother's arrival than one of a mere business oriented ETA. Adrianne nodded quietly. Kharet turned towards me, "My brother works with my father, but is an artist at heart. Adrianne represents him . . . I suppose one could say. He is not nearly as talented as you, but he is an A-level artist nonetheless. Wouldn't you say, Mrs. Spence?" The moment of discomfort could not be missed. Adrianne looked as if she wished to do to Kharet, what I did, or rather, didn't just do to Cooper. There is too much going on tonight. I glanced at my watch. An hour and a half left. Seemed like an eternity. People were either taking seats or being seated at small round tables throughout the showroom.

"He is seated beside me, yes?" she asked Adrianne.

"I am not sure that seats have been designated," Adrianne answered.

"Oh, of course they have," Kharet took my hand and led me to the table.

26

Everything at the table moved like a movie that I was in, but not. Questions. Answers. Talk on world matters. Art. The seventy-eight million pound Klimt piece that was just auctioned off. Blue chip versus contemporary art. Weddings and royal affairs. Africa and oil. The prime minister of England. The president of France. I listened but didn't. The same would go for eating. The table seated eight. Adrianne and Cooper sat at two o'clock, Kharet at six thirty-five. There were two older couples present. Friends of the family, I was told. Lovers of art, simply here for the showing. I'd pretend to ignore that I was struggling with the sight of Cooper's hand on Adrianne's leg under the table. Kharet's beautiful face, (and other aspects of her) were the only saving grace.

"So, Islam, have you always been a fine artist?" an older woman asked.

"As far as I can remember, yes," I answered.

"And have you always painted women?"

"I've worked abstractly in other areas, but women have kept my interest over the years." I responded quietly. I've gotten it down to a science. Focus on the women at the table. Old. Young. Beautiful. Beautifully challenged. It didn't matter. They all had something to offer. And the check. Focus on the money. It was the best way to ignore what I was hearing. Adrianne's moans from the morning were in surround sound.

"What is it about women that has kept you so interested? Surely there are other subjects," she asked.

"Change," I replied quickly, happy for the diversion. "Women change with the wind. Even the same woman is never truly the same day to day."

"Indeed. Are you sure that your work will transcend cultural impediments? We have properties worldwide."

Kharet was in business mode. I wanted to bring her back to communicating with me personally. I worked more efficiently that way. "A beautiful woman cannot be denied in any culture."

"And the inspiration for your work, Mr. Ian?" Kharet probed further. Why was she so transfixed on that question? The inspiration for my work is sitting across from me, with another man's hand caressing her upper leg. I didn't want to talk or think about her.

"As I said, I will answer that at a later date."

"Sooner than later, I hope." Although the young curator maintained her posture, she was flirting.

"Yes, sooner," I replied.

"Answer it now," Adrianne interjected. Her abrupt and curt interruption caught Kharet and I both off guard. So did her tone of voice. It seemed to catch her off guard as well. Cooper conversed with the older men at the table, and the older women were enthralled in each other. There was just us three, in the most interesting conversation at the table. I addressed Adrianne, but kept my eyes on Kharet.

"Inspiration is natural, free, it comes of its will, as does its explanation of existence." I turned to face Adrianne. "At the moment, I am not feeling free. Or natural. I would like to give the lady an accurate response, but an uninhibited one. So, I will answer her at a later date." I said in the final tone of voice that Adrianne often used with me. I'd ignore the fiery darts circling her eyes and try my best to block out any intimate thoughts of us. Cooper's hand was still on her leg. It moved as he spoke and was unnerving me.

I checked my watch. Under an hour left. I just need to make it out of here in one piece, a millionaire, and sort my life out later. Kharet turned to Adrianne.

"Well, Adrianne, what do *you* think of his work?" It seemed like a direct question, but nothing was direct or straightforward tonight. Adrianne glanced downward at the gold and ruby bracelet on her wrist, then looked Kharet directly in the eye.

"I am representing him. What more is to be said?"

"One can represent another and not necessarily be passionate of their work. I know what *I* think of Mr. Ian. The question is simply, what do you?" She was better than Adrianne at masking the personal and professional, tying it all up in one neat sushi roll. If looks could kill, Kharet would be in a flash, a hanging duck in an Asian bistro.

"As I said, I am representing him. That as well as his work, speaks for itself. Wouldn't you agree?" Adrianne asked.

"Have you ever represented one you were *not* passionate about?"

"Kharet . . ." I know that look. Adrianne's had it. The exchange was gratefully interrupted by a voice and language that I didn't recognize.

"Sabahir nahaar yaa, jameela," a good looking man, hair and skin identical in color to Kharet's had approached the table quietly as to ward off the disruption typically caused by one of the most powerful sons in the world entering a room. As for the exchange, I didn't speak Arabic, but I knew the word *jameela*. It meant beautiful.

"Sabahir nahaar," Adrianne answered perfectly, in dialect to match his own, accepting each one of the three kisses he gave her with a slight smile.

"Kaif haaliqui?" he spoke directly to the center of his attention, as if the rest of the table didn't exist.

"Quais," she answered calmly. They were eye to eye, the

longer the stare, the softer his gaze on her. In his eyes were a lot. Pain was the easiest to see. Eyes were averted, Adrianne turned her attention from Mohammed to the table and business was back to its usual.

"Cooper." Mohammed extended his hand.

"Mohammed." Cooper stood, responded with a handshake. Mohammed turned to the group.

"Greetings family and friends, apologies for missing what I'm sure is an excellent showing." He properly addressed the elders at the table and walked over to his sister. A kiss on either side of her cheek. One more as was customary, then he turned to me.

"I am Mohammed Siddiq. You are the artist?"

"Yes."

"I am enjoying what I have seen so far. Your pardon for the brief attendance, I have a previous engagement to tend to. Rest assured Kharet will brief me on all that is to be known of your work," he said.

I wanted not to, but I watched Adrianne. Her gestures and motions were that of fatigue from trying to keep up with a world that she usually excelled in, but today was passing her by. Cooper rose from the table, kissed his wife, then looked at me. Mohammed looked at Adrianne. Kharet at Mohammed. Me at my love. Adrianne simply put her head in her hands. She appeared to be mentally and emotionally exhausted.

At that instant, I didn't remember much about arguing or art or unmet desire. I just wanted my baby, my darling, to feel better. I decided to answer Kharet's question on inspiration. Allow Adrianne time to gather herself from whatever had just taken place.

Cooper and Mohammed left the table, the older couples reclaimed their arbitrary chatter, and I began, "On inspiration. You say you are looking for passionate work, Ms. Siddiq. Of my own, I am not sure of how much passion is injected into each piece, or how it is come about that a work is passionate or emotional to start. I like to capture the strength that is weakness, the look in one's eye when they allow themselves surrender. Many of the women that I've painted share this trait. As an artist, I wish not only to encapsulate the feelings of my subjects, but allow myself into them. Relieve them as well as myself, in a sense." Adrianne raised her head. I felt her eyes on me. "Take the large painting to the right of us," I gestured towards Kharet's favorite work, the abstract of Adrianne. Everyone turned their eyes to it. Adrianne's remained on me. "My relationship with the subject is expressed in color. I may not be able to express it, but I paint what I want to say to her, how I want to hold her and make her feel. If she is troubled, I paint a horizon of understanding, if no one understands, I do. If she is frustrated, I paint solitude. If she is without love I paint love. If she is without passion, without freedom, I give it to her. When I am inside of her, heart and soul alike, I feel like a god of sorts. Creating a world where she can exist as she wishes. Not as she is."

The table was quiet. In circles and dinners of this sort, emotion, anything other than a bland directorate was unexpected. I didn't want to, but I glanced at Adrianne, whose own sterile look had been replaced with one of warmth and tenderness, followed by a quick one that I knew well. *Love me gently.* It was cursory and transient. Arriving and leaving me as she often did.

"Well! When you put it like that one cannot resist!" one of the elder women exclaimed. "If you are granting wishes, I wish to be Marilyn Monroe in love with Johnny Depp! We can begin the session at once!" Everyone laughed except Adrianne. The ill and nauseating look from this morning replaced the warm one. The older woman turned to Adrianne. "Are you not feeling well?" she asked with concern.

"I am okay. It's the fumes. They are making me nauseous." Adrianne placed her hand lightly over her mouth. "My god . . . what do they use to clean this place?" she asked to no one in particular while excusing herself.

A dessert and a fine coffee later, I was about to make a grand exit. It took almost all I had, but I'd managed to get through the night. All I wanted was to sit in the steam room at Sezz and do nothing. No painting. No love. No women. No Paul. No anything. Of the showing, I did what I could. I held back feelings. I could hear the light clicking of heels behind me, I knew who it was. I held back all night and I was still holding back.

Making my way through the grand courtyard of the museum, I was happier to be leaving than I had been upon arrival. I was looking forward to the company of the common man on the Parisian metro. Kharet, about to step into her chauffeured vehicle, signaled for my attention.

"Are you heading back to your hotel?" she asked politely.

"Yes."

"Would you like a ride?" I wasn't sure if it were a direct or an indirect question. Nothing was as it seemed with these people. I honestly just wanted to catch the train. Adrianne walked over to where we were standing.

"Montmartre tomorrow for the studio visit?" she asked me. Her voice lost the edge of earlier evening.

"Yes. I will meet you at the penthouse," I answered. Adrianne stood there, ringlets of dark hair blowing in the wind with the rain. Her eyes were lasers between myself and her childhood friend, or adversary.

"Are you coming along?" Kharet asked. You know what? This wasn't as hard as I am making it out to be. Here was a gorgeous and intelligent woman, offering me a ride, maybe literally, maybe figuratively, and another offering me anguish and frankly driving me insane. I opened the door and slid into the car.

I would ignore the look on Adrianne's face, or the fact that it seemed harder for her to mask her feelings than it used to be. Maybe freedom, the feel and experience of it was irreversible for her as well. Maybe the exhausting look from earlier was her dealing with her own feat, her own airs of freedom and sanity. For a split second, I weighed the implications of that. The second came and went. She asked me to leave her. She does not want me. Not enough. It fucking hurt. A quick look at the wondrous creature sitting beside me, a signal to the driver, and I'd resolved to make the best of the night that I could.

"Six fremiet d'avenue, Sezz d'hotel s'il vous plait," I said, taking a last glance of a woman who had more of me than I knew to exist.

"Oui Monsieur," the driver replied dutifully. We sped off.

I loved her. I wanted her. I missed her already.

27

"You want to paint me?"

"Why not?" I answered, reaching in my bag for the appropriate brushes.

"It's so sudden."

"Are you nervous?"

"Should I be?"

"You are in the best of hands."

"That is what I am worried about," she smiled slyly.

I walked over to her, and directed her towards the bed. Tea and conversation had turned into something else.

"Would you mind loosening that?"

"How much?" she asked.

"Enough to make you comfortable." I was focused on cleaning brushes and unrolling canvas. What I saw when I turned around was worth a portrait of its own.

"There. I am comfortable." Her tiny black dress hit the floor quietly, but with as much emphasis as a paper weight. With black lacey bottoms and more cleavage than I'd given her credit for, I was viewing the splendor of a woman who would never hear the word no, in any language.

"What am I to do?" Kharet asked innocently.

"Whatever you wish," I answered.

Lace was near my nose, inviting me to shred it like licorice. My mouth watered. The scent was wonderful, and parts of me— the most obvious one—responded as it was designed by God to. The scent of her, the spicy vanilla one, blanketed me, and I couldn't see the color on the canvas in front of me.

"What is desire?" A sly hand ran through my hair.

"What is longing?" It lingered at my chin.

"What is love?" I grabbed her. It was only right.

"Are you alright?" A more jasmine-flowered scent crept in over the spicy vanilla. The air loosened. The voice changed. Kharet sat, legs crossed and removed her heels. My senses were thinning, and if I didn't know me, I'd swear I was high. For the third time tonight, Adrianne has been with me, in my space but not. I was doing and feeling things that apparently weren't there. No, I am not sure that I am okay.

"Come closer." I said. Kharet smiled.

"Why don't you come to me?" The closer I got, the more beautiful my subject became and the clearer my objectives. *Get Adrianne out of your mind.* Simply, get her out. That was it. It was all I could think of. I stood directly over Kharet. A small wet brush traced the sensitive area under her belly button.

"So, you are painting me." A statement-question.

"I am." I answered.

As she moved her body beneath the brush, I positioned myself to do what came naturally in the presence of a beautiful woman. *Desire is . . .*

The only thing standing between myself and bliss was a part of me that's never let me down. I tried again.

The sister of pain . . .

"Are you alright?" Kharet asked. A quick glance downward confirmed a fear I've never known. Limp? I was too excited. That was the problem. It had to be.

I sat up, walked back over to the canvas and applied a stroke of deepest blue.

"Yes, I am fine."

* * *

Latest night found me in the comfort of a stunning woman. A portrait and a sunrise later, I'd learn many things about the woman who looked to acquire passionate art. I'd also learn something else. I am not—or rather do not feel as strong as I've always believed I was. My determination to purge all of Adrianne from me in a single night was simply a stupid idea.

Earliest day found me awake but exhausted, walking the west bank of the Seine, tossing pebbles into the river, trying for a moment of solitude, as the notion seemed too much to ask of the universe these days. Another pebble into the water. I am mesmerized by the ripples in the river. Who knew that one small thing—being free—could cause such a big splash in one's life?

The walk to the penthouse from my hotel was not a long one. If it was, I was so out of it that I hadn't noticed. I did however, see couples lying on the grass at the base of the tower, some embraced, others simply staring upward. As if the key to the life they've chosen to live was dangling on top. I'd look up too, hoping for answers.

Turning left onto Avenue Emilie Deschanel, the penthouse rested neatly on the corner, taking its own splendor for granted. I waited downstairs for its owner, unsure that I was welcome up. She appeared at the top of the marble stairs, the same but different, as if there had been a visit from Gabriel overnight.

"Good morning," I offered.

"Good morning," she replied. We stood there. And I'd pinpoint the difference. Withdrawal. But on a different level than before. Disconnection. A first, our energies weren't whole. Auras were not connected as two bubbles managing to find each other mid air.

"Right this way, Madame, Monsieur . . ." The driver gestured towards the vehicle and she walked towards it. I touched her arm.

"It would be better to ride the Metro, yes?" I hoped she wasn't set on driving. Today was the only day of real vibe and people that I had scheduled. I wanted to experience it front and center. Not from a skybox.

"Metro?" she said, as if she'd never heard the term.

"Yes. Montmartre is not far, and is better experienced by foot," I persuaded. She looked unsure. Twenty-four hours ago she knew me well, in the biblical sense. Right now, I was a stranger offering her candy. "Trust me." I added.

She signaled the driver and we walked the ten minutes to Ecole Millitaire station in silence. Today was a long day, there was the visit with my favorite Parisian artist and a surprise studio visit. I didn't know how long she'd planned to be out, so I thought it best not to assume.

"How much time do you have today?" I asked.

"I don't have anything on the schedule," was her reply.

"It's possible that we'll be out all day."

"I don't mind," she answered quietly, as we trotted down the old stairs into the station. Of habit, I was about to place my metro ticket through the card reader when I realized she's never been on the train. Adrianne stood still, transfixed by her surroundings. She raised her sunglasses.

"Where do I pay to ride? I assume it's there?" she pointed to a small scratchy window with a young woman behind it issuing directions to an older couple. I nodded. She stood in the queue patiently. I waited for her at the turnstile. "L'aller- retour a Montmartre, s'il vous plait?" she asked the young woman for return travel to Montmartre. Adrianne walked towards me with the small purple ticket, placed it in my hand and waited patiently for me to operate the turnstile on her behalf. I did as was requested. She slid past me, through the slim double-doors, allowing more intimate areas of hers to touch mine as they would normally. I had to stop my hand from taking its usual position at the small of her back. I could see that we'd both try for friendship, but it wasn't natural for us.

The old train pulled into the station, and I pushed the button to open its doors. I pulled a corner seat down for Adrianne, and one for myself.

"You good?" I asked.

"Yes, thank you," she answered, keeping focus on a small advert above her for a small show in St. Germain.

"This is your first time, yes?" I was referring to the train ride. She nodded quietly. I know we had a rough day yesterday, but it was her idea to call things off. These cold shoulder bollocks weren't a part of the deal. Adrianne sat beside me and acted as if I were merely a stranger on a train. I couldn't go on like this all day. A man got onto the carriage and began one of the most unique solicitations for money I'd ever seen. A puppet show.

"Good morrrrrning, Paris!" he spoke in French, pulling an odd looking puppet over a small black piece of material wedged between the carriage poles. Everyone either laughed or smiled. It was creative. Adrianne stared out of the window. She was in another world. I had an idea.

"Good morrrrrning Puppetman!" I answered. It startled the puppeteer, as I'm sure he's never included crowd participation as a planned part of his morning show. To my surprise, he answered back.

"Monseiur! How are you this morning?" I stood up to reply. The people on our carriage chuckled. It took a second, but Adrianne finally realized that I'd injected myself into the show.

"Islam!" She gasped. I had to keep myself from laughing at the look on her face. She was mortified. Despite her hand on mine, attempting to pull me back into my seat, I continued.

"Oh puppeteer! I am distraught! I've just arrived in Paris this morning, in search of the most beautiful woman in the world!" I turned to face the passengers and heard Adrianne mumble under her breath. *Oh my God . . . Oh my God . . .* she almost died. I had to hold back laughter. "She said she would meet me on your carriage this morning, but she is not here! What to do!" I proclaimed. My arms were stretched out, and I faked anguish. Everyone laughed. It was the most horrible acting in the world. The puppeteer took a look at Adrianne and smiled. He'd caught on. Wiggled the puppet a bit. Made dramatics in Adrianne's direction. She chuckled.

"Why, I think you are sadly mistaken, Monseiur! There is a beautiful leg—I mean woman, possibly the most beautiful, right beside you!" The carriage roared. The puppet's winks and excitable come-on gestures took me out of character. I laughed. So did Adrianne.

"But she does not fancy me! She won't say a word! Is it my trousers?" I pointed towards the large holes and tattered parts. The passengers were having a ball. As was the puppeteer. Our stop was next. I signaled to Adrianne. She stood, smiled and shook her head.

"You're mad," Adrianne said playfully. After all that's been happening, I won't object to that, but I know one thing. I got what I wanted. She was smiling. I removed twenty euro from my pocket and handed it to the metro performer. On a scale of one to ten, he'd receive ten for creativity and ten for execution.

"Merci," I offered. We shook hands.

"You're welcome," he replied in English.

The carriage doors opened, and we'd walk the narrow corridors and steep stairs to Place des Abbesses. The weather was beautiful. There was so much activity. Park benches. Flowers. Terrorist pigeons. Jugglers, children and carousels. A jazz band on a small stage nearby. Beautifully designed windows and moldings on old Parisian buildings. Cafes and brasseries packed with artists and summer flow. The music was fresh and airy. The small shops and boutiques were trendy. This is what I'm talking about. Adrianne's smile was a mile wide.

"I love it already," she beamed. "Have you eaten?" she asked. I hadn't. I asked her what she was in the mood for.

"Demitasse, Pain au chocolat, . . . anything but pressed duck," she'd say of the arrangement of duck from last night's dinner. "There's but so much *haute monde* one can take." Adrianne mocked the high-class waiters of last night's showing, facial expressions and all. It caught me off guard. I laughed out loud. My sentiments exactly.

*   *   *

We'd decided on brunch at Le Saint Jean, a café in the heart of Montmartre. At the small wooden table, Adrianne and I speak richly, as if each of us inherited the other.

"I am interested in your perspective on this . . ." Adrianne leaned inward and wiped baguette crumbs from the corner of my mouth. We were speaking on the differences of Christianity and Judaism.

"So, you are saying that these two groups are reading from the same books and thus should be implementing a singular practice and faith?" I asked.

"Yea," she answered in my signature filler. I chuckled. She blushed.

"Are you Christian or Jewish?"

"I am well read," she stated simply.

"Well then, this is what I think." Everything about her gaze invited me to be as free as I wanted with my interpretation. "I would agree that the practices of Christians and Jews should be better aligned. I do not think however, that it is possible for certain groups, no matter the religion to allow change—admitting flaw—as it would shake, possibly crack the foundation on which they've built their lives as well as the lives of their children . . ."

"Um-hmm."

"And if this is so, if alternate realities and perspectives are realized and furthermore validated, then guess what? It will be just fine to be short, or poor, or gay, or deformed, or obese or uninterested in business matters, or interested in polygamy. It would be fine to love who you love. It would be fine to speak your mind, to show hurt and feel pain. To scream in the streets. To be passionate. To extract those freedoms would not be at the expense of one's survival. It would be the norm. A madman would be one who engaged in the opposite of those practices, as the majority would be free to choose and change as they wished. Insanity as we know it, perhaps it wouldn't exist."

She sat quietly staring at me. A wondrously glossy look in her eyes that I hoped—no prayed was love, shined through the deep violet halo that has been there all morning. After several moments of silence, the bill came. She reached, I intercepted it. Inserted my card into the slim jacket and handed it to the waiter.

"Are we ready for brilliant and innovative art, Madame?" I asked.

"Absolutely," she replied. We gathered our things and were off.

28

Cobblestone streets and beautiful windows greet us as we make our way up the steep hill that is Rue Ravignan. There are many small shops in a row, and I remember them all. A shop with a bright yellow awning catches Adrianne's eye. She wants to stop inside. I chuckle at the irony of her choice. Prechi Precha is where I first met Victoire, the Parisian artist who captured my heart during my residence here. The one we are on our way to see.

After a few small purchases, we continued the walk up Rue Ravignan, talking arbitrarily about the differences in Parisian and English architecture—the beauty of both—until we'd arrived at Gallerie Chappe. We were welcomed inside by a petite short haired woman with multicolored plastic spectacles who went on about new artists, old art, expressionism, fauvism, neo-classicism, so many isms, that one suspected disease was the topic of conversation as opposed to fine art. I took a look around the small store-front gallery in awe. Victoire was better than I thought. Much better than her portfolio suggested. Better than me, for sure.

"This is good." Adrianne inspected a large piece, in more shades of blue than I knew existed. I just nodded my head. Good is an understatement. I could tell that Victoire was still the passionate and caring person of years past. But she'd matured. Her style is effortless and true. I knew that she was doing well in Paris. I wanted to make sure that she was appreciated world wide. It was the least I could do.

"Bonjour." A modest voice rang lightly through the room. I turned around.

"Bonjour, Mademoiselle. Cet a ete trop long," I tell her it's been too long.

"Oui." She ignored me and turned her attention to Adrianne, who was knee deep in a painting of hers. "I am Victoire. You are Adrianne Spence?"

Adrianne stood and shook Victoire's outstretched hand.

"I am. It is a pleasure to meet you. Your work is amazing." She turned back towards the Monet-like painting. "There is so much pain in this," Adrianne added. I knew that tone and language. She'd become entranced in the work.

"Pain is there, yes."

"What is it called?" Adrianne probed.

"The Color of Allah." Vic answered as her eyes bored through me. I saw the damage I'd done. Now that I knew how it felt, I was sorry for inflicting that sort of pain on anyone.

"What was the inspiration for this?" Adrianne asked, turning back towards us. Vic didn't hold a punch.

"Heartbreak," she said evenly, as if she'd merely mentioned the word plastic. I remember leaving her. With nothing. No note. No card. No last goodbye. I didn't know what to say.

As women often do, Adrianne picked up on things instantly. I could feel her eyes on us. I wanted to reconcile with Victoire so badly. I knew that I was different than before. But honestly, I truly didn't know how. I feel, yes. But putting things into words . . . I was still working on that.

"I am going to walk through the gallery," Adrianne said.

I decided to take the time to at least find out how Vic was doing. That I could do. "How are you?"

"I am managing," she replied.

"You are doing better than managing," I gestured to the work hanging on the gallery walls. "You are better than me now." We both let out a chuckle. We used to compete. Just to compare technique and style. We'd argue about who was better, then make up in the way that young lovers do.

"Merci. And you?"

"Me? I am trying not to stir up trouble," I answered sheepishly.

"Failing flagrantly I suppose." She half smiled. Memories of us smearing each other in paint clouded me. Instead of a heart-felt apology, I focused on the issue at hand.

"Listen Vic, take this offer. You will do well in the States," I proposed.

"I am not a fan of America, but I will take it because it will make you feel better," she answered. There was a slight smile in her eyes that said it all. *I loved you. I hated you. And I've reconciled.*

"I have seen all that I need to see. Are we ready?" Adrianne asked, startling us both. I didn't know how long she'd been standing there, but my skin was on the other side of the room.

"Yes," I answered.

"Victoire, your work is excellent. We will be in touch with you shortly." Adrianne's all-business tone was back. I kissed Vic on both cheeks and hugged her before exiting.

"Ready for our next showing?" I asked. Adrianne was facing the street, staring quietly into nowhere. Her entire demeanor had changed. I wondered why.

"I thought there was only one today," she said quietly.

"Oui, madame. One *scheduled* visit, yes. This one is a surprise."

"You are full of surprises today." Adrianne's tone was mellow and subdued. The hollow look in her eyes had returned. What had I done?

"Well, this one you'll thank me for—I think." I added playfully. There was no play in her voice or disposition. She was distant and remote. Moody. Perhaps the moodiest person I'd ever met. "Are you sure you're up for it?" I reassured.

A simple head nod from her was it. In fact, Adrianne walked beside me, en mute, for the duration of our journey. She is bothered. But does not pour out her heart. Does the fact that she won't communicate her feelings make her a slave to a society that frowns upon and punishes free expression? Or is she free because she has decided not to express herself by choice? Is freedom in the action? Or the ability to choose when and how one acts? If the latter were true, I'd be the slave and not she. I'd think about it until we arrived at our destination.

"Is this it?" she asked hesitantly. We'd stopped in front of a building that looked like it could be bulldozed any minute.

"Yea. Are you scared?" I asked. She looked it.

"No. I am not scared."

"You sure you want to go in?" One couldn't see indoors, only dark, degenerate walls soaked in mildew, broken glass and pavement at the entrance and the dim flickering of candlelight in the distance. Hearts were being sung out in Portuguese, one couldn't help but nod to the cadence of hands and spoons playing tables like drums, along with the foot stamping of the patrons, or should I say residents of the space. Samba School was in session at this unique squatter spot. We'd reached the favela of Paris.

"Yes, I am sure. I want to go," she replied anxiously. We hadn't spoken more than two words to each other since the gallery visit and since she wasn't in the mood to communicate, I couldn't tell whether the look in her eyes was fear or fascination.

"It's not the Louvre, Adrianne," I said sarcastically. Before I could finish the sentence, she took off. Left me standing right where I was. I had to laugh at that. Truly a piece of work. I trotted, caught up and followed her through a dim corridor that opened up into a massive space. The building was gutted and filled with art. Weirder than weird sculpture. Paintings. A hanging bathtub. Colored ribbon. Old mannequins. And artists. Not just any artists. Aside from being musicians, chefs, painters, sculptors, dancers and designers, they shared a unique trait. They were homeless. I wondered if Adrianne picked that up. It was so far from her world, I doubted it would click.

A toothless gentleman asked if we were hungry. He directed us to an open grill area where food was being prepared, and water served. Organized squatter spots like this one ran differently than most. An abandoned building was conquered by people who had more in mind than slumming. Inhabitants were technically homeless, but they ate. They shared music and art. They'd find a space, christen it, get shut down, move on to the next one. Life was a party. Rent free. Adrianne's eyes were wide as saucers.

"Are you okay?" I asked her.

"Of course I am," she answered as if the question were the most absurd thing she'd heard all day. "What is this place?" She seemed mesmerized. I must admit I sought to surprise her, but I was most surprised. I'd expected discomfort, uneasiness, but got just the opposite. Adrianne walked toward the metal bin that served as the open grill and pulled out a large bill.

"Two bottles of water, please," she asked a woman as slim as the cigarette hanging from her mouth.

"A. Everything here is free."

"Free?" Another unfamiliar term. Metro. Free. We were building her vocabulary today.

I had to stifle a laugh. "Yes, they're homeless. Food is purchased with money that is gathered collectively during the week," I explained. While her mouth formed a giant 'O', the Virginia slim handed Adrianne two small cups of tap water.

She didn't get it. I was laughing for real this time. "No Evian. No Fiji. No Volvic," I teased, removing the cups from her hands. "Just good ol' Parisian tap." She peered inside of the cup as if expecting a sea monster to erupt from its bottom. It was hilarious.

"It's alright. I am thirsty. I can drink this," she answered, and even more astounding was her locating a cup on the table, and placing the large bill inside.

"They take tips, right?" she asked.

I smiled. "Yes babe, I'm sure they won't object to it."

My lover-turned-friend sipped what could possibly be the most distasteful water she'd had in her life and tapped her foot to the welcoming rhythm and voices in the air. She looked good in candlelight.

"I love this place. The music is beautiful," she added. Without warning, all of the work, the distractions, the rationalization, every step I'd taken towards friendship with her evaporated into thin air. I loved her right then more than I had on any other night. Seemed no matter how many steps taken forward, only a tiny one was required to send me spiraling backward. It was as if the slightest snag of a loose thread unraveled an entire knitted sweater. I needed a distraction before I began breaking rules. Quickly.

Scanning the room for a diversion, the most obvious one sat tables over, eyes closed, hands moving rapidly over the table top, head nodding to the cadence of the Samba drummers.

"Excuse me for a moment, I will be back." Adrianne was too enthralled in music to care either way. Making way through small groups of people, a man jumped up and down to the beat. Another sat quietly in a corner in diatribe with himself. A remote image of the Hare Krishna people dancing through Soho Square in London flashed through my mind, and I thought maybe I was wrong to judge them.

"Pablo?" I asked a wiry man completely absorbed in the table rhythm he was creating. I hated to disturb him. No answer. Maybe this wasn't Pablo. The large tattoo of Fidel Castro on his right arm, and one of Che Guevara on his left, gave me my answers. "PABLO!" A second or two of intense focus, and we were in an embrace of old war comrades.

"Amigo! Que paso amigo! Islam! Ahhhhhhhhh!" We hugged again. I hadn't seen him in years.

"Pablo! Mate! Do you know what it took to locate you? You move as a fugitive!" I exclaimed.

"I try!" he replied. We both shared a laugh.

"How'd you find the place?" he asked.

"Nate. He said you were here, and that your art was better than ever." Nate was a transplant, an American living in Paris. He moved after the election—or should I say pre-appointment—of their current president. We all met years ago, while I was here. Pablo and I were a part of the same program, Nate was an actor on location of his current film. "I am curating for Spence Galleries, and am here on special visit," I grinned.

"*The* Spence Galleries?"

"Yes."

"Who'd you fuck?" he asked in jest.

I laughed out loud. If he only knew. "When one of *us* gets into an organization like that, either you've fucked someone or hell is an iceberg," I laughed at the irony of his statement as well as the Cuban-Parisian accent. It made everything funnier. Sort of like Ahmed's weird dialect.

"It was a freak accident." We both shared laughter. Something I'd been missing lately. "As I said, I am on a special visit tonight. Nate told me you were sculpting. He sent a photo via e-mail, and I am here to see the rest. This is a professional visit, Pablo."

"Para mi?" All laughter ceased and Pablo's voice settled into a more serious tone.

Adrianne approached the table wearing the cutest, most playful look. She was enjoying herself. "I was looking for you, I've been dancing." She smiled. Everyone was having way too good of a time. I wanted to settle down and focus on signing Pablo. He's homeless now, but one of the most talented sculptors I knew. Including Paul.

"Pablo Munez, Adrianne Spence." His eyes widened and he began adjusting his attire, as if anything could be done to alter the state of a bullet-holed Assata Shakur tee.

"It is an honor to meet you," Pablo extended a dirty hand.

Adrianne shook it more heartily than she had those at the Louvre dinner. "The pleasure is mine," Adrianne responded. "Are you the artist?"

Pablo looked at me for confirmation. His eyes said: *Am I?*

"Yes . . . yes you are the artist, Pablo." I let out a light chuckle. "This is a studio visit. Now show us the goods." I told him.

"Follow me," he said, leading us into a crowded space filled with the good, the bad, and the ugly. Adrianne was enthralled. Pablo was a nervous wreck. And me? I just wanted to see her differently tonight. As a friend. As a boss. As anything but the love of my life.

29

We were an hour later, stunned, shocked and frankly flabbergasted by what we'd been shown. At a small table supported by crushed soda cans, Adrianne and Pablo were engrossed in each other. She, with questions to rival any award-winning journalist, and he, with as many answers as she had questions.

Pablo excused himself, and Adrianne pounced. "I want to sign him immediately," she pulled out her checkbook.

"Slow down." I placed my hand over hers.

"Of course you think he's worth it." The tone she used dared me to disagree. Of course he was. We wouldn't be here if he weren't. That wasn't the issue.

"Adrianne. Put the check book away."

"You cannot be serious." She was passionate and intense for all the wrong reasons. "We cannot let an artist of his caliber remain—"

"Where will he make the deposit?" I asked of a bank account that I knew not to exist. Another 'O' shaped her mouth.

Pablo returned to the table. Adrianne took matters into her own hands. Cut right to the chase. Offered my friend what was, in his world, a whopping sum of money to start, a decent royalty split, gallery to artist, and other extras that were new to me. Pablo was white as a ghost and I had to explain to him that we did things a bit differently at Spence, offering artists advances and such, to ensure productivity. It was a system I'd come up with, as many artists stressed and starved waiting for galleries to sell their work. Although still white-faced, he understood and hugged the both of us repeatedly. I know the feeling.

"I am unsure of his residential preferences, but there is a small flat in Saint Germain that is not currently occupied. It had been previously used for storage, but I will have it cleared for Pablo. *If he is interested in the accommodation,*" Adrianne said as we made our exit. She really liked him.

"I'm sure he will not object to the offer. Pablo is a skeptic, not an idiot." I was happy that she was impressed with the work of my friend, but I had a question for her. She handled this acquisition differently from the last.

"So you love Pablo Munez." I probed.

"Absolutely. I already have purchasers in mind. His debut collection may not make it out of Paris." She answered matter-of-factly.

"And Victoire?"

A sigh. "Yes, I thought her work was excellent as well," she said slowly.

"But you signed Pablo instantly." Stillness. Thought. She had an affinity for avoiding issues. Mine was for confronting them. At least now it was.

"Yes, I did," was all she said.

"But not Vic."

"Vic?" she asked dubiously.

"Yes. Vic. Victoire. You did not sign her. Why?" We had approached a dimly lit street corner and stopped. Another sigh. "Do you not think she is as talented as Pablo?"

"I have to think about it," she answered defiantly.

"What do you mean you have to think—"

"What is the nature of your relationship with Victoire?" she interrupted.

"She is the artist, I am looking to acquire her work."

Adrianne turned towards me. We were eye to eye. "Islam. What is the nature of your relationship with her?"

"Why?"

"Answer the question," Adrianne urged.

"I just did."

"Alright." She fiddled with the fringe piece on her bag. "It seems the question needs rephrasing. What *was* the nature of your relationship with her." A simmering Adrianne placed her weight on one foot, determined to compile answers before steps forward.

"She was my girlfriend."

A wince. A slight change in posture. The digestion of words. A composed reply. "Do you think that is good for business?" she asked squarely.

Good for business? "Fuck—I mean, what the hell do you mean, is it good for business? What type of question is that, Adrianne? She was my girlfriend almost ten years ago and she's talented, and I can't believe we're having this conversation! Good for business? Shit. Are *we* good for business?"

"We?" she asked as if the thought had never crossed her mind.

"Yes, we. You and I. I and you. Are we good for business Adrianne?" I was incredulous. Couldn't believe we were ruining an evening with this nonsense.

"There is no you and I."

"Is that why you signed Pablo and not Victoire? Is that why we are on a street corner in Paris arguing over foolishness? Because there is no you and I?"

"No! That is not the cause of this argument! I am simply becoming tired of drawing lines between you and every woman in the room! Islam and Victoire! Islam and the singer! Islam and the sales clerk! Islam and bloody candy striper! You're a fucking slot machine, for Christ's sake!"

"Slot machine?" I asked between chuckles. A slight laugh betrayed her. I didn't want to argue. I just wanted to enjoy the remainder of the night.

"I don't want to argue. You are not good at it."

To be honest I didn't mind the outburst. At least she wasn't completely numb when it came to me. It's been hard to tell. Just as we'd began to walk, my mobile rang. I glanced at the screen. It was a call that I couldn't ignore.

"Islam, here. Yes . . . no. I've been on studio visits all day. Tonight? That is possible . . ." Kharet. The striking young curator had mastered the art of communicating in a way that most artists wished to. To say but not. A simple inquiry of my availability resembled an invitation to engage her for the night. In paintings. In positions. One could never truly tell. "Yes, Ms. Siddiq. I will try. Alright . . . I will more than try . . . Yes. Yes. I . . . recall that, yes." Kharet's ways cut through anything solid. Marriage. Friendship. Piety. It wasn't what she said, but how she said it. "Yes, tonight. Until then." I closed the slim casing and was greeted by eyes that held more contempt than inquisition.

"Was that Kharet?" Adrianne asked.

"Yes."

"Have they made their decision yet?" Her foot tapped lightly to an unheard rhythm.

"You would know before I, wouldn't you?" I replied.

"Would I?" The response was laced with derision. What was that supposed to mean? I decided to ignore the cynical tone of voice.

"Would you like to stop by the artists' square in Place de Teatre?"

"Take me home," she snapped.

"What is bothering you, Adrianne?"

"I am not bothered," she stated flatly.

"Yes, you are."

"No, I am not." She was sharp and irritated. The last time I coerced her into a discussion, she tossed at my forehead every object excluded from Noah's ark. This time I would let it go. She stopped mid step.

"Did you sleep with her?"

There it was. The ton of bricks. They were impossible to hold for an entire day. I thought about her question. And the look in her eyes. *Lie to me.* Women. When they do not want you, they don't want anyone else to. "Why?"

"Did you sleep with Kharet?" she repeated.

"Did you sleep with Mohammed?" The question was arbitrary but I was caught off guard. Any diversion would do.

"We were involved," she answered briskly. Her focus was more on receiving answers than giving them. Now stop the nonsense and answer me. Did you sleep with Kharet? Did you bed her?"

"Are you asking as my agent or as my woman?"

"ISLAM!" What instinctively begin as a rant, instantly calmed into a long exhale through clenched teeth. A low and even toned voice cut through the bullshit. "I am going to ask you once more. Only once." Her eyes closed momentarily and the retort was slow and seething. "Did . . . you . . . sleep with her?" she asked. Black licorice lace. Ringlets. Heels. Intentions good and bad. They all swirled around in my head like bottom shelf liquor. "I called you twice after dinner last night." There was the cue not to waste time in elaborate fabrication. Don't lie but lie. Women were complicated creatures.

"No," was my answer.

"You're a fucking liar," was hers.

"I don't understand what you want from me. Are you asking as my agent, Adrianne? Or as my—"

"Why can't you tell me the truth?!?!" she screamed.

"Why can't you tell me you love me?" I matched.

"Tell me, Islam, tell me right now . . . tell me you slept with the bitch."

"Tell me you love me."

"Tell me what you did. Did you touch her? Did your put your bloody hands on her? . . ."

"Tell me you are in love with me, Adrianne . . ." We were speaking simultaneously, neither of us able to hear the other over our own voices. Back and forth back and forth. "What do you want from me, A? I don't know what you want. What you say and do is never the same . . ." I went on. As did she. My love was fuming. And changing right before me. She was so beautiful. The street lamps made her more enchanting than I'd remembered.

Before I could stop myself, I'd silence the source of my intoxication as would a lover. Not a fighter. Lips were packed into each other. Hands moved across my neck, over my head and up and down my back. Souls flowed into and out of one another without reserve.

"Stop it." She pulled away. I stopped. She pulled my face back to hers. What was first a heated and feverish episode turned into a slow and deliberate kiss.

"Damn it!" she exclaimed.

"What?" What was wrong? I reached for her. She backed away.

"Don't touch me. Do not. Touch. Me." A mantra of don'ts. "I am finished with you. I . . . I am finished. I cannot—I *will not*, see you like this anymore . . . I will not allow it . . ."

The rose of me reasoned with herself, and all I heard was, *"Kiss me. Kiss me, love . . ."*

That is what I did. A hand hit my chest gently.

"We are finished," she said softly.

"Finished?" Adrianne looked at me sternly. She was serious. I didn't believe her. I leaned into her again.

"Islam. Stop it!" she scolded. A simple statement. A blow to the stomach. I felt rejected.

"You're serious."

"Yes, I am." I scanned her eyes for fault, for ambiguity. An image of her pinned to the bathroom wall of the penthouse flashed before me. She's not serious. I pulled her close, eye to eye, so that she'd see that I was.

"Adrianne. You are forever joined to me. There is no such thing as finished. Nothing can be done about it. This . . ." I motioned between us, ". . . is out of our hands." I said simply.

"I am married."

"That is what I am trying to tell you," I answered.

"To Cooper."

"You do not wish to be."

"But I am."

"He is not God."

"Some would beg to differ," she said.

"You can do as you please, Adrianne. You do not wish to be with me?" I asked.

"This is my reality. And you can not even tell me a simple truth." There was hurt in her voice. A first. My phone rang again. It was another call that would prove difficult to ignore.

"Good evening."

"Islam. Where the hell is Adrianne?" Cooper asked incredulously.

"She is standing in front of me." I was tired of this. Whatever he asked of me I would answer.

"Would you place her on the phone?"

I handed it to her.

"Hello," she said solemnly. "I shut it off . . ." Her voice rose an octave. "Well I am sorry that I am not as attached to this electronic leash as you . . . Yes, it has been all day . . . I have. . . . we've been on visits. Cooper . . . Cooper! I am not having this conversation tonight. Why? Why do you wish to speak to him? Will he say any differently? No, I am not. It is of no importance. Yes. We will. Yes . . . Love." She closed the casing and placed it into my hand. Raised her hands to her forehead. Let out a long-winded stream of air.

"Adrianne, look at me." She did. Glassy eyes met mine, and the man in me wanted to protect her from hurting. But truth was truth. "Is whether I'd slept with anyone a matter of importance if you do not love me enough? If you do not love yourself enough to love me? Kharet. Would it even matter if I had?" I wanted to hear her say it. Say that I mattered to her. That there would be no Cooper, no Mohammed, no weekend love. Just us. I wanted more than anything, for her to give herself to me. I had her heart. I wanted her soul.

We walked. Adrianne looked ahead, as if the answers she sought were on sidewalks and city streets. On the metro, we rode in silence. Upon our exit, I took her hand, more of courtesy than possession, and we walked the mile run of Place de Resistance to a beautifully lit tower that told our story more vividly than we ever could. I loved her. She loved me. Under the Eiffel Tower or the Brooklyn Bridge. But it was not enough. Forever love wasn't enough somehow.

"Goodnight, Adrianne," I offered. I stood politely at the gated entryway, watching her take each stair one at a time. She paused halfway to the top.

"Care for tea?" she asked quietly. Never turning to face me, or confirm my acceptance of her invitation, she turned the key and stepped inside. She was sure that I was behind her. I was.

30

"You sit there. I'll sit here." Adrianne motioned toward two chairs and placed a small silver tea set onto the table.

"What type of tea are you having?" While she fumbled around with ceramic, herbs and steam, I attempted to make myself comfortable in the small chair. I shifted and fidgeted a bit. It wasn't working. I was uncomfortable with her being so close, yet so far from me. I reached for her. She intercepted my hand. Used the other to light a single candle on the small table.

"Just tea," she said. The serious look in her eyes prompted me to straighten up a tad. Put my urges and feelings aside and respect her wishes. The thought of being nothing more than friends with her made me sick, but if it was what she wanted, I would try. Maybe we'd simply talk tonight. Adrianne pressed a button or two and the smooth, soulful falsetto of Robin Thicke's voice gave the candle lit room a warm feeling.

"I can do better, than make love to you . . ."

"Who does he sound like?" I asked. If she knew her music the way she knew her art the answer would be on the tip of her tongue.

"Everyone who sings in soprano over soul is not Marvin Gaye," she rebutted her own answer. Her eyes dared me to challenge her.

"But he is close," I replied.

"As are quite a few young men who love the legend. It's inescapable, the influence," she answered astutely. She raised an eyebrow. I chuckled. Too smart for her own good. I wanted to ask her if she'd done something different today, possibly a facial or new skin cream. There was a unique glow about her. It wasn't that of love, I've become familiar with that sort of light. This was different. Maybe it was the tan. As I tried to pinpoint the cause of radiance, we sipped and spoke of matters arbitrary in nature, memories of family and quirky friends. Since my Brooklyn spillover I'd found it easier to speak of my mum, and Adrianne told easily of her own family's ways.

"As I said, Daddy loved his daughters." She was in the middle of a story that I'm sure was to be an interesting one, when a lone thought crept in. Daughters? I thought she was an only child?

"You have a sister?" I asked. Another one of those dark waves flashed over her and the free, comfortable manner in which she spoke to me retreated back into its shell. I'm not sure of why the dark side of her comes and goes as it does, but I do know one thing. It has been with her since we've met. This secret, this thing, this undercurrent that presents itself as composure and resembles reserve, feels like something else to me. Calm and collection is what she displays to the world but what I see in her, what I feel is torment.

"I. . . had a sister, yes," she responded solemnly.

"What happened?"

"Suicide."

"Why?" She took her usual route and didn't answer. And although the look this time was unusually frantic, it was familiar. She was in a box. Not a coffin. Not a hole. But a box. She was screaming, but there was no sound. Crying but there were no tears. Everything in her was shaking, but the box stood still. I knew the feeling. I knew darkness well. I wondered if sunrise for her would ever come and if it did, would it bring freedom, insanity or both?

The disc in the CD player changed and the sound of soft violin, light piano strokes and Fiona Apple's depressing but heartfelt voice told the beginnings of Adrianne's life story as if she were there herself.

"Your first orgasm?" Adrianne asked as a smile appeared over a soul that I knew felt like crying.

"My what?" I wasn't in the mood to change the subject.

"Who granted you the first one?"

"A thirty-year-old art instructor," I half smiled at the memory of her climaxing before I did. "I was fifteen."

"You're smiling," Adrianne said as we both let out a light chuckle.

"I am. And yours?" I figured it must have been Cooper, since they'd known each other from childhood. Adrianne shifted slightly, swirled the remnants of herbs and warm water at the bottom of her cup, and stared inside, seeming to wish the vortex was strong enough to take her with it. "Who was yours with, A?" I asked again.

She paused before answering, "My father," she said plainly. I knew I hadn't heard her correctly.

"Pardon me?"

"Daddy. We had a governess and I was home schooled for years. Always thought it was our special time together. One of the special things we kept to ourselves. I had no idea that it was wrong until I left for boarding school."

I was speechless. There were many lurid tales of crude, heartless experiences that hurt young girls. Never had I heard of one that gave pleasure. What type of sick shit is this? "You climaxed?" I felt myself sinking into a place that I'm sure Adrianne feared most. Judgment. Misunderstanding. Part of me wanted to stop the conversation. I wanted to see her as purely as I always had. Her demeanor changed. Her guard was up. She dared me to do as she expected. To judge her. To leave. Since this was completely over my head, trust me, I wanted to. The old me who didn't know love well enough to suffer—didn't know that it was mostly suffering, wanted out. Anyone who could enjoy sexual encounters with their father was far more capable in creating their own reality than I ever was. Too capable.

"Yes, I did. More than once. My love for my father was different from my sister's. Although we never spoke of it, she hated him, and took herself out of her misery as soon as she could. I enjoyed the exchange and felt closer to him. Until I learned the truth." A piercing stare tested my loyalty. I wasn't sure of how I felt. If I had the capacity to deal with something like this. She continued. "When I questioned his habits, his way of showing love, he shut me out of his life. Accused me of all types of things. All I knew is I didn't want to partake of the exchange ever again. He made me pay for that by taking his love with it."

Adrianne saw the doubt, the confusion in me, and the tough piercing glare she held, melted almost instantly, like soft ice cream on a hot summer day. She looked depleted. At that moment, I knew love. I didn't want her to feel alone. Protecting her from hurt was all I wanted to do. I knew that I'd never leave her for any reason. I couldn't.

"How did he die?"

"Cooper walked in on Father attempting to force himself on me one night and shot him."

"Shot him?"

"Once in the head. Cooper's always loved me. And he's always been a tyrant. It can be an admirable trait in most cases, but in some, it can be quite callous."

"He loved you that much?" I asked.

"To Cooper, love is ferocity. It's what he understands best. Of this incident, we said that Father was robbed by an outsider and that I barely escaped. Since I was already bruised, it stuck." As my love continued, I was speechless. "I didn't want Father to die. I just wanted him to stop." This was a lot. I was a nervous wreck. But with Adrianne, there wasn't a tear in sight. "At times, Cooper takes pride in reminding me in so many ways that the case is still open. Father was a high-ranking government official. If the truth is ever found, repercussion would be endless. Especially in the case of inheritance. The pension my family receives would be cut since I was the cause of death."

"You weren't the cause, Adrianne."

"Yes, I was." We were still. I wanted to reach out to her, to comfort her, to be free enough to do those things. I should be able to do that. Love her pain away. Instantly, I hated that I was unable to. I knew she didn't want to be touched. I knew that. And she wouldn't look at me. Should I reach for her? Should I stroke her hair? What would make her feel better? If life was truly about passion, connection, spirit and freedom then the height of it had to be love. Tonight, things in me are wired differently. The current of this woman runs through me so that it doubles my strength when we are both in accord, and depletes it when we aren't. Right now, I just wanted to alleviate the pain. For her. For me. She was tormented, but I felt it most. Part of me wanted to surrender the connection. It was too much. The other part, knew that I may not ever be able to.

"Come here." I was standing at the foot of her bed.

"I can't." I'd pretend not to notice the quiver in her voice, or the slight trembling of her fingertips. She will never know how much I love her.

"Not for that," I answered, "Come here and sit. I'm going to sketch you." It was the only other way I knew to connect. While I fumbled and arranged rock-like pieces of soft charcoal, Adrianne placed her cup down, and walked tentatively towards me. "Here is fine," I gestured to one of the four neatly arranged corners of the bed. We sat. Me on a small footstool and she, facing me. I pulled her closer. Eye to eye, there would be no hiding place. If she wouldn't cry out, the rocks would.

Our unique means of communicating silently began,

"*You are fragile.*"

"*I am strong.*"

"*I love you.*"

"*I know you do.*"

"*You love me.*"

"*I do not want to.*"

I adjusted her face, as to allow more light into eyes that needed all the illumination they could get tonight. As I stared into her, I wished for the natural light of hers that had been covered by clouds all day.

I won't leave you.

You don't know that.

I won't hurt you.

How can you be sure?

I love me too much.

Smile. It was good to see. My hands moved quicker, to capture a full moon smile that was rare as it was beautiful. I sketched and stared and sketched. She stared back into me. I stopped mid stoke to gather a better understanding of my subject. The intensity of her glare. The small beads of sweat forming on her upper lip. In a flash, we were in my hallway, lying on the floor, staring into each other's eyes. I, searching for truth, for love, for light, and she, for a morning that never seemed to come. I wanted her to know that I'd bring sun in as many ways as it existed. In freedom, in lilies, in lullabies, in love. That I'd accept her. Accept everything. Even what I disliked of her I loved. That there was no other, that she was all of me—in fact, the best part—and that my definition of love would hold true, under any magnification, under any scope. It would have to. It was the only way I knew to live. A light hand on mine stopped the back and forth motion of my own. *Love me gently.* I knew the look well.

Unsure if the look in my love's eyes was genuine, or a figment of an imagination that had overtaken me, I looked for affirmation in other ways. I stood, took her hands, stretched them upward until her fingertips rested comfortably at the base of my wrists. I inhaled. She exhaled. Our arms moved outward, and then downward slowly, as they had on a first night in a London hotel. There was no rush for possession or physical intimacy. No contracts, or containment. Just stillness. And us. Inhaling the scent of a love that took no prisoners and made no mistakes.

As inspiration often does, the notion of just being, experiencing her spirit, sharing in a perhaps more powerful way, hit me without warning. I wanted her, but differently. Unable to express it, I'd resolved to simply stand with her hands touching mine and let go. Breathe. Breathe what I want to say to her, how I want to hold her and make her feel. If she is troubled, breathe a horizon of understanding, if no one understands, I do. If she is frustrated, breathe solitude, if she is without love, breathe love. If she is without passion and freedom, give it to her. I realize that I am inspired, I am inside of her in another way, and upon this realization, I feel like a god of sorts. Creating a world where she can exist as she wishes. Not as she is.

"I'm here, babe. I'm here," I whispered as I wrapped my arms around her tightly. A hug was all I could offer to protect her from the cunning of a man who would prey on the innocent love of a child. Forehead on my chest, Adrianne's hands drifted upward, and placed mine in an area where just an hour ago would have been sweet nirvana. I was hesitant.

"Please," she said softly.

"Are you sure?" I asked.

"Yes."

I didn't know what to do. Virginity is of will, not of occurrence. No matter what was taken from her as a child, Adrianne's was still, a virgin soul. Hers I wanted. But as a gift. Not as an acquisition or conquest. It was important for me to know the difference between myself and Cooper. Myself and Mohammad. Me and her father. I needed to know that she trusted me with the most important aspect of her. With the only thing that transcended time.

Adrianne sat on the bed. The glaze in her eyes was warm and wanting. I laid her down, and did the reverse of what I've always done. Instead of jumping into her, I took a step backward.

The candlelight in the room flickered, and although I've been here, in this position many times past, with Adrianne, with Yasara, with countless other women, I felt like a virgin myself. Palms were sweaty. My heart was racing. To be honest, aside from waking up to her every morning, I had no idea of what I wanted to do. I was however, sure of one thing. As for connection, as for the freedom and passion of love, I've become unsure of the tipping point. If I accepted what she offered, I'd be too far in. I felt it.

I laid next to her, but still. Adrianne's hand found mine, and what initially began as somewhat of an awkward gesture, turned into a fluid and beautiful kiss. There was no rush. For the first time, I felt as if I had forever with her. Another nerve wracking feeling. Forever is a long time. What if I can't keep the promise?

Her legs were closed tight. One might as well say they were clamped shut as compared to their usual position. Wanting to assure her of my intentions, I initially resorted to the first thought that came to mind, *I love you*, as that was the only thing I'd become sure of over recent months. Realizing the powerlessness of the phrase to her, how much it didn't mean, I'd cut through the distrust, the grey, the protective sheath Adrianne's held to herself for all of these years, and prove my definition of love another way. I stopped everything. The kisses, the movement. With no interchange, no back and forth inside of her, she was forced to open her eyes. I wanted her to see me for who I was. To see sunrise.

Determined to lie there until she did, I passed time by taking smaller pleasures. A nudge of a cheekbone. A fingertip on an eyebrow. And although my love was underneath me, I wrapped my arms around her frame tightly, as the look in her eyes wasn't of calm or reserve. It was of crystal in an opera house awaiting a final note.

When heart and legs loosened, and I'd received the invitation of life from her, I didn't take it lightly. In fact, I didn't take at all. I gave.

We moved together. Not against each other, not for desire or passion or selfishness. We moved as one, ours a wave of giving and receiving as a single entity. The friction, or lack of, gave a different type of pleasure. There was no tingling, no cloudiness to fight. With no control of anything, I'd simply resolve to allow the complete energy, the strength of us, to flood my entire body. Adrianne moved into me and I into her. The heated feeling that normally gathered at the center of me, had seemingly run its course through my entire body. I felt it at my fingers, at the tips of my toes. And Adrianne seemed to be overwhelmed by the same. We moved so slowly, and so closely together, that it was hard to tell if the throbbing, the heart beating pulse I felt was from she or I.

Seconds passed, and it became easier to tell the difference.

"Babe . . . b-baby . . . n-not yet . . ." Adrianne's stutters and cries were flagrant. I felt the throbbing, the shakes. I could feel her struggle against the pleasure I gave, for to succumb would be to give herself to me fully. Her cries weren't loud, but they were frantic. Attempting to ward off the inevitable, Adrianne seemed to take as many short breaths in a row as her body would allow. Her determination in any other case would be admirable, as that of a bloodied contender who wouldn't go down without a fight.

I kissed her deeply. The light, the heated energy had spread to every corner of me and I couldn't fight it anymore. I didn't want to. I gave in. In a moment that seemed like an eternity, Adrianne fought hard. I saw the fight in her eyes, and also saw that she was losing it. I heard my own cries and sounds mix with hers. There were things of me that I would be forced to give. Some of which I wanted to keep to myself. Nightmares. Cold sweats and nights without heat or love. The hanging doll with the half-smile and the gift that was never given. In this room but out of this world right now, I understood her struggle. The unknown was a great fear for all of us. But I gave. All of those things from me to she, came and went with the pleasure like a west wind.

We were eye to eye when she cried out. Although the movement between us was slow as molasses, she scratched. Bit my lips. Pushed me off and back onto her. Through her uncontrolled cries and unstoppable pulses and shakes, I'd hold her tightly, and she'd enter a similar tunnel of freedom. The eruption of arbitrariness in feeling, seeing, and hearing. The enjoyment of the mind's lack of discipline, the joy of human unreason. She trembled and cursed and agreed with Nietzsche more than she knew, but would continue to fight a war that couldn't be won. As she convulsed and quivered and twisted her face into a million expressions, the look in her eyes said that she wanted to be stronger than she was, but couldn't do anything about it. Surrender is sweet for one who has fought an entire lifetime. Unaware if she knew this or not, submission *was* strength.

"What is love?" After minutes of sweating and lying still, Adrianne posed the question as if she'd never heard it in her life.

I smiled. Placed a simple kiss on her forehead. "I don't know. Why don't you tell me?" I asked. She moved closer to me and positioned her face to mine.

"Love is light," she said calmly. "It's light. It's liberty. It's freedom. It's what it means to be you. To be loved is to be accepted. To be accepted is to be free. It means there is no repercussion for being who you are." I nodded slowly, taking in the meaning and its definitions, trying hard not to grin. "Are you free, Islam?" she asked.

"Are you asking if I am loved?" I replied playfully, watching the light that she spoke of, dance freely through smiling eyes.

"I am asking if you are accepted for who you are," she said smartly.

"You are asking me to define what cannot be defined from my point of view," I responded to the light-hearted sarcasm with a kiss on her collarbone.

"I am asking a simple question," she said. "Are . . ." Kiss. "You . . ." Kiss. ". . . Loved?" I returned each one of her kisses heartily. Adrianne's funny. She could just tell me herself.

"Are you?" I asked.

"Am I?" She answered the question with a question in her typical manner except she was blushing terribly. I chuckled at her ways. Reverse psychology 101. She knew I loved her and more importantly, she knew that she loved me. Expressing it freely was something she'd have to get used to. I moved her from my side and placed her on top of me.

"Would you do something for me?" I asked.

"What would you like?" she replied happily, while making herself comfortable in her customary manner.

"Close your eyes, forget that I am here, and imagine yourself at your purest moment." An inversion of her request on a Brooklyn park lawn, caused the appearance of a peaceful smile. Eyes closed momentarily, then reopened.

"What's wrong?" I asked.

"Do it with me."

"What?"

"Close your eyes and imagine," she said. Eyes closed, heart and soul open, we'd entered a world where there was no pretense. No pressure. No politics or need for asylum. Souls who'd become used to dancing on their own, darted through playgrounds and kicked sandcastles together without reserve. At my purest moments in life, I am virgin. I am free. I remember love.

She sleeps peacefully, on top of me. There are no words or imagination. Just the stillness of the room. My love shifts. Climbs me like a mountain in her sleep. At this moment, at sunrise, I don't face the east. I don't get on my knees and pray. I make a single declaration. I will not move from her. That is my position. If I needed to be patient I would be. If I had to hold back at times, so be it. If I had to grow a bit more, to stretch, to alter my perspective, I would. I'd do whatever it took. Unsure of what that meant, I'd decided to simply stay long enough to find out.

I'd say to sunrise, that it is most definitely strange. Tiny rays of light peek through blinds and drapes. I feel the heat from Adrianne's breath as she snores lightly on my chest. I feel myself giving into sleep. Happily so, because I am where I want to be. In a world where what matters most to me counts. I sleep with that notion on top of me and smile. The sun is up.

31

I am between slumber and consciousness, in a place where thoughts and dreams play, each unaware of the differences of the other, like small children discovering friendship for a first time. While night and day touch faces, I thoroughly enjoy this semi-conscious state, aware of the presence of sleep, yet able to hear myself think, and see the color behind my lids take shape and form. I see a few things. New paintings and color. Inspiration and ideas. And Adrianne and I, in morning conversation over tea, light years from today, in a state of calm. There is no coming or going. No north or south. No having or being had. All that rests between us is stillness and comfort. That's what I hear and see while consciousness taps me lightly on the shoulder this morning. Behind closed lids, I am seeing peace. Something I've never known before.

My arm reaches about a foot or so right, to what has become Adrianne's usual place beside me when I wake. I want to pull her onto me and relax myself into consciousness, but I don't feel her.

"Adrianne." I call. No response. "Adriaaaaane." She must be on the other side of the flat. "Baaaaaabe. . . ." I yell. Still, no response. I look at the clock beside me. It's late afternoon. She must have stepped out. Hopefully she's due back shortly, I'm due to CDG in under two hours. My flight leaves at six.

A shiny silver place setting on last night's tea table caught my eye. Grapes, apricots, kiwi and berries filled a small plate. Fresh croissants, assorted jams and a sterling pitcher filled to the brim with morning juice greeted me with a smile. Completely famished, I slid into my boxers and sat. Facing me, was a small note in familiar handwriting.

Good morning sweetie,

You are sleeping quite peacefully and I do not want to wake you. Plans have changed. I am not taking the jet back to the US. I am instead, flying commercially. This meant an earlier than planned departure. Please eat breakfast, as I know you often skip it. If you are not too tired, we will have our time together this evening in New York. I will miss you until then.

-A.

Damn. Twelve hours door to door. I have to wait that long to see her? I crushed a strawberry, took a swig of juice and sulked. Then chuckled. Can't believe me. I'm what my brother calls whipped.

Having eaten heartily, I wipe my mouth, gather my things, and head back to the hotel. I'm always running ridiculously late. Today is no different. Unable to count the number of flights missed on a mere technicality, I alerted the penthouse staff to my departure and almost flew past the tower, into my room and into an awaiting taxi. Tonight. Me. My lady. It was all the incentive I needed to fly.

On the same carrier that always got me to where I needed to be safely, I prepared myself for landing as was suggested by the captain. The applause this time was sincere, as I could hardly tell if we'd touched ground in New York. I liked this pilot. Wished I could fly with him every time. He's gotten me seven hours closer to my love without making the evening news.

New York was New York. Hard accents and harder stares hit me directly in the chest as soon as the plank met the gate. A smiling face from a beautiful friend greeted me at the terminal exit.

"Well hello there, mister! Welcome back!" Lydia exclaimed,

eagerly attempting to remove the small carryon from my shoulder. She was so sweet.

"Thank you," I stopped her before she could grab the bag and gave her a big hug. "But no thank you. I'm sorry, but I cannot have a beautiful woman carrying a bag through an airport on my behalf. I'd be some sort of joke you told a girlfriend while you were pissed with me," I laughed.

"Oh whatever, Islam!" she laughed along.

"Lyd! Of course you agree! You know how you women are . . . girl . . ." I sucked my teeth, ". . . his broke ass had me carrying that bag all *through* that airport! . . ." As I continued my female impersonation, Lydia cracked up.

"Islam, give me the damn bag." She held her hand out to me and I placed a small paper bag of chips and bottled water squarely into her palm.

"You're giving me French fries to carry?" she asked incredulously.

"Chips." I answered.

"Fries damn it! You Brits and your complicated English!" Lydia and I snapped right into character, walking, talking and laughing about as usual. It was good to see her.

"So how'd it go?" she asked eagerly. Images of my Parisian trip—the museum, Adrianne's anger, Kharet's wonderful face and figure, and last night's confession—if one could call it that, flashed in and out of view.

"Honestly Lyd, I am not sure how it went. I showed up. Everything else is out of my hands," I replied.

"Well did they like your work?" she asked as we threw the first set of real luggage I've ever had in the back of the large truck.

"It seems *she* did," I emphasized.

"Oh lord," Lydia started the car, but stared at me through the corner of her eyes. "What, or rather *who* did you do?" Badu's smooth voice filled the interior with warmth, and we both nodded our heads to the beat.

"What mix is this?" I asked of the unfamiliar blend of drums and sounds playing over the familiar voice. It sounded like she and Zap Mama, the Afro-Euro futuristic soul group. Hard to tell, as their voices were almost identical.

"Don't change the subject!" she laughed openly. "If there's a she involved, there's usually a penis hidden somewhere in the story!" she exclaimed. I had to laugh at that one. She was cute.

"I'm not changing the subject. The curator was a woman, I think she liked my work but it can be hard to tell. You know how you women can be," I offered, grinning impishly.

"Yes, I do. We can be especially hard to read after we fuck you the first night we've met and never hear from you again," she said playfully.

"Lydia!" I yelled.

"Islam!" she yelled back. "Don't act like you don't know what I'm talking about! Your brother's always told me there was something with you and women," she chuckled. "I had to see it myself to believe it . . . poor Lia." I busted out laughing. That was a mistake. But Kharet . . . whew. Lucky I'm a one-woman man now. That's what I tell her.

"I am a one woman man . . . apparently," I offer.

"And what is this woman's name, Mary the Virgin?" she asked sarcastically. I had to laugh at that too.

"She is *definitely* not a virgin," I replied. "Her name is Adrianne." It felt good to say her name. To associate it with mine.

"The woman from the park?" Lydia asked.

"Uh, yes. She would be the one."

"So, you didn't sleep with the curator?" she grinned.

"I . . . had some interaction with her, yes. But only enough to paint." I said sheepishly. "

Jesus Islam!" She was cracking up. "You know they were stoning guys like you in the Bible days," she said. We merged onto a traffic-ridden Belt Parkway. The brake lights of about a million New Yorkers glowed like Christmas bulbs in front of us. We'd be in traffic for a while. I thought about Adrianne coming by and didn't want her to have to wait outside for me. Besides, I wanted to do something special for her tonight. Maybe I'd cook dinner. The thought of it made me laugh inside. Me? Cook?

"Lydia, I'm going to need your help with something tonight." I began.

"I refuse to be an accomplice to some young lady's untimely demise," she said playfully.

"I've never done this before, but I figured I'd try and make dinner tonight. She—the main one—is coming to see me and . . . well you know the rest." I offered sheepishly. Lydia gave me a weird look.

"Which one is this again?" she asked.

"The only one." I answered. "And although I know what she likes, well at least somewhat, I am unsure of how to prepare it. I mean, I've never really utilized the kitchen much . . ." I stammered.

"Oh my god, Islam . . . you're really in love."

"Something like that," I winked at her.

"Okay . . ." she said slowly. You have to tell me everything. Don't leave a single detail out," she said as we veered off the parkway and made a b-line towards Manhattan. "This is possibly a moment in history." As she pinched my cheek, I saw the smirk and playful grin spread across her lips and decided to give as much as I could in earnest.

"Well, there was an artist's party at a warehouse in London . . ." She listened from Queens to Manhattan, through grocery aisles, and over the Brooklyn Bridge about freedom, passion, and how I felt like I had no control over me anymore. She smiled as I told her how unsure I was of everything other than wanting to be with Adrianne for a lifetime and frowned when I told her that she was married. Above all, Lydia didn't say, speak or judge. As we climbed the stairs to the brownstone with grocery bags and luggage, she did only what I needed her to. She listened.

A lone white candle dressed a table that spoke volumes of the chef. Lydia was amazing with freshly grilled salmon and vegetables, not to mention a wonderful dessert that I had plans for way beyond spoon to mouth tonight. I checked the time. Adrianne should be here soon. Her flight should have landed a few hours before mine.

The passing of an hour brought worry. I didn't know what carrier she flew, so I couldn't check her arrival time. There were no reported taxi accidents from any of the airports. But then again, she would be chauffeured anyway. Another hour gone by, and I rung her up relentlessly. Sometimes I'd hear ringing on the other end, other times it went straight to voicemail. The food was cold. But I left it out. I did the arrangement myself and wanted her to see it. I didn't know if I could do it again. When the phone rang, I'd be disappointed, as it was only Paul, checking for my safe arrival, and to see if "we" had become rich yet, and if it were okay for him to take a celebratory shopping trip. Where the hell was Adrianne?

Another hour in, and worry turned to anger. If she weren't okay I would have heard by now. The least she could do was call and say she'd be late. I couldn't attribute the episode to my own karma, as no matter what situations I've been in with women, I've always at least called if I were going to be late. A quick glance at the time. Hours gone by felt like minutes. Time read: two fifty seven a.m. She's selfish.

There was no excuse. A call took less than two minutes. I'd fall asleep, and awaken at the kitchen table, candle burned to a nub, the aroma of old fish and kitchen cleanser creating a nauseating stench throughout the flat. No missed calls. No note on the door. She didn't show. Pissed wasn't the word.

I reached into the small tin container where I keep the contact numbers of women who catch my eye. A bit of searching and I find the one I am looking for. Lauren. The porcelain doll with the waist length locks, beautiful brown eyes and long legs. We chat and I invite her to one of the biggest art parties of the year.

Adrianne doesn't love me. If she did, the things that came naturally to me, would come naturally to her. I'd sum all of that up in two words. Fuck her.

32

The meatpacking district of New York City reminded me of Shoreditch in London. Warehouses, gutted and gentrified lofts, artsy, well-designed restaurants, good-looking people in interesting exchange. Home of APT, otherwise known to forward party-goers as The Apartment, it's one of the few areas that can actually cope with London's gritty tech-contemporary art scene.

Ninth Avenue looks good tonight. People headed in every direction, I double-check my wears in the glass window of one of the best brick oven pizzerias in the city. No fashionistas. No designer jeans. There is no one in there that catches my eye. Anyone who normally would, I suppose, is on the rooftop of a multi-million dollar industrial loft, the one I was en route to. Even I had to throw on the crocodile cowboy boots, tattered Rock and Republics, and expose a tattoo or two.

A lone man protected a steel door as if it were the Garden of Eden.

"Your name?" I'm greeted inhospitably. I've gotten used to it.

"Islam Ian. My guest will arrive within the hour." He checks my wears before he checks my name on the list and circles hers. Apparently I've made the cut.

"And you are here for?"

"Aperture," I offered the code name for Dissident Display, a multimedia art group who'd basically become the poster boys for trendsetting worldwide. Although most popular for their eclectic video visuals, Adrian and Ayo had mistakenly conquered the worlds of fashion, film and contemporary art as well. Just a look around at the guests of the evening would tell the story. Models, actors, film directors, musicians and the world's most forward thinking creators were spreading vibe and stimulus through the air of the rooftop loft.

There were Mohawks and spikes. Prada. Puma. Large projected images of runway shows from New York and Milan on white walls. A vintage camera took random snapshots of guests in compromising positions. A large poster with endless sexual positions informed the artsy-chic crowd of the accepted behaviors of the night and a glowing sliver of a pool that split the loft in half was the cherry atop the ambience. This was wicked.

"Hi," a sweet voice offered as she and a friend made way through the crowd with twin martinis.

"Hello," I offered back. Aside from business—and there was much to tend to tonight—what determined a good night overall, was the quality of the female demographic of the event. So far there's one . . . two . . . three, four . . . six . . . a red headed brown girl made eye contact with me and . . . damn it I lost count.

"Are you enjoying yourself?" The red head asked coyly.

"So far I am," was all I said.

"Love the accent," she smiled and walked away. The walk. It was a blessing. I hope she is being paid well to walk like that. A mental note. Don't leave without her. I'd perish the thought as soon as it appeared. I forgot. Lauren's meeting me tonight. Sand to the beach. A curse.

On an elevated deck, I recognized a favorite DJ of mine out of Berlin, DJ Synflood. He was busy, wetting the ears of the sardine like crowd with futuristic techie soul of everyone from Spacek to Flying Lotus. Exactly what I needed.

"Jack and ginger ale please," I needed a drink. More than one. A week has gone by since I've heard from Adrianne. She has not reported to work. She hasn't called. Cooper says she's well so obviously she has no interest in me. A part of me wondered what she'd wear tonight if she were here. The other part simply reminded me of my philosophy on life. Fuck her. I ordered an extra shot. If I were going to get this woman out of my system once and for all, it would take more than one drink.

Two artists that I had hopes of acquiring were in conversation on the other side of the loft space. Normally, I'd ease into business, but considering I've started with a double shot, I figured the time to talk art was now. One was actively listening, nodding her head, while the other painted a vivid picture of whatever he was trying to say with antics that would give Paul a run for his money.

"Pardon the interruption, but this will be quick," I offered. "You are Dawn Okoro, yes?"

"You must be Islam Ian." She smiled and extended her hand for a shake. The other looked at me like I was piece of lint on his shirt.

"And Kehinde Wiley I suppose? We spoke the other day," I clarified.

"Oh! Islam with Spence? What's up? You're back from Paris! Pleasure to finally meet you," he offered.

"I don't want to take up any more time than I already have, when either of you get a moment, give me a call at the gallery so we can talk." I extended a card to them both. Kehinde was already doing well commercially, but with Dawn there was room for development. Artistically she was amazing, commercially, her paintings are worth more than they're being sold for. I want to change that. Dawn chimed in.

"The work you're doing over at Spence is great."

"Thank you, we are trying to—" something caught my eye. I hoped for hallucination, but it was entirely too early for that. Was it? Adrianne? She, in a corner, in conversation with a guy who looked like an artist but I couldn't be sure. I recalled the mantra. Fuck her. I decided to ignore her and focus on Dawn, but the guy grabbed Adrianne's hand. *Oh really?*

"Handle your business." That was Kehinde to me, as my face must have given me away.

"Pardon me," I offered. Maybe it was the extra shot of Jack, but I almost flew across the loft. Counting to ten was the most popular way to boil down. I made it over there before reaching the final number. Big mistake. The look on Adrianne's face pissed me off even more. Guilt betrayed her. Deep breath. Ask nicely.

"Excuse us for a moment, will you?" I asked the man who held her hand as nicely as I could stomach. I only had one of those in me. Hoped he knew that. The half-artist moved closer to her. I resumed counting. Ten seemed a long way away.

"Do you know this guy, Adrianne?" He asked. Know me? That's it.

"Does she know me, bloke? Does she *know* me? Motherfucker I swear to god if you don't—"

"Yes," Adrianne answered him swiftly. "Please pardon us, if you will." Before she could finish the sentence, I grabbed, or rather yanked, her fine ass across the large flat. She could hardly keep up with me. Seemingly causing a scene, I slowed down a bit and found a corner on the rooftop. A quick once-over almost melted me. I missed her. My hand softened around hers. It seemed she had gained a pound or two, but her skin glowed even more than it had in Paris. She looked damn good in a short Missoni knit and boots, but that was neither here nor there. Focus Islam! I coached myself back to where I needed to be. Her eyes were dark but they weren't cold. They were tinged with warmth. And stressed. That surprised me. I felt myself softening against my will. Who the hell is this woman, Medusa?

"Isn't there something you wished to say?" I asked incredulously. Adrianne stood there quietly. As if the moment would pass if she could just be patient. While she stood there en mute, her eyes traveled every curve of my face, as if she were somehow evaluating me.

The phrase I've heard, but have never, ever had to say, tumbled out of me in one sweeping breath. "You couldn't call?" She didn't reply. It was pissing me off even more. "Adrianne! Say something! You couldn't ca—"

"Give me a moment," she said quietly. I heard her but continued my rant. People looked our way. We were spoiling highs and breaking buzzes. I moved her closer to me. "There is a reason," she began. After a deep breath, she asked, "Can we speak privately? There are so many people around."

"Adrianne, just say what you have to say," I answered. I wasn't in the mood to get caught up in her shit. I still loved her. As I stood here, every blood vessel and nerve ending of mine told me just that. But I was done with this.

"Alright," she sighed. "You may have noticed that I haven't been too well lately. Especially in the morning . . . feminine events haven't been timely . . ." I shifted impatiently. If she wasn't abducted by aliens I didn't want to hear it. ". . . Immediately on my return from Paris, I scheduled an emergency appointment . . . there were so many things to consider at once . . ."

"Adrianne." I interrupted. "You left me hanging for over a week. Fuck does a doctor's appointment have to do with anything?" I asked wildly. If there was ever an emotional sociopath, I was staring her in the face.

"Please . . . settle down. I am trying to tell you why it was hard for me to phone you." Eyes glassy, she looked the most stressed, the most unsure of herself I've ever seen. I was too mad to care.

"You know what Adrianne? Never mind the excuses. They are not my problem anymore. Leave your shit to Cooper, I've become tired of it. This thing between us is as you said it best . . . finished." I gestured with my hands. The expectation was for verbal lashing—for argument, as was typical of Adrianne's temper. The lashing never came. She was soft and more fragile than before, it seemed.

"Islam . . . if you would just listen to me . . . there is an excellent reason . . . I found out that I was—"

"There you are," a beautiful woman with soft locks approached us with a smile. Lauren. Just what I needed. "I brought your favorite," she said of the small glass of Jack Daniels she held. Adrianne need take note. *This* is how you keep a man.

"Splendid you could make it," I said, as I pulled Lauren to me and planted a firm kiss on her lips. If she was surprised she didn't show it. A pro.

"You were saying something Mrs. Spence?" I asked sarcastically. It took a second for Adrianne to gather herself. But she managed an answer.

"N-no. You are correct, Mr. Ian. Things of the sort are not your problem anymore." Adrianne tried to manage her all-business tone as easily as she always did but failed miserably. She looked shattered. For a moment I felt bad. Only for a moment. Her eyes traveled from Lauren's to mine. She continued, "I will . . . I will handle the matter on my own." If I thought it possible, I could have sworn I saw a tear threatening to fall. Not Adrianne. Impossible.

I grabbed Lauren and left Adrianne standing there. My heart was in my stomach and I wanted to turn back around and hug and kiss my baby, I wanted to take the horribly stressful look off of her face, I wanted to dance with her at the party, get her drunk, take her home, feed her, give her water to drink and laugh at the off the wall things she'd say before she fell asleep. She'd gained a bit, but I loved the extra pounds, they made me want to stay in bed with her longer. I found the bar, and chased all of those thoughts with shots of Jack and whatever else Kehinde passed me.

"Don't think! Drink!" He'd say every time I signaled 'enough'. The world was spinning. I concentrated extra hard on stopping it. I'm no wanker. I can hold my liquor. I needed to perspire. I don't dance. There is only one way of breaking a sweat for me. There was the red head brown girl in one corner, the twins in another. Red head. Twins. Red head. Twins . . . Ini, mini, miney. . . . red head. Lauren chatted with another artist at the bar and Kehinde patted me on the back.

"I've heard about you!" he yelled in my ear. He'd seen it all. The eye contact. The silent signal to meet in the bathroom.

"Good to see the master at work!" He laughed. Five minutes later with a pardon to Lauren and a Pope's blessing from Kehinde, I found myself unzipped in the unisex restroom, hands clenching the tops of either side of the stall, the ambient drums and sensual voice of Uschi Classen's meditative flow oozing through the speakers, adding ten times the feeling to the redhead's lips on my manhood.

I threw my head back and relaxed into the rhythm. While red attempted to suck me dry, I pushed back into her and tried to keep from choking her to death. A hand met the top of her head and moved with the tide.

"Mhmm. Stop." I asked. "Just for a second." I was where I needed to be, but entirely too soon. Maybe it's the liquor.

"I love the taste of you," Red said. I loved to hear her say that. The break was obviously arbitrary, as a few minutes and a serious effort later, the pleasure centers of the body began to speak up, and my head spun for a different reason.

While the wetness and warmth of her mouth left no escape, there was no leg shaking, or feeling radiating from toes or fingers. I moaned but didn't yell. I rocked steadily into her but didn't cry out. It felt great, but I didn't even have the courtesy to divert myself from her face when the moment came.

Shit. Adrianne was better. I was pissed at that. I want this whatever it is . . . this thing . . . for lack of a better word out of me. I'm sick of thinking of her. I'm sick of loving her like this. While red cleaned me up, I checked for the small square packages I always keep in pocket. Much thanks to the adventurous gal, but I needed something stronger tonight. I'll have to try the twins.

33

"What's up bro?" Micah said. "We've been trying to call you. Pick up your phone," he said.

I didn't recall hearing it this morning. "It didn't ring," I replied. "What time is it? Isn't it early?" I asked. "Lydia and I aren't due to do our thing until later in the afternoon," I yawned.

He laughed. "It's four pm. Get whatever chick you've got up there outta bed so my wife can do this painting shit you've got her all excited about. If I didn't know better I'd swear y'all were fucking," he added nonchalantly.

"What's all this?" I asked of bags and boxes being carried upstairs.

"Food. Lydia is tired of pizza and beer. She went grocery shopping. And yo, start inviting me to shit. Why don't you invite me to shit, man? I want to fuck model chicks too . . . well you know what I mean," he laughed. I didn't.

"We have different tastes," was all I said. "But I'll keep it in mind." I brushed Micah off as usual and if I didn't know better, I'd think he was a bit hurt by it. Lydia walked into the kitchen and smiled. I gave hearty thanks. I needed the company. My brother left us to our own devices. As we unpacked fresh vegetables and herbs from paper bags, Lydia asked,

"So how was last night?" If she only knew.

* * *

"So, let me get this straight." Lydia stopped applying brush-strokes to what looked like an abstract of something tangible, but I couldn't be sure. "In Paris, she told you she loved you."

"Yes. Well sort of," I answered.

"She got back to the States and didn't call."

"Yes."

"You saw her last night, and she looked different. But the changes began overseas."

"Yes." I answered.

Lydia paused. "She's sick in the morning, gaining weight, and glowing."

"I believe that is it. Yes." A hand popped me across the back of my head. "Owwwh!" I yelled.

"She's pregnant, Islam," she said.

"She's what?"

"Have the two of you ever had unprotected sex?" Lydia asked.

"What?" I asked again. I was still hanging on the initial statement.

"Have you been together unprotected?" she asked. No. I never have unprotected sex. If there were a model Trojan, it would be me.

"No. Never," I answered.

"Any accidents?" Lydia probed. She wouldn't let the pregnant thing go. Accidents . . . yes. Adrianne caught me off guard before Ahmed's concert with the belly waves and wax. Shit.

"Yea. Once. Here. A couple of months ago." I put my hands on my head. My love couldn't be pregnant and I not notice it. Impossible.

"But Lydia, she is not pregnant. Why would she keep it from me?"

She immediately placed her finger in the air in a way that said the answer was a simple one. "Islam, if I were married, in an affair, in love for Christ's sake and possibly pregnant, by a man who was *not* my husband . . . AND. . . . my spouse happened to be the Escobar of the oil world . . . I might take a week or so to come around myself. That's project—or how you Brits say, council estate—drama right there," she laughed. I didn't. It wasn't funny. The look in Adrianne's eyes, her acquiescence, and the tear all came to mind. Along with the way I treated her.

"Shit!" I yelled. Got up. Walked toward the window of the studio. "Shit! Shit! Shit!" My fist pounded into a wall that could only take so many punches at once. "I am so fucking stupid! I am so stupid!" Lydia wiped her paint sodden hands on the cloth next to her and stood. "Lyd! I have to see her. I can't believe I acted like that!"

"Well how did it end? What did she say?" Lydia asked. I thought for a second. Something about . . .

"She . . . would handle it herself." I said. "Lydia. What does that mean? She would handle it herself . . . she would handle it herself . . ." I repeated the mantra until it all made sense. "AHH-HHHHH!" I dove across the table for the phone, clearing every single item off its top. Brushes, tins and other knick knacks tumbled onto the floor.

"Islam! Calm down!" Lydia called. I had to talk to her. My baby, literally and figuratively speaking, I've got to let her know that I'm here, that I'm not going anywhere. That I was just upset with her. That's all. I love her too much to leave.

"I am calm!" I yelled back.

"You've just flown across the table, your hands are shaky and you're acting a bit manic. Calm down," she repeated.

Calm down. Calm down. I hit speed dial one. Yes, my hands were shaky. My palms were sweating. She had no idea. I *was* calm. *"You have reached the voice mail box of Adrianne Spence . . ."*

I dialed again. "You have reached the voice mail . . ." Again. "You have reached . . ." Again. "You have . . ."

"FUCK!" The mobile shattered against the wall before I'd even realized it left my hands. While Lydia's mouth formed a large O, I tossed sofa cushions and articles of clothing in the air. Where's my jacket? I stopped for a second to think. Where did Lauren put it? The bedroom. Had to be in there.

"Islam." Lydia said softly. As if a decibel more would cause civil war.

"Yes?" My tone matched her own.

"What are you doing?" she asked cautiously. What the hell did she think I was doing? Book education can be entirely over-rated.

"Getting my jacket?" The questioning tone of voice from me was patronizing but I couldn't help it. She was acting strange.

"Your jacket," she gestured towards the stool that I used to sit while we painted, ". . . is right here," she said flatly.

I trotted to where she was sitting and grinned. "Yes, this is it. Thank you," I picked up the slim hooded sport coat, slid it on briskly, ran through the flat to find one shoe, and back to the front of the studio to put on the other. Under the arms. I reeked. But that was neither here nor there. Keys. Then I'm off. I hope Adrianne's home. I hope she's off her feet and comfortable. I hope she hears what I have to say. I know she doesn't want children. I hope I can change her mind.

"Islam?" Lydia's tone of voice was unnerving me.

"Yeeessss?" I answered her just as Martha Stewart-like as she'd asked. She was truly acting bizarre.

"Would you mind sitting with me for a bit?"

"There is some place I need to be," was my response. She knew that.

"Seriously. Just sit. For a minute." She patted the cushion next to her. I sat on the arm of the sofa instead. "Where do you need to be?"

I love my brother's wife, but she is wasting my time.

"Where do you think?"

"You can't do that."

"Says whom?" I responded.

"You haven't spoken to her."

"So what?"

"How do you know she—"

"How do I know what Lyd? That's what I'm going to find out!

Now, I must be going. Let yourself out when you're ready." I stood and headed toward the door.

"Islam stop! You're displaying manic behavior. Now, settle down. Please." If she suggests that I calm myself once more . . . wait. What did she say?

"Manic?" I asked incredulously.

"Yes. What are you going to do if she isn't there?" Lydia placed the question as if it were a vowel on a money wheel.

What am I going to do? That's easy. "I'll wait."

"And if she doesn't want to see you?"

"She will." It was a simple answer. Lydia shifted a bit. Along with a deep breath, she took a different approach.

"If what we've hypothesized is true—and again, it is a hypothesis—then you're going to need that two million more than anyone we know. So again, calm down, or rather sit down for a while. Think it over."

Damn. She was right. Keys were tossed onto a now bare table top, and I sat hands to head in one of my tattered armchairs. I missed her. I wanted her to have my baby. I can't believe I treated her the way I did. Thoughts of Adrianne—of my predicament with her, eclipsed the bare notion of communication or exchange between myself and Lydia. I just wanted to sink into me and be still. The feeling was that of slowly ripping a tight bandage from a hairy chest. Moments turned to minutes of stillness. If the room could claim color, it would be blackest black. Half past an hour later, I was on the ocean floor of my emotions. The weight of a titanic effort on my shoulders, stillness and void were all I could manage. I thought Lydia would leave, but she didn't. I laughed to myself. It was all I could do.

"I think you're bipolar." Lydia stated quietly. I am not in the mood for her psychobabble tonight.

"Bi-what?"

"Bipolar. I think you're bipolar, manic depressive, obsessive compulsive, a tad borderline, and sex addicted to name a few. And that's just what I can see from here," she finished. Names of personality disorders and line items from morning train adverts flashed quickly in front of me. Manic. Obsessive. Borderline. Insomnia. Anxiety. Symptoms. *If you have five out of ten of these* . . . Is she serious? I busted out laughing.

"Explain this," I said between laughs. She didn't flinch or grin. She *was* serious. It made me laugh harder.

Lydia waited until I settled down. "Okay . . . for one. Your mood swings are instantaneous. Just as instantaneous as they are intense. Anxiety levels shoot up and down like mercury. You can go from being highly active to an extremely depressive state in a matter of seconds." I thought of Adrianne's swinging moods. Mine weren't that bad.

"I see. Further engage me," I encouraged. I was trying to keep my composure. Didn't want her to think I didn't respect her line of work. But I don't know how one's personality can be disordered. Who is the model person? Whose persona is orderly enough to even construct a counter-definition of *dis*order? We are all different. We adapt and change. We grow and interpret things and behaviors on an individualized basis. I'm not denouncing her hypothesis, just considering it may be misplaced. Passionate? Yes. Personality disorder? What man isn't addicted to sex?

"Your relationship with this woman. The back and forth. It's co-dependent. A disorder based on highs and lows. Ups and downs," she stated firmly. "And all the women."

I thought about the subjects of the Eteri paintings. Of Frida Kahlo and Diego Rivera, their 'manic' marriage and masterpiece works. The back and forth. Highs and lows. Passion, pleasure and pain. The endless cycle. Picasso and his women. Modigliani and his models. Van Gogh slicing off his own ear after an argument. And the young American pop singer who burned down her boyfriend's mansion for a little Tender Love and Care. Expressive. Manic. Free. I chuckled inside. It's who we are.

"Lydia. I am sorry to break this to you, as I am sure American schools have greatly prepared you to recognize things of the sort, but you are sitting in the presence of an artist. By law, and structure of humanity, we are high, low and sex addicted. I don't know any one of us who isn't. I am recent in my own development, but a member of the sect nonetheless. I am who I am." I shrugged. "Now, I have a woman to see, wait for, whatever. And a baby to love. Possibly. We can talk about sex addiction later," I said as I grabbed my keys off of the table. The door slammed shut behind me.

34

The public telephones of Gotham city were hilariously disgusting. I cursed myself for shattering my mobile, placed the receiver to my ear, and prayed I didn't end up with anything ending in *osis*. Adrianne's mobile just rang and rang. I spoke after the beep.

"Babe. I'm so sorry. I know I've said this a million times by now, but I am. I want to hear everything you have to say if you'll have me. Please. Let's talk. Love you, Ciao." I placed the phone on the hook and waited. Ten dollars in quarters already. I looked upward. The lights were out. Maybe she was asleep. I've heard pregnancy makes one lethargic.

I played around with the key to the gallery, and the upper loft space where Adrianne lived. It was for emergency purposes only. This was an emergency.

Sliding the key card through the small reader reminded me of a last visit to the ostentatious loft. It's been a while since I've rounded the slate stairwell, but I took each flight like a champ. The cherry wood and steel planked door dared me to do what it knew I would. Careful not to wake her if she were sleeping, I turned the key slowly. A shot of adrenaline to the abdomen gave way to a nervousness that I hadn't noticed earlier. I hoped she accepted my apology. I hoped for more than that, actually.

Although the lights were technically off, the loft was well lit by large street lamps welcomed by larger than life windows. Unaware that they were in front of me, I tripped haphazardly over small leather cubes that served as chic ottomans. I wasn't completely sure, but I didn't think Cooper was here. If he was, I'd deal with it all as it came. At this point, he was the least of my worries. Navigating through the large open space, I walked a slim passageway, made a first left, a sharp right, and traveled up a grand spiral staircase to the small room where Adrianne worked. A slim black case with an illuminated apple logo sat half closed on a glass desk. The small red light on her mobile flashed as if it were in its own state of emergency. I looked left into the large space that posed as a bedroom and my heart jumped. She was here. Under a bushel of down feathers was a head of loose black curls that caused me to stare for longer than I thought I would. She shifted in her sleep, and a lone foot peeked out from under the down.

"Adrianne," I whispered softly. She sleeps so hard. "Adrianne," I tried again. Nothing. Maybe I'll just wait until she wakes. Quietly, I moved closer to the bed. Unsure of where to sit, I figured I'd just kneel beside it, as she was furthest left of the platform and it would be easier to see things of her I never truly get a chance to. Lips less than half an inch from hers, I could feel the heat of her breath on my face, and I wondered what a baby of ours would look like. Would it have my hair or hers? My complexion? Her eyes? Would it be a boy? It would have to be. A girl would kill me. Minutes of night watch passed, and Adrianne stirred. Stretched. Eyes of hers fluttered gently, then opened slowly. There was a quick moment of disorientation, the rapid closing of her lids to regroup, and the popping open of her eyes once again. Shock, horror, panic, all of those things appeared at once, before she screamed like the leading lady in a horror film.

"AEEEEEEEWWWWHHH!" She jumped up so quickly that her head bumped mine. I didn't realize I was that close. "Ohhhhhhh my goddddddd! Oh my god! Oh my god . . . oh my goddddd!" she carried on in a state of utter panic. My love sat up in bed, her hand over her heart, chest heaving like an exacerbating asthmatic.

"Relax, A. It's just me." I said softly, moving toward her legs. I didn't want her to be cold. Or get too wound up. "You shouldn't be getting so excited, babe. It's just me. Relax." I stated calmly. She looked at me as if I'd just been released from an institution. Her eyes said simply, *Relax?*

Head shaking slowly from left to right, she clutched her chest. And although her breathing slowed, I could tell she was still shaken up.

"What . . ." She swallowed a lump. "What. Are you doing here." I reached for her. She moved away. "Don't. WH-How did you get in?" Why was she acting like that?

"I used my key." Another huge breath outward from Adrianne made me sorry I startled her like this. "I called first," I added. She attempted to respond, but it seemed she could hardly catch her breath let alone regain her composure. "I didn't mean to scare you, baby. I just wanted to say sorry for the way I acted at the party. The girl was nothing . . . I mean no one. I was worried, then upset when you didn't show to the house. I love you, you know I do. Now, will you please tell me what you were attempting to? Please?" I'd found her feet and began to massage them. Kissed one. I wanted her to be as comfortable as she could be.

"Islam."

"Yes?"

"Stop it." I did. "Listen to me carefully," she began. "This . . . this is mad. It's bloody insane for Christ's sake. You can't just— what if Cooper were here?" she asked incredulously.

Cooper? Fuck Cooper. "He isn't."

"What if he was? You . . . that key is for—it is not for this," she scolded.

"Adrianne. Yes. You're right. It's not. But can you do me a favor and reprimand me after you tell me what you were going to last night?" I asked. One of those infamous dark waves passed over her eyes. Can't say I was in the mood to pull teeth tonight.

"There is nothing to speak of, Islam."

"You said that you were not feeling well," I offered additives to the beginnings of a story that I wanted to hear. "Are you still sick?"

"I am fine," she stated coldly.

"What was wrong?"

"I am fine, Islam. There is nothing wrong."

"Yes, Adrianne, yesterday you said that there was and I think I know—"

"That was yesterday. As of today, there is nothing to know." She was concrete cold. I searched for warmth, the warmth from yesterday, from Paris . . . there was none. "In fact, I cannot believe I ever got wrapped up in this . . . this nonsense." She stood, placed a bright white terry cloth robe on a naked body and headed into the main space. I stood still. She's not going to tell me?

"I am seeing you to the door," she stated flatly. "If you knew what was good for you, you'd gladly exit."

"Adrianne."

"Adrianne nothing. We're finished correct? It was the best decision you could have made. I don't know what the hell I was thinking. This has all been so . . . I don't know what to call it but it's over."

"Adrianne. Just tell me," I egged her on. She was in another place. I pulled her face to mine. She wouldn't look at me. "Tell me, babe."

"I cannot fucking believe you. I can't. Can't believe I even— and from today on, call me by my full name. Or rather my last. Goodnight, Mr. Ian."

"Babe . . . come on," I wanted to hear it so badly.

"I'm serious. Do not call me that."

"You love me right?" I asked.

"No." Her tone was sharp and arctic.

"Then tell me . . . tell me, A . . ." I begged and continued on oblivious to her response.

"Cooper and I are renewing our vows. Your invitation is in the mail."

I heard that clearly. "You're renewing what?"

"Vows," she snapped.

I busted out laughing. Good one. Funnier than Lydia's earlier rants. I will give her some time. Maybe try again tomorrow. "Okay, love. I will come back when you're feeling better. Be ready to tell me then." I laughed down the stairs and all the way back to Brooklyn. Cooper and vows. Right up there with manic artists. Bullshit.

No matter what I thought about apologies or stories untold, truth was, it's been more than a week since I've made love to Adrianne and I'm craving her. My body and spirit is craving the nourishment. Unable to quench the thirst with a hand or another woman, I'd found an outlet—a minor one, in my dreams. They were vivid and soulful, she and I, the impact of a tidal wave on my stomach each time I awakened. Dreams of unmet desire can easily turn into nightmares. Seemed I couldn't close my eyes without loving her, and waking up more deprived, more starved, more famished than before. No matter how much I wanted to rid myself of it, at least in hopes of thinking clearly, this thing was all over me. An hour into sleep and I'd dream. An hour into awakening I'd imagine. Her body on mine was like oxygen right now. I'd most definitely have to resolve this tomorrow. I needed her love as soon as I could get it.

35

Here I sit outside your door . . .
Talk to me . . .

Nights of tossing turning, anguish, Red Bull and Meshell. She says what I mean, but never seem to convey. Gentle piano strokes, delicate chords and airy tenor notes brought a morning full of imagination and requirement to ascent. On repeat, the expressive artist says she'd sit hours through a rain shower, that she'd be content to just listen to her love's voice. I close my eyes and hear the longing in her own, the petition to be loved, to be understood—even coped with and tolerated—rings true. The DC native expresses indulgence of the tenth commandment with so much piety it becomes blasphemous to consider it a sin. She wants a deeper connection, she wants to be loved as the only, she wants small things that are big in everyone else's world but hers. One of my favorite artists expresses me this morning. She covets love.

I face the east.

Memories of a famous story of a young king and his regretful plea, asking forgiveness of his deep love, lustful drive and affair with the wife of a warrior of his army. I think, maybe, the impulses—the drive to love like this is not singular to me. David was King. He was also a musician and a poet. An artist. That he was of sin, was a strong and much preferred consideration. That inner impulse of the human heart overtook him, and he sought freedom outside of the very law he taught, is also a possibility. Beautiful verses in which he begs a wrathful God to blot out his transgressions, to create in him a clean heart, to spare him of His judgment, come to mind, and I pray, summoning the God of David—the forgiving one, to help me overcome this. I hope that He understands. I don't believe in adultery. I believe in following one's heart.

I pray to the artist of all artists.

"Barukh Atah Adonoi Elohanu . . .

Vihiratzon milfaneykha, Adonai Eloheinu, velohei avoteinu . . ."

David. Nietzsche. DaVinci. Me. I pray for us, the freedmen.

"Ve'al tevi'einu lo lidei chet, velo lidei averah . . .

Ve'avon, velo lidei nissayon, veto lidei vizayon,"

The sinners,

"Ve'al tashlet baru yetzer hara . . .

Barukh atah Adonai . . .

Amein."

Covered in sweat, I repeat the verses,

"Blessed art thou O'Lord our God, King of the Universe,

May it be the will before you Lord, Our God, and the God of our Fathers . . .

That you lead us not to the hands of sin, nor to the hands of pride and perversity,

Nor into the hands of temptation or scorn . . .

Blessed art thou O'Lord . . .

Amein."

I pray and wait. The sunken feeling in my chest does not subside. Nor does the emptiness of spirit. Laying, tracing the ceiling for anything other than anguish, I don't know what to do with the state of me. I'm not hungry. I'm not thirsty. I am not interested in daylight or inspiration. Just the warmth of her. Relaxing into the confines of an imagination that keeps mind, body and spirit from draining completely, I lean backward into a pillow filled with her scent and drink caffeine as if it were love; basking in the only state of being that allows me to touch her. I awaken from dreams in a state of emotional and physical poverty. I don't have to awaken from imagining.

The song began again, and I willed myself to the shower. No avail. What the hell is wrong with me?

"ISLAAAAAAMMM!" I heard him, but nothing in me could get up to answer. I've got to shake whatever this thing is. This building pressure in my chest. I've got to get rid of it. Staying in bed all day without female company has never been my forte.

The phone, the story of my life, rang. And rang. And rang. Paul. He wouldn't let up.

"Hello."

"You have no idea what I've just been through with Ahmed . . ." Paul started instantly.

I didn't have the strength to deal with it all. "Paul, not now." He continued without even so much of a breath between words. "Paul . . ."

"What the hell is the matter with you?" he asked.

"Not feelin' well."

"Bird flu? SARS? Mad cow disease? What?" he joked.

"It's a long story."

"Adrianne." He chuckled. "I thought you were finished with her?"

"I was."

"Then what happened? Because you sound like a friggin' girl. Fix yourself up man," he said jokingly. "No, seriously what happened?"

"Paris."

"Sex?"

I didn't even want to think about it. The more I did, the worse I felt. "Yea. It felt different. I've never felt that before, it felt free . . . like we could do anything we wanted, like she wasn't going anywhere." I recalled the session where Adrianne and I were closer than close, and wondered how she could just stop it all on a whim. "But now she won't talk to me, I messed up man . . ."

"Islam."

"Yea."

"How many women have you had since you've started this thing with Adrianne?" he asked.

"I dunno. Two. Three the most?"

"This week?"

"No. Since I've been in the US."

"That's the problem right there! No wonder you're ill, your body is withdrawing! Get your ass some ass!" he joked.

"Paul . . ." I didn't want to hear anything other than how to remove this sunken feeling from my chest. My woman was leaving me stranded. I didn't ask for this. She approached me at the party in London, not the other way around.

"Islam, listen. This is a dead-end affair. Move on. The women are plenty. Get one of those educated Black American types, they're crazy but not as crazy as artists. Give up."

"I can't."

"Why?"

"I don't know. That's what I've been trying to figure out." My head was killing me and I really didn't feel like talking but maybe my mate could figure this out. "I'm telling you, there is something between us. It's not just love it's a . . . a thing. This thing, whatever it is, is killing me. When I'm with her I feel it. When I'm not, all I can think of is feeling it again. Tell me how to get rid of the thing and I've gotten rid of Adrianne." The most I'd said all day came out slow and pathetically. "This can't be normal, Paul. I feel like I'm losing it."

"You are, my friend. Three women only? You could put that down in a day here in London," he laughed. I tried to join him but failed.

"I'm tired, man. I don't feel well. I have to figure out what to say to her. I messed up, Paul."

"Well, just stay out of Cooper's way. Adrianne's smart. She'll choose wisely." Paul said assuredly. We said our goodbyes and disconnected. I hoped he was right.

Hours passed, and I'd only managed to change the track on the CD player, make it to the toilet and back. While Marvin

Gaye sang of love addiction, I dug deeper into the pillow on her side of the bed. I need my baby. Her smile and encouraging words. This is not about sex. There is something else between us. The longer I went without it, the worse I felt. Imagination, caffeine, sleep. Nothing was working.

A quick glance at the time and I wondered where it all went. Eight o'clock. She was working late at the gallery tonight to accommodate international hours. I popped out of bed, grabbed my jumper and was on the C train to Manhattan in a flash.

"Adrianne . . . Babe. I know. I can't help that. No . . . no! You don't do the same. All it took was a call. Tired? Tired! How do you think I feel? Well what do you want me to do? Woman? Oh . . . wom-*en* . . . they're nothing . . . what do you mean . . . you're the only one who does this! Yea? Yea? So come home with me . . . no . . . today. . . . yes Adrianne . . . Yes! . . . Calm down? WHY DOES EVERYONE KEEP TELLING ME THAT—"

"CUT!"

"Cut?"

"Yea, Osama, cut . . . I need more passion!" My trash alley friend, the one who lived in the passage across from the gallery, gestured to rival Al Pacino's award winning facades. "Why does everyone keep telling me that. . . . at the end you go flat. Rocky. Again, from the top. ADRIANNE!" she yelled. I laughed for the first time today.

"You want me to do it again?" I asked.

"Do it do it do it!" she yelled. "If you want your wife back— yes—you'll do it. Why she leave you again? She don't like your other wives? Well then sorry about that," she answered her own question. I realized that the plump, toothless woman was not a nutter, or as Lydia would say, manic, she was accelerated. Her mind worked faster than her mouth. She'd ask an original question, then ask a third, having already used logic and her surroundings to answer the second. It was a bizarre form of genius. Frequently misunderstood, I'm sure. She insisted that I practice what I wished to say to Adrianne.

"But I should be going, yes?"

"No, no, no, no . . . time? Yes, she's still downstairs." She offered the response to the question I'd typically ask of the time as well as my follow up on Adrianne's whereabouts. I've asked the former but never the latter. She's good.

"Thank you. That was exactly what I was going to ask." My eccentric friend smiled. If I could ever repay her for putting a smile on my face today, it would be in teeth.

"Okay, practice again?" she asked. "CUT!" she belted out. I hadn't even begun.

I tried again. "Adr—"

"CUT!"

"Adr—"

"CUUUUUT!" People stopped and looked at us. I started to comment but she cut me off.

"I already know you're going to mess up," she said with a playful look in her eyes. I busted out laughing. Folks stared. Some gave hideous looks. I know I am not looking my best. My hair is uncombed. Her teeth are missing. We both smelled bad. However, I could care less. This was the best I'd felt all day.

"G-go now no boyfriend isn't left afternoon no bags."

"What?" I responded. That went completely over my head. I had to take a minute to replay staccato sentences and verbiage. Four questions ahead. Two word answers. It's safe to go in. Cooper isn't there. He left during the afternoon, but wasn't carrying any luggage. Damn, she's good. Is she psychic? Those happened to be my next few questions for her. She adjusted the dirty blanket used as a shawl and nodded toward the gallery as to say, *what are you waiting for?*

"Alright pretty lady," I kissed her on both cheeks. She beamed. "Wish me luck," I said, as I headed across the street to the gallery. At the window, I could see through to Adrianne's office. She sat on her desk, legs crossed kindergarten style, wireless piece in ear, tapping away on her laptop. My reflection showed the state of me, and I realized that it may be smarter to wait upstairs, as this is my place of work. Wouldn't want anyone to get the wrong idea.

Managing to stop at an independent book shop nearby, I was proud of my selections. I've never purchased children's books before. Children's anything. But I think I did a pretty good job. All of Curious George's bollocks. Charlotte's Web. And Toni Morrison's illustrated book for tots, in case it's a whiz kid. You never know. I also bought *Beyond The Indigo Children*, a book about the children of the new age, their hyper-intelligence, near-psychic abilities, and propensity to be classified as manic, ADHD, or personality disordered. I didn't want my child on Ritalin. So I picked this one up for Adrianne.

I sat in my love's favorite reading chair and waited. I know that waiting up here will not make me favorable, but technically, it is a corporate flat and we need to get to the bottom of things so, I'll deal with the consequences later. The keys to the large door made entry noise, and I put Curious George to rest. Adrianne chatted, or rather listened and vaguely responded to whoever was doing the chatting and I waited quietly. The spicy vanilla scent of hers, which I'd narrowed down to classic Cartier, filled the loft and I inhaled deeply. She was in the kitchen. I couldn't wait.

She, standing arms crossed, engrossed in conversation, left her waist wide open. I slid my arms around her center. No horror flick-scream, just a sharp, piercing yelp that deafened the deaf. Adrianne turned, slapped me across the head and grinned. On instinct, her fingers found their usual place in my hair. She listened and detangled for moments that I melted into. In a flash, she jolted her hand backward, as if she'd been burned. The comfortable grin turned to a scowl. It would be fair to assume she'd forgotten she was upset with me. I didn't mind the brief encounter. At least there was hope.

She answered the voice on the phone. "No . . . no I am fine. It was a small bug. The revelries of New York," she chuckled. Her eyes said otherwise. I reached for her again. She moved. I didn't

want to play this game anymore. "Yes, until then . . . good night."
Adrianne closed the mobile casing and stared at me hard. It wasn't
a difficult look to interpret.

"Good evening," I smiled.

"What are you doing here?" she asked callously.

"I've come to talk. Or rather to listen," I replied.

"How many times have I got tell you that there is nothing to
talk about, Islam. There is *nothing*. If you do this once more, I am
going to call the police," she said.

"Call them."

"Is that a challenge?" she asked with contemptuous eyes.

"No, I am not challenging you, I just do not want to leave until
we speak openly. Talk to me, babe. What is on your mind?" I was
being as patient as I could. Tackling her. Loving her until this
world was a figment of our imaginations was at the forefront of a
spirit that needed her more than it needed to be fed. But I'd be
patient tonight. I wanted to hear her say she was having my baby.
That and a kiss. One step at a time. "I've purchased a few things."
I retrieved the bag of books from the main space and brought
them to the counter.

"Islam. Please. You are making this harder than need be. Where
was all of this on the weekend? When *I* wanted to talk? Tonight?
Your selfishness is blinding. I can't trust that. Other than business, there is not a thing between us to discuss."

"Love, I'll admit to being a tad immature at the party. But I
am working on that. I love you, Adrianne. I don't really know
what to do with all of this. It's hard for me."

"You're a loose cannon. I cannot trust it," she said flatly.

"As are you. But I trust you. Despite all of this," I gestured
openly to the space around us.

"No, you don't. You expect the worst from me," she said with
disdain.

"I've only known the worst. Show me better, Adrianne and I'll
accept it. I'll accept whatever you give, babe." They were the
truest words I'd ever spoken. She remained silent. The sound of

keys on cold tile provided the soundtrack to lives that were vacant without each other.

"You want me to trust . . ." She shook her head back and forth in a way that suggested she was reformatting her words. I know Adrianne. She's angry. She doesn't want to show it. "You want me to trust you enough to have . . ." A sigh. More recomposing. A response that was almost a whisper, "If you are left alone for a second, if I turn my head or you are displeased you act like a child . . ."

"You left me hanging, Adrianne. What was I supposed to do?"

"WAIT!" she yelled. She didn't mean to. Wait. The thought hadn't crossed my mind. Apparently waiting was something else I wasn't good at. There is so much to learn. Startled, I watched her shift items, keys, salt and pepper shakers from left to right. "Let's just say everything cannot be on your time, Islam. This is one of those times. Now please . . ." She gestured towards the door. I stood still. Why was she so upset? She's headstrong, but she's never been *this* headstrong. As vivid as my imagination was, I couldn't imagine leaving her.

"You really want me to leave?" Adrianne nodded. Although I recognized the effort, I can't say I recognized the look in her eyes. But I can say it unnerved me. She looked, for lack of a better word . . . conclusive.

I am sorry. Conclusion is something I will not accept from Adrianne. I decided to take a different approach. "Alright. Before I leave, a request. And I will not bother you anymore." I offered. She was quiet as usual but gave me the edge I needed to ask, "May I kiss you?"

"Absolutely not." She shook her head.

"Just once. A last time. And I promise I will leave." I wasn't looking for positive response. I was looking for conflict. Conflict portended care. I also know it's Adrianne's weakness. It's not sex. It's in the kiss.

"No. And that is final." She placed her keys down on the kitchen tile and waltzed that ballerina walk into the center of the loft. It almost killed me. Resolve, rationale was not working.

"Babe. Please. Just a kiss." I was losing the composure of just minutes before. More than conversation, I needed a kiss badly. "Just one."

"What is the matter with you Islam? I said no." She tossed her hair upward into a ponytail. The weakness, the sunken feeling flooded me all at once. No from her tonight was something I couldn't seem to take like a man. I needed so much to feel her . . . I couldn't leave without it.

"Please, Adrianne . . . I need—I just want one more. I promise." I felt powerless and pathetic. Trying desperately to keep it all together, I leaned against the countertop and waited. That didn't seem to work. Fuck. If I could just touch her, some of this horrible feeling—this thing—would subside. "Come on . . . just a kiss." I was begging and quite frankly ashamed. This wasn't of my nature. But I didn't know how else to make my point.

"I can't trust you," she said out of nowhere. "I can't trust you and I want you out of my life."

I was starved and unfocused. This was not turning out well. "You can trust me, Adrianne."

"I don't want this. I am renewing my vows with my husband. I want my old life back," she reasoned with herself.

"Do you?"

"Yes. Now please. Will you go?" she asked earnestly.

I can't. I've tried that already. New life, contracts, love . . . everything else, I can figure out later. For the moment, nothing mattered as much as a kiss from my darling.

"A . . . just a kiss. Just—"

"No! What part of no don't you understand!" she raged. "No! No! No! No!" An angry hand slapped the counter violently. "You want what you want when you want it! No, Islam!"

A male voice interrupted her rant, and I wondered how long he'd been here, how much he'd heard. "Such a harsh word from such a beautiful woman!" Cooper kissed Adrianne from behind, on the cheek, then turned her towards him. "I am glad I am not the only one who Adrianne says no to," he said kissing her on either side of her face. "She." Kiss. "Loves . . ." Kiss. "Saying . . ." Longer kiss. "No. It's quite frankly, genetic. Her mum said no so many times that her father was forced to look elsewhere for entertainment, isn't that right honey?"

If I weren't so completely obliterated, Cooper would be dead on arrival of his last comment. That was a shot to her womanhood. However, witnessing him come out of nowhere and easily acquire simplicities that I had to fight so hard for—a kiss, open affection— infuriated me and I couldn't think clearly enough to respond.

"Islam! My god, look at the state of you!" Cooper exclaimed. "Surely you must be immersed in one of your artistic spells . . . as I've heard hygiene can take a back seat to inspiration in these cases." Was he fucking with me? "What's in the bag honey?" Cooper was the only one with words here tonight. Adrianne went grey as usual, and I simply waited for Gabriel to read me my rights before committing another cardinal sin. I was up to three in under twenty four hours. "Let's see, we have *Charlotte's Web* . . . ah . . . *Curious George* . . . I've always loved him. Such a rascal of a monkey," Cooper laughed as he haphazardly tossed books I spent hours agonizing over, aimlessly onto the countertop. I was in too much agony—if that's what one could call this—to respond to anything. Apparently, so was Adrianne.

"What's wrong, Spence?" Cooper called Adrianne by his pet name for her. He had such a way about him. One never knew what he truly thought. What he'd witnessed. His Machiavellian ways were such the opposite of what I offered. Adrianne's mouth was wide open. We stared at each other.

"Have you told him?" he asked.

"Yes, Adrianne. Have you?" I followed up. We could do this right here, right now. Tell him you are having my child and coming home with me. A simple statement. However he wanted to deal man-to-man we'd deal.

"Adrianne. Does he know? What is the problem?" Cooper reiterated. I already knew of an alleged vow renewing ceremony. That would happen over my dead body. She shook her head.

"There is none, I . . . I am a bit overwhelmed." She replied, sifting lightly through the books on the countertop.

"I know it'll be hard, but he's going to have to know sooner or later," Cooper said.

"My sentiments exactly," I added. Adrianne ignored us both, sitting down in the main room.

"She's leaving," he stated. Now he was speaking my language. "The gallery here will operate as a satellite office effective two weeks from now. We've already hired someone to take Adrianne's place. Islam will report to them, right honey?" Cooper yelled towards his wife.

I walked over to where Adrianne was sitting. Hands covering her face on either side, she sat as still as a statue. "She will do business from London," he offered squarely. There are responsibilities and important events, one in particular . . . things needing her immediate attention. Have you called Mohammed, Adrianne?" With her eyes closed, she shook her head gently, as if it was too heavy for her neck.

"When were you going to tell me?" I asked her.

"I tried," she answered quietly.

"Not to worry Islam, your contract is still on the table, and the personnel change shouldn't be too much of an adjustment. Change is good. I know it won't be the same as working with my wife, but some things are just a temporary fix. London's home." He walked toward me, patted me on the back, and smiled that weird smile. "Curious George . . ." he chuckled. "I know you two have managed to score quite a kinship during her tenure here. I'll leave you to sort it all out," he said as he walked confidently away from us. I closed my eyes. This was not happening.

"When are you leaving?"

"Tomorrow," she replied barely above a whisper.

"Adrianne, we need to talk." She's just as volatile as I am. I know this was all done in a huff. My love's not leaving. She's just upset. I can fix that.

"I will brief you on the details of the personnel change." Adrianne's voice went in and out of hoarseness. "Your contract with

Siddiq was awarded . . ." Her voice cracked, and I listened, but didn't. "Pending signatures from myself and Cooper . . . outstanding contracts with proposed artists will be honored . . ."

I didn't—or refused to hear anything she was saying. My contract was awarded. If all went as it should in the next few weeks I'd be two million dollars richer. I should walk out. Walk out right now with a Jack Nicholson smile and say to hell with all of this. I'm rich. There should be toasts and fine champagne and the finest of female specimen for my mates and I. Walking out, never calling her again, celebrating the rest of my life, I should engage in all of those things but I do not. I can't hear reality over the noise in my heart. As Adrianne speaks, my head swims in wanting and confusion. I am strong. I am successful. I have what I've always wanted. Walk out. That is what I tell myself but it doesn't resonate.

My chest hurts. Soothing the ache becomes the priority, which meant one thing to me. I just needed to be close to her. I needed her body on mine, laying, sleeping, breathing . . . whichever. If I could manage that, all things would fall into place. We'd deal with everything else as it came. "Come to Brooklyn tonight," I offered. We can fix this.

"I can't," she whispered.

"So this is it?" My love nodded, and I . . . I didn't know what to do. Blurbs and fragmented thoughts replaced grammar and poise. Staccato verbiage was all I had left. "I know at the party . . . and in Paris . . . I'm sorry. I didn't mean it. It meant love, Adrianne. . . . It meant love, you know it did. Stay here. I will clean the flat. I will do the dishes. I will make sure you never want . . ." There was no care of Cooper, or contracts or being found out. Just her with me for as long as we could be. She couldn't leave. Didn't she know? She was all that mattered.

"I don't know what to do. Tell me what to do, Adrianne."

Eyes the color of fire, she removed her hands from her head, stood and stated simply, "I want you to leave."

36

I walk aimlessly through Manhattan, city lights and life a figment of my imagination. The feeling of being a small dot on a
crowded map covers me entirely, and I walk with my eyes closed
to recapture my place in this world. Beneath my lids the dark
works overtime. Opening my eyes proves no different.

Trains are ghosts. People are phantom. I don't notice the spirit-
less or love dead, as we've blended into one another on the crowded
carriage. There was no life on the R or the C train tonight. If
there was, I simply hadn't noticed.

The turnstile I'd chosen to exit the station was inoperable,
and to me it signaled the end of human life as I've come to know
it. My veteran friend sits in the stairwell, invisible guitar in hand,
and tells me of a civil war break out after the next election. I nod
but I am numb. The calm before what I've come to know as the
storm portends but I can't do anything about it but wait.

The door to my flat greets me indifferently, completely unaware of change. Unable to recall what I've done moments prior,
the turning of a key, a step or two forward, they all get lost in the
shuffle. What to do with this information? Removing shoes and
socks, trousers and boxers, I lay and wait for riposte like inspiration. It doesn't come.

Stillness is deafening me, and I get up to paint, to visit my feelings, but find myself still in bed. Body here, spirit there, judgment tests my sanity as I swear I am looking down on me from a happier place. I want to leave here and go to where I am painting vividly, to where the good feeling awaits. Unable to read the writing on the walls of my reality, I am choosing to pass through them, an apparition, evading the inevitability of its fate. She is leaving me. The words are here in spirit, but in truth, what do they really mean?

My stomach stirs. My chest sinks further into me. This is not pain. I remember pain and this is not it. Dizziness. Mouth waters. I jump up and run to the toilet. I don't make it. Yesterday's liquor and today's ache fill the flat with a repugnant stench. Will and ability to clean the floor are wherever inspiration is.

A repaired mobile, and a note from Lydia to call a.s.a.p. sat neatly on the kitchen table. The strength to dial laughed me in the face. Maybe I wasn't alive. It was a possibility. I decided to test the theory. I cleared my throat.

"She is leaving," I said out loud. "She . . . is leaving." A bit louder this time. "Adrianne is leaving me . . ." Maybe if I sang it I would believe it. "She's leaaaaaving . . ." no avail. I can't really figure it all out. More dizziness. More mouth watering. More vile and bile on the kitchen floor.

There is heat, cold and the chattering of nerves. In bed, a simple rocking back and forth motion stifles the convolution. The sheets hurt. Anything to stop the pain . . . I rock and repeat the mantra, as the rhythm of my leg keeps time. Hours of this. Who can withstand it?

Morning comes, and I do not pray to a God who has forsaken me. I am more concerned that I will die of this, and He, unable to face a broken promise, will arrange for my position in this state to remain, as the question that He did not answer of his hanging Son, may be the only one he cannot.

The mobile flashes and blinks. There are missed calls from Paul. Danny. Lydia. Lauren. There is no strength and nothing left of my stomach lining. I feel like less than a man, but can't seem to do anything about it. Bones of mine vibrate aimlessly, and the cold contradicts the dampness of my shirt. I think, maybe this is what mum felt. Maybe it's why she twitched and turned as she hung. Maybe the movement dulled the memories. I wanted to be sure.

"Nine-one-one, may I help you?"

"Yes . . . I am ill. I need to speak to a doctor."

"Do you need an ambulance, sir?" the voice asked.

"That is what I am trying to figure out," I reasoned.

"False 911 calls are a felony," I heard the voice say. I am not a felon. I am sick. That's what I try to convey. The sound of heels on hardwood startled me.

"Islam, your door was wide open. I've been calling you all night. What's the problem?" Lydia asked as she gently removed the mobile from my hands and closed its casing.

"I don't feel well." I stated simply. She placed a cold hand on my hot head.

"You're not running a temperature. Open your mouth," she checked for whatever doctors do when they ask one to almost bust a jaw bone.

"I am not fine."

"I know," she answered empathetically. "What happened last night?"

"I am unsure."

"What did she say?" Lydia asked.

"Nothing."

"Surely she said something." I didn't answer. I wouldn't until I figured this out. Adrianne's leaving me. I won't feel her body on mine, or see that full moon smile again. Ever? A gentle laugh escaped me. More of reflex than resolution.

"Well, glad to see you're doing well. These things take some working through, but ultimately you get over them. Time heals all wounds," Lydia said casually, as if she's never seen or spelled the word love in her life. "I on the other hand, have had better days," she sighed. "Your brother has spent yet another night out. He doesn't call, doesn't give me the consideration one would a friend let alone his wife," she said with insult. I wish I could respond but I don't care enough to breathe.

"Have you slept?" There was so much concern in her voice.

"I don't remember." I half-answered.

She dug into her shoulder bag and pulled a purple box from its pocket. Returning from the kitchen with a paper cup in hand, she placed a small pill in front of me. "Here. Take this. It will help you sleep. Only for a couple of hours though. Enough to recharge the brain." Lydia offered intelligently. I wanted to say thanks for the concern and the pill, but I am not interested in advancing what seemed to be a stabbing feeling in my chest. If I slept I'd dream about her. Too much to risk. All of that tumbled out with the shaking of my head from left to right. Lydia sat beside me on the bed. "Islam. This isn't debatable. Your door was wide open. Your kitchen's a mess. You need to go to sleep. I am not working today, and will be here until you do." She removed her shoes and jacket, opened a magazine and said, "Move over."

I made room for my brother's wife, hoping that maybe she had the answers to this. Maybe they were in the little pill that I've swallowed. Maybe this is a dream and the pill was my portal out of this horrible matrix, where people couldn't live and love as they chose. Any series of answers would do. Anything to stop the pain. I said it until my dreams became reality.

The position of the sun confirmed the notion that I've slept longer than I'd wanted. Something was all over me. I remember pain, but I also remember kissing Adrianne, taking vacation in the shape and softness of her lips. Remnants of both feelings are still present, that of excruciating pain and an eternal sense of peace and arousal. I try and force clarity through emerging consciousness. Which was which? I do remember a dream—a nightmare that I don't ever wish to revisit. Life without my love. What bullshit.

Unable to recall if we were in Paris or New York, I reached a foot or so to my left nervously, hoping that the nightmare was just that. A nightmare. Holding my breath, I stretched my arm out, in attempt to pull Adrianne onto me, and wake up the way I wanted to—with her body on mine. If she was here beside me, the way I remembered, then it was all just a bad dream.

A warm body, much further than Adrianne's normal twelve inches from me stirred, and I wondered why she was so far. Eyes shut, I reached a bit further and pulled a different but pleasant scent onto my chest. Adrianne felt different this morning. Good but different. I kissed her as I would any morning she was with me. It was natural for me to desire her at the first sign of day-break, no matter how long we'd been up the night before. She was hesitant, much more than usual, but eventually let her lips and tongue wander mine in an exploratory fashion. It all seemed so new.

"Mmmmh," she moaned. Her voice wasn't as raspy, and her intonation lacked an overall feminine quality that belonged to Adrianne only. Too lazy and much too aroused to care, I kept my eyes shut, moving on autopilot, gestures that I knew by heart taking control of the situation, making the transition from man to woman more habitual than calculated. I needed my baby this morning. I didn't care that she smelled different, or sounded less like herself. The need to be connected to her overrode any nuance.

She gasped. The sound of surprise added pitch to her voice the moment my manhood made its presence amongst the wet-ness. We moved against each other as two who had yet to master the secrets of the other's stride. I positioned myself between her, enough to move deeply inward but not to ignore the small pole north of her, the orb that would make her head spin. That tiny button was my focus.

"Oh my god . . . O-oh . . . my goddddd." She repeated the phrase enough to hypnotize herself into a state where pleasure didn't drive one insane. "Yes . . . oh my god . . . yes . . ." the com-mentary was fledgling but loud. Not sadist sex in the window loud but loud enough. Something was different. The tingling in the bottom center of me made me care less of smaller differences and more of the tidal rhythm that caused her legs to shake.

Strokes, moments, incoherent stutters. She was there. Love, cried and moaned like a porn star.

With fistfuls of my hair in her hands, I allowed her to move and do as she wished. Wetness ran down the sides of me, bringing an ethereal moment to the forefront. Breath deepened. Muscles clamped and tightened. Another climax. Words, broken and caught in the center of her seemed to take a back seat to impulsive reflexes and she begged me not to move an inch.

"Are you alright?" I asked.

"P-please . . . d-don't m-ove . . . I can't t-take it . . ." Breath left her body in a small steady stream, and I wondered why she was so sensitive this morning. Maybe it's the hormones. There's so much about pregnancy that I've yet to learn. She's normally used to my presence on that spot. Another difference. And I am unfulfilled. A first. Adrianne moved back onto her side of the bed. It's more typical for her to fall asleep on my chest. What's all the difference?

"You act as if you've never felt me before." Silence. "Adrianne. Why are you so far from me?" I was fully awake now. If there was a problem—which I was certain there was, then we should talk about it now. I have never been denied a climax from her. We typically come together.

"I am not Adrianne," she said flatly. Shit.

"Kharet?" I asked in disbelief. If so, I'd need Moses *and* Houdini to get me out of this. Without warning, the daggers, the ache, the memory of words that I couldn't bear flooded me at once.

"I want you to leave . . ."

It wasn't a nightmare. The pain told me so. I could have cried, but it would hurt too much. Something else came to mind. I jumped up, stepped over the different Adrianne and dialed out to the real one. She said today was the day.

"The number you have reached . . . has been disconnected . . ."

I dialed the number to the gallery.

"Spence Gallery of Contemporary Art, New York," the receptionist answered.

"It's Islam. Is Adrianne in?" I asked.

"No, Sir. She's out to London. I thought you knew . . ." Damn. It's real. I walked from the bed to the front of the studio, from the studio to the kitchen. From the kitchen to the toilet and sat.

"Tell me what happened, Islam." Lydia appeared at the bathroom door, half dressed. Lydia? What th—. Did I just . . . that wasn't Kharet? Shit. I am losing it. I am fucking losing it and my chest is killing me. Stop the pain first. Deal with the other stuff later.

"She said she wanted me to leave." I answered.

Lydia sighed. "Did she say anything about her physical condition?"

"No. She said there was nothing to speak of. That there was the other day, but not now, and that she was going back to London." The more I spoke the worse I felt. "What did you give me? I missed her departure."

"You needed to sleep."

"I needed to see her," I snapped. "FUCK!" I could hear my voice echo out to adjoining streets and blocks. Lydia shifted feet.

"What did she do to you?" she asked quietly. "I mean, what is it about her that makes you this way?"

The ache once reserved for my chest and stomach, spread across my body evenly. I resumed my rocking motion. It was the only thing that helped. "I'm sorry . . ." I mumbled.

"It was an accident. No need to ever speak of it again," Lydia proposed of a session I'd like to forget. I'd respond, but mentally, I wasn't even in the room right now. Walking into the studio, I thought about the various ways I could die and return after this all blew over. Nothing came to mind.

"I need to be alone, Lydia." I opened paint canisters and wet brushes as would a serial killer preparing his show.

"Come into the office tomorrow, I'll be in all day. There is a friend—a physician that I want you to speak to," she said as she slipped trousers over long legs.

"For what? Will it bring her to me?"

"No, I just want to make sure you're okay," she answered.

"I'm fine. As soon as I can get the pain to leave my chest I will be alright." If God couldn't help, psychoanalysis would surely fall short. A stroke of blackest blue along with hope for either healing or having her appeared on canvas. Whichever came first would be greatly appreciated.

37

Daybreak again. Five or so paintings in. I move brushes across canvas until my arms cramp. The painting doesn't speak to me, it doesn't allow me to move pain. It instead, sits and stares limply, like a detached nerve.

"ARRRGGGGGGHH!" I yell in frustration, and the nerve dead piece topples off of the easel, onto the floor, along with other cans and tins. Hands grip my head and a tear threatens to fall but decides it is also going to die before I can make anything of it. "I can't deal with this . . ." I say to no one in particular. "I CAN'T DEAL WITH THIS!" The roar only intensifies the pain. I pick up the phone and dial the toll free for Virgin Atlantic. I have to get to London. I can get my mate Terrence to hit me with some acupuncture. See if that helps.

"Good morning, Virgin Atlantic may I help you?" a kind voice offers.

"I need your earliest out from JFK to Heathrow," I say.

"Sir? Please speak up a bit. I can't hear you."

"JFK to Heathrow, your earliest please," I reemphasize and wait. The kind voice offers empathy as she tells me that there are no flights into or out of London, as a code red terror alert has been posted by both the US and British Governments. Other rhetoric and arbitrary facts escape me, as all I can think of is a possible conspiracy for my untimely death, as it is surely known that I cannot sustain myself at this pace. Movement, literal physical movement has been the only solace for the pain. Shattered, yet unable to sit still long enough to sleep or fully dress, I head out. Maybe someone out there can put me back together.

As I walk, people stare, and I am uncertain as to why. I am however, positive that I will never do this again. There was not a moment like this for me before Adrianne. Maybe I wasn't passionate, or connected or free, but I didn't hurt. The pleasure pain cycle is a coaster that I do not wish to ride again. The highs are wonderful but the lows . . . this cannot be natural. It is understood why free expression is not a popular practice. It hurts. People, regular people can't make it through life on these terms. The spirit, the stronger part of me wants to face the tide but I am broken. So I resolve to conform. I will hide my feelings, I will nod and smile, I will do whatever it takes to remove the noose from my neck.

There is a small group outside of what seems to be a storefront church on Washington Avenue.

"Jesus saves, sweetie," a thin grey-haired woman says softly enough to be sweet but loud enough for me to hear. She signaled for me to come to where she was. I've never been inside of a Baptist Church, only synagogue when I was young. Maybe Jesus was on duty there since He wasn't at the flat. It was worth a shot. "Baby? Are you alright?" the old woman asked. For the first time in months I had to think about my answer. Answer freely or safely? I nodded. Lied.

She smiled wisely. "Well then where's ya' shoes?" she chuckled. I hadn't noticed I'd stepped out without them.

A twinkle in her eye and a gentle pat on the back made me want to tell her everything. How I used to be so on top of things, how I met a woman at a party and began to change against my will. How I felt so free and painted so brightly . . . about how my paintings were from the deepest part of me, and how Adrianne made that part of me a safe place to be. As the old woman commented on the bags under my eyes and putting meat on my bones, I thought to tell her that my love has left me wounded in a sea of sharks, as it seemed as though I was caving in, and subsequently expressively misunderstood or as Lydia put it *manic*, and that no one seemed to accept me for me. I wanted to ask the old woman who offered me macaroni and cheese, seasoned meat and vegetables, if she'd ever weathered this storm, if her chest ever hurt as much as mine did. She placed a hand on my forehead and said, or rather sang, a quick prayer, and I thought maybe in English as opposed to Hebrew, maybe sung instead of spoken, God would, as she so feverishly prayed, *"forgive him for his sins . . . heal him Father . . ."* Her Amen, much like my *Amein*, yielded more hope than results. I am still in half.

As I leave the small storefront building, a child runs at top speed towards me. His mother chases and scoops him up expertly, chastising and further reminding him about *what she told him about crazy people.* I am tired. I am crushed and defeated. I am walking it off. Didn't know that made me crazy. A clear thought of a well dressed man roaring in Fort Greene park came to mind. Maybe that would help. Standing at the corner of Fulton and Atlantic Avenues, I inhaled deeply and yelled as thunderously as I could. It didn't erase the pain but it relieved a bit of the pressure. There's hope. I yelled louder, and as soon as I'd developed a rhythm, I was interrupted.

"Sir, you can't do that here." A man about my age, with short locks and black plastic framed glasses attempted to grab me by the arm and direct me elsewhere. He was condescending and rude.

"Announce yourself before you touch me," I stated calmly. His face gave him away. Shock. My accent and perfect English threw him off. I continued, "Please explain to me, what it is that I cannot do and perhaps I will consider your request." A simple, even statement. He readjusted himself, as proper British accent and intonation will cause even the most uneducated to straighten their spines and stiffen their lips.

"I-I'm sorry, Sir. I thought you were . . . you know."

"Crazy?" I responded.

"N-no. Not at all," he responded sheepishly. "It's just not every day that a man stands on the corner and yells."

"I'm sure." I replied. "May I be left to my own devices?" He squinted, apparently attempting to recall the phrase and its meaning. I clarified it further. "May I be left alone," I explained. I was tired, hurt and depleted but not about to be escorted any-where by a man who couldn't manage simple conversation with an alleged lunatic.

In the window of a nearby boutique were shoes that I know Adrianne would wear, and a dress that she'd be stunning in. I wanted to reach out and touch the mannequin, but thought against it, as any eclectic behavior seemed to have one escorted from the premises. Church revivals, psychics, yoga, free media-tion—signs of the times called out to me from storefronts and street corners alike, offering healing and deliverance to a society that simply needed to open its mind.

I walked further and what appeared to be an upstanding woman, offered to sell me a piece of rock, hereby noted as a healing crystal and I busted out laughing. Happiness that I could indeed manage laughter was overshadowed by perplexity of world-sanctioned behaviors that seemed to consistently reward the truly insane. Now unsure of a previous declaration of mine—to give in—to re-join a society like this, I wandered about in torment, searching for a better way. There has to be a way to move the pain. Nothing I know is working.

"Aye! Get your crazy ass out of the middle of the street!" A hostile voice screamed my way. It hadn't crossed my mind that I was on the yellow traffic divider on Atlantic Avenue. Also to my surprise, were glowing traffic lights and a dark blue sky. Where did the day go? I stood still for a moment and looked towards the sky. Everything seemed to be escaping me. Light. Love. Life. I didn't know what to do.

One last hope. I headed east, down Fulton to Greene Street.

"Where've you been," Danny asked in an aggravated fashion. Quietly, I walked the long corridor of his gallery behind him. The pain. It's still here. "I've been calling your ass for days!" he exclaimed. "Did you hear about what happened? Plane full of state officials and executives got clipped. Shit fell right out of the sky. All of Heathrow is shut down. I was hoping you didn't get caught up in that—what the hell is wrong with you?" His attention shifted to the state of me, and I realized that I'd have to tell him a story that would drain what little energy I had left. "Where the hell are your shoes?" he asked incredulously.

"Back at the flat," I replied.

"I swear, between you, Kehinde, and Basquiat, I can't decide which of you is the most outlandish." He chuckled, shook his head, looked at my feet and chuckled again. Did everything but call me crazy. He waited unassumingly as was typical of him.

"I fell in love with Adrianne," I blurted out. "Now she's in London and won't talk to me, she might be pregnant but I kissed a woman in front of her so she's upset and doesn't trust me and I have no idea how to stop the stabbing pain in my chest. The shit just will not stop . . . not even if I paint . . ." I rambled. While I told him about full moon smiles, freedom and late night paint sessions he listened. Guess hiding my feelings didn't work anymore.

Danny stood, fumbled around with glasses and bottles in the kitchen and returned with a small glass. "Drink. It'll relax you," he pushed the goblet in front of me. I did as he said. A button on a high-tech remote moved channels up and down the large screen. It landed on CNN.

"A high profile hijacking turned into a fireball in the sky as a number of state officials and oil executives attempted to thwart what had initially been designated an act of terror. Intelligence has confirmed the deaths of sixty percent of the passengers of which top executives from at least five foreign oil companies including Mohammad Siddiq and Nahir Al-Haaq of Saudi Aramco oil are amongst the casualties. Both, popular amongst human rights activists for silently sledging the oil market by intensively lowering the price per barrel of crude oil out of Saudi Arabia, Iraq, and the United Arab Emirates . . ."

"Told you if he was here he had a plan," Danny assessed. Conspiracy theories were last on my list of things I wanted to hear today.

"Danny. I have to get Adrianne back."

"You need to wait this out."

"I can't."

"You'll have to." He pressed buttons, flipped back and forth. The saga was on every channel and was pissing me off. I know I should care, but I don't. When the fate of the humanity is in the hands of a bunch of loonies, shit like this happens.

"Terror is being ruled out . . . foul play is suspected . . ."

"When did you say she left?" Danny asked.

"This morning."

"No one left this morning."

"She did. I called her phone," I told him.

"Smoke screen," he replied. My head is killing me. And he won't stop with it all.

"Danny! Will you please stop it with the conspiracy bollocks! I'm fucking dying over here!" I exclaimed.

"She must be really good. I've *never* seen you this excited before." He laughed and patted me on the back.

"Seriously. I have to find a way to fix things." I looked at him intently. Danny shifted and his demeanor changed. He was concerned.

"Well then seriously, you're going to have to wait. Cooper's part owner of the airline whose plane went down. Mutherfuckers start connecting dots . . . and BAM," he clapped his hands, ". . . It's all she wrote. Good thing is, no one can leave and there is business here for Cooper to take care of—the UN is in session," Danny added, as if I should be able to draw lines as clearly as he could. ". . . So chances are, your lady is still here."

"You think so?" I asked.

"I'd bet money on it." He reached into a small barrel-like container and pulled out a cloth-covered object. "With two of his buddies running the two most powerful countries in the world, Cooper's crazy ass is in rare form. They all are. Since I recommended you consult him for work, and I know you're going to do what you're going to do with the other situation, I feel responsible." He handed the cloth to me. "Don't make me sorry I gave you this. Protect yourself. That's a crazy mutherfucker. Not free. Crazy." He shifted a bit, fed a small treat to a canine without a care in the world. Surprised by the weight, I placed the cloth carefully in back of me. "Change of subject." Danny said. "I looked up that . . . what's her name? The Arabian curator?"

"Kharet?"

"Kharet . . . gat dayum she's fine!" he yelled. "Isn't she making the decision on your Paris showing?" I nodded. "Tell me this. Did you get your money?" he smiled knowingly. On the Kharet or the contract, I hadn't thought about much with all of the hoopla. Curves, lace and doe-like eyes danced briefly in front of me, and despite how I was feeling, a slight grin formed.

"Possibly," I responded guiltily.

"Possibly?"

"I believe so," I grinned.

Danny cracked up. "I knew it! Soon as I saw the photo I knew it, man. Contract was in the bag. Did you . . . you know. Sleep with her?"

"Yes and no," I answered grinning.

"Yes and no?" He threw his hands up and laughed. "Fucking painters, I swear. Congratulations." The first hope I'd had in what felt like a decade gave me a bit of strength. I stood. Danny and one of his two canines walked me to the door.

"Call me as soon as you get straightened out. We'll toast. And remember, don't make me sorry," he said.

"I won't." The first deep breath in a few days escaped me and I walked home with a tad more pep in my step.

She was still here. That was all I needed to know.

38

"*Yes. Yes, thank you. Is she aware of that? Please . . . no, I'll call myself. Yes . . . I have it. Jumeirah-Essex House Hotel, Central Park South.*"

My stomach swirled acid around like it wished to make a cake out of it. Hands dialed, but the heart wasn't sure it could deal with more of the same. No, wasn't on the menu for tonight. I wanted Adrianne to look into me and tell me that she wasn't happy with me. I knew she couldn't do that.

A cheerful voice politely declined my request to be transferred to the Spence suite at the Essex House Hotel in midtown, as I lacked the proper codes and special sequences for access. On fifteen minutes of pressure, and a promise of a dinner date, the receptionist at the gallery forwarded the information I needed to stop Adrianne from making a terrible mistake. If she knew how I really felt, that I wasn't as volatile as she thought, if I could show her that I'm in this thing for the long haul no matter how many tantrums I throw, maybe she'd stop this stupid vow-renewal-move-back-to-London bullshit. Proving a point to oneself shouldn't lead to unhappiness. I would do whatever I needed to in order to make that clear.

I tried the hotel again, and a different voice gave an identical answer. Damn high profile residences and their protection bollocks. Ten calls in and I can't get through. No matter who I speak to. There's only one person who can side swipe situations like this. I dialed him immediately.

"Ahmed"—There was chatter, noise and arbitrary rhetoric over thumping music. "I need to speak to Paul," and there was me, trying to get my point across. It was taking a while. "Ahmed!"

"Yea . . . he is uhh . . . watching purple legs," Ahmed blurbed and laughed uncontrollably. I'm sure he was seeing the world from a bird's eye view right now. Getting him to understand and execute my request would prove almost impossible. But I had to. It was the only way I could possibly speak to Adrianne tonight. I looked at the receiver. Three minutes. Fifty-seven seconds. I'm losing patience. "AHMED! PLACE PAUL ON THE BLOODY—"

"Yes?" Paul answered happily.

"Paul. I need you to do something for me." My request fell on deaf ears.

"Ahmed, would you take look at those . . . yes, right in front of you. No . . . she is not a mannequin," Paul was laughing just as haphazardly as Ahmed had been. A twinge of jealousy felt at the carefree nature of my friends' night—whatever they were engaged in—reared its head.

"Where are you?" I asked.

"What?"

"Where are you guys?" The music was too airy for a super party. Too chic for a festival.

"Oh. At the Prada spring show. The—whoa! Ahmed look at that! That's the one from backstage, no?" He rambled on about what I gathered was a woman. Or rather a series of them. Damn, I forgot. September. Milan. Fashion week. They were shopping, but not in the way women shopped. Paul paid absolutely no attention to me or my dilemma.

"Paul. I need you to call Adrianne. Please. I don't think she'll speak to me and I only have one chance at—"

"Islam, hold a second. . . . wheeeeeeww! Write that one down, Ahmed. What do you mean you've already had her! In that case write her name twice . . ." I could hear the two laughing, arguing playfully as was typical of us at a fashion show. Damn. I wish I was there. Doing what they were. Being the old me. But I wasn't.

"Paul. Please. I need you to do this."

"You do realize that Miuccia Prada has nothing but bare legs calling out to us from the runway this season, don't you?"

"Paul. It'll just take a few minutes."

"Islam. She loves you, but not enough to leave her lunatic husband and even if she did, you're going to drive yourself mad trying to force her. Now there's a slew of eligible women here in Milan with your name tattooed on the inside of their thighs. Give up. If Spence doesn't want you, someone else will."

"I can't give up, Paul. We were almost there. In Paris . . . well I can't tell you what she said but we were closer than we ever were, then she saw me with the girl . . ."

"What do you want me to do?" he asked.

"I need you to call the Essex House hotel on Central Park South, and pretend to be Cooper."

"I beg your pardon?" Paul asked in his obnoxious fashion.

"I know it sounds crazy but I can't get through to Adrianne and I can't get the pass code either, but I'm sure they'd let Cooper up so . . ." What made perfect sense to me tumbled out of my friend in a bundle of laughter and disbelief.

"Have you been to a doctor?" Paul asked sincerely.

"I called one earlier, and Lydia, my brother's wife checked me out and said—"

"Because you must be out of your bloody mind!" he interrupted. There are planes falling out of the sky, planes that your woman's husband owns nonetheless and you want me . . . your best mate, to call a five star establishment and *pretend* to be the terminator? Has Mrs. Spence fucked your brains out literally?" Paul ranted. I know it sounded a bit off, but I just needed to get through to her. He laughed and chided with Ahmed in the background.

"Paul, please. She may be pregnant."

"Are you certain?"

"No. That's what I need to find out," I replied honestly.

"Ahmed! Call my mum, Tony Blair, the Pope, and Scotland Yard. If you can't find me after the show, I'm at the bottom of a ditch in Bogota begging for a home cooked meal and a Penthouse magazine . . ."

"Thank you, man." If I didn't feel so gutted, I'd laugh. Paul was . . . Paul. I dialed the number to the hotel from memory. We waited.

"Good Evening, Essex House," Friendly voice number one from my earlier attempts answered as if we were the first call of hers all evening.

"Yes, Cooper Spence here . . ." Ahmed busted out laughing. I almost blew a fuse. Paul kept his cool as usual. "Is my wife upstairs? I need to speak to her at once," he asked-stated as if there were centuries of royalty behind him.

"The pass code, sir?" The voice asked just as politely as she had minutes ago.

"Pass code?" Paul asked indignantly. Even I had to grin slightly. He sounded just like Cooper. "I am in a Turkish bath with an inflamed penis and a prescription for Viagra which has shown up in my travel bag disguised as box of tampons! I NEED TO SPEAK TO MY WIFE!" Paul exclaimed. Ahmed roared. I sat still, the tips of my fingers playing each other like piano keys. "Now if you cannot help me, I will be forced to appear in all of my finery in your grandest of lobbies . . ." Paul continued.

He was swiftly interrupted. "Suite eleven forty five at once, Sir," the voice made its exit and a series of buttons, sounds and beeps followed an award winning performance.

"Did you get that?" Paul asked.

"Yea."

"Be careful, Islam." I didn't know about being careful, but I was nervous. Paul disconnected and I was left with a ringing phone and a swirling stomach. Man up, Islam. I egged myself on. The worst was over. The phone rang and rang. She's not in. At least I have the suite number. All of that nervousness for noth—

"Good evening," a familiar voice answered. She sounded groggy.

Must have been taking a nap. I got a little tripped up on the raspy sexy thing in her voice and couldn't answer. "Good evening . . ." she said more clearly.

"Love . . ." was the only word that slipped through all the thoughts and questions fighting for space. After a few more moments of silence, I thought she would hang up. But she didn't.

"Yes," she answered softly.

It's been a long couple of days. I'm worried about her. I want to wake up to her. Is she still feeling ill? Thoughts and questions fought for space in a crowded funnel. "I . . ." Words were a luxury. I didn't want to hear no again. The possibility of it stunted everything I'd planned to say.

"How do you feel?" I asked for lack of better to say.

To my surprise, she answered. "Tired." She yawned.

"May I see you tonight?" As Adrianne seemed to weigh the option, the slightest bit of hesitancy gave way, and it took what I had left not to hit the panic button.

"Tonight is not—"

"Please, A. Just to talk, nothing else."

A few moments of heart thumping silence and the first glimpse of light I'd seen all day. "At the gallery in an hour?" she asked.

"Yes. I'm on my way." I replied. A shot of adrenaline ran straight to my gut, and my body responded in a few different ways. I wondered if she was as affected as I, if her body responded in the same way. The pain in my chest was replaced with a thumping that gave me the energy I needed to hop into the shower, tidy up my hair and find something fresh to wear. Common sense whispered, *there was no need to be excited, nothing is promised*. We could end up in bed, or walking separate ways. Nothing in me paid attention to the latter possibility. I'm going to see her tonight. We are going to work this out. It was the best news I'd had in weeks.

I trotted down the noisy stairwell of my brownstone and paused to check for my keys. Got 'em. Alright, man. This is it. I began the pep talk that I'd continue on the train ride to Soho.

Stay focused. Don't let her or your emotions get to you. Talk, or rather listen instead of kiss. Nod instead of grab. Be what she needs you to be, in earnest. The second chance alone lets you know where her heart is. Whether or not she'll follow it, is to be determined.

The old lock spun twice to the left, and a half, and outdoors was fresher and brighter than it had been in days and nights past. A female voice startled me. I wasn't expecting visitors. It was Lydia.

"Hey, Lyd. I'm on my way out right now. If you want to go upstairs and paint, or just get away from my brother, feel free." I signaled towards the stairwell. The weird look in her eyes threw me off. I didn't have time to be thrown off. I had less than thirty minutes to get to lower Manhattan.

"How are you feeling?" she asked in a tone of voice that wasn't her most natural.

"I am fine. Better than earlier," I said in a huff.

"Why didn't you come by the office?"

"I didn't know it was mandatory."

"I didn't say it was. I was worried though. Did you take the medication I left?" she asked in an almost patronizing fashion.

What's her deal? I truly didn't have time to find out. "No offense, Lyd, but that medication had me thinking I was in Paris when I was actually in New York. The remainder of it's on the nightstand. I have to be going."

"Where are you headed?"

"To Manhattan."

"To see Adrianne?"

"Yes."

"Have you spoken to her?"

Why all the questions? "Yes, I have. Now the paint's upstairs in the studio, I actually left some of it out. We'll talk when I get back."

"Are you sure you've spoken to her?" she reiterated.

"Lydia. What's the issue? Yes. She and I have spoken. I am on my way to rectify things as we speak." Two men the size of American football players appeared from the side of my brother's truck. They both eyed me suspiciously. "Are they your friends?" I asked.

"They work with me. Listen, I need you to come into the office."

"Is the office at Four twenty-one Broome Street?" I joked. She didn't offer a smile. Alright, women are most definitely the most unstable creatures I've ever encountered.

"No, Islam. I need you to come in for an evaluation."

"Now?"

"Yes."

"I can't. Adrianne's waiting for me at the gallery."

"She and her husband were just on live television a few minutes ago. There is a Spence Foundation Gala tomorrow night. It's all over the radio."

"What does that have to do with anything?"

"Are you sure she's waiting?" Lydia reiterated.

"Come on, Lyd. I have thirty—excuse me, twenty-five minutes to get downtown. Yes. I just spoke to her. She should be there. It was her idea."

Lydia didn't budge. Neither did her sumo wrestler friends. "Islam, don't make this hard, just come with me and if nothing's wrong, we'll let you go tonight. I promise," she said sadly.

She promises? What type of primary school bullshit is this? "Lydia! What the hell is wrong with you? Have you taken one of those bloody pills? I'm not getting into any vehicle. I need to get on the train." I tried to side-step her without bumping her in any way that would seem disrespectful. At the third step in, sumo one and two jumped on me.

"Lydia?. . . ." I was calm. As calm as she and everyone else suggested I be under these types of circumstances. While one of the men pulled out silver cuffs, the other maneuvered my hands behind my back. This was the second time today. My fuse was short. Breathe, Islam. I spoke cautiously, as not to tip the alarm inside of me that I'd become recently acquainted with. "Lydia . . . tell them . . . to get their fucking hands off of me . . ." Still calm, and counting to ten slowly, it was hard to figure out why everything in the known universe wanted to work against me today. The men, apparently under Lydia's supervision, patiently awaited instruction.

Okay, think quickly. They have made a mistake. Correcting it means you will be late. Call her. It sounded simpler than it was. She'd changed her mobile number and I'm sure she'd already left the hotel. Even if she hadn't it would be impossible for me to be connected to the suite this time. Alright . . . do not panic. Breathe. Get out of this situation.

"Apologies for raising my voice, it's just that I have an appointment in approximately twenty minutes," I said pleasantly.

The sumo wrestler men looked at each other and snickered. "Yea, this one is a nut," one said to the other. Assuming he was speaking of the sudden change in the tone of my voice, I thought to offer an explanation. The effort was interrupted.

"Okay, let's go." Lydia stated firmly.

"Go? Where?" I was completely outdone. She was about to have me miss one of the most important meetings of my life. I'd already fucked up once. I couldn't afford a second time. If I stood Adrianne up, it would be over. They escorted me to the truck in the way one would a serial killer. "No. No! No! Nooooooooo! Come on, Lydia! What are you doing! I'm not a madman!" I shifted and moved, the orderly's grip tightened as he attempted to place the cuffs on my arms. A quick glance at one of the men's watches. Fifteen minutes. If the trains were running on schedule I could get there. Fuck this. They'd have to take me swinging.

"Islam. Calm down."

"Calm down! I'm sick of people telling me to calm down! *You* fucking calm down!" I'd had it. The patronizing tone in her voice was the straw that broke the camel's back. Stress, love, ups, downs, mum, Micah, I'm sick of it all. "What type of bloody doctor are you, fucking piece of shit profession . . . it took *all day*

Lydia . . . no actually it took longer than that . . . months! . . . and I finally got her to speak to me . . . FUCK YOU!" the bass in my own voice surprised me. The orderly smirked. I spat in his face. He cuffed me in mine.

"Stop!" Lydia screamed.

"I bet you go home and fuck your son at night don't you? Yea, your wife mentioned it but I could hardly hear her with my stiff in her mouth," I said, staring him directly in the eye. There was no respect or reserve left of me. I was tired of making pleasantries, of making excuses and explaining my behavior. Tired of conforming. Or justifying why I chose not to.

In the back of my brother's super-sized truck, the same one that brought me into this rubbish, now the one that escorted me to wherever "let's go" was, I vented and ranted and ranted and vented. Fuck Lydia, the orderlies, the fucking bullshit system that wouldn't allow a man to express himself while he was hurting. I cursed and spat and kicked the back of the seat in protest. Fuck close-mindedness and beaucracy and the rules that say a painter can't love a rich woman. Fuck capitalist right-wing pedophiles who make it so that anyone considering life freely, on the outside of their navy blue box would rather hang themselves than take on their burden of their judgment. Fuck them.

"AHHHHHHH!" I yelled in frustration. Three minutes past the hour. Adrianne was waiting for me. I hated everyone who took a breath. Fuck the Brooklyn Bridge. Fuck the truck. Any hope of reconciliation, of possibly having a child—a family— with the woman I loved had just been muted by their inability to understand and acknowledge difference. I am different. What is so difficult to understand? But then again, they don't have to understand it. It's their world.

"Islam, watch your head," Lydia said softly as we stepped out of the truck.

"Fuck you," I replied. I was seething.

"Yes, Islam, fuck everyone." Lydia patronized. Oh really?

"That seems to be how you like it, milady." I spat over my

shoulder as grayish walls and horrible yellow tiled floors greeted me with an evil grin.

BELLEVUE HOSPITAL CENTER

I was in society's petri dish. Honestly I cared not to leave or stay. The life that I wanted was out of reach by now anyway.

39

"And can you think further back to when you were a child? . . ."

Wheels, carts and nurses' behinds were far more appealing than answering questions of who I'd find to be Lydia's partner in psycho-whatever.

"Listen, the quicker you answer the questions, the easier it will be for you to leave," he said. I stared. Wondered how long Adrianne waited for me, or if she was perhaps still out there. For a quick second, I thought to oblige the stout man in black metal frames and a white coat that had seen one too many sub sandwiches. Maybe if I indulged in these arbitrary bollocks I could get out in time to see her. The time suggested otherwise, so I decided to sit en mute. He could insult my intelligence until he was blue in the face. As of now, I had all night.

He moved a leg. I moved a leg. He twiddled his thumbs, I twiddled mine. While I was bored, having fun mocking the man, and watching him grow in nervousness, he seemed to spend the last few minutes of my evaluation wondering where I bought my clothes. The differences between us were apparent. He, in a beige, or what used to be white button-down shirt, crusty semi-leather belt, and brown pants older than us both, sat opposite me in pinstriped trousers, sleek rubber soles, and a hooded Dolce and Gabbana sport coat. I was not what he expected. We were Archie Bunker and The Fonz, in an exchange that was going nowhere. Bunker shifted and moved as if he were the one in the hot seat.

"Is that your wife?" I asked of a pretty woman whose photograph was prominently displayed. The doctor jumped out of his skin. I chuckled.

"Yes, she is."

"Seems like she has her pick of the litter, yea? Ever stop to wonder why she chose you?" I asked squarely. His face, red as a tomato, threatened to burst into flames. I laughed. "Tell Lydia to send someone more qualified in for the job," I tisked.

"I am qualified. Are you going to answer the questions?" he shifted impatiently.

"Haven't I already?" I motioned towards the photo. Enough was enough for the egg shaped doctor. A button and an SOS disguised in medical terms, later, I was facing more doctors, more red faces, more deficiencies. Some angry words, some calls for security but no answers to questions they asked. I knew what my issues were. They were tattooed on the front of me, displayed colorfully in my art—my expression—as a decoration of pride and overcoming. My issues and perspective were in plain view. The question asking was coming from the wrong side of the table.

"Islam!" An exasperated Lydia entered the small office, ready to strangle me. "Why can't you cooperate! This is for your own good!" she exclaimed. Another look at the clock. Any hope of Adrianne even staying an hour past our meeting time had gone flying out of the window. She'd never forgive me for leaving her out there like that. As of Lydia, this was her fault. Or rather mine for being foolish enough to express myself freely in front of a close-minded woman. "I told my colleagues this was a simple evaluation. Now they're suggesting we place you in a more developed ward," she said angrily. "Just answer the questions."

I motioned for her to sit. She did. "Ask what you wish," I said more gently than I felt.

"Alright. What is your earliest childhood memory?" Lydia asked.

"Breastfeeding."

"And your happiest?"

"In Paris with Adrianne."

"Childhood, Islam."

I've had enough. "I can't believe this shit, Lydia. This was the only time I had to tell her how I felt before she left. I can't *believe* you. My own good? Is this the only way for you to understand me? What is the purpose of this shit?" I was disgusted. Tired. Stressed.

"Have you taken the time to notice your behavior lately?" Lydia asked impetuously. "You had a breakdown."

"I did not."

"You're obsessed with this wom—"

"I'm fucking HURT!" The bass in my voice echoed through the halls. "I'm hurt, Lydia! How am I *supposed* to act? You wanna talk notice, eh? Have you taken the time to notice your own un-happiness? That you wake up every single day the same? Self-loathing pity . . . you're swimming in it for fucksake! Does the fact that my brother doesn't love you—that you don't love you— that you wouldn't know yourself if you walked the streets with a mirror taped to your nose make you unhappy? Well it should! Obsessed? Consider Adrianne lucky! I wouldn't give up. If Micah were more obsessed with you . . . if he made you feel more like a woman, you wouldn't be sleeping with me!"

"What? Don't you dare—"

"Dare what, Lyd? Dare what? I was a bit delusional, and I can't stand my brother so pill or not I might have still let you ride me. Sick? Yea. But I know me. I confront my issues. You, of sound mind and body, fucked, squeezed and grabbed me like a champ then said it was an accident. A multi-orgasmic accident? Acknowledge your shit, Lydia! You fucked your husband's brother with a smile on your face! And you're calling *me* manic?" Tears rolled down her cheeks. I wanted to feel bad but I didn't. "Are you crying for me? Don't. I will not be held to your standards. I am not the one pretending. In my world, *you* are the lunatic," I pointed an angry finger at a woman who I once called a friend.

"Dr. Blackwell to station one," a tear-faced Lydia placed a finger on the intercom button. "Transfer the patient to ward three. I'm unable to break through . . ."

The walls were barren. In fact, color boycotted every aspect of the government building as if it were protesting the rights of the sane. No color. No freedom. No art. I had to beg for chalk, paper, and ask to engage in short rights, as relieving myself here. With the exception of a small radio playing old tunes, vacancy and void were loud, from the offices to the patient community room. If I've truly lost my sanity, this would be the last place I'd find it.

A lady with a heart shaped face claimed to be Joan of Arc of Queens. A man, just a few years older than I, rambled legal terms and 'approached a bench' that none of us could see. Assuming they both were victims of holding in matters that plagued them most, I sat amongst the two apathetically and drew. Understanding them more than I did Lydia, I colored and shaded, wondering when her day would come.

"Pretty girl." A slim yet familiar-looking man, with curly black hair and a cigarette that hung from his lips as if it were an extension of him, motioned towards my rapid moving left hand. I wasn't in the mood for conversation with anyone, let alone a loony. He dressed eclectically, in a colorful jacket, distressed denim, shoes that were obsessively shined to perfection and stood quietly by my side, as if he had all day to wait. "I said, pretty girl," he repeated. "That your woman?"

"Yea," I responded half-heartedly.

"And kid?"

"N-yea, I mean . . . I don't know."

"I know all about that." He coughed and laughed. "May I?" he stood impatiently, almost with a quick jitter, as if he and I shared the same temperament. He took the remaining seat at the small table. I guess I was having a conversation tonight no matter what. "What's her name?" he asked.

"Adrianne."

"And her last?"

"Spence." Another laugh.

"Why the laugh?" I asked.

"Let's just say I know the name," he said with an "I am God" smirk that seemed to be taped to his face. We both sat still, the back and forth motion of my hands creating a hypnotizing distraction from a conversation I didn't want to have. I couldn't place where I'd seen him before. It was fucking with me. I decided to entertain the guy until I could place the face.

"Why are you here? If you don't mind me asking."

"Why is anyone here?" I replied indignantly. The look the colorful curly-haired man gave said, *Come on*. I obliged him. "I was off to see my woman, to fix something that I'd screwed up . . ." I gave him the short version of a long story. "Let's just say someone seems to think I'm insane."

"Are you?" he asked.

"Are *you*?" I replied.

"Depends on who's judging today," he laughed. "No, honestly. Are you, you know . . ." he made looping circles around the right side of his head. I was becoming sick of the exchange already. The eclectic man with too many colors in his clothes, took notice of the look on my face, which I'm certain revealed more than I probably wanted it to. He cleared his throat, calmed his laughter and said seriously, "I know what they think, but what do you?"

"Me? I don't know. Maybe a bit unconventional, but not insane. Free." I answered assuredly.

"Your name?"

"Islam."

"Well, Islam. I don't know if you know this but insanity . . . it's like being a genius. A genius can go insane at any point. It's when he goes about it in an intelligent way that makes him a genius instead of a fool. Take you for example. You're an artist. Passion is an everyday thing. Painting, drawing, writing a song can be the only thing standing between you and Riker's Island in some cases. That sort of channeled expression can help avoid slitting a throat, bombing a building, you know," he gestured with his hands. "The genius expresses that intelligently, because he understands the true meaning of freedom. The fool doesn't."

"Explain."

"The art of freedom—understanding it—is knowing less of what to say, and more of when to say it. Intelligent versus unintelligent expression. It all comes down to timing." He clarified.

"Like the Nietzsche quote."

"Exactly. See, freedom is a psychological thing. People think they're free because they can come, go and say as they please. That is a fool's interpretation of liberation. And oxymoronic to say the least." I nodded quietly. "These people, are acquiring their definition from the same group they wish to separate themselves from. Even the free conform to the habits of the free. Which is why this place and profession exist. Any behavior that can be categorized, boxed etcetera is not free behavior. The idea that living freely is simply 'letting go' is a foolish one. A group of people who express themselves flagrantly and by any means, is simply that. A group. A cohort whose rule is to use bad timing in expression and be proud of it. Use your genius, man. Paint, draw, sketch, lose your sanity in those moments. Take insanity to acquire the mental freedom you need, dip into and out of it. Come and go with it. Don't stay."

I twiddled my thumbs and he pulled on his cigarette as if it were the last one he'd have in life. We were both still. What he said, I'd never thought of before. A colorful drawing on his shirt caught my attention.

"Hey, what do you know about Dub Ell?" I asked of worn tee with graffiti art that I was all too familiar with. The artist was a genius.

"What do *I* know about him? I should be asking you that," he replied. I raised my shirt to reveal an identical graffiti art tee, boasting the work of one of my favorite activist-artists. My friend laughed and asked, "Do you remember the last work of his? On the inside wall of one of the World Trade Center buildings?"

"Yea! The only one that went unsolved. It used to take us so long to decode his work. Now, *he* was a true madman. Rumor had it that he was a high level government official, an attorney or something, who'd kirk out every now and then and go crazy with graffiti cans. Government secrets, intimate ones, sprawled in color across walls of the world's most famous buildings. And they would all prove true," I said in admiration. "W. Ellington something . . ."

"Felton," he answered, smiling brightly while I ranted about the legend.

"That's it. Felton. He was ridiculous with color. Let's see, there was the multicolored fresco on the White House's side wall that read backward: *Bin Laden Cooks With Exxon*. Shit was hilarious. And the last one at the Trade Center, I can't remember it now—was some sort of color code in Latin. I always wished to be the first to crack it, but they whitewashed it immediately after it was found." My new friend took a small piece of paper, one of my chalks, and scribbled away. When he was done, he slid it gently across the table.

"How'd you know that?" I asked. It was the World Trade Center drawing, etched out and broken down into fragments. What was originally a replica of an elaborate illustration was deconstructed into a simple sentence that read: NY: WTC FLT 175, 11 DC: PENT FLT AA 77, RIP.

"It was my best work," he said.

"And The Mona Lisa was mine," I replied sarcastically.

He shrugged his shoulders and said, "Check it out for yourself. There is one photo, a small one, at the Deutsche Museum in Berlin. Let me know if it all matches up." He smiled.

"Impossible. That man was a genius." I shook my head. There was no way one of my favorite artists was in the mad house. No way.

"I can't be a genius?" he asked.

"Not saying that. It's just that if what you're telling me is true, although I have my doubts—but if it is, then you are a hero. You're an activist and a genius artist who played the game just right. From both sides." I said. I still had my suspicions, I was after all, in a mental hospital. But the drawing, the precision of it, was swaying me. Not just anyone can replicate that. While I further examined the small piece of paper, the tail end of a radio commercial caught my attention.

"Brought to you by the Spence Foundation of the Arts . . ."

I let out a long deep breath. Seemed like the more I wanted to forget about something I wanted but couldn't have, the more it teased me. There were reminders of Adrianne everywhere. Whether at home in Brooklyn, the madhouse in Manhattan, or even on the toilet for Christ's sake, I couldn't shake this thing. Dub, or whatever his name was, looked at me and smiled.

"Love is a motherfucker ain't it?" he said while blowing a cloud of smoke in my face. Just that tiny sentence—the mention of the name Spence—brought the chest pressure back. And the nausea. I hate this. He continued, "It's worse when the you-know-what is good. When the Mrs. left me, I was fucked up, and had no help from the environment," Dub laughed. "Seemed like she was everywhere. Fuckin' radio, television, damn it my own dick reminded me of her. It's like trying to wean yourself off drugs. When you're lovestoned . . ."

I didn't want to talk about Adrianne or being stoned by love. It literally made me sick. Fingering the paper with the drawing on it, I asked him what he asked me earlier. "If this is who you are, then what are you doing here?"

"Vandalizing."

"Is that a crime?"

"Excuse me. *Obsessive* vandalizing." Dub shrugged. Smiled.

"But you're an activist." He shrugged again. "And you speak your mind." Another shrug.

"As I said, it all comes down to timing," he suggested.

"Don't you think that at a certain point, timing is not even a factor? If people don't want the responsibility of their own freedom, timing will never be right."

"Good point but we're not talking about people, we're talking about you."

"No, I'm talking about you. If what we know of humanity is true, timing has not been and will never be right for people like us. Expression, whether personal or for the masses, fighting for, exerting freedoms of speech and basic human rights are at the right time and place consistently. It is always the right time for equality. It is always the right time to expose treachery and speak out against injustice. It is always the right time to be passionate, to be connected, to be you. To be free to choose how and when you handle how you feel. When is it not the right time for that? But you are here. So has it ever been the right time for you? Have you chosen intelligently or foolishly? And if you cannot answer that, what is one to do? How are we to survive?"

"You keep talking like that, and we're going to grow old together," Dub laughed. I didn't.

"Surely you can get out of this place." Him without color was a waste.

"Leave? For what? That's the jail house." He nodded toward the barred window.

We were interrupted by a nurse and two orderlies. Different from the ones that arrived with Lydia earlier.

"Islam Ian?" the nursed called out. "Time for you to go."

"Go?"

"Yes. Go. You're being released."

"I'm going to look that info up at the museum," I said, as I placed the small paper square with the alleged code to a classic work in my back pocket. "I'll let you know my findings," we exchanged handshakes and smiles. This was the best conversation I'd had in a long time.

"Uh . . . Islam."

"Yea?" I turned back. Dub took a last pull of tobacco, put his cigarette out on the edge of the table and smirked the 'I am god' grin he seemed to wear with his trousers.

"Go and get your woman. Spence is a pussy."

40

Giving up is hard to do when love comes from a place that we know not how to get to or from. As I stood at Central Park South across the street from The Plaza Hotel, the venue of tonight's Spence Foundation Gala, I willed myself control and discipline. Ten plus paintings, two weeks of undefined illness, one psychological evaluation later, and here I was, leaned against a shiny vehicle, attempting to talk myself out of doing what I knew I would. Insanity, passion, determination, foolishness—whichever plucks your fancy, I will not let her leave me like this. Tonight, we will talk. Or I will listen. I didn't care, as long as she was with me.

Diplomat tags and bright blue headlamps arrive dutifully to the mouth of Fifth Avenue, matching the magnificence of the city's lights and announcing subtly, the importance of its passengers. In a beautiful flowing dress, Adrianne looked most like a portrait and I struggled to give her the basic human qualities that we all share. Watching her smile beautifully, as she was issued compliment after compliment from entering guests, I knew, by the dissipation of the pain in my chest that I was doing the right thing. Ache had turned into a radiant energy that spread from my chest to my hands and feet.

By process of elimination, I'd resolve that it was she who

added true value to my life. She accepted me for me. And whatever I wasn't she was. There was half of me with Adrianne. And half of she with me. The half, is an important one, because the motivation that I have to get up and paint, to make a living, to provide her with the stability and security she deserves, comes from it. From a simple look, a sparkle in her eyes that says *I love you anyway*. The look, the feeling . . . it's what I cannot get from red heads, fashionistas or million dollar contracts. Wealth, women, weekend love, none of them made me feel whole. Now that I know for sure, the feeling—my feeling—the one that my love brings to me, is completion.

Guests flood into the legendary grand ballroom, and I follow suit, trying to blend into the fabric of the hotel inconspicuously, as an assassin attempting to configure his next move. I want to lay with her and talk. That's it. Making it happen was the hard part.

"Sir, will you be joining us?" a kind man with dark hair and an Italian accent asked. I was dressed in the same clothes from yesterday, black sport coat and soles. Luckily, the pinstripes and sleek nature of my wears helped me blend into the sea of black. Standing in the vestibule, I was blocking the flow of traffic both in and out of the venue. The man was being nice about it.

"Uh . . . shortly, yes." I answered unsurely. Although my name appeared on the guest list as Spence gallery staff, I had no idea of how to approach the situation. Go inside, sit down and ask Adrianne to talk? Wait for her to leave the ballroom on her own? I was swimming in ideas but no solutions. A parade of voices made feminine chatter noise as they approached the grand lobby.

I heard her before I saw her, and that wasn't good, as I'd like to have a plan before I lost my footing the way I always seemed to. While Adrianne listened to a woman chat on about society lunches and shoe sales, our eyes met in passing. To my dismay, she looked immediately away, as if I didn't exist. Unable to blame her, I took on the additional challenge without complaint. I'd stood her up. I deserved that.

She and the others waltzed into the ladies room like a parade

of schoolgirls. My feet moved in their direction, and I found myself standing outside the restroom like a voyeur. Maybe if I asked,
she'd talk to me here. On her way out, I touched her lightly on
the arm.

"Adrianne."

Without breaking stride, she gently pulled her arm from me
and continued to ignore my presence. This time, I grabbed her
softly by the hand. Before turning to face me, she paused and I
thought it meant she had been positively affected by the touch. I
was wrong.

"I am going to say this once, and never again. You can do whatever you wish with the information," she tisked apathetically,
like she could care less that I was breathing. "There is nothing
between us. If the matter is not business related, do not call me,
do not request to speak to me," Adrianne said calmly. The look
in her eyes was surreal and resolved, like she'd come to the conclusion of a life-long journey. "I do not love you, nor do I wish to
speak to you about it." Attempting to raise her chin so we were
eye-to-eye, fingers of mine were intercepted and pushed away. I
wanted her to look into me and say that. I knew she couldn't.
"You are a hazard. To me and to yourself. Anything that tran-
spired between us was a mistake. I am clear on that. I want you to
be as well," she spoke clearly and purposefully, as if she were
giving a presidential address.

"I am sorry about—" before I could get the words out of my
mouth, she was halfway down the hall. This wasn't going well.
I'd have to figure out a better way.

Ladies and men dressed to ballroom perfection, glittering crystal chandeliers, high-end cuisine and a well dressed, overzealous
hotel staff gave the gala a sparkling flair known to the richest of
the rich. There were tables lined in a row, elaborate string instruments, an elevated wooden platform that served as a dance floor
and me, in a corner, trying to figure out what to say and when to
say it.

Adrianne looked marvelous. For two hours, I waited and

watched, happy that the only person I knew in the room was ignoring me. It gave me time to think. Apparently time was not what I needed. A decent idea mustn't have gotten its invitation to the event. Unable to figure out if my lack of ingenuity stemmed from watching and wanting Adrianne all night or the overall lack of sleep and nourishment, I continued to lean against the wall farthest from gala civilization, and wait for inspiration, the other entity seemingly missed in action.

Something caught my eye. As she nodded and laughed and played along, there was a long-stemmed glass of dark something-or-other in Adrianne's hand. A sip. A nod and smile. What is she doing? She can't drink in her condition. She must be crazy.

"Adrianne. What are you doing?" I was there before I could say my own name. Startled, she turned immediately to face me, leaving the previous conversation hanging mid-air.

"I am speaking to Mrs. Trump," she said evenly.

"No, what are you doing with that?" I signaled towards the glass in her hand.

"I am drinking it."

"No, you're not."

"Yes, I am," she said defiantly. "What is the matter with you?" What's the matter with me?

"Me?" I was incredulous. "What's your problem? You're not to have alcohol in your condition." Mrs. Trump gave us a surprised yet knowing look. Adrianne noticed it and took a small step backward. Apparently the only one who could care less of what this looked like, I continued where I left off. "Come with me. We need to get this talk over with. Now." I grabbed her hand. She flinched. In no mood for games or resistance, I tightened my grip. How the hell is she going to drink in her condition? If smoke could exit my ears, it would.

"Let go of my hand," Adrianne whispered through tightly clenched teeth.

"No. Let's go."

"I am not going anywhere with you. Get your hands off of me," she was whispering, but glaring and clearly seething.

"No. Not until we talk." We were causing a scene. I knew it. Ask me if I cared. She wasn't going to pump what may or may not be my child with bourbon. The more she attempted to squeeze her hand from mine, the tighter I held on. For a second, I thought I saw a flash of fear in her eyes, but eagerly dismissed the notion. Adrianne could never be scared of me. I love her too much. What were originally fleeting looks and glances were now unadulterated stares from gala guests. What were people staring at? This was between she and I.

"Are you alright, my dear?" a painted lady in red approached Adrianne as if she were a battered housewife. What does she mean is she alright? She's with me, of course she is.

"Yes. She is fine." I answered firmly. Adrianne stared at me half-defiantly, half in pretension of a man she'd told was a hazard to himself and to her. I'm not a hazard. I'm not insane. I just want to talk. I'd show her just that if she'd let me. After making me fall for her like this, for turning my life upside down, a conversation was the least she could grant. An idea. Finally. Not sure if it were a good one or not, I swiped the first idea I'd had in a while, more thankful for its presence than quality. "Let's go."

Arbitrary to hearing, feeling and thought, apathetic to dropping jaws, gasps and fainting lady noises, I scooped Adrianne into my arms in one swift gesture. Too surprised to cry out, she twisted and turned, but to her dismay I had her locked in. "All I want to do is talk. Now is just as good a time as any," I said, and was surprised at how calm I was. Of how easily the words flowed. I wasn't frantic or heated. Just wanted to talk. That's it. Although I truly couldn't tell with my hand over her mouth, my love looked scared to death. She knows I'd never hurt her. Not like she was hurting me.

The closest exit was a door to a staff stairwell. We were a tight fit, but a fit nonetheless. Adrianne having long since given up twisting and turning, preferred to attempt communication through a muzzled mouth.

"Mmmh. Mmmh. Cmmp." Sounded like Cooper something. Fuck Cooper. I've had enough of him too. We can discuss all of that after the main event. Stairs were taken at top speed. At an exit door, I navigated through hallways and corridors, some better lit than others, and I'd be careful not to squeeze her too tightly, as health in her condition was paramount. We'd reached our destination.

BOILER ROOM.

The last place anyone would look.

I removed my hand from her mouth, pressed the door handle and opened sesame. A rusty chair sat in a corner, and I thought to seat her there, but it would ruin her dress. I placed her neatly atop an old wooden table. The room was small and stifling but served its purpose. Adrianne looked at me like she'd never seen me a day in her life.

"I love you. You know that right?" She looked too uncomfortable to talk. I wanted to fix that. Slowly, I moved my hand from hers and ran it across her cheek. She, motionless and completely void, gazed at or rather past me with a sheet-white look. The most emotionless I'd ever seen her. My hands found their way around her waist, and I stood between her legs, the only spot that was ever a comfortable fit for me. The muscles in Adrianne's body stiffened, and it seemed she'd completely gone empty.

"Adrianne. Look at me." She did but didn't. Her eyes were on mine, but every bit of her body and mind was elsewhere. Of all the known looks of coldness, reserve and vague, I've never known Adrianne to be as detached from herself as she was now. Her hands were trembling and I wondered why she so nervous. We talked like this—in this position—all the time. "Love. Say something." She wouldn't. The silence unnerved me, because it meant we'd never have this conversation. Maybe if we were closer to each other. Maybe if she felt the warmth—the love, she'd break through. I pulled her to me. "Hug me, babe," Adrianne limply placed vegetable-like arms around me. She wasn't here. I'd have to try something else if I were to ever warm her up enough to talk to me. I placed her hand in mine, locked fingers and asked as lovingly as I knew to, "Kiss me."

The trembling spread from her hands throughout her body.

She gave me a weird look, hesitated, then placed a dry kiss on my lips. Although it was the most passionless kiss I'd ever received from Adrianne, I wasn't surprised at my body's instant reaction to it. She noticed it too.

"I miss you," I explained.

"Islam, please . . ." she whispered.

Please what? "No, you don't understand, A. It's been too long without you. So *he* . . ." I motioned towards a balloon-like bulge making its presence known to the room through my pants. ". . . misses *her*," I pointed what was now a wrapped sausage towards the 'V' shaped area that was making me sweat. There was a second where I'd blur, where I'd feel the warmth and softness of my love's body on mine. A moment where I'd hear her ask the questions that I loved to answer.

What is desire?
What is freedom?
What is longing?
What is love?

Adrianne shifted backward, and I moved closer to her. Every inch traveled away from me made me want her more. With my love's body so close, it was hard to focus on the true purpose of all of this. Talk. I placed a soft kiss on her lips, and each time I kissed them after, I had to remind myself of why I was here. Talk not love, Islam. It was so hard. Even though my love's lips were barren and lifeless on mine, it was hard to stop. I forced myself to.

"Are we ready to talk now?" I asked. A teary-eyed Adrianne nodded her head, and I wondered why she looked so . . . petrified. "Baby, what's wrong?" As was typical of her in uncomfortable situations, she declined an answer. Maybe she needed a change of scenery. The boiler room wasn't exactly the most comfortable.

"Let's go somewhere more comfortable," I offered. Tears that never fell, collected in the corners of her lids. As impatient as I always was, I felt like shaking the conversation out of her. When her lips finally began to move, my body dealt with weeks of not having them on me harshly, and I was so . . . aroused—for lack of a better word, that I didn't hear anything she said. I didn't know how much longer I could control this. Adrianne repeated what seemed to be a mantra of sorts.

"I can't trust you . . ." she whispered.

Can't trust me? My life is upside down. I want her to have my child. She is the only one that matters. How can she not trust that? Anger rose to the surface and I forced myself to swallow it whole. The softer approach seemed to work best with Adrianne. That is the one I'd resolve to take. I reached for her, and she hit a nerve.

"No!" She wiggled and moved her way into a seizure-like state, the no's becoming more resounding by the second. "No! No! No . . ."

Anything other than no. I was tired of hearing it. "I'm tired of hearing no, Adrianne. Tired of it. Now let's get this on," I said firmly. She kicked and moved and I held her. There was just my love and I in a damp cold room, me, attempting to get from her, what I needed to survive. She had to trust me. There was no other way of doing this.

"No . . ." Adrianne kicked and pushed and fought me to the best of her ability. "I can't trust you . . ." she said over and over again. I can't work like this. Pinning her to the table proved more difficult than I thought. She was strong. Determined to connect with her no matter what, I placed myself between her legs and held her there. With nothing to lose, I went for what I knew best.

"Adrianne, love . . . look at me. You can trust me. All of this is because you can trust me . . ." I began. "You can trust me to love you. You can trust me to provide for you. You can trust me to act out when I am upset sometimes. You can trust me to look at women as they walk by, but you can trust me to love you only, as deeply and truthfully as you need me to . . ." A tear fell, the only one of Adrianne I'd ever witnessed. ". . . You can trust me to listen always, even when it appears that I am not. You can trust me to never treat you as a possession, to always love you as I love myself, possibly better, because you are the better half . . ." As words were plenty, my own voice reverberated in my chest, and I had to swallow tears and other proof of how fragile I was without her, "You can trust me to be unconventional in my approaches to life, to love, but please, do not confuse unconventionalism with instablility, Adrianne. You can trust me to be your rock. Your foundation. You never have to put off a conversation, or a request. You can trust me to live through any hardship life brings us, to overthrow it before you even know it's a part of your world . . ." Minute drops, one could call them tears, made wet lines down my love's cheeks. Small drops turned to larger ones, creating a puddle in the nook of her collarbone.

"Please . . ." Adrianne whispered. "I don't want to . . . Please, don't . . ." she stammered and begged, and I cursed myself for not catching on earlier. Shit. I finally got it. My heart sank at the notion of her thinking I might do anything to hurt her.

"I only want to talk, A. Nothing more, sweetie." I reasoned with who was now an unreasonable woman. At this point, she kicked and punched and bit my hand and the only remedy I could apply was to hold her as tightly as I could. To rock her back and forth. "Babe. I love you, I would never hurt you . . ." I continued to hold her close to me. Maybe I could love all of this away.

"Adrianne. Listen to me," I said softly. "All I want to do is talk. You can come to me, love. You can say anything and I won't leave. That's what love is, remember?" Whispers in her ear went unnoticed as she used every bit of strength she had to push me away.

"I can't trust you." A more aware Adrianne spoke clearly and definitively, and I was happy for her return. Even if it meant the same thing as it did seconds ago.

"I love you, Adrianne."

"I can't trust you," she repeated.

"I love you . . ."

"I can't trust . . ." As we spoke simultaneously, I could almost feel my heart breaking in two. She couldn't leave me. My mum left. Micah left. I didn't know if I could take it again.

As I continued to hold her, things seemed to only get worse. A thought came to try the opposite, to step away, to give her space to come to me. The thought was interrupted by multiple shouts and voices, all coming our way at once.

"STEP AWAY FROM THE WOMAN AND PUT YOUR HANDS UP!" A parade of red dots lighted streaks on grey walls, creating a dance floor of maddening screams and beams. The dots were multiplying by the second. "I SAID STEP AWAY SLOWLY AND PUT YOUR HANDS IN THE AIR! . . . UP! . . . OFF HER! . . ." the voices yelled together. It was hard to focus. Adrianne was still beneath me.

Instinct prompted me to raise my head, but the loud gunshot sounds above me negated the notion. Bullets pounding into old plastered walls caused a smoke-like abyss in the room. It was enough to choke on.

"Don't move." Adrianne said soundly. She was back. The rose of me was back from wherever she was minutes ago, the surprise visit jolting us both into reality.

"THAT WAS A WARNING . . ." a hostile voice yelled. "RE-MOVE YOURSELF . . ."

I am not a madman. This is not what they think. I wanted to tell them that. As I moved slightly upward, Adrianne's legs clenched tighter around me.

"Let me handle it," she whispered. Men in black, some in suits, circled us like flies. A more familiar voice joined the ranks.

"Lower your firearms!" A formally dressed Cooper spoke loudly to the men behind us. Red dots quickly moved south. He tapped me on the shoulder. "Face me, Islam." Cooper said casually. With Adrianne's legs still clamped around me, it was difficult to move. "I said, face me. If you can," he reiterated. Standing slowly, I surveyed the scene. Men in tuxes with guns, federal agents, officers, Adrianne's tussled hair, tear-stained face and hiked up dress. Cooper flashed his own red dot contribution, a small black piece situated smartly in his waistband. "Dejavu . . ." He said to himself. "Islam! I said stand up! Get the fuck off of my wife and face me!" A harsh hand grabbed me by the hair and yanked me off of her. The force almost snapped my neck. To my surprise, there was no reaction from me. Everything stood still. Men in black rushed to Adrianne's rescue, as if I were the one she needed protection from.

I could hear Danny clearly,

Protect yourself . . .

The metal gift of his was nestled neatly in the small of my back, but I didn't make a move.

"I am alright," Adrianne said. "It is not the way it—"

"Shut up!" Cooper snapped at her.

She continued. "Cooper, it's not what you—" An angry hand came across her face, slapping her so hard she almost stumbled backward. But Adrianne was strong. She didn't give into the force. I looked for a reaction from me. Still, none.

"I want to hear from Islam," Cooper said calmly while read-justing his tie. "Take that fucking smirk off of your face!" he ordered. I wasn't aware that I was wearing one. The room was quiet. I could feel Adrianne to the right of me and see Cooper in front. Everything else was a blur. "Take Adrianne upstairs, I will deal with her on my own," Cooper ordered.

"She is not going anywhere." The first words from me came out easy as Sunday morning. I was calm. I was still. I knew she wasn't leaving me.

"Oh?" Cooper replied in surprise. I shifted feet. A million red dots responded instantly to the movement, canvassing my body's most vital areas. "Lower your fucking firearms," Cooper said to the officers. He laughed to himself. "You know . . . I think we're all forgetting a minor but imperative fact. You see, no matter what type of whore Adrianne was with you, she is *my* wife," he pulled the black metal piece from his waist belt and pointed it towards his chest. "She belongs to *me*. Is that well understood, Islam?" I was still unmoved. "God damn you! Take the fucking grin off your face before I blow your head into the wall!" Cooper screamed. Agents and officers shifted uncomfortably with their guns. Dots hung haphazardly on the concrete floor, bored with waiting. I wanted a reaction, but couldn't find one to save my life. "He doesn't get it." An incredulous Cooper spoke to himself.

"Come here, honey." He extended a free hand to Adrianne. I placed an arm in front of her.

"As I said, she is not going anywhere." We could settle this however he wanted to.

"Okay, Islam," he chuckled. "I will be patient with you. As I mentioned, I've had you checked out. I know your mother was a crazy bitch who didn't care enough about you to off herself in the way that any decent lunatic would. In front of her children? How did she do it again?" He tipped his head, bugged his eyes and pulled his arm in a hanging motion. "See, Adrianne and I are *family*. I know you couldn't find the word in a dictionary with a magnifying glass and an extra pair of hands. She is my *wife*. I am her husband." He scanned my face for a reaction that never surfaced. "That smirk is getting on my last nerve. You're not comprehending this. Honey!" Cooper walked towards Adrianne, "Let's help him out. Show your lover boy how a wife treats a husband."

"Cooper stop." Adrianne ordered.

"Stop? Is that what you told painter-boy over there? Is that what you said while he was ramming you up the ass in the bed that I paid for? Is it honey? Now, look. I know you have special talents. Your father rest his soul, was a great coach . . ." I felt myself turning towards them, but couldn't feel anything else. My hands, feet, everything it seemed went numb. "Stop acting as a virgin. Get on your knees and show Islam who your husband is." As Cooper jolted her head downward, a bolt of lightning raced through me. That was it. Before I could convince myself otherwise, I—

"Get your fucking hands off of her." The bass in my voice shook the metal pieces in the boiler and seemed to awaken red dots that had previously fallen asleep. "I will *kill* you. Do you understand that Cooper? I will fucking *kill* you . . ." My hands were on his neck. Both of them squeezing and twisting, ringing him out as if he were a wet towel on a hot day. "I will *kill* you . . . I swear to God . . ." People were screaming, red dots were flying everywhere. I heard and saw some things, but in my world there was only the man who would take my love away, and me, snubbing the orders of a thousand guns. Unaware that I'd lifted him by the neck, and more so unaware of the fact that I'd thrown him across the room, through glass, metal pipes and whatever else made up the boiler, we were pinned to the wall at the far end of the small room. He, gasping and clutching his throat for air, and me, unable to awaken myself from this nightmare as I did in Paris.

"DROP HIM!... HANDS OFF!... YOU HAVE UNTIL THE COUNT OF THREE!..." The same voices from minutes earlier yelled. I heard them but didn't.

"You're going to hurt her? Really? I will fucking kill you Cooper..." I repeated, as laughter resonated from my chest. Everyone wanted me to calm down. I *was* calm. Seemed I was the only person in the room who wasn't screaming. As I whispered, the words flowed smoothly. It felt good.

"Islam! Stop! He's turning blue..." Adrianne pleaded. I will myself to stop but it doesn't happen. Cooper is instead, pushed deeper into the concrete wall. His head tilts and the tips of his shoes pound into my shins like the nose of a woodpecker. My love is crying. She wants me to put him down. I do, but don't.

"RELEASE HIM! OR WE'LL FIRE!... ONE!"

Play a game with Mommy...

There was my mum's face. Adrianne's voice.

"TWO!"

Go ahead Micah,

Kick it...

There is twitching and foaming and wiggling, just like mum. Cooper's hands swung aimlessly in circles, fighting for small cups of air that seemed to allude him. He grinned, and I pressed harder into a half-smile that said he understood my orders. That he would never touch her again.

"Islam, please.... you're killing him..." Adrianne's voice mixed in with the others, screaming and pressing for change. All I wanted to do was talk tonight. It was all I could think of. Guns. Dots. Paris. Brooklyn. The Soho Hotel. So many images. So many things to decide.

"Are you free, Islam? . . ."

Yes, I am. I have never felt so free in my life. Shouts and screams were crowding me. As I smiled, Cooper smiled back.

"THREE . . . AIM . . . FIRE!" A piercing scream from Adrianne followed by the deafening sound of red dots blooming into gunshots jolted me into a different state of mind. The burning sensation in my arms and back made me more aware of myself, and I pushed a limp-necked Cooper further into the stone.

"She is not going anywhere . . ." I could hear me whispering to a man who cared less of my orders or considerations. As the burning and pain spread through my legs and chest, I blinked back red, and tried to ignore Adrianne's cries. I've never heard her cry before. It was a beautiful sound.

"Don't cry babe, I'm here . . ." I assured her as plastic masks and other apparatus were pressed onto my face.

We need an ambulance on a ten seventy one, multiple gunshot victim . . .

Can I get a ten forty five on the patient?

Condition of the patient is critical . . .

She doesn't have to worry. She can stop crying. She can trust me. I will not move from her. It is the only thing in which I am certain.

Report on patient two?

Yes, ten fifty four . . . Coroner's case. Choke victim . . .

I am calm. I am peaceful. I am without worry or care. It feels different, but good to me. Unfamiliar with the setting, or the things going on around me, I do however, love the feeling. For the first time in my life, I am not in a box. Or a hole. Or a coffin. There is no reason to scream or shake or cry. There aren't any nightmares of containment. Just love. Acceptance. Freedom. For so long, I've wanted to get out of myself. Happiness is here because I did.

"Can you hear me?" A voice says. As cloth and hands are pressed into my chest, arms and legs, red tears are wiped from my eyes. They, along with the rest of me are on fire. Burning too much to hurt, dizziness takes over and I want to give into whatever is pulling me. Oddly enough, the pain brings peace. A peculiar sense of pleasure washes through me, like painting a greatest portrait. Like the feeling. *My* feeling. The one I get from loving Adrianne. "I said can you hear me, son." A man in white says to me. I nod. "Well then. You have the right to remain silent . . ." I continue to nod. It is all I can manage. "Anything you say, can and will be held against you . . ."

My favorite paintings and moments are before me. My mother and I playing in paint, Adrianne and I playing in peace and loving. Reds, blues, purples, they all say that I am okay, that I am forgiven for taking so little of life for so long. Sleep falls, but I am more awake than I've ever been. Color upon color appear and reappear in the kaleidoscope of soul, offering me more than I can say I bargained for in life. There is sunlight, a warm feeling, and I hope it is the feeling of Adrianne's smile, of her hands and heart. Of her encouraging nods and inspiration. I hope it's the feeling of forgiveness when she doesn't want to forgive, of love when she doesn't want to love, of passion and connection and spirit. Of the dancers in the park and the look in her eyes when I've reached the very inside of her with the stroke of a brush. Hope it's the feeling of freedom. The light of love. Hope it's me, becoming who I already am . . .

Epilogue

"*And can you think back further, to when you were a child? . . .*"

A few people shifted in their seats, awaiting an answer. Often times I've been without reply, but after a few months of much needed physical and mental therapy, I've found myself sitting center circle, full of response, amidst a group of people that I'd actually come to love. There were smiles and encouraging nods, prompting me to dig as far back as I could, for memories that I've never claimed to have.

"Yea. I can remember. We didn't have much. But there was lots of love in our house. My mum loved us without fear. We could speak and love freely, without worry or care. My brother and I were not normal children. We'd paint and draw and laugh all day, talk of aliens, my brother swore he'd see them—friendly ones," I emphasized. The room laughed. "And I was never good in school. I hated it. Mummy never doubted us though. She never questioned or made us feel lesser than for being different. Love in my house was acceptance. It was freedom." I thought back as far as I could, until I saw the face of a beautiful woman who smiled even when she wanted to cry. "Although she'd cry at night sometimes, we never noticed anything other than love while we were awake. I guess that was the shock in it all. We never knew she was unhappy."

Newfound friends and fellow group members quietly offered support, as they too knew how tough it could be to speak from the heart. Unlike the rest of the world, the people at The Bellevue Hospital Center offered each other a safe environment to express innermost thoughts and feelings without judgment or fear. I've been here for months that seemed like years. But it's all been worth it.

The door at the front of the room creaked open, and I smiled at the arrival of a wanted guest.

"That is my brother, Micah." I motioned towards the doorway. My loving but sometimes overly-emotional friends offered applause, and Micah reddened in embarrassment. I shrugged. We laughed. I continued. "Since this is my last day with you, I wish to share something." A small piece of paper made crinkling noise, as I retrieved it from my back pocket. "Normally, I'd leave a painting, or an illustration or sorts, but this time, I decided to write what I felt instead." Smiles greeted me warmly, giving the encouragement I needed to read the writings on the walls of my heart. I cleared my throat and began.

"There is no truth in the game we call love," I began. "Not honesty not fact or frank. There are frauds and fakes and pretenders, those who liveth and loveth a lie . . ." This is what I recall. That there is no happiness in love. No harmony no calm. There is no love in a game that everyone plays, but no one seems to win . . ."

"Bravo!" an older man yelped before I was done. We all laughed. He was such an expressive person. I continued to read from the journal I'd kept on what I felt of my experiences from the last few months.

". . . So I will say to you all, fellow freedmen, that although these things do not exist in the love that mankind seems to offer us, they exist in you, in me, in all of us. In those who are connected. Spiritual. Passionate. Free . . ." Everyone smiled. ". . . Choose intelligently but please, live freely. Enjoy the gifts of the universe. Bask in your differences. In your art. Shout, feel, be you, no matter the opposition or recourse. For we are the spiritual safe keepers of humanity . . ."

Thunderous applause spread throughout the room, I nodded in acceptance of the love given and headed towards the doorway, careful not to look back into an empty past.

"You ready?" Micah asked.

"Yea." I answered. "Have you heard anything of the charges?" I wasn't worried, I just wanted to know. Things I'm sure, would happen as they were supposed to.

"Well I've already mentioned that we've gotten the murder one charge reduced to involuntary manslaughter—that came along with today's completion of therapy. As for everything else, don't worry we'll talk about it all later. My firm is handling things. Tonight's New Year's Eve," my brother said and smiled.

"Alright," I nodded.

We slid into his truck, and the first real music I'd heard in months made me feel good inside.

It's so hard for me to say this . . .

The soulful voice of the Philadelphia native comforted me. Allowing myself to melt into the words of the song, I closed my eyes and allowed sister Jill to lead me wherever she wished. Thoughts landed on Adrianne, and I wondered how she was.

"Have you spoken to her?" Micah asked, obviously reading my mind. I shook my head, and instead of changing the subject, I sat still with the thought. Minutes passed, and we turned right onto twenty-third street instead of veering left onto FDR drive, the main vein to the Brooklyn Bridge.

"We're going to Brooklyn, yea?" I double-checked as my brother fumbled with a small piece of paper.

"Yes, but we have to make a stop first." Fine with me. With no work, love or flat for me to return to, I reclined backward into the music.

Micah maneuvered the large luxury vehicle onto Fifth Avenue, into lights, hordes of people and New Year's Eve traffic. As we came to a stop, a man dressed in bright red, asked politely for the keys to the truck. Another greeted me at the window.

"Good evening Mr. Ian. Welcome to Cipriani," a sparkle in his eye, and a grin my brother couldn't hold back led to a suspicious reply.

"Good evening, Sir." I shook the valet's hand and turned towards my brother. "Where are we going?" I questioned. Micah placed an arm around my shoulders.

"Walk. Don't talk," he smiled like a Cheshire cat. We entered a grand lobby, filled with lovely candles, and exotic plants. The lobby led to an even more magnificent room, where round tables, glass pillars and beautiful balconies greeted us along with a sign and scene that was more confusing to me than the look on my brother's face.

CONGRATULATIONS ISLAM
PERCEPTION ALTERATON REALITY GAMES
THERAPEUTIC CLASS OF
2007

People stood and applauded. And I was more confused than ever. What the hell is going on?

It was the most bewildering thing I'd ever seen. Mark, Julia, Ahmed, Paul. There was the receptionist at Spence, my trash alley buddy and veteran friend. To my right were Lia and Lauren in light conversation. Then Lydia, who stood patiently at the top of the room awaiting the opportunity to speak into the microphone in her hands. What type of craziness is this? Lydia began.

"I'd like to take this time to congratulate Islam Ian . . ." the applause became more thunderous and I, more stupefied. ". . . Into Perception Alteration Therapy Games' class of Two thousand seven . . ." As she spoke brightly into the room, I surveyed the scene—my vet friend dressed to the nines, and the young girl who delivered the invitation to the loft party in Shoreditch talking to Ahmed. As I viewed the ultimate in insane, I had to remind myself of a few things. Yes, I lost my mum at a young age. Yes, I found freedom in love. And because of it, I was a bit off and such. Yes those things were a part of me. But this . . . this is some crazy shit. As Lydia continued, I thought, I really *have* lost my mind.

"Hellooooo," Paul sang and laughed as he came and stood next to me.

"What the hell is this?" I asked him.

"Shhhh. Listen," he advised. Lydia went on about how I'd been nominated as a candidate to play the ultimate life sport, a reality-simulated alternative therapy game designed to push its players to their mental, spiritual and emotional limits. She explained that all of the people that I'd interacted with in the past six or so months of my life were either graduates or players of the game and that everything I'd experienced from the loft party in London to my showing in Paris was simulated reality—planned, organized therapy that mirrored real life, and forced me to confront my issues in a condensed yet safe environment. Lydia noted that while mild, more traditional therapies were recommended for typical trauma, in most cases candidates who qualify, who are inducted as 'players' have experienced unusual trauma and repression, and that PA games—as she put it—were a gift from the people who loved them most.

While she continued, I looked around for the bar.

"Inspired by the reality simulation games of San Francisco and Seattle, Perception Alteration Therapy has altered the lives and perspectives of thousands of candidates. Nominated by Paul Salzonne, and sponsored by Micah Ian and Ahmed Iranai, join me in welcoming our newest member, Islam Ian." Lydia finished. As people clapped, she stepped off of the platform and walked towards me. I didn't know whether to sit or stand. This was unbelievable. "How are you feeling?" A poised, more confident Lydia spoke with a British accent. Fucked me up entirely.

"Lydia . . . wh-what, is this for real?" I asked.

"Yes, it is," she smiled. "When Paul brought you in for the personality assessment, you tested at levels that surprised us all. Your session was specially designed for you," she said.

I shook my head. Couldn't believe this shit. "You people should be jailed." It was a natural response.

"Don't fret, Islam." Lydia's accent. It was perfectly British. I laughed out loud at the absurdity of it all. She spoke to me as if she were a guardian angel. "The Game of life, of love is one of perception. Or rather perception alteration. If the powers that be can alter our perspectives, can convince us to believe in war, in caste, in racism, then we figured we could do the same for matters of the heart, mind and spirit. Whether simulated game or of one's own cognizance, perception alteration is a healing technique. All we do is bring it to you. In the game of life, our experiences are set in motion by how we perceive. What one's perception is of what it means to love or be loved. Of what it means to go insane. To be free. When one's perspective changes, so does the game and how we play it," Lydia added intelligently.

"How did you do this?" I asked. No matter how much she explained, I was still completely baffled.

"DNA sampling," she added. "With a sample, we run a model that tells us what your concerns are, your fears, traumas, even your perfect love match and we feed you messages to alter your behavior and beliefs."

"DNA?" I asked incredulously. The young fashionista who delivered the invitation to John Martin for the loft party in Shoreditch smiled bashfully. Lydia continued.

"You wanted to be free. To be passionate, spirited and connected. You've wanted it for so long, but truly couldn't express it and didn't know where to start. That's where we came in. If you were presented with the ultimate life decisions, ones that forced you to change, grow and deal with your issues, if those choices were made available to you, how would you choose? It is our job to place them in front of you."

"Look at his face!" Paul busted out laughing. People lined up behind Lydia as would a baseball team congratulating its competition.

"What is the line for?" I asked.

"They want to shake your hand," she answered sweetly. This was a dream. I assured myself of it.

As I shook hands of people I either knew or didn't, all I could think was, "Never again." I said to no one in particular. It was a Freudian slip.

Lydia laughed. "You don't have to worry about that. You've come through your session quite well. Your friends and family love you very much."

"So you're not my brother's wife?"

"No."

"But you're a doctor," I added.

"Yes."

"A very rich one, we might add! One could buy several thousand Nike child laborers for the cost of this!" Paul ranted. Ahmed and my brother were at a nearby table thumbing through paperwork. This is mad.

Lydia laughs and says, "I'd love to take all the credit, but *he's* the mind behind the magic," she pointed to a slim, black-haired man in a colorful jacket standing obscurely in the corner to the right of us. Dub Ell grinned that 'I am God' grin and winked at us. Get the hell out of here. An implausible laugh escaped me. I'm done.

"Sorry, man. When Paul called and asked me to participate, I couldn't resist. And the check was nice," Danny laughed while patting me on the back. "Can I have my gun back?" he joked.

"I can't believe you." I said to Danny, smiling despite myself. "How in the hell did you find time to manipulate the television networks?"

"DV-R is a powerful thing." He grinned.

"Fuck off, Danny." I joked a bit, but I still didn't feel too good about it all.

"Vet. I can't believe you took part in this," I saluted my veteran friend who promptly corrected me.

"Uh . . . actually my name is Larry. I'm an attorney. Your brother and I work together," he smiled honestly. I had to laugh at the large diamond band on his ring finger.

"My name is Susan . . ." My trash alley friend greeted me with a smile.

"And what is your story?" I asked her.

"I'm an actress. And a mother of three," she grinned. Lights were dimmed and dance music rushed through the room, raising the vibe from social soiree, to discotheque. Ahmed saluted me from the DJ booth and played what he knew to be one of my favorite songs from Cinematic Orchestra's classic release. The only one in the room who looked somewhat normal in cashmere, tailored trousers, shined shoes and a classic timepiece was Cooper. Or whomever he was.

"Cooper?" I asked doubtfully.

"Yes, I am Cooper Spence. Spence family executor and Perception Alteration therapy, class of nineteen seventy-six," he smiled evenly and extended his hand. "Take the look off of your face, son. Such as life, if the game doesn't kill you, it makes you stronger. Besides, one would certainly say you faired quite well to make off with my wife," he raised an eyebrow. "Sometimes I'll admit to wanting to kill her, but I'm no Michael Douglas," he added playfully.

Paul rushed us with two dark green bottles with gold labels.

"Perrier Jouet Belle Epoque?" he said in his finest French accent. Classic. Paul is pouring thousand dollar bottles of champagne while I tried desperately to piece my life back together. He interpreted the look from me correctly. "We had to do it, man. You're our best mate. I'd never heard you scream or saw you cry a day in my life. Hate to see you on America's Most Wanted Serial Killers on a technicality. So, we thought to free you up some. When you decided to move to the US, it gave us the perfect opportunity."

"Paul . . . you shot me."

"Garcon! Two of your finest crystal flutes!" He ignored me.

"How could you do this?" I asked him. I was for real. Something didn't sit well with the only love I'd ever had in life being a product of a simulation game.

"How could I not?"

"You shot me, Paul." Attempting to reason with a man who'd already had one too many drinks was an exercise in futility. He aimlessly passed champagne around the room.

"Ah . . . bollocks to that! A gunshot and a beautiful woman! The only things on God's green earth that'll get you into therapy. Besides, you're painting and fucking like you never have!" Everyone laughed.

"Lydia, but we . . ."

She half-smiled. "Most of the therapy is planned, but some of it is completely spontaneous, Islam. It is all decided by the perception shifting, the mind opening and progress of the patient. Sex is natural for you. So our encounter . . . all a part of the job," she winked.

"Yes, it is too natural for him." A recognizable voice came from behind. It was Adrianne's—if that were even her name. If all of this were truly a fake, she was the last one I wanted to see. Deciding to ignore her, I turned to my brother.

"Micah. How much did all of this cost?"

"I'd never done anything for you, this was my chance to do something, man. Sorry about ma. Or as you say . . . mum. I didn't mean it. And then you shut down so hard. I felt like I lost my mother and my brother on the same day, so I just took care of myself. Sorry, bro . . . hope you'll forgive me."

This is all too much. I needed several drinks in a row. The music thumped and a large digital clock counted down to the upcoming year. Pieces that I've painted hung proudly. There was my collection from Paris, the abstracts of Adrianne along with the more intense pieces I painted while I was in pain—those were the best—and the gift for my mum. I stood still for a moment—a long one—attempting to replay the past months of my life. Trying hard to decipher what was real and what wasn't. I walked back towards Cooper.

"Are you alright?" I asked him.

"I've seen younger years but I am well," he smiled that awkward smile, the one that never truly revealed what he thought.

"Sorry about the . . . you know." I made choke gestures with my hands. Cooper laughed. "Oh, it is of no concern. Crimes of passion. They are what they are," he smiled knowingly. Someone wishes to speak with you," he motioned towards a beautiful woman with dark hair and darker eyes, staring in our direction. My heart still melts when I see her. I can't believe it wasn't real. She looked great in a black dress that fit her loosely.

"So what is your part in this?" I asked, while trying to ignore the thumping of my heart. "Are you even called Adrianne?"

"Yes. I am Adrianne."

"Cooper's wife?"

"No. I am his niece."

"What?" Visions of half hugs and bland cheek kisses flooded my memory. "Is what you told me . . . any of it . . ."

"Yes. What you know of me is true. I am the executor of my family's collection. I love art." She half-smiled. I was blown.

"Cooper and your father are brothers?" It was getting more ridiculous by the moment.

"Yes. They *were* brothers. It happened as I said it did," she said solemnly.

"What about the contract?"

"No, that was a simulation. But I've managed to capture interest in many of your works from collectors, that is if you are willing to sell them."

"What's true, Adrianne?" I said in frustration. "How I felt . . . I felt so connected. My spirit . . . it felt so free. For the first time I felt like I could breathe. Can't believe it was all a lie." Adrianne placed an even hand on my cheek.

"It can be overwhelming, but it wasn't a lie. All of it is inside of you. Art. Love. Life. It's there for whenever you wish to express it. You are not a slave to this society, Islam. You are naturally passionate, expressive and free. You're a beautiful person."

"This game. It's a sick one." I added.

"We live in a sick world. One must do what they can to survive. Perception Alteration Games, they're a gift from god. Sometimes it's all you need to re-establish your place here," Adrianne said meaningfully. While I looked around and tried to ingest all of this, those dark eyes of hers penetrated me like daggers. It was the same look from the loft party. And from the museum in Paris.

The feeling—freedom, connection, whatever this was, ran through me and I didn't want to believe what I knew was true. I still loved her as much. Having to stop myself from instinctively reaching for her, I took a step backward. Gunshots. Group sessions. Months away from my love. They all did nothing with how I felt.

We stood quietly, as was typical of Adrianne and I. After a minute or two, she continued where she'd left off. "My uncle granted me the gift of this type of therapy about a year ago. I am still dealing with my issues. Many of them I confronted during your session. Each time one participates, they live and learn as does the patient. Your session . . . it was freeing for me too, Islam." Adrianne paused, seeming contemplating the next stream of words. "There is something else," she said quietly.

"Oh? Can there possibly be any more?" I was sarcastic and surprised that I was taking this as well as I was.

"I was engaged to Mohammed when we met."

"Siddiq?"

"Yes. We were to marry shortly after Paris." I sat still, twiddling my thumbs, waiting for the rest of my life to be excavated with a pitchfork and thrown aside. Adrianne continued nervously, "We are not supposed to get emotionally involved with the client, Islam. I was only supposed to lure you to a certain point. But I . . . it was unplanned," she stopped.

"What was unplanned?"

"The . . . the way that I love you. I didn't mean to—I mean . . . I couldn't marry him because I've never felt—" She'd barely gotten the words out before I launched into her. As I kissed her, Adrianne melted into me, her body, her spirit, everything that I wanted to feel and touch gave itself freely. Her soul was mine for the loving. Not as a conquest or acquisition, but as a gift. As lips and fingers and breath moved into and out of each other, people danced and partied and toasted and I wondered if I could ever live another way. With my head nestled deeply into the small of her neck, I was unsure of how much time had passed. I knew for sure that we were minutes into the beginning of a new year, a new life together, as confetti, champagne and the cheering of our families and closest friends brought Two Thousand Eight in, in style. Adrianne smiled that full moon smile and looked into me.

"I love you," she said clearly. I knew she did. I knew from the moment she came to me in London. From the look in her eyes the night at The Soho Hotel and in Paris. From the expression she wore in paintings of mine, portrait and abstract alike. I knew, based on who she was and allowed me to be that she loved me. The light, the special look that started all of this radiated throughout my entire body and I kissed her again. It was the only way to express how I was feeling.

"Oh, come up for air! Get a room!" Paul exclaimed. As Adrianne hugged and allowed her hands recess over my entire body, Cooper, on his way out of the ballroom, gave me an unmistakable look that men interpreted plainly as, *take care of her.* I nodded in promise.

"Can we leave?" I asked my love. I wanted quiet time with her away from all the hoopla. Moving as sensually to the music as she always did, Adrianne chuckled and whispered in my ear,

"Baby, we cannot leave. It would be rude and Paul would kill us both."

"In an hour?" I placed a very attentive salute to her womanhood in its most desirable position and Adrianne tossed her head back displaying two beautiful rows of white teeth.

"Maybe in an hour," she responded to the arousal with a gentle kiss on the lips that made waiting harder than I was. As I pulled her closest to me, she grinned and said,

"There is another unplanned event that we need to discuss . . ."

Nietzsche said that a man is called a free spirit if he thinks otherwise than would be expected. With all that has happened in my life, there is no choice for me to think or be any other than what an artist should be—liberated, passionate, pained, spiritual, expressive, unconventional . . . loving each of those traits as one would a first born child. Tonight, as I place my hands on Adrianne's belly, and feel the small bulge beneath her navel, I feel freedom—I feel loved and inspired. I breathe deeply and feel the light radiating from within. She smiles, and I thank God for sunrise, for the chance to begin again. Reminding myself of a promise I've made to me, that each day, as the earth awakens with new perspective, I vow to take responsibility for my part in the chaos we call life, probing myself of the role I've chosen to play. Am I accepting myself in truth? Living from within? Do I love me for me? Or am I a slave to the impulses of a society who assures us that we are insane for daring to be different?

Although I am unclear of how my life will unfold from here, I am certain of a few things. Each time we choose to live life to the fullest, to express ourselves freely, to live passionately and colorfully without abandon, we choose liberation over death. We soar above what even ourselves could've ever imagined and create our own masterpiece of human spirit. We rise. We change. We stake our claim in humanity's game. Each morning, with the rising of the sun, we are given a second chance at life. Each night we dream of winning. Each day we play the game. Again.

Dear Readers,

Thank you so much for reading Lovestoned. I hope that you have enjoyed it. I also hope that I have grown as a writer, as I am always striving to do the best I can for my readers. As with Behind Those Eyes, Lovestoned was based on premises that are debatable—there is no wrong or right, just sharing! I hope Islam's story has opened your minds and hearts to a different type of personality, one that may not be popular or understood in today's society, but loved nonetheless.

Till next time,
—T.P.

LOVESTONED

T.P. Carter

The following questions are intended
to enhance your group's discussion of
this book.

Discussion Questions

1. Whether defined by society, psychiatrists, or characters in Lovestoned, everyone has their own definition of what it means to go insane. Lydia felt that societal norms, along with psychological theory, defined insanity. While Islam slightly agreed, he mostly felt that the ruling majority tended to misunderstand eclectic personalities and unfairly place them under psychiatric care. He also felt insanity was a by-product of a repressed society. What do you think? Does insanity truly exist? Or is it a figment of our imaginations?

2. Islam loved passionately and freely in his eyes, but everyone else thought he went crazy over Adrianne. Have you ever loved anyone deeply enough to feel like you've lost yourself? Have you ever done anything that would be considered "crazy" during one of those moments? How far has a lover gone to get your attention?

3. Adrianne and Islam spent much time defining what it meant to be loved. Islam's definition of true love was giving the gifts of freedom and acceptance—allowing each other to be themselves in truth, to do as they please without repercussion. Adrianne said that love by his definition cannot exist because no one is truly free. Do you agree with Islam or Adrianne? What is love to you? What is freedom? What roles do both play in shaping our desires?

4. In terms of passion and eclecticism, how would you describe your personality? Is it free flowing? Do you say what first comes to mind? Do you live for the moment? Or are you more reserved? If you are a more eclectic spirit, how often are your personality traits and characteristics misunderstood? If you are more reserved, is it because you

feel there is a proper time and place to do/say everything? Or do you find yourself holding back words and actions in fear of being isolated and/or characterized by society's majority?

5. Name your favorite artists (painters, musicians, writers, poets, dancers, filmmakers etc.) What are your favorite works of art? How did they make you feel?

6. In the epilogue, Lydia says, *"The Game of life, of love is one of perception. Or rather perception alteration. If the powers that be can alter our perspectives, can convince us to believe in war, in caste, in racism, then we figured we could do the same for matters of the heart, mind and spirit. Whether simulated game or of one's own cognizance, perception alteration is a healing technique . . . When one's perspective changes, so does the game and how we play it."*

After reading Lovestoned, has your perspective changed? Which characters, quotes, and/or experiences affected you the most? Do you see anything differently than you did before reading the book? Share your thoughts with the group.

Acknowledgments

Thanks to The Creator, for helping me play "the game" to win, and for giving me the words . . .

To mommy for loving all of me all of the time. To my brother Corey (I'm so proud of you) thanks for giving me Lil' Corey and thinking for me (and Islam) when I began to crash and burn. You are truly "free" lol. My little bro Mikey, thanks for reading and tearing my work apart like a true expert. I love you both! To Proph. B. Odino, thank you always for the prayers. My friends: Latifa, Kiana, Katrice, Danielle, Shelly, Gia, Camille, thanks for always being there for me. To Nic, thank you much for the growth and love. Thanks for watching Islam grow up and reading everything I've ever sent you. To W. Ellington Felton, for the inspiration and the killer conversation that day in Tryst. To Kayle and Cymantha, for the instant feedback and love. To Danny Simmons for helping me start all of this. For the phone calls and stories, and introduction to killer art and artists. Thanks for leading by example. To Derek at Rush, thanks for the talk! A special thank you to the neighborhood I grew up in—Brownsville, Brooklyn, for preparing me to play "the game" to win. And for always welcoming me home.

My London crew: Terrence for always being a big brother. Thank you for opening up your space and making me feel at home. Jean Claude for the music, inspiration and the aspects of Adrianne's life that made her come alive. Aaron Jerome, Samantha & Cyndi, Peter Brown, Uprock (Darren and Adam esp.), Femi, Moms & Pops (for making me feel like a part of the family), The artists and management (J. :0) at John Martin Gallery, for spending time with me and teaching me the ins and outs of gallery work. The Louvre, Tate Modern, Museum of Modern Art, Nate in Montmartre for showing us reality in Paris. Dissident

Display, for keeping me on my toes and defining the cutting edge artistically. Brook Stephenson for the encouragement and Eric Jerome Dickey for the adventure. To the city of London, thank you for making each time unique, for the constant growth and change. (what's up with dual citizenship??? Can we get on it or what? ☺)

After the 30 hours we spent editing this book, I know why people thank their editors. Selena James, thank you for the time you put into making me a better writer. Greatest appreciation and thanks to my wonderful agent, Sara Camilli for always listening and explaining and listening. Thanks for allowing expression and freedom in my work. You are the best!

Inspired by/dedicated to: Grandma Nicholson for spreading the philosophy of love, acceptance and freedom. I miss you already. Nietzsche, for timeless works that make me feel understood. All of my philosophy professors—both in and out of the classroom. Frida Kahlo, Picasso, Modigliani, Braque, Van Gogh, Issac Newton and DaVinci. Eteri, Mark Adlington, Dawn Okoro, Kehinde Wiley, Bjork, Fela Kuti, Lauryn Hill, MeShell N'degeocello, Lisa Lopes, Kanye, Sean Carter, Spike Lee and every artist and free spirit out there, changing the world one song/dance/film/painting/word at a time.